Praise for *Comrades in Miami*

"[A] sexy little noir novel . . . I loved it. . . . It's a timely study of life in the waning days of Castro's Cuba. . . . Hugger-mugger is mixed with wit and style." — Margaret Cannon, *Globe and Mail*

"An impressive mind-bender." — *Entertainment Weekly*

"Beautifully crafted from start to finish." — *Library Journal* (starred review)

"An exhilarating espionage tale." — *Financial Times* (U.K.)

"An exhilarating and chilling read, this powerful book stays in the psyche long after the last page has been read." — *Ireland on Sunday*

"Victoria Valiente may well be one of the most fascinating characters to appear in a crime novel in my memory." — *Baltimore Sun*

"A well-plotted compelling tale of the infrastructure of spies, politics, and ordinary people. . . . Latour takes the reader on an armchair trip from Miami neighborhood to the heart of Havana, delivering a cityscape that is as multi-layered as his plot." — *Houston Chronicle*

"With a native's sense of place, [Latour] delivers a finely textured Cuban noir." — *Miami Herald*

"Latour writes about the island with an unmatched verisimilitude." — *Booklist*

"[A] subtle and complex chess game of a thriller, with an interesting insider's view of contemporary Cuba." — *Kirkus Reviews*

"Latour's fascinating book remains a thing of beauty." — *Publishers Weekly*

Praise for *Outcast*

"If you like hard-boiled, suspense-filled fiction with a twist, *Outcast* is your read."
                                                                — *Sun Times*

"José Latour's decision to write his noir mysteries in English was our good fortune."
                                                      — *Globe and Mail*

"*Outcast* is a remarkable novel. . . . An absorbing thriller."
                                                   — *Washington Post*

"A rich, satisfying novel about a driven man."   — *Quill & Quire*

"Latour writes thoughtfully and subtly on the agonizing trade-offs implicit in joining the Cuban exodus."   — Montreal *Gazette*

"*Outcast* is warm, human, often funny and consistently interesting – a fast, rich read."
                                                     — *Los Angeles Times*

Praise for *Havana Best Friends*

"A wildly entertaining, plot-driven page turner that's as difficult to put down as a cool coconut filled with mango daiquiri. . . . I loved this book."
                                                        — *National Post*

"Different, colourful and utterly beguiling, *Havana Best Friends* is a delight."
                                                   — *Irish Independent*

"A stylish, sexy thriller."   — *Winnipeg Free Press*

"Latour's superbly atmospheric thriller, with its eye-opening portrait of contemporary Cuba, is one of the most original and exciting crime novels I've read in ages."
                                                     — *Mail on Sunday*

"Filled with greed, lust, broken necks, neighbourhood spies, corruption, stifling heat and a good cop on the case."   — *Globe and Mail*

"[*Havana Best Friends*] delivers everything one could ask for in a mystery."
                                                      — *Quill & Quire*

CRIME OF FASHION

ALSO BY JOSÉ LATOUR

Comrades in Miami
Outcast
Havana Best Friends
Havana World Series

JOSÉ LATOUR

CRIME OF FASHION

McCLELLAND & STEWART

Library and Archives Canada Cataloguing in Publication

Latour, José, 1940-
Crime of fashion / José Latour.

ISBN 978-0-7710-4659-9

I. Title

PS8623.A814C75 2009   C813'.54   C2008-904223-9

We acknowledge the financial support of the Government of Canada through the Book Publishing Industry Development Program and that of the Government of Ontario through the Ontario Media Development Corporation's Ontario Book Initiative. We further acknowledge the support of the Canada Council for the Arts and the Ontario Arts Council for our publishing program.

Typeset in Janson by M&S, Toronto
Printed and bound in Canada

ANCIENT FOREST
FRIENDLY

McClelland & Stewart Ltd.
75 Sherbourne Street
Toronto, Ontario
M5A 2P9
www.mcclelland.com

1 2 3 4 5   13 12 11 10 09

To Marcial, Maria José, and Juan

"Taught from their infancy that beauty is woman's sceptre,
the mind shapes itself to the body, and roaming around its
gilt cage, only seeks to adorn its prison."

– Mary Wollstonecraft (1759–97),
A Vindication of the Rights of Woman

July 31

The man who sashayed into the Pair-A-Dice Bar & Lounge straddled the stool next to the gloomy-looking Tommy Jones and asked for a beer. He took a couple of swigs, extracted a pack of cigarettes from the left pocket of his shirt, shook one free, then started patting the pockets of his jeans.

"Fuck," he said, then looked over at Tommy. "Gotta light?"

Tommy picked up his lighter from the bartop, handed it over, and cast an incurious glance at the guy. Medium height, copper-coloured skin, beaked nose, raven-black hair. Short-sleeved green shirt over a grey T-shirt, jeans. A Mohawk, Tommy guessed.

"Thanks," giving back the lighter.

"It's okay."

The newly arrived took another swig. "Saw you earlier at the wheel. Bad day, right?" turning his head to eye the mark better.

Tommy detected an unfamiliar accent. "Bad for me; not for you, dude." Then said again, "Not for you," shaking his head and eyeing the wet circles he was making on the bartop with his glass.

"Whaddaya mean?"

"You guys are making a killing here."

"You guys?"

"You Mohawks."

"I ain't Mohawk."

Tommy frowned, let the glass alone, stared.

"You're not Native Indian?"

"I'm Mexican."

The white man shook his head and chuckled. "Well, sorry 'bout that. You looked Mohawk to me."

"I know. Up here people think anyone looks like me is Mohawk, or Iroquois, or Oneida. But I'm Mexican. You're Canadian, right?"

Tommy smiled, nodded, sipped from his Molson, puckered his lips.

"Yep. From Cornwall. You've been to Canada?"

"Every year for the last five. From August to October, I tend bar in Quebec. Make some money, haul ass back home. Patricio Tirado," the man said and extended his right hand.

"Oh, hi. Tommy Jones." They shook.

"Like the actor?"

"Minus the Lee."

"And minus the pineapple face too." Patricio said it with an engaging smile.

Tommy nodded and took another sip; Patricio drew on his cigarette. The Akwesasne Mohawk Casino, on Route 37, was a mostly pink, single-storey building with a green roof, the sole attraction in Hogansburg, a New York state town close to the Canadian border. Operated by the Mohawk Tribal Council, it had almost a thousand slot machines, tables for roulette, craps, poker, blackjack, and a money wheel. Those actively playing on the gaming floor could order alcoholic drinks at a reduced price. Tommy Jones was correct; by tossing together gaming, spirits, food, and state-of-the-art security, the Mohawks were making a bundle.

"I'm not a gambler, you know?" Patricio said, "But every year, just before going into Canada and when I head back home, I come here, gamble a hundred or so, and watch other players. Mostly watch.

Relaxes me. And you know what? I'd never seen seven blacks in a row before."

"You were there?"

"Right behind you. It's like tossing a coin and getting tails seven consecutive times. I mean, what are the odds?"

Tommy Jones considered the question for a few moments, then launched into a four-minute-long tirade on randomness: red/black, odd/even, three columns, oo to 17, 18 to 36, proving he knew nothing about the law of independent trials.

"How much did you lose?" Patricio asked, once Tommy's outburst on the vagaries of luck concluded.

"Almost five Cs," with a sigh. Then he lit a cigarette.

"Wow. Oh, well, next time. What do you do for a living?"

Once he'd ordered his third beer, Tommy said he owned two bed and breakfasts, one in Cornwall, the other in Hogansburg.

"So, you have one foot in Canada, the other in the U.S., right?" Patricio said, smiling.

"That's right."

"Lots of driving."

"You bet," agreed Tommy.

"You are in the Nexus, I suppose."

"'Course."

Patricio nodded approvingly, ready to make his pitch.

"Tommy, would you like to make five Cs?" Crushing the butt.

Tommy Lee frowned again in confusion and stared at Patricio. The cash he had lost belonged to his wife and his sister-in-law, co-owners of the bed and breakfasts. The women occasionally transferred dollars across the border to take advantage of fluctuations in exchange and interest rates. He was supposed to hand the greenbacks he'd lost to his wife for her to deposit in the company's U.S.-dollar account at the TD in Cornwall tomorrow morning. Two days earlier, after he'd blown $325 at this same casino, Emma had given him a stern warning: next time he gambled away her and her sister's dough, she would sue for divorce and find a new guy to do the rooms and take out the trash at both B&Bs. For this Tommy was paid $200 a week; the 1996 Buick LeSabre in the casino's parking lot was his sole material possession. Before the talkative Mexican came in, Tommy had been considering which used-car dealer would pay most for his jalopy and what good reason he could give Emma for selling it, so she wouldn't suspect it was because he had lost the $460 Darlene had given him that afternoon.

Patricio – real name Valerio de Alba, a Peruvian national who had never set foot in Canada – didn't know all this, but he and his lover, Chris Dawson, had spent three days checking out vehicles entering the U.S. across the St. Lawrence Seaway. In their 2003 Cadillac DeVille they had followed cars with Canadian plates to the casino, scrutinized the drivers as they parked, then tagged them inside. Quickly discarding the noticeably affluent, those who bet small amounts for fun, and the big, mean-looking ones, they focused on the easily identifiable pathological gamblers: folks who were excited when winning, depressed when losing, and desperate when the loss was insurmountable. Chris had spotted Tommy on their first scouting day, when the dude lost $325. They tailed him when he left, jotted down the plate, watched him cross the bridge to Canada, and the following morning saw the Buick return to New York state.

In his early forties and not too bright, Tommy wore his shoulder-length hair in a ponytail, shaved maybe once a week, didn't seem particularly keen on showering daily, and dressed in cheap pants. In denial of his thirty-eight-inch waist, Tommy kept buying thirty-four-inch pants – the size he wore in his twenties – and fastened them three inches below his navel.

The Peruvian and Chris had watched with great interest as Tommy emptied the bed and breakfast's garbage cans, took orders from a tall, overweight woman in her late thirties, and later wolfed down hamburgers at Wendy's. Two hours earlier, as he hurried into the casino, Tommy had ripped open a white envelope, pulled out a sheaf of bills, and lost it all in an hour and a half. Then he had padded to the Pair-A-Dice to brood. From the slot machine where he'd been dropping coins to pass the time, Chris had stared at Valerio and raised his eyebrows, wordlessly asking his partner whether this was the right moment to make their move. Valerio, standing thirty feet away, had given three fast nods. Then Chris had shrugged and nodded once.

"Of course I'd like to make five Cs," Tommy said, wondering if, for the first time ever, God was showing compassion for him, "but it depends on the risk. I'm not going to prison for that kind of money."

Valerio shook his head and averted his eyes to show how sad that remark made him. No decent Mexican would ask anyone to do anything illegal.

"I'm a good judge of character, Tommy," he said, struggling to overcome his sorrow. "You ain't stupid. I can see that. Only a stupid man would risk his freedom for five hundred bucks. On the other hand, I come from a poor but principled family. They raised me right. I have a conscience" – tapping his chest with his right thumb – "and I don't want to end up in jail either. Other Canadians have done what I would've asked you to do today ten times over, and nothing bad happened. But if you think I would ask you to do something that'd get you in trouble, I withdraw my offer. It was a pleasure to meet you. Barman!"

Valerio pulled a thick wad of fifty-dollar bills from the right pocket of his jeans.

"No, wait," Tommy said, and Valerio knew the little fish was hooked; now it was just a matter of reeling it in gently.

"Sir?" The barkeeper.

Valerio eyed Tommy questioningly.

"Bring my friend a beer and put it on my tab," Tommy said.

Valerio's tale was simple. He had lost count of the times he had crossed borders. It wasn't his fault. American and Canadian authorities made it extremely difficult for Mexicans to obtain working permits. He had been turned down twice. Yet, as surely Tommy knew, private businesses in the U.S. and Canada needed immigrants to carry out the jobs locals were unwilling to do. Since 2002 he had crossed the border ten times, five each way, in the trunks of cars driven by Canadians in the Nexus. The regular fare was five hundred bucks. Other undocumented Mexicans spent a whole year picking oranges, grapes, and tomatoes in the U.S. to net the seven or eight thousand he made in Quebec in just four months. Therefore, forking over a thousand to get in and out wasn't a steep price. But if Tommy considered it too risky . . .

Ten minutes later, after he settled the bill, Tommy said he needed to take a leak before hauling ass. Valerio kept his eyes on the dupe until he entered the washroom, then hurried to Chris's slot machine and whispered in his ear. It was almost 6:00 p.m. when, at a deserted country road not far from the casino, Valerio got out of Tommy's Buick and lowered himself into its trunk.

The Nexus highway program simplified border crossings for low-risk citizens and residents of the United States and Canada who frequently travelled between the countries. At the border, participants entered designated lanes equipped with licence plate and ID card readers and bypassed the usual customs and immigration inspections and questioning.

Tommy crossed unmolested into Canada. Less than a minute later, Chris showed his driver's licence at the Canadian Customs and Immigration booth, opened the trunk for the inspector to examine the contents of two suitcases, and was allowed into Canada. At half past six, following Valerio's instructions, Tommy eased the Buick alongside a lawn of the Nav Canada Training Institute in Cornwall; a hedge blocked the view from the cluster of buildings two hundred metres away. The Canuck got out, looked around; not a soul. He opened the trunk and a smiling Valerio climbed out, ten Ulysses Grant portraits in hand. Tommy pocketed the money, said goodbye and good luck, got behind the wheel, and drove home in high spirits. He had not only covered his losses but discovered a great way to make easy dinero.

Valerio ambled to the intersection with Montreal Road, where he dropped the pack of cigarettes in a trash can and waited ten minutes for Chris to pick him up.

"How did it feel?" his partner asked as the Peruvian buckled up.

"Like a womb. Fetal position, dark, defenceless."

Chris nodded. "We'll reach Toronto by midnight," he said.

"You know what? I'm tired," Valerio said. "What do you say we hit the road now, spend the night at the first motel we find, and drive to Toronto in the morning?"

"Good idea. Maybe it will have a pool and we can relax and sip margaritas; blow off steam."

"Blow we will, darling, but not steam. Look, the sign says 401 West."

August 1

Elliot Steil said, "And you think that's correct?"

Fidelia, on a loveseat across the room, lent an ear. She hadn't been paying attention to his voice in the background, but the word *correct* fired synapses in the lawyerly section of her brain. She lifted her eyes from the newspaper, gazed at Elliot.

"Oh, really?" he went on, looking at the top of his desk. "You charge me the monthly rate over the whole balance because I didn't pay eight cents, and you think that's correct?"

Fidelia's mind flashed back to when they started their relationship. Back then, he'd reacted to unfairness by clicking his tongue, forcing a smile, shaking his head sadly, and glancing sideways. Over the years, the competitiveness of capitalism had changed him. Right now, Elliot's face was flushed with anger.

He listened for a few moments, then said: "I know computers don't think. But I expected a person would realize this is absurd and fix it."

Short pause.

"Well, thank you very much" – dripping sarcasm – "I'll mail you a cheque first thing tomorrow. Oh, by the way, cancel my card."

Couple of seconds.

"You bet I am."

Brief silence.

"Nothing else, thanks. Goodbye."

Elliot stabbed the end key and returned the cordless to its base.

"What was that?" In Spanish, as always at home.

"Bandits. They are all bandits."

"What happened?"

Elliot took a deep breath, rolled himself out of the desk's kneehole, turned in the swivel chair. Dressed in pyjama bottoms and a T-shirt for lounging at home, he was now as relaxed as a tuned violin string.

"My credit card. Last month they billed me $478.08. But I missed the eight cents and cut a cheque for $478.00. This month they billed me a finance charge of $7.87. So, I called and punched like fourteen keys and listened to a stupid song for five minutes and several of those 'your call is important to us.' Finally I got a guy, in Mumbai probably, and asked him why the $7.87. He said that because I didn't pay my previous bill in full, they charged me the monthly interest over the whole amount, $487.08. Can you believe it?"

Fidelia shook her head in disbelief, folded the newspaper, set it beside her on the seat. "You sure the guy understood you owed eight frigging cents?"

"Well, I don't think call centres employ mentally retarded people. And he commiserated, 'Sooo sorry.' Said the computer automatically charges interest over the whole bill if you don't pay it in full. And he couldn't make it right."

"That's outrageous."

"It's why I cancelled the card."

Elliot turned to face the desk, opened a drawer, grabbed a pair of scissors, cut the credit card in three, threw the pieces in the trash can. "Bandits, that's what they are."

Fidelia kept her eyes on him.

"Everybody gets offered two, three credit cards every month," he said, fuming, as he opened a chequebook. "What happened to cash and cheques? Why do we need so many damned credit cards?"

He had gained around twenty pounds over the years, Fidelia reckoned. Had gone from a thirty-four waist to a thirty-six, from M to L, from briefs to trunks. There was a bald spot on the crown of his head, much more body hair on his chest and back. Well, she wasn't getting any younger either; it was almost three months since her last period. And despite the dieting, the aerobics, and the pill-popping, her breasts surrendered to gravity when she unhooked her 34-C. Would he adjust? All men want their women to stay young, beautiful, and sexy until death do us part, and adjustment implied acceptance – or resignation. She was not in the least turned off by the waning of his physical powers, but she was a woman. Fidelia deemed females more mature. After eleven years practising marital and family law in Miami, she firmly believed that, in lifelong spousal relationships, most women are psychologically attuned to bodily decline, whereas most men aren't.

Still peeved, Elliot tore the cheque from the stub. "*Hijos de puta*," he mumbled.

"Let it go," she said. "You've cancelled the card, so move on. Come, sit here," moving the newspaper to her lap and patting the seat.

Elliot stood, hitched up his pyjama pants and sat beside her on the loveseat. Thirteen years earlier she had chosen this one-bedroom apartment on Virginia Street in Coconut Grove. The house she owned, where her seventy-nine-year-old mother and twenty-three-year-old son lived, was in the northwest section of Miami. Most nights she slept here, with Elliot.

"Guy like you, signs multi-million dollar contracts on a weekly basis, getting all worked up for . . . How much was it?"

"$7.87."

" . . . by a seven-buck swindle? How come?"

"It's the principle, Fidelia."

"I understand that. But forget it. Let your pulse drop back to normal. It's not worth it."

"I can't help it."

"Yes, you can. I've seen you play it cool in much more stressful situations."

He remained silent, staring at the floor. Fidelia believed she knew the underlying cause of his irascibility these last few days.

"It's nothing, Elio. Think what Willy Cardenás is going through," she began in a neutral tone, setting the trap with feminine astuteness.

"Yeah."

"Or Henry Nicholson."

"Hum."

"Or Humberto Marrero."

Elliot lifted his eyes from the floor and stared at her. The wife and two teenaged sons of Willy Cardenás, a prominent Miami realtor, had died in a traffic accident a week earlier; Henry Nicholson was a television producer standing trial for child molesting. Total strangers to Elliot and Fidelia, but their stories were all over the media. Humberto Marrero, however, was a Miami Seaport official accused of getting kickbacks, gifts, and paid holidays in exchange for turning a blind eye to smuggled goods and banned substances. The scandal was front-page news and several police officers had been suspended and were under investigation, among them Tony Soto, a friend of Elliot's.

The hint of a smile tugged at the corners of his mouth as he fixed his eyes on her. It was crystal-clear. She wanted to discuss the case. She wanted him to admit that Tony, in addition to being aggressive and intimidating, besides being an alcoholic, and a guy who thought little of women in general and of his wife in particular, was a corrupt bastard.

Innocence shone on Fidelia's face as she added, "Speaking of Marrero, the paper says Tony Soto has been suspended from the police force, pending investigation. Allegedly he was one of the cops that bribed inspectors."

She unfolded the newspaper, pointed at a paragraph.

"I know," Elliot said. "I read it."

"What do you think?"

Elliot forced a smile, shook his head.

"What's with the head-shaking?" Her tone was confrontational.

His smile vanished. "I don't want to discuss Tony's case with you."

"Oh, no? Why not?"

"Because for you, Tony is guilty as hell. Judge Fidelia has already sentenced him to ten years in prison. So, what's to discuss?"

Her face froze. She stood and dropped the paper onto the coffee table. "You are right. There's nothing to discuss," she snapped. "It's your problem, not mine. I'll turn in now. Good night."

Elliot followed her with his eyes as she stomped out of the living room and slammed the bedroom door.

He sighed. One hundred per cent guilty, Tony was. For many years he had been the cutoff man for Imlatinex, the company Elliot currently managed. Before Elliot arrived in the U.S., the late Ruben Scheindlin had recruited Tony, then at the Biscayne Boulevard Police Mini Station, Bayside Detail, to grease the palms of customs officers who expedited the clearance of shipments, post-clearance audits, and the resolution of disputes. As a result, certain merchandise shipped to Imlatinex cleared customs without being sniffed by dogs or X-rayed. After Scheindlin died, Elliot and Samuel Plotzher, the firm's senior shareholder, had kept Tony on their secret payroll. Whenever "expediting" was necessary, Elliot called Tony, provided details about the shipment, gave him the cash. Later the cop talked to his contacts and lined their pockets.

It had got costlier and riskier after 9/11. Retirements and firings, plus the stepped-up rotation of inspectors among various cargo stations, had forced Tony to scout for new recruits. Elliot and Plotzher had made it clear they didn't want to know names or positions; all they wanted was for Tony to expedite. In conversations, they referred to him as "the expediter."

Nothing really dangerous had been smuggled. No drugs, explosives, or firearms. Chlorofluorocarbons, yes, by the ton, but that had ended around 1996; also products containing asbestos, banned hydraulic fluids, pesticides, that sort of thing. Elliot quieted his conscience by reasoning that the products would be reshipped to Latin American countries where they were not banned (or where customs inspectors were fixed, too). He suspected that other import/export firms were doing the same, but should Tony cop a plea and rat on them, the company would be in serious trouble. He, as general manager, would be charged and maybe fined, or sentenced to prison.

Which was why an unfair credit card charge made him seethe. Why Fidelia wanted to discuss Tony. Why he couldn't.

She knew he was at the helm of a company where dealing with customs was a daily occurrence; she knew Tony Soto was a cop, a friend of his, and a frequent visitor to Imlatinex. She was a lawyer and read the papers; you didn't have to be a mental giant to figure it out.

And Tony was on the brink of collapse. No one who had known him at fifteen, a lean teenager at the Havana institute where Elliot once taught English, would recognize him now. Nobody would believe that the 275-pound, six-foot-one, thirty-nine-year-old cop, who looked forty-nine, had been a 185-pound, pumping-iron hunk in the mid-1990s. Eating like a goombah and guzzling ten beers a day had spoiled his physique. Elliot suspected him of womanizing too. He had twice spotted Tony coming out of bars on Collins Avenue, arm in arm with women who looked like hookers; the sort who will give hot leads and free rides to cops in case they ever needed to call a friend at Miami Beach's Police Department.

One of Elliot's guiding principles was not to give advice on personal matters to anyone. But Tony had been so supportive when Elliot first arrived from Cuba that two or three years earlier, for a minute or two, he contemplated warning his friend about the risks of a life of excess. But how could he? Ask the man to bribe people, and in the next breath moralize on broads, booze, and junk food?

Elliot shook his head. His sense of right and wrong had degraded substantially. He no longer stole cars or sold banned refrigerants, but now he bribed people, paid experts to find loopholes in tax laws and accounting regulations, cheated on his income tax return, donated to Democrat and Republican candidates to have a finger in each pie, overcharged clients on shipping and handling, kept a secret cash fund and . . . He searched his memory for other transgressions in vain. So, who was he to get on his high horse? Was he any better than the credit card company?

Who could get on their high horse these days? Scientists? Artists? Judges? Maybe. Most, not all. The Fidelias of this world? Possibly. And, regardless of what they did or where they lived, lots of people among the billions of the dispossessed. But no one on Earth who held a position of authority in politics, government, business, the military, or the media could even access the horse's stable. Every single one, at some point, started to bend rules, make compromises, cut corners, cheat, contravene the principles their parents and educators had tried to inculcate in them.

So what the fuck was he whining about? According to the rules of the game, if Tony blew the trumpet on him, he would retain the best lawyer he could afford and face the music. And if worse came to worst, he'd try to leave the Glades penitentiary with his ass intact.

Elliot Steil got up and went to the bedroom. The lights were out. He slipped into bed, turned on his side, closed his eyes. After a minute:

"Elio?"

"Yes."

"You know how old my mother is?"

"Eighty-something, I guess."

"Seventy-nine. She's frail. She forgets things."

"It's normal at her age."

"Yeah."

Nothing was said for a while.

"Soon I'll have to start spending some nights there."

Elliot opened his eyes. His payback for refusing to discuss Tony? Possibly.

"You feel you should care for her, go ahead. I understand."

"I knew you would. I'll do it gradually. Just two or three nights on weekdays, for as long as possible. But should she get worse, I may have to stay there every night."

"You won't consider moving her to a home?"

"Not while I can keep up with my work. When she reaches the point she needs round-the-clock care, I'll find a home."

"Let me know if I can help."

"Thanks, Elio. Good night."

"Good night, Fidelia."

August 4

Valerio de Alba eased the Cadillac into a parking lot near Richmond and Sherbourne a few minutes after 9:00 a.m. He got out and read the instructions on the parking meter before dropping in a two-dollar coin that bought him one hour. He looked up: limpid blue sky, temperature feeling in the mid-nineties (was that thirty-something in Canada?) on account of the high humidity. By the time he placed the ticket on the dashboard, Chris Dawson was already tapping on the computer resting on his lap.

"You found one?" the Peruvian asked, as he closed the driver's-side door.

"Are you kidding? This is downtown Toronto," Chris said. "Hundreds of offices, thousands of routers. Most people don't encrypt. I've found six. Let me see . . . Excellent connection. Now, what should we surf first?"

At Valerio's indication, Chris googled "gay community Toronto." With the Peruvian peeking over his shoulder, he clicked until he found a map.

"Write this down, dude."

Valerio opened the glove compartment, pulled out a notebook and a ballpoint, wrote *Places to Avoid* at the top of the first page. "Ready," he said.

"Gay territory. Limits: Yonge, Jarvis, Bloor and Carlton."

Next Chris dictated the names of three hotels, four restaurants, and two bed and breakfasts considered gay-friendly.

"What now?" he asked.

"Areas of violent crime?" Valerio proposed.

It took Chris a little over six minutes to find out: "The club district, downtown; the general area around Jane and Finch; and the Junction-York area."

"Not good enough. Try recent shootings and stabbings," Valerio said.

Less than two minutes later Chris started rattling off street names. "Richmond Street near John Street; Flemington Park in the Don Mills area; Jane and Lawrence Avenue; Weston Road near Eglinton Avenue West . . ."

Valerio wrote down forty-two places where violent incidents had taken place in the past two months.

"I'll be damned. I thought this city was a lot less violent," Chris said with a puzzled expression.

"And I thought it was cooler in the summer. Okay, let's find out 'race of murdered men.'"

The best they got was a vague "mostly young black men."

"Search for neighbourhoods with more drug dealing and drug use."

Finding this took longer. Eventually Chris started reeling off city areas.

"The downtown core of Toronto and the neighbourhoods of Malvern, Jamestown, Jane-Finch, Kingston-Galloway, Lawrence Heights, L'Amoreaux, Markham and Eglinton . . ."

Valerio had to drop two more two-dollar coins in the meter to finish the first phase of their research. They drove back to the unexceptional hotel on Harbour Street where they had spent their third night in Toronto, had lunch, and went to their room. After spreading a city map on the floor, Valerio produced a red marker and sat cross-legged. Chris sat beside him and started reading addresses that the Peruvian located – first in the street index, then in the grid – before circling or dotting the areas and places they would avoid.

An hour later they were done. Valerio contemplated the map. "The east seems quieter than the west," he said.

"Except for a few trouble spots in . . ." Chris leaned forward, "Scarborough."

"Right. But see, this area here" – Valerio moved his forefinger over the map – "let's see . . . between Bayview to the west and Victoria Park to the east, north of . . . Danforth and south of . . . Lawrence seems less problematic."

"Uh-huh. And it's not too far from downtown."

"Yeah. Lots of green spaces. See? Parks, rivers; looks promising. Let's start looking for houses in that area. C'mon, let's go."

Back in the same parking lot, Chris googled "Toronto houses for rent." Checking the map for each address, they found none in their chosen area.

"I guess we'll have to go there and drive along the streets; try to find For Rent signs," Valerio said.

"Remind me why an apartment is out of the question," Chris asked.

"Would it be possible to ride an elevator feeling absolutely certain no one will step in?"

"No."

"Walk a hallway absolutely sure that no neighbour will come out?"

"Okay, okay."

"The Professor said privacy is a must. A house in a quiet street with a garage and the least neighbours possible, as far away as possible. We don't find the perfect place, then we put up with neighbours; may even have to take one in a noisy street, but a house with a garage is absolutely essential."

"Understood. You want me to search used-car dealers next?"

"The kind of wheel bandits we need don't advertise on the Web. See if there's something on Arab clothing stores."

Ten minutes later they had compiled a list of eleven stores, their addresses and phone numbers.

"What now? Video stores?"

"Nah. Any camera will do."

"So, what next?"

"What do you say we do some scouting in the east?"

"Sure. Let me study the map first."

They took Queen Street to Bayview, north to Eglinton, then meandered through Leaside. One- and two-storey detached homes prevailed, the oldest made of honest-to-goodness brick and wood; the most recent of plywood, plasterboard, and faux brick or rock panels. Well-tended lawns, hedges, garages, chimneys, one or two cars in the driveways. Power and phone lines overhead, impeccably clean streets and sidewalks. A lady picking up her dog's poop on this block; a guy mowing his lawn on the next; an old man tending a flower bed two hundred metres farther along; across the street, a twelve-year-old on rollerblades hitting a puck. A Korean couple living alongside a Jewish family, next to an Iranian family, adjacent to a Canadian household, flanking a Chinese home.

"Is this a rich neighbourhood?" Valerio asked.

"Middle-class, I guess."

The Peruvian nodded. "This would be considered Fairyland where I come from."

They said nothing for the next four or five minutes.

"Are these people onto something?" Valerio again.

"What do you mean?"

"Coexistence."

"What?"

"Living in harmony. Not like you guys. You live in patches. The Latino patch, the Irish patch, the Italian patch, the Jewish patch. The white patch, the black patch, the yellow patch. Melting pot? Give me a break. I'm seeing a true melting pot here."

"That's bullshit. We've been to Chinatown, Greektown, Little India, Koreatown," Chris countered.

"Those are business areas. It seems to me, after closing time people from all those places drive home and live side by side."

"I don't think so."

"Well, you are entitled to your opinion. That's coexistence too."

They didn't find a single sign advertising a home for rent and gave up around 8:00 p.m.

"Good day," Valerio commented on the way back to the hotel.

"We haven't found the house," Chris objected.

"Things click into place in five minutes only in the movies, my love. And this isn't a movie."

Valerio

Having illegally crossed the borders of ten countries in twelve years without ever getting apprehended made Valerio de Alba a specialist in clandestine migration. To pull it off, he had – with more successes than mixed results or clear-cut failures – manipulated scores of people. Along the way, he learned a great deal about human nature.

When he was born, in 1976, his father had been a cashier with the Wong Supermarket chain for six years. He could afford to rent a modest house with electricity and running water in the Cono Norte neighbourhood of Lima, Peru, sparing his family the awful deprivations experienced by most descendants of Quechua peasants who had moved to the capital. Valerio finished grade school at the San Felipe public school, where he found his vocation for drawing.

At secondary school Valerio discovered American and European fashion magazines. Perusing the slick colour photos and ads, it suddenly came to him there was a world out there he knew nothing about. It had megalopolises jam-packed with steel-and-glass towers and wide avenues chock-full of shiny cars. Mostly young, white, and beautiful people looked, dressed, and probably smelled like no one he had ever known. They lived in mansions or enormous apartments furnished in magnificent styles. From the clothing and swimwear the models wore, Valerio deduced that their summers weren't cloudy and foggy like his and that people vacationed at beach resorts where the seawater was warm enough for them to dip in practically naked. Their winter took place during the Peruvian summer, and many longed for snowy Christmases. It seemed to be a world free of poverty, crime, and injustice. Valerio started sketching the dresses, faces, and bodies he admired most.

In those same years his father was promoted to store manager and the government started a program of sex education and AIDS prevention in which Valerio learned about homosexuality, a subject taboo among relatives, neighbours, and friends. The teenager realized that although he was fascinated by the beautiful faces and lean bodies of female fashion models, he was not sexually attracted to women. The models he longed to touch were the extremely handsome, perfectly proportioned men, especially those in sportswear and underwear ads.

Valerio's second eye-opener happened when he visited the Gold Museum and gaped at the numerous treasures of pre-Columbian Peruvian civilizations, including Moche ceramics and pottery and Incan pieces of gold. A later tour of the National Archaeology, Anthropology and History Museum convinced him that he was descended from great people. Artistically, the Incas had been second to none.

To broaden his horizons, he started visiting Barranco, the heart of Lima's contemporary arts and nightlife. Valerio wanted to find more about fashion designers and models, painters and painting, photographers and photography, sculptors and sculpting. He found all that, and something else. One evening, in the restroom of a discotheque, a handsome guy in his thirties, a *muñeca* – a derisive term used in Lima for a delicate but not effeminate homosexual man – at the next urinal started relieving himself. After a few seconds he turned his head, lowered his eyes, gaped at Valerio's penis, gasped, and covered his mouth with his free hand.

At that moment, six things clicked into place for the seventeen-year-old: first, until then sex had been masturbation; second, he felt attracted to white, blond, handsome males, and this guy was all that; third, he had learned at school that homosexuals were not degenerates; fourth, the parish priest had said a person could be homosexual *and* Christian; fifth, his weekly allowance was only two *nuevos soles*; and lastly, two margaritas had considerably softened his inhibitions. When the *muñeca* offered Valerio twenty *nuevos soles* to take a shower at his apartment while he watched, the young man considered it. The blond man grasped that he had stumbled upon what many gay men dream of: a virgin and closeted gay youngster with a big cock. He assured Valerio that all he would do was watch him shower; he wouldn't make his new friend uncomfortable in any way.

"Okay, let's go," Valerio said, zipping up.

The *muñeca* knew damn well that should others in the community learn about his marvellous find, there would be a fierce struggle for the teenager's favours. He decided to keep him for himself. But he did tell his confidant, the older, sweet, and supportive basketball coach he had known since high school, the man who showed him the delights that may be experienced in dark, empty locker rooms, who was presently his personal trainer. Five or six weeks later, Valerio was well-known in the Lima gay community as a *chala*, slang for big dick, or the man who has one. A lasting friendship between a gym devotee and his trainer shattered into animosity. A few months later, Valerio was a *moderno*, a gay man who enjoys both pitching and catching. After a year or so, he was downgraded to *flete*, someone who would trade sex for money.

It was true, he had become a *flete*.

Valerio now hung out with other fashion devotees, hairdressers, make-up artists, photographers, and models; devoured *Vogue, Harper's*

Bazaar, Elle, Vanity Fair, and other fashion magazines; and feverishly sketched costumes. His burning ambition was to gain entry to the world of fashion, but he knew that, being Quechua, he would never achieve that in Peru. He had to go to Paris, Milan, or New York, where racial discrimination was negligible or non-existent and some rich cognoscenti thought that supporting and promoting exotic individuals was chic and modish. A round-trip plane ticket to Paris or Milan, however, cost between $1,500 and $2,000, the cheapest to New York around $1,000. He owned nothing; his family barely scraped by. What could he sell to make money? His body, nothing else.

After high school, Valerio ran a stall at the Indio Market, in Avenida La Marina, during the day. He sold works of art carved in wood by a friend and got paid a 10 per cent commission. Monday through Thursday evenings he took English courses, the most popular second language in Lima; in his free time he took care of a select clientele. Three years later, in 1996, the *neuvos soles* he had saved, at the prevailing exchange rate, amounted to only $700, give or take a few. The fees to obtain a passport and to apply for a visa to France, Italy, or the U.S. added up to over $300. Valerio grasped that even if he managed to save enough for all the fees and airfare, he would arrive penniless in a country ranked among the most expensive in the world. His dream seemed impractical.

Then he met Manuel Serrano and Gladys Suárez de Serrano, a married couple from Guayaquil, Ecuador. Respectively gay and lesbian, they came from rich and extremely conservative families, and shared a taste for luxury cars and travel. Six years earlier they had agreed to get married to relieve the pressure that Ecuadorian high society brings to bear on people in their thirties whose close friends are all same-sex. Manuel and Gladys frequently felt like making new friends and spending time where not a soul knew them, so they had flown to scores of places. They didn't think much of

Ecuador's southern neighbour and had never been there, but on an impulse decided to take a shot at it.

From Machu Picchu the couple drove to Lima, took a presidential suite at the Miraflores Park Hotel, explored the city, and while browsing the Indio Market met Valerio. A glance sparked instant mutual recognition. Manuel took a liking to the Peruvian. He learned of his ambition to travel and offered to take him to Ecuador.

"I can't accept your offer," said Valerio. "I don't have a passport."

"Not a problem," Manuel said.

Six days later, an impressive-looking, late-model E-class Mercedes-Benz crossed the international bridge over the Lagunilla River, on the Peru-Ecuador border, where the customs and immigration officers of both countries had an unofficial gentlemen's agreement not to waste time checking out the papers or vehicles of foreigners *leaving* their country; inspections were the responsibility of their counterparts across the border.

Their colleagues on the other bank believed that smugglers and illegals do not attempt to slip through an adequately staffed border crossing in broad daylight, in brand-new, seventy-thousand-dollar Mercedes sedans with all their papers in order. Neither do smugglers surrender valid passports full of stamps from all over the world, nor do they wear expensive clothes. They had also learned that if you treat rich people courteously and respectfully, they may slip you a twenty-dollar bill, and their salaries are meagre. Would you ask this affluent couple to get out and perform a thorough search of the vehicle's interior? Demand they open the trunk? Of course not. It was how Valerio de Alba, lying on the floor of the car's back seat, covered by a grey alpaca blanket, left his country of birth unnoticed.

After five months in Ecuador, Valerio paid a steep price to cross into Colombia. For two weeks he had to screw nightly an obese, fifty-five-year-old masseur from the thermal baths of Aguas Hediondas.

In exchange for Valerio's services and the promise he would return
in a month, the masseur paid a guide to take Valerio around the side
of the Chiles volcano into Colombia.

Carrying a small, very old suitcase with his best clothes, hitch-
hiking on all sorts of vehicles, travelling occasionally on foot or as a
fare-paying passenger on stinking buses with as many goats, pigs, and
fowl as humans, or as a stowaway in freight cars, Valerio pressed
forward. Drenched to the skin during thunderstorms, sweating to
the point of exhaustion in summertime, shivering with cold in winter,
stung by mosquitoes, watching out for snakes, hungry most of the
time, and frequently thirsty, he watched the breathtaking South
American and Central American scenery slide past.

Playing a gay or straight card according to circumstance, picking
fruit in season, painting walls, mowing lawns, Valerio earned money.
Sometimes he bribed folks. On many occasions he made up stories.
Depending on the mark, he was variously: searching for his wife and
son, who had gone missing; keeping a promise he made to the Virgin
of Guadalupe, who healed his little girl's cancer in nine days; tracking his parents' assassin; hoping to get a job with his uncle in the
capital; joining the rebels in Chiapas, Mexico; exploring the migra-
tory patterns of birds (or fish); or looking for a miraculous herb
that the Archangel Gabriel had assured him cured AIDS. But to
keep moving up north he also had to give or receive blow jobs,
bugger or get buggered, which occasionally required putting up
with some difficult men.

Valerio flew to Panama on the helicopter of a cattle rancher from
Antioquia who swallowed the Virgin of Guadalupe story hook, line,
and sinker. He entered Costa Rica on the roof of a freight car, then
reached Nicaragua via a jungle trail. Sixteen months had gone by
since the day he left Lima.

On a very hot and drizzly afternoon, Valerio found his way to the
town of Nueva Guinea. He was coughing, short of breath, and feeling

feverish, and his chest ached, but determined not to spend a cent on doctors and medicines, he kept padding along. Nothing if not strong-willed, he had the luck this time to be in the right place at the right time. He lost consciousness at a gas station across from El Reposo, a non-governmental centre for the rehabilitation, care, and instruction of destitute and abused children. Two gas station attendants hauled Valerio up by his underarms and feet and took him to the centre where, coincidentally, a Catholic pediatrician was holding pro bono consultation that afternoon. The doctor suspected the Peruvian had pneumonia, but lacking a chest X-ray and lab results, he couldn't be sure. Despite the patient being an adult and a foreigner, the centre reached into its meagre stock of donated antibiotics and properly treated and nourished Valerio until he was pronounced in good health six weeks later.

Such display of human compassion tugged at his heartstrings. He repaid the director's kindness by becoming the centre's unpaid jack-of-all-trades seven days a week. For ten months, he cleaned floors, ran errands, taught illiterate children the alphabet and the elements of drawing, read them stories, nursed the sick, and comforted the suffering. Valerio stuck to masturbation, abstained from manipulating anyone, and learned to love the humble and destitute farmhands of Nicaragua. The young and the middle-aged and the old expressed their appreciation in countless ways, including the donation of a less battered suitcase full of used clothes to replace Valerio's rags. Three women considered him a saint and asked him to bless them. There were abundant tears the day he resumed his trek.

Along the way, as Valerio saw how scores of poverty-stricken, bare-foot, malnourished, and illiterate Hondurans, Guatemalans, and Mexicans lived, he concluded that God had meant the world to be as it was. Donations and compassion would alleviate, not end, poverty. His burning ambition to be a rich and famous fashion designer grew all-consuming; more than ever he wanted to leave behind poverty and sickness. Once he made enough money, he promised himself, he would return to Nueva Guinea at the wheel of a tractor hauling a twenty-ton trailer full of food, pharmaceuticals, toys, books, paper, and crayons. He would spend a couple of weeks with the people who loved him like his mother and father loved him, those who were clueless concerning his lack of scruples, the kind souls who had believed him a saint. But first he had to conquer the world of fashion, be acclaimed the new Dior, sashay the catwalks at the end of the shows, bow to the standing ovations of audiences in New York first, Milan next, and, finally, be crowned king in Paris.

It took Valerio over three years to sneak into Casa Grande, Arizona. On November 4, 1999, he felt pretty much what Christopher Columbus must have felt the day he set foot on a small tropical island.

August 16

Jenny Scheindlin smiled and shook hands with the attractive woman pushing forty, noting that the daughter had inherited her mother's genes. The girl's father, one of her Upper West Side apartment building's doormen, was courteous, obsequious, discreet, tidy, probably honest, but as plain as an electricity pole. Jenny had noticed that many beautiful women date, marry, or live with physically unattractive men. Movie stars seemed to be the exception that proves the rule, maybe because they share their orbits with leading men, not because handsome guys are superior in any other respect, she had concluded years earlier.

"You are *so* kind to give me a few minutes of your time, Ms. Scheindlin."

"Jenny, please. Come in, come in" – stepping aside and waving her in – "your husband asked me if I could see you and I said, With pleasure. I owe it to him; he's willing to lend a hand anytime" – closing the front door – "This way, Mrs. Moretti."

Virginia Moretti, the wife of Phil Moretti, a third-generation Italian-American, gazed around as she crossed the short hallway and entered the living space. A huge, exquisite Persian rug graced the floor; an antique French tapestry hung on one long wall, opposite a very old mirror framed in dark brown wood. Below the mirror was a two-drawer, hand-painted stand with bronze inlays. Jenny waved Virginia to a small French-style sofa with gold mouldings and sank into a bigger one, upholstered in fine tapestry, opposite her visitor. Both seats were flanked by elegant side tables supporting Venetian rose vases.

"Oh, Ms. Sch– . . . Jenny, what beautiful décor."

"You like it?"

"Oh, it's lovely."

"Thank you. Make yourself comfortable," Jenny said. "Would you like a cup of tea, coffee, a cocktail maybe?"

"Oh, no. I'm fine, thanks."

"You sure?"

"Totally."

"Then, let me know how I can be of assistance."

The visitor pressed her lips together, interlaced her fingers, and gazed at the tapestry on the opposing wall. Her inexpensive pantsuit looked classy on her, Jenny noticed. She had learned years earlier that clothes don't make the woman, or the man.

"Well, Jenny," Virginia now locked eyes with her hostess, "I suppose Phil mentioned that our daughter, who is as mule-headed as her father –"

"And as beautiful as you."

"Oh. C'mon, *you* are beautiful," taken by surprise. Then, "You think so?" smiling and batting her eyelids.

"I do. Your husband showed me pictures of . . . Donna? Is it Donna?"

"Danette."

"Right, Danette. Tell me you didn't look like her when you were her age."

"Oh, well, she looks a little bit like me, but I wasn't half as beautiful as she is. Danette was, oh, I don't know, ten or so, when people started saying she was so beautiful and tall and had such lovely eyes and hair that she could be a fashion model. At that age, she had no idea what a fashion model was or did. But at twelve she, you know, awakened to her beauty and started flipping the pages of fashion magazines and since then she's been, like, obsessing about becoming a model."

"She's fifteen now, right?"

"Right. Sixteen next March." Virginia fidgeted, slid to the edge of the sofa to get to the point. "And you know, Ms . . . I mean, Jenny, about a year ago – seeing she talked about nothing else and spent hours in her room with a book on top of her head and, like, modelling clothes – I started reading all I could find: magazines, newspapers, I even went to the public library and borrowed books. And I've come to believe that it's . . . a fine profession, sure, with many fine people, like you, but . . . it seems to me, as an outsider, that a minor is not prepared to deal with this travelling all over the world and posing semi-nude, and going to parties where there's a lot of drinking, and maybe drugs, and sex, too. And because you are a famous model –"

"I was," Jenny said, feeling forced to interrupt. "I quit modelling two years ago, but I'm still in the fashion industry, considering business opportunities."

"Oh, I didn't know that."

"But I know the world of fashion pretty well. Go ahead, please."

"Anyway, since you were a model for several years, I was wondering if you could, well, you know, advise me on how to make this child see that it wouldn't be in her best interest to be a model."

Jenny let a few seconds slip by, as her father had taught her. *Always make sure the other person is through*, he had repeated over and over.

"I see. Now let me ask you a couple of questions. Are you religious, Virginia?"

"Yes, I'm Catholic."

"And you've raised Danette as Catholic, right?"

"Right."

"You have a job?"

"Yes, I'm an accountant at a moving agency."

"Okay. What would you like Danette to be?"

"Oh, I don't know," again raising her eyes to the tapestry. "Any profession that's . . . standard."

"Would you like her to be a nun?"

"Oh, no," emphatically.

"Glad to hear that. Then, do you want her to be a doctor, a lawyer, a hairdresser, a business executive?"

"Oh, any of those; whatever she prefers."

"Aha. Now, are you aware that, regardless of the profession she chooses, a young woman as beautiful as Danette is going to be asked out on dates by dozens of guys that hope to have sex with her?"

"I suppose so."

"No, don't suppose. How many guys asked you out when you were young?"

Virginia blushed and lowered her eyes to the floor. "A few."

"Don't be modest."

"Well, yes. A lot."

"And now?"

"Now?"

"Yes, this month, last week. C'mon, I'm sure guys are putting the moves on you on a daily basis."

The blush turned into beet red. "Sometimes . . . guys . . . like, you know, insinuate they would . . . Tell me, Jenny, what's the matter with men? I mean, a stranger, I can understand. But neighbours? Phil's friends? Jesus!"

"Now we are talking. Listen, Virginia. Regardless of the career she chooses, Danette will get invited to parties where there are drinks, and drugs, and people have sex. A guy I know says that if you could vacuum up all the cocaine Wall Streeters sniff in a single working day, you'd probably gather two kilos of the thing. Imagine Danette doing an internship at the New York Stock Exchange; your baby moving among the wolves there."

"Oh, my God."

"Yes, you better pray she doesn't. So, is Little Red Riding Hood out of the woods? No, Virginia. If Danette chooses to be a dental assistant, any straight dentist, married or single, is gonna come in on her. Secretary of a business executive? The guy will try to dip it in too. Whatever line of work Danette chooses, she's going to have to fight off ten guys every single day."

"I suppose so, yes."

"You suppose?"

"No, you're right."

"There's no perfectly safe environment for your daughter or for anyone else in Manhattan. Predators are everywhere, Virginia: the Red Cross, the Boy Scouts, Homeland Security, churches, among doctors and nurses and teachers and sports trainers and government officials. Sex is the most primeval of human instincts, and most men and some women have a hard time controlling their sexual urges.

"Now let's discuss modelling. You are right; it's not the most appropriate environment for immature and inexperienced young women. Nor young men, I should add. You send a baby animal out in the wild alone and anything can happen; the chances of getting torn apart are considerable.

"There are predators in the fashion industry, among agents and photographers and designers. But there are ten decent people for

every predator. Just as in a hospital or a church you find ten decent
doctors and priests for each sonofabitch.

"Let me tell you something else. Some kids are pretty mature and
educated, but some are like animals. These young animals, girls and
boys, are willing to do whatever it takes to make money out of fashion
for the rest of their lives, and they can be like predators, too; predators on the system. For the right kind of money they are willing to
make love to a giraffe or an eighty-five-year-old; they will sniff coke
if asked to, do a porn movie –"

"Oh, my God."

"Yeah, but maybe God has better things to do. Sometimes these
kids give more than they get. I've met some that peaked early and
then they were gone; lost as a consequence of drugs and alcohol."

Virginia covered her mouth with her hand.

"I had no clue what it was like when I got into modelling," Jenny
went on and crossed her legs. "No clue *at all*. I got lucky, though, for
two reasons. My parents brought me up like all parents, you know,
don't steal, don't lie, say your prayers, the usual. But they never said
'we forbid you to have sex' or 'we forbid you to smoke grass.' They
weren't moralists. My mother, though, explained the dangers of
unprotected sex, promiscuity, and taking drugs very clearly to me. I
saw my first condom at twelve: my mother slipping it on a banana,
can you believe it?"

Virginia chuckled, then said, "I did that to Danette two days after
her fourteenth birthday."

"Good. But you know what? All dicks I've seen since are smaller
than that banana."

Virginia doubled over and the smiling Jenny waited until her
visitor calmed down, took a Kleenex from her purse, and dabbed at
the corners of her eyes.

"The second reason is that my late father was quite comfortable
and he loaned me the money I needed to make a book. He paid the

balance of my credit cards, and if I needed cash all I had to do was go to the nearest ATM. But 99 per cent of the girls that start in fashion don't have rich parents. In fact, some from Eastern Europe, Africa, and South America are dirt poor; entirely dependent on agents and penniless most of the time. And, you know, when you are abroad, homesick, broke, and somebody offers you two hundred bucks for ten minutes of your time . . ."

"Oh, my God."

"You asked me to advise you, right?"

"Oh, yes, please."

"Have you tried to dissuade her?"

Virginia nodded.

"Many times? Over the years?"

Two energetic nods.

"Take it from me, Virginia. The worst thing you can do, the absolute worst, is to be at odds with your daughter concerning her choice of career. You should tell her that you'd prefer she opted for a less uncertain occupation, one where people are not considered old in their early thirties. But maybe you should also offer her a deal. The month she finishes high school, you'll take her to a modelling agency for a casting. I'll recommend you a good agency. Then, I'm willing to have a long talk with Danette so as to, you know, open her eyes to the realities of the business. She'll believe everything I say because she knows I'm speaking from experience and because I'm not her mother."

"Would you really do that, Jenny?"

"I would, Virginia, if you do as I recommend."

"Wow, I didn't even dream that you'd volunteer to help me out to such an extent. I can't begin to say how –"

"Wait, wait," Jenny raised her hand to impose the pause. "She still has to finish high school and you still have to take her to a casting.

That's two years away. I'll keep in touch but don't thank me for a promise. Not counting that she may disregard my advice. Now, come to the kitchen, let's make some tea . . ."

August 31

Elliot had preserved Ruben Scheindlin's office space with quasi-religious veneration.

"Guys, I propose we keep Mr. Ruben's desk as it is. He was a good boss and died there. Sam's okay with it. What do you say?" he had asked the office staff a week after Scheindlin's interment.

Grief hadn't worn off yet, so the other three office workers had said no problem. But by the third month, behind Elliot's back, they debated whether or not their manager was a little wacky. Keeping the desk of a dead man unoccupied was absurd. Couldn't Elliot see they were cramped in the glassed-in cubicle? They sat side by side and had to sideslip between pieces of furniture and step out of the way of each other. Besides their own desks, there were tables for fax machines and printers, four filing cabinets, a double-door cabinet for office supplies, two chairs for visitors, desks for Elliot and Sam, plus "the altar." The only change Elliot had made was move the credenza and the four land lines at the rear of the boss's swivel chair to behind his own. When all of them were inside the cubicle and visitors came in, especially the gorilla, the walls threatened to burst open.

The gorilla was Tony Soto. The moniker had more to do with the man's manners than with his height and weight. As did many employees in extremely hierarchical organizations – like the armed forces and the police – Tony had developed instinctive respect for superiors and a similar, unthinking disregard for subordinates. The exception was beautiful women. However lowly their jobs, he treated gorgeous babes like queens until he was certain they would never have sex with him.

Consequently, Tony ignored Imlatinex staff and hardly ever said hello or passed the time of day with any of them. This morning he came into the cubicle and went directly to Elliot's desk. His friend froze.

"How you doing, Teach?"

"Fine, and you?"

"Not too bad. Have a minute?"

Elliot noticed the knowing looks his employees exchanged. *They are on it*, he realized, then scribbled "bug" on a notepad and turned it for Tony to read. The cop frowned and moved his eyes to Elliot.

"Sure," Elliot said, "give me a minute. Why don't you wait for me outside?"

"Okay."

Tony stomped out of the cubicle without a glance.

Elliot slipped the notepad into his jacket pocket and hurried to the back of the warehouse, opposite the entrance where Tony waited. Behind a storage shelf for power tools, he drew out his cell phone and speed-dialled a number.

"Hello."

"The consignment is here," Elliot announced.

"Okay. Be sure to package it and ship it like I said."

"I told you I can't do that," Elliot said through clenched teeth.

"Well, it's your hide. Sorry, but I'm in the middle of a conference. Bye."

Elliot stared at the phone for a second – *damn lawyer* – then holstered it. On his way out, he tore off a handful of pages from the notepad, ripped them, dropped them into a trash can, and returned the pad to his pocket. Tony was waiting by the huge entrance for trucks.

"Let's ride my wheels," Elliot said.

They got in and closed the doors before Elliot turned to Tony and, eyeing his friend knowingly, pressed his forefinger to his lips. Tony nodded.

Elliot turned the radio button, the volume up full, and quickly and unprofessionally frisked Tony's chest, belly, and underarms.

"Hey!" the cop said. It was the first time someone had done to him what he had done to others thousands of times.

Again Elliot stared at his friend and made the keep quiet sign. He buckled up and turned the ignition, wondering where the hell he could go to minimize the chances of their conversation being recorded. He opted for the Presidential Country Club, a semi-private country club on nearby Presidential Way. A Nicaraguan neighbour of his worked there and several times had invited Elliot to visit the place and take a long, quiet walk around the oaks and ficus. He would fall in love with the spectacular setting, and golf was a great sport; the Cuban should give it a try, the neighbour had said. Hence, after hands were shaken, greetings exchanged, and a new sales pitch listened to, Elliot said he and his friend would like to look the place over. No escort was required, thanks.

Finally alone and outdoors, at a place neither had been before, Tony asked: "Your office is bugged?"

"I don't know. I'm assuming it is." The well-tended lawn smelled wonderful and Elliot took a deep breath.

"Okay, I can understand that," Tony said, nodding. "But why did you frisk me?"

"Listen and listen good, Tony. I don't know when our next session will take place. I'm acting against our lawyer's advice. He said you could admit you bribed people for Sam and me, plead guilty, and agree to wear a mike to tape either one of us."

"Who's the sonofabitch?"

"I'm not saying."

"And you thought I was wired."

"Tony, you don't read the papers but you watch the news. You know it happens every day."

"Goddamn it, Elliot. We're friends. You've known me since I was a kid. You think I'm gonna rat on you?"

"Tony, you know much better than me that even Mafia hit men cop pleas, wear wires, and get their mothers on tape ordering them to bump off people, if doing it gets them into the witness protection program."

"But we are –"

"Jesus, Tony, you're a cop, for Chrissake. *You* should be telling *me* that lawyers don't believe in friendship and don't trust anyone. Lawyers only believe and trust in evidence. It's why ours has advised Sam and me not to talk to you, in private or in public, about the customs investigation, your suspension from the force, your visits to Imlatinex, or anything of the sort until the investigation ends and you are cleared or charged."

"And you are following his advice."

"You bet. This is the last time I'm talking to you in private. Until this is over, what you can't tell Sam or me in the presence of witnesses, keep to yourself. So, now, come on, what's on your mind."

Elliot watched Tony nod three times and read him like an open book. The head bobbing said he understood, and it also said one of the few people he thought would back him up, no matter what, had failed him, and that everybody covers his ass when the heat is on. For a few moments they strolled in silence. Tony clasped his hands behind his back and raised his eyes to the top of huge oaks. Despite feeling a bit sad and very responsible, Elliot noticed the lush lawns, the white sand traps, and the bluish water traps. A beautiful place to saunter and breathe clean air. As for golf, Elliot didn't think much of hitting tiny balls with a club into little holes. They started to feel the sun on their heads and backs.

"Customs Internal Affairs has joined forces with our IA people and –"

"Customs IA? Like in the police? Our lawyer says there's no customs police force."

This made Tony chuckle. "Really? Uniformed law enforcement officers with badges that arrest people, take fingerprints, have canine units, not a police force? Give me a break. And yes, they have an IA unit."

"Okay, okay. Go on."

"Their IA and our own have teamed up. I never dealt with Marrero directly; he was too high up the customs food chain for me. He got cuts from the people I dealt with. But maybe he's ratting on the guys I took care of and they may rat on me. That happens, I'd be real lucky if I just get kicked off the force. If I'm out of luck, I'll get ten years. But I won't rat on you, buddy. Word of a Cuban."

Elliot sighed. "Okay. Have you admitted to something?"

"I've never bribed anyone, not customs, not anywhere."

"But you've been asked about the firm and me."

"True."

"And you've said . . . ?"

"That you were my English teacher in Havana, when I was fourteen. I helped you when you got here, I found you a job with Mr. Scheindlin, we are buddies. It's why I drop in once in a while."

"And as to why you go frequently to customs?"

"I spent two years at the Bayside Detail. I made many friends in customs back then. I visit those who haven't been transferred or retired; like I visit you."

"What about Sam?"

"I know the geezer; we've never been close. 'Hi, sir, how are you doing?' is the longest conversation I've had with him. Nothing more."

"Okay, sounds plausible. But suppose a customs guy swears you bribed him. What'll you say?"

"It'll be my word against his. Is there any proof? Is there a video? An audio tape? If there's none, I'll walk."

"You think they may have taped you or something?"

"I don't think so. They would've confronted me with the evidence by now if they had proof, try to make me cop a plea. So hot here."

They were sweating now, Tony like a pig. He pulled a handkerchief from the back pocket of his jeans and dried his face. Elliot patted his back pocket and found he had none. After rounding a water trap he spoke again.

"Should they charge you, how are you going to cover your legal costs?"

Tony pocketed the hankie. "The PBA has a team of –"

"Whoa. What's the PBA?"

"Police Benevolent Association. They have a team of in-house attorneys that provide good legal assistance as part of your membership dues. The problem is, they do it if you are accused of something related to the job, like you beat the shit out of a klepto bro, or shoot him, and the NAACP wants your ass. But they wouldn't represent me because the investigation isn't job-related. So, I would have to retain counsel."

"You have money for that?"

"I could take a second mortgage out on my home."

Elliot took a deep breath. "That would be better; I can't give you money now. Money is traceable and we don't need a DA showing that a deposit of several thousand dollars reached your chequing account, or Lidia's, through circuitous routes."

"What's circuitous?"

Elliot stared at Tony and let out a big rolling guffaw. Tony, puzzled, chuckled anyway. Finally Elliot controlled himself.

"What did I say?"

"Nothing, Tony. It's just funny that in the middle of this mess we find ourselves in, you want to learn the meaning of a word."

"That's not funny."

"I know."

"Jesus, Elliot, you are fucking crazy, you know?"

"Yeah, I know. Circuitous means indirect. You transfer money to ten different accounts in ten different banks before it reaches the person who collects."

"Just a fancy word for money laundering."

"Not exactly, but close. Now, if you get charged, take the second mortgage and retain a good lawyer. If you are acquitted and remain in the force, I'll take care of the second mortgage. If you are sent to jail, I'll take care of Lidia, the kids, and the second mortgage. If you are acquitted and fired, I'll tide you over until you find a job you like. None of that will be possible if you cop a plea and implicate me or Sam, because we'll all be in the same cell. Understood?"

"Understood. Don't worry about it, Elliot. They got nothing. They can't prove it in court."

"I hope so."

"And thanks for the helping hand."

"We are in this together. You helped the firm, the firm has to help you."

"Appreciate it."

"Okay. Now, is it clear that this is the final private conversation you have with me or Sam until this whole mess ends?"

"It's clear."

"You are charged, you come to the office and in front of everybody tell us that you are being framed by your enemies. You are cleared, you come in with a bottle of champagne to celebrate. Everything overboard. No more 'Have a minute, Elliot?'"

"Understood."

"Let's get the hell out of here. We are so conditioned to air-conditioning we can't enjoy nature any more. I'll be damned."

September 15

Jenny Scheindlin stirred when her radio alarm, perpetually tuned to WNYC2, a classical music station, went off. Rich, single, and childless, she enjoyed pleasurable awakenings. So, she had made a habit of setting the alarm or, when abroad, asking to be called half an hour before the time when she could no longer postpone getting up.

Jenny stretched and yawned, rubbed her eyelids, examined her fingernails and cuticles, picked up an oval hand-mirror to inspect the almost invisible lines on her forehead and in the corners of her eyes. Then she went over the day's schedule in her mind, all the while listening to Mozart.

Her eclectic musical taste included a sizeable collection of pop, from the 1990s to contemporary. Alongside fashionable hip hop and classic jazz, she owned the whole lot by Marc Anthony, the Backstreet Boys, Shania Twain, and Mariah Carey; Diana Krall alleviated her moody moments, and she even had a few rarities, like three Cuban CDs by Camerata Romeu. But to remove the cobwebs of sleep she preferred the masters of bygone times.

She watched Tico Monerris snoring softly for a few seconds, then glanced at the clock, turned on her side, and gently shook her lover's shoulder.

"Uh."

"Get up, sleepyhead; it's 10:12."

"Oh." Joints cracked as he stretched his arms and legs. Jenny let a few moments slip by.

"Will you fix me breakfast after I shower?"

"Sure."

"Okay."

Tico watched her get up and walk to the bathroom. With a fine eye for forms and movements – albeit not a hand, as his lousy watercolours proved – he had chosen *glide* to define how Jenny moved when she got out of bed. Her naked body swayed like a reed as, on the balls of her feet, she walked across the bedroom. Except that reeds didn't show such arousing contrast between a narrow waist and softly curved hips. Reeds were deprived of perfectly rounded firm asses as well. No water plant had anything that could remotely measure up to the dark cranberry shock of hair cascading down to the middle of an unblemished back. Reeds also compared unfavourably with his lover because they only swayed when a gentle breeze blew, and Jenny moved gracefully all the time.

Tico sighed admiringly, got up, put on a velvet robe, and marched to the bathroom to pee, shave, and brush his teeth. He knew Jenny wouldn't reach the kitchen before eleven, so he had ample time to get her simple breakfast – tea and toast – ready.

Twenty minutes later, as he was inserting a slice of wholegrain bread into the toaster, the phone rang.

"Ms. Scheindlin's residence."

"Mr. Monerris?" a woman's voice.

"Hey, hi, Rose. How are things?"

"Things are fine. Is Ms. Scheindlin available?"

"Nope. She hasn't come out yet. Is it urgent?"

"No. Just tell her . . . Can you write this down?"

"Gimme a sec."

Tico grabbed a notebook and a ballpoint pen from on top of the fridge.

"Shoot."

"Tell her I got her return ticket from Paris for October 13, as she wanted. And the ticket to Toronto for the 14th."

"Good."

"And I'm sending the e-tickets attached to my email, as always."

"That's fine. Anything else?"

"No. Thanks, Mr. Monerris. Bye."

"Bye, Rose."

By the time Jenny entered the kitchen, Tico had finished eating the American breakfast that most immigrants born in abject poverty love to have: four strips of bacon, two scrambled eggs, and two pieces of buttered toast, all washed down with two mugs of coffee. The instant he saw her come in, he transferred the teakettle containing a half litre of Evian from the warming area to a hot plate whose dial he turned to max. A can of M&P's English breakfast tea and a strainer were ready.

"Make my day, Tico," Jenny said.

"Oh, well. Let me see. Umm. The guy forgets his wedding anniversary. His wife says, 'Tomorrow I expect to find a gift in the driveway that goes from zero to two hundred in six seconds and *it had better be there*.' Next morning the guy gets up early, leaves a gift-wrapped box on the driveway and goes to work. An hour later the wife wakes up, looks out the window, sees the box, puts on a robe, and brings the box into the house. She opens it and . . . guess."

"I have no idea."

"A brand-new bathroom scale."

Jenny's chuckle placed tiny parentheses around the corners of her mouth. How could he come up with a new one every morning? The teakettle whistled. Tico turned the dial to zero.

"Rose called," he said and passed the notebook to Jenny. She read. "Oh, okay."

Tico dropped a spoonful of tea into the pot. Then he pushed the toaster's lever down.

"Have you made out all the cheques?" she wanted to know.

"Yeah. The chequebook is on your desk. You just have to sign."

"Fine. But I have to write one more. To the Carnegie Corporation of New York, program for training the homeless."

"That's a great program. Give a man a fish and he will eat for a day. Teach him how to fish and he will sit in a boat and drink beer all day."

This had Jenny in stitches for almost fifteen seconds, once again amazed by how he could come up with the right joke instantly. By the time she was shaking her head and smiling, Tico was straining the tea into a mug. She had no clue he spent no less than an hour a day trawling Internet joke sites. He placed the mug in front of her after the toast was done, then used plastic tongs to put it on a plate that he positioned by her right hand.

"You feel like something else?"

Jenny considered it for an instant, then remembered certain words of wisdom her mother had said to her many years earlier and decided not to tell Tico she felt like making love.

"No, I'm fine," she said instead.

September 23

After much scouting, Chris and Valerio concurred that it would be difficult to find a more appropriate place than a detached house on Halsey Avenue, a four-hundred-metre-long cul-de-sac close to the ravine named Taylor Creek Park. The very last dwelling on the north side of the street had a living room with a fireplace, two bedrooms, two bathrooms, an eat-in kitchen with a stove, a fridge, a microwave, and a brand-new dishwasher, all above a two-car, ground-floor garage. The rent was $1,500 plus utilities. To rent they needed IDs, so they befriended two drunkards whose wallets they lifted after buying them enough rounds to make them insensitive to amateur dippers. Nonetheless, Chris had to take a shot at charming the landlord because all government-issued Canadian IDs have photos, except for the Social Insurance Number card.

Chris told the proprietor he would lease the home for six months and advance him $10,800 in cash – $9,000 for the full rent plus $1,800 to cover the utilities, because he didn't want to be bothered with bills – the moment they signed the lease. With a conspiratorial wink tempered by his engaging smile, Chris said he was sick and tired of the government taking so much of his hard-earned money. Wasn't Mr. Singh? The hopeful proprietor nodded energetically. Chris then made known that should the proprietor wish to forget this income when filling out his tax forms, he would never admit to having paid a cent to Mr. Singh; should anyone ask him, he'd say he lived there as a rent-free caretaker. After he had counted a stack of one-hundred-dollar bills, the owner filled in the name from the Social Insurance card – Donald Whitmore – on the lease form, signed it, and gave a copy to Chris without asking for a photo ID.

Next day, a Wednesday, Valerio and Chris packed their things and checked out of the ninth Toronto fleabag where they had stayed. At a Goodwill store they bought basic furniture, mattresses, and a few plates that a self-employed mover hauled to the house in an ancient F-350 truck. Later Chris went out again for bed linen, towels, and toiletries while Valerio assembled the beds. On Thursday they shopped for food, plastic cups, and cutlery; after sex they felt settled in. On Friday Chris googled Toronto sex shops. At the first one Valerio walked into, on Queen Street, he found the handcuffs and ankle restraints they needed. Cash, no questions asked.

They felt they were living in the forest. In the evenings, as Chris studied the manual of a GPS watch and Valerio surfed the Internet, crickets chirped, owls hooted, frogs croaked, and raccoons climbed up and down trees. During otherwise silent nights, especially after thunderstorms, the murmur of the swollen stream reached their ears. After dawn the twittering, chattering, and warbling of sparrows, robins, orioles, and cardinals was punctuated by the honking of geese and the barking of dogs being walked by their owners. One evening, to their total amazement, they watched a white-tailed doe calmly munching leaves from a tree.

"In the middle of a city of 2.5 million?" marvelled Valerio.

"That's Toronto."

To buy a used van in passable condition they rode the subway to Islington and took two buses to Mississauga. After pacing through three used-car lots, the couple opted for a 1993 Mazda minivan with 275,000 kilometres on its odometer. The test drive proved it was in acceptable condition and Chris forked over $1,800 cash for the clunker. At a hardware store, Valerio purchased tools and a small toolbox. After supper Chris parked the van in a side street and they walked to a nearly empty Mississauga motel five blocks away. Awakened at 3:00 a.m., as requested, they settled the bill, then stole four licence plates from vehicles parked in the vicinity – two cars, two vans – using the hand tools. Before sunrise they were back in Toronto. Partially overhauled by way of new tires, battery, spark plugs, and fan belt, the van was always parked on a different quiet block one or two kilometres from the rented home.

Exploring the ravine came next. People strolled, jogged, cycled, or walked dogs on the asphalted walkway that sinuously followed the creek's southern bank, from where trails ascended to rather populous neighbourhoods. From the dirt path on the opposite bank, wooden stairways led to private homes on secluded streets. Every four or five hundred metres, short bridges connected the walkway and the hiking trail.

"Is that the O'Connor Drive bridge?" Chris asked on the second day of exploration.

"According to the map."

"It's huge. Look at the arches."

"Yeah. How high would you say it is?"

Chris slowed down to work it out. "A hundred and fifty feet?"

"Probably. What's up that paved road? Let's go see."

A week later, based on a Toronto Parks and Trails online map, and drawing from memory, Valerio sketched a quite accurate scaled diagram of the ravine, from Victoria Park to the Don Valley Parkway. It included parking lots, public washrooms, points of access, and bridges from the online map, plus symbols for the maintenance sheds, stairways, drainage manholes, and benches.

One of their better discoveries was a trail on the right side of the creek wide enough for cars and vans. However, at its entrance, on Glenwood Crescent at Glenwood Terrace, a sign prohibited vehicles. The trail wound down the side of the ravine for three hundred metres before it reached a flight of concrete steps flanked by a handrail made from soldered metal pipes. The steps descended to a narrow trail where, turning right, the couple reached a second concrete staircase with a handrail. They climbed its sixty-five steps and found themselves on O'Connor Drive's eastern sidewalk.

For two weeks, the only motorized vehicles they saw on the park's asphalted walkway were riding mowers and trash collectors operated by park attendants; but one morning they spotted a police cruiser creeping along the blacktop.

"Uh-oh," Chris said.

"Keep going. Don't look at them," said Valerio, who considered the situation for a few moments before adding, "It's understandable," gazing at a treetop, beaming, the harmless birdwatcher enthusing over a lovely mockingbird. "This is a park. Mothers with their babies, other cunts jog or walk dogs; it's a rapist's paradise. So, cops let the bad guys know they are on the alert. Are you a bad guy, dear?"

"I'm a lily-white, nature-loving, gay photographer," tapping the camera hanging from his neck.

"That's the spirit. But you know what? We must spend one or two full nights here."

"Are you out of your mind?"

"I don't think so. This is probably deserted at night, but we gotta make sure. Maybe some weirdos come here to, you know, deal the goodies, make love, smoke pot, tell stories, have a drink, and if that happens, a police cruiser marking the territory makes sense. Remind the black sheep they should behave."

Chris considered it, then: "You may have a point. But we'll get bitten by mosquitoes, peed on by bats, and maybe mugged, for God's sake!"

"Well, honey boy, the payoff is worth a few mosquito bites. But there's repellent for that, you know?"

That same afternoon, Chris decided he was ready to strap to his left wrist the Suunto X9i, a Finnish watch that included, among its many functions, a GPS receiver. Three days later he had recorded the coordinates of twenty-two points in the ravine.

Once they felt Taylor Creek Park held no secrets for them, the couple began scouting the neighbouring streets. To the southeast of Taylor Creek they found more semi-detached, smaller houses than they'd seen northwest of it, where the sort of dwellings they'd first seen at Leaside predominated. They paced the parks – Donora, Webster, Stan Wadlow, Cullen Bryant, and Coxwell Ravine – to map public phones and bus stops. Gradually it dawned on them that the O'Connor Drive bridge was the best place.

Chris estimated it was 250 metres long and 22 metres wide. It had eight lampposts on each side, and approximately forty metres below the sixth lamppost on the eastern side, counting from Woodbine, lay the park's asphalted walkway.

"What do you think?" Chris asked.

"Very good."

"And we know where that stairway ends."

Chris tilted his head toward the north end of the bridge.

"I think the time has arrived, you beautiful man, to go get us our weaponry," Valerio said.

Chris

The backgrounds of Valerio de Alba and Chris Dawson could not have been more different; yet, as if to confirm that opposites attract each other, the two men had become inseparable.

Coming from a long line of WASP ancestors, the six-foot-one, 190-pound, thirty-five-year-old blond and blue-eyed American hunk made women of all ages, and some men, turn their heads in admiration. Chris was a silver-spoon native of Colorado Springs, a city that tourist brochures describe as "blessed with the stunning backdrop" of 14,110-foot-tall Pikes Peak. A number of residents, however, figure that the blessing is offset by the three air bases that configure the North American Aerospace Defense Command, a centre of military space operations at spitting distance from the city and its four hundred thousand people. NORAD is why hundreds of spy satellites orbiting the United States and Canada scrutinize these bases 24/7. For this reason local pessimists like to think that, the day a nuclear war starts, the first city to disappear from the face of the Earth will be Colorado Springs.

Chris had an MBA from U of C at Boulder, traded in his Jaguar for a new one every summer, wore the priciest clothes, watches, and colognes, sipped the most expensive wines, and enjoyed gourmet foods. He was so good at photography that his application for membership in Professional Photographers of America was approved and he made fifteen or twenty thousand dollars annually as a fashion photographer. He occasionally played tennis, and drank whatever cocktail was in vogue. He tried cocaine and marijuana at the university, but finding the effect of both disconcerting, never got hooked.

From 1993 to 1997, Chris spent a quarter of a million annually, the sum his father, who made between fifteen and twenty-five million dollars a year as CFO of a chain of rehabilitation hospitals, deposited in a chequing account of the FirstCaribbean International Bank, in

Grand Cayman, each January of those five years. But this came to an end when a whistle-blower disclosed to government regulators that the corporation was concealing hundreds of millions in losses through sophisticated accounting tricks. In a matter of days the share price plummeted, Chris's father was indicted, and his bail was set at ten million. To get out on bail, Mr. Dawson had to offer all his assets as collateral.

Although Chris was not down for the count, his living standard dropped precipitously. He had to rent a bedroom and a bathroom of his Greenwich Village apartment to an Italian fashion photographer for eight hundred a week. The man requested the right to develop and print at Chris's home-based processing lab, too. The monthly payment of the two-year lease, however, was six thousand, so the first toy he sacrificed on the altar of survival was the Jaguar. He applied for full-time jobs at banks, insurance companies, brokerage houses, and other businesses employing MBAs, but not once made it beyond the first interview because he was the son of a publicly disgraced man and had never practised his degree. Chris concluded that fashion photography would have to be something more than a pastime that put him in contact with trendy people. He called in favours from friends and mere acquaintances with influence in New York's high-fashion crowd.

Eventually Chris learned that rich amateurs were tolerated by professionals for their money, but they better not fall on hard times. Should that happen, revenge would take multiple subdued forms. Once the disturbing news did the rounds, you would arrive at any of the places in which the soigné meet and no one would conceal the sneer in his expression and tone. People would shake your hand and blow you kisses, ask *how are you doing*, say *heard about your dad, so sorry, but that's life. Hope for the best.* Then, the same guys who in the past had always asked you to join them, would renew their chit-chat and ignore you.

Next morning the phone would ring and you'd learn that Linda specifically asked for you to do her Hawaii photo shoot, which starts tomorrow. You wouldn't ask Linda who; there is only one Linda in the world of supermodels. So you'd max out your credit cards and fly to Oahu and stay at the hotel where they told you she will stay. One day goes by, two, nobody gets there. You'd call the agency and they'd tell you to chill it, there's been a change of plans, Linda will get there tomorrow. And when Linda does arrive you'd find it's a sixteen-year-old, recently discovered anorexic who will be doing editorial for a knitwear manufacturer that sells shoddy clothes to the teenaged underclass. The bastards will pay you a couple of thousand after a four-month delay and you'd be four grand in the red. Back in New York, you'd complain meekly only to be told, "You thought it was Linda Moss? For God's sake, sister, why would Linda Moss ask for *you*?"

Chris had expected the gays in an industry where they abound would show solidarity with one of their own. Dead wrong. Many envied him for being A-list, and others for his looks, clothes, freedom to travel, and the studs he had bedded. Most of the flamers in design, photography, and modelling resented him because, in the past, Chris had kept his distance from the limp-wristed and the flamboyantly effeminate.

In March 1999, his father was sentenced to seven years, fined five million, and transferred to a minimum security prison. His mother was devastated. Several months later, one evening at the Cubby Hole bar, alone and gloomily staring into his *mojito*, Chris brooded over his options. Returning to Colorado Springs in defeat was one; moving to Miami Beach, where he had friends and fashion photography was big, was the other. Then an exotic, attractive man came into the place. Dressed in bargain-basement clothes and carrying a small, battered suitcase, he had a haunted expression and seemed to be hungry and cold, a gay-for-pay out of place, Chris assumed. But then he dropped his eyes to the bulge in his tight-fitting jeans and frowned in disbelief. Was this (what? Cherokee? Navajo? Mayan?) wearing a packer, the artificial flaccid penis some use to create expectations? Or was that package for real? Unless he acted fast, Chris knew, in a minute this pitcher would have ten catchers vying for his attention. He jumped to his feet and approached Valerio with a charming smile.

"Hi," the American said.

"Hi."

"I'm Chris."

"I'm Valerio."

"Glad to make your acquaintance. I absolutely hate dining alone and feel like a T-bone steak. Would you like to join me? My treat, of course."

Given that Valerio had been sipping water at public restrooms since a cup of coffee at seven in the morning, and that the money in his pocket consisted of three quarters, he smiled gratefully and nodded. The Peruvian was playing the gullible immigrant country boy who, knowing nothing about Manhattan, Greenwich Village, and gay bars, had stumbled into one by accident, to ask for a glass of water.

Chris sensed the backwoods jockey might not be familiar with Greenwich Village directness and used a standard approach. *I am a photographer. I need a model for ads the Yucatán Tourist Commission will run at* Travel and Leisure. *It doesn't matter; no U.S. WASP knows the difference between an Inca and a Mayan. I could pay you fifty for two hours of your time. You need a shower and some shut-eye. My studio is nearby.*

Having reached bottom, Valerio was willing to take anyone: a daddy or a boy, a bear or a chicken – to be top or bottom, rim or be rimmed – but a gorgeous blond gay photographer in his late twenties or early thirties? A photo shoot for a magazine? Fifty dollars? Was this fag for real? In case he was, Valerio decided to bet seventy-five cents to win on this horse.

He gasped when Chris, camera in hand, drew open the shower curtain and took several shots of him naked, covering his privates with both hands. When the photographer set aside the Nikon and started touching and kissing him, Valerio resisted mildly and faked moral scruples. This was sinful, no, no, please, oh, oohhh. While Chris seduced the Peruvian, he took the precaution of covering the package in plastic before lubricating it generously.

The next morning, during breakfast, Valerio told a variation of story number four – his uncle in Boston needed someone for his hotdog stand's night shift; problem was, he'd lost the piece of paper with his address and phone number. No problem, not for nothing was it called the Walking City; he would find his uncle if he had to cover every single street on foot.

But surely he wouldn't leave today, Chris said. He was exhausted, needed to rest. Valerio argued that taking advantage of his new friend's hospitality would be wrong. Not at all, feel at home, stay a few days. *If you insist . . .*

Six months later, the relationship had progressed to the point they had no secrets. Initially Valerio experienced a combination of sexual attraction and self-interest, which gradually incorporated warm feelings of affection, sympathy, and concern as he learned of his lover's present predicament. To make the American realize that his plight wasn't so bad, little by little he recounted his life experiences, including the many cons and homosexual adventures.

The evolution in Chris's feelings began when Valerio started doing chores for free, returning the change after buying the groceries, asking him a thousand questions about photography and the fashion industry. It progressed more when he learned that the Peruvian had spent three years of his life trying to reach America and become a fashion designer. Having a soft place in his heart for Valerio, he tried to persuade him that his dream was unrealistic and unworkable. His feelings developed further as Valerio, assisting him at photo shoots, made clear to other gays who asked him out that he was going steady with Chris.

Valerio was already seriously unaware of the most recent technology when he left Peru; a gap aggravated by his prolonged trek. So Chris started with cell phones and computers, moved to the Internet, all the while giving him books on photography to read and explaining the workings of his six cameras. To the American's amazement, his lover absorbed everything like a sponge. Chris also taught him studio and outdoor lighting tricks, poses for sportswear, work clothes, menswear, and womenswear. At the processing lab, Valerio was initiated into the mysteries of chemicals, developing, retouching, and printing.

The forging of an additional, solid link in their bonding occurred in August. A very well-known fashion designer offered Valerio two thousand dollars to spend a long weekend with him in Big Bear, a gay-friendly hotel. They were hard-pressed for money, and two grand would tide them over for a couple of weeks, but when the Peruvian asked his partner's opinion, without an instant's hesitation Chris said Valerio was a free man and could do as he pleased, but he wouldn't, under any circumstance, touch a cent of that money. The fashion designer who never got to open Valerio's package spread the word that he wouldn't do business with anyone who employed Chris or his assistant. Work dried up, but their relationship ascended one more step.

By November the couple had grown close enough to openly admit to each other that their future in New York seemed pretty bleak.

"The lease ends on the thirtieth," Chris said.

Valerio nodded, then said: "Winter is coming."

"And?"

"Winter is milder in Miami Beach."

"I know."

"You've been talking about moving there since we met."

"I know."

A few seconds' pause ensued.

"Aren't rents cheaper in Miami Beach?" Valerio asked.

"Not for a place like this and not in wintertime. But if we take a studio –"

"Don't you think the time has come for you to sell all you have in the darkroom, both enlargers, the easel, developing tanks, the whole enchilada, and move to Miami Beach?" Valerio asked.

Chris mulled it over. "Would you like to?"

"Very much so."

"Then we will."

In six years, Chris and Valerio had it made in Miami Beach. The Peruvian bought a fake Social Security card and obtained a legal driving licence, learned photography from his lover and made between twenty-five and thirty thousand tax-free dollars a year at the weddings, birthdays, baptisms, graduations, coming-of-age parties, and other rites of passages of Spanish-speaking families. Chris kept doing fashion photography, and because he was good at it and his New York colleagues had consigned him to oblivion, he carved a niche for himself and cleared between eighty and a hundred grand a year.

October 2

Crossing the bridge from 5th Street to Dodge Island, Elliot remembered his first visit to Miami Seaport, in the cab of a rented flatbed steered by a tough black man. They had picked up a shipment of twenty drums of cup grease and taken it to a warehouse not far from the international airport. Sam Plotzher, posing as a fork-lift operator and helped by another guy, had unloaded the truck; it was the first time Elliot had seen him. Many months later, he learned that each drum contained, buried in the grease, a twenty-five-litre cylinder of R-12, the gas used for domestic refrigeration. Chloro-fluorocarbon had been considered largely responsible for the depletion of the ozone layer and the U.S. had banned its importation. Ruben Scheindlin saw an opportunity to make money.

And here he was, fourteen years later, summoned to a meeting at the Seaport's customs office that Sam, he, and their lawyer suspected had to be about the bribery scandal. He hadn't been there since . . . when? 2000? 2002? From atop the bridge the place seemed quite different. The white roofs of new passenger terminals glistened in the afternoon sun; there were new maritime terminals and buildings, dozens of new cranes flanked thousands of containers along the island's southern coast and eastern tip. A ship blew its horn. He remembered reading about a new detection system that screened every cargo container by irradiating it with something he couldn't remember, protons, neutrons? As a child in Santa Cruz del Norte he had taken for granted the smell of the ocean; not any more. He filled his lungs with it.

Over the phone Sam had been asked whether he, as the firm's senior partner, would come in for a friendly meeting with officials from the Miami Field Operations Office of the U.S. Customs and Border Protection Agency on this day, at 4:00 p.m.

Stanley Greenberg, their lawyer, had advised Sam not to attend unless he was told beforehand of the agenda. If he showed up, the attorney had elaborated, it would insinuate the company felt at fault; that Sam might be willing to admit wrongdoing and negotiate a solution. If the regional Field Operations Office had convened the meeting, why wasn't it being held at their 1st Avenue office? But Plotzher had waved aside his worries and said he would attend and bring Elliot with him, because not asking Imlatinex's general manager to be present gave him the impression that something would be laid at Elliot's door. Stanley should limit his participation to warning them should an answer to a question be legally compromising, the old man said. Let's hear what they have to say, he had added. Jenny Scheindlin, in Amsterdam, had no clue what was going on.

At the wheel, with Plotzher in the passenger seat humming a tune, Steil followed Greenberg's chauffer-driven, brand-new XLR Cadillac until both vehicles reached a parking garage in South America Way. They got out and ambled into the administrative building, where the customs offices were.

Plotzher entered the meeting room first and was greeted with courteous smiles that slackened when Greenberg followed him and froze the instant Steil stepped in. Plotzher took a seat and motioned Greenberg to his right and Steil to his left. Introductions took place, business cards were exchanged, and Elliot learned they were sitting opposite Don Winslow, Special Agent in charge of Internal Affairs, Manuel Portela, Chief Counsel, both from the CBP's Miami Field Office, and Robert McAvoy, Special Agent in charge of customs at the Miami Seaport.

By accident or by design, Winslow – in his forties, white, over-weight, sandy-coloured hair – addressed Sam Plotzher as though he were the only person in the room. He had been told, the man said, that due to the deaths of the founder of the firm and his wife, Imlatinex's majority shareholder was their daughter, who, apparently, did not participate in the day-to-day management of the firm and was currently abroad. He also had learned that Mr. Plotzher was the senior shareholder and one of two decision-makers.

Sam nodded.

Mr. Plotzher was probably aware, the man went on, that a Miami Seaport customs official had been charged in a bribery case. As Imlatinex's lawyer surely knew (glancing briefly at Greenberg), according to U.S. Code Title 18, paragraphs 201 to 219, bribery of public officials was a crime, and both the suborner and the suborned might be tried. If found guilty, they might be sentenced to heavy fines and as long as fifteen years in prison. Four officers from the Miami Police Department had been suspended and were under investigation for possible implication in the scheme. Antonio (Tony) Soto was one of the suspended police officers. The investigation had revealed that Officer Soto was a close friend of Imlatinex's general manager (who merited no glance from Mr. Winslow) and frequently visited the firm.

Imlatinex, the Internal Affairs man continued, was a trading company with a high volume of shipments arriving in or departing from the Miami Seaport that were contingent on U.S. customs regulations and procedures. The purpose of this meeting was to remind Mr. Plotzher that all import/export companies should cooperate with U.S. Customs. It served the interest of said businesses and their brokers to forge bonds of mutual trust. Should Mr. Plotzher collaborate with the investigation and reveal anything he might know concerning the bribing of customs officials, CBP would find ways to prove its gratitude.

The CBP, for instance, might put in a word for a legal resident in the U.S. found guilty of a crime. Guilty citizens and residents are sentenced to prison, but once the sentence is served, the deportation of a legal resident is possible and likely. (Feeling Steil tense in his seat, Plotzher reached for the Cuban's knee and squeezed it.) Both CBP and USCIS are under Homeland Security, the IA man went on, so any resident wishing to collaborate in the investigation might cop a plea and avoid deportation.

Neither he nor his colleagues (wrapping it up) expected Mr. Plotzher to make a decision on the spot. He should think things over, consult with his associates, and call him back should he wish to further strengthen Imlatinex's good standing with CBP.

When a short silence made clear the man had finished, Plotzher nodded twice, kept his eyes on the Formica-topped table, then took a deep breath and raised his head.

"Dear Mr. . . ." – he hurriedly put on his reading glasses, shuffled the business cards in his hands, read all three, smiled, lifted his eyes to Winslow –"it's Winslow, right?"

"Correct," said with tautened face muscles.

"You must forgive me. Old age. Well, Mr. Winslow, I can't even begin to tell you how honoured and grateful I am – should say *we* are – for your kind invitation to come here today and learn this important information from the horse's mouth. I had read about it in the papers and talked it over with Elliot, our general manager. Isn't it true, Elliot?"

"Yes, sir."

"So, I asked Elliot if he knew anything concerning that, didn't I, Elliot?"

"You did, sir, yes."

"And what did you tell me?"

"I told you that I had read about it in the papers and that my friend, police officer Tony Soto, had been suspended and was under investigation."

"Now, I want you to be perfectly frank with these dear friends of ours from customs. You know that having good relations with customs in this port is very important to the firm. Additionally, you are a legal resident in the U.S. and you know the terrible things that this gentleman has said can happen to residents who, given the opportunity to cooperate with Customs IA, fail to do so. *Should they be* charged, *should they be* found guilty, *should they be* sentenced to prison, *after they serve* their sentence, *they might be* deported. You understand what the man's saying, Elliot?"

"Yes, sir, I do."

"Do you want to be deported to Cuba, Elliot?"

"No, sir."

"So, please, Elliot, answer truthfully, did Officer Soto admit to you that he had bribed any Miami Seaport customs official?"

"No, sir, Tony, I mean, Officer Soto, said somebody was trying to frame him but that he had never, ever, bribed a public official."

"Have you ever asked Officer Soto or anyone else to bribe a public official, Elliot?"

"No, sir, never."

"Well, I haven't either. But I'll tell you what I'll do, Mr. . . . ." – fresh peek at the business card – "Winslow. I know a few people in my line of business. I'll tell them about this interest customs has in finding informers and give them your number. Would that be okay?"

Winslow attempted, but failed, to conceal his irritation; his two colleagues appeared to be a little embarrassed. Greenberg was fighting off a smile and thinking this was the sort of big-balls client most lawyers look on with disfavour, yet admire. He preferred non-confrontational approaches, but Winslow had crudely tried to intimidate Sam and Elliot and had gotten what he deserved. He had enjoyed the old man's denial of guilt because he loved seeing the bureaucrats seethe, and because any adverse consequence would not be his fault. If things went south, he could tell Plotzher, *I advised you not to go.*

"Yes, that would be okay, Mr. Plotzher," Winslow said, standing up. "Would you excuse us? We have other things to do right now."

"You are the host, but you are excused, Mr. *Winthrop*," was Plotzher's last barb. "Have a nice day."

Fifteen minutes later they were cruising Miami Avenue on the way back to the warehouse. When Plotzher said, "Take a right at 125 Street," Elliot knew what they would be doing once they crossed into Miami Beach. After Ruben Scheindlin's death, Sam had laid new rules. Nothing compromising would be discussed in the warehouse, over the phone, or in the presence of others. Today, as on many other occasions, Elliot would take the turns the old man ordered, park where he said, and both would go for a saunter along the shore. Plotzher always picked a different spot, on impulse it seemed, to be sure no one could have anticipated where they would be having their private conversation.

Once Elliot had expressed doubts about such precautions. He had argued that, according to press reports, the evolution of listening devices and wireless recorders had reached a stage in which they could tape, with excellent quality, conversations taking place a thousand metres away. Elliot was right, Plotzher had admitted, but the old man added that cutting-edge technology, due to its high cost, was used only for matters of national security, not to tape a couple of businessmen talking shady deals. And given the run-of-the-mill technology police departments and most federal agencies had at their disposal, Plotzher had ventured that, in Miami, should they try to get on tape people cutting corners, cheating, and bamboozling others, they would have to record fifty thousand conversations daily, which was impossible. He and Elliot were just two little fishes in a gigantic shoal. Nevertheless, alertness and precaution were their sole weapons, so they would use both generously.

This time, Plotzher chose a stretch of public beach on Ocean Boulevard, between Poinciana Drive and Kings Point. Both were wearing sport jackets and they started sweating the instant they got out of the car. The sun reflecting off the sand made it even worse. There were a number of beach bums hanging out, a few pleasure boats and a couple of luxury yachts sailing along, and clouds to the east, over the Bahamas. Elliot filled his lungs; why did Cuban beaches smell so different?

"How you think I did?" Sam asked.

"Excellent."

"Really? Well, I don't know. The guy seemed pretty pissed off. But now we have to be careful. They can't single us out, because too many people were bribing inspectors. But every time we have a shipment delayed, an audit, or a dispute, they are going to lean heavily on us. Know what I'm saying?"

"I know."

"So, I want you to check out all the pending contracts we have to expedite. Negotiate, arbitrate, conciliate if necessary, but get us out of them."

"There are four, all under 250,000. I'll keep you posted."

"Good."

"Thanks, Sam," Elliot said.

"For what?"

"For backing me up like you did."

"Well, Ruben recruited Tony; we just kept the ball rolling. But I think we should keep our noses clean for a year or two. Don't you think?"

"You know what? I've been going back in our records and I think in the future we should not get into contracts that need expediting. They seldom exceed a million dollars and the profit we make is, what? Four per cent, five? It's not worth it."

"Maybe you are right. When you took Tony to this golf club . . . was he mad at you?"

"A little."

"Well, Elliot, when this ends, I think you should cut loose from Tony, know what I mean?"

"No, Sam, I don't know what you mean."

"Get rid of him."

"I can't and won't do that, Sam. You know he's my friend. You know he helped me a lot when I got here. You know it's thanks to him I'm working for you. I can't turn my back on him now that he's having a rough time."

"The Tony I met sixteen, no, eighteen years ago," Plotzher said, "no longer exists. He's an armed drunk and armed drunks are dangerous."

"He's suspended. He must've surrendered his badge and gun."

"C'mon, Elliot. You know Tony. He has probably three or four handguns and a couple of hundred rounds at his place. One day he gets loaded, loses his mind, nobody knows what can happen. But you want to help him? Okay, that doesn't concern me. But tell him he's not welcome at the firm any more. So hot. Let's get back to the car."

October 9

The client was insisting on a 3 per cent discount; Elliot had decided not to budge, for if he did, Imlatinex's margin would be a mere 1.2 per cent of the quoted price. He was trying to be diplomatic, though. A vibration at his waist signalled an incoming call on his cell phone.

"Could you hold on for a second, *Senhor* Cavalcanti? I need to consult with my partner about this. Thank you."

He put the Brazilian on hold, answered the cell.

"Steil."

"Elio. It's me."

"What's happened?" he blurted. Fidelia had called him at the warehouse just five or six times in fourteen years.

"Lidia's hysterical. Tony beat a neighbour to a pulp and got thrown in jail."

"Beat a neighbour? Why?"

"I don't know."

"You didn't ask Lidia?"

"I asked. She doesn't know."

"Was he drunk?"

"I don't know."

"Where did they take him?"

"I don't know that either. I'm driving over to Lidia's to find out what happened. Can you join me?"

"I'm talking to a client in São Paulo. Then I've got to call Houston. I can't leave now."

"Okay. I'll call you back when I find out what happened."

She hung up and Elliot slowly returned the phone to its holster, his unseeing gaze lost on the ceiling. Tony had totally lost it. *Must've been blind drunk.* Remembering the client on hold, he punched a button on the corded telephone.

"*Senhor* Cavalcanti, thanks for holding. Listen, the best we can do is shave 0.5 per cent. Would that be amenable to you?".

"I don't think so, Steil. It's 3 or no deal."

"Well, sir, I regret to say it's no deal then. Sorry for that. Got to go, now. Please remember that we are always ready to do business with you."

"Wait, wait. What about 2 per cent?"

"I'm sorry, sir. I can't improve on 0.5."

"Give me 1 per cent and the deal's yours," the Brazilian said.

"Just a second. Let me check some numbers here."

Again he put the guy on hold. What had Tony done? Was he loco? He could understand that his expulsion from the force and not finding a job to his liking would make him feel like a caged lion. But escaping a bribery indictment, remaining free and with a clean sheet were pretty solid reasons to count his blessings and walk a straight line, figuratively and literally. He felt sure Tony had guzzled a couple of six-packs, picked a fight with someone, then beat the shit out of the guy. Well, there was nothing he could do except keep providing the moral and financial support he'd been providing for a couple of weeks.

Punch. "*Senhor* Cavalcanti?"

"Yes?"

"Thanks for holding. Considering that you've been doing business with us for six years, we are willing to sacrifice most of our profit on this deal and give you a 1 per cent discount on the quoted price. But I've got to tell you, sir, we quote good prices because we take smaller margins than our competitors. However, if you make a practice of requesting discounts over our quoted price, we would be forced to inflate our margin estimate before quoting you, to protect our bottom line. Then we would readily agree to your request and we'd both be playing a game. Do you follow me?"

Elliot wrapped it up, called Houston, and exited the cubicle a few minutes after midday. Leaving the warehouse he ran into Sam, who asked if everything was okay. Elliot explained. Sam just nodded, but his eyes said *I warned you this would happen* before he turned and walked away.

At Tony's home, Lidia was clueless as to what had caused the brawl, so Elliot called Carlos Casamayor, a cop friend of Tony's, described what had happened, and asked him to find out which police station Tony'd been taken to. Within twenty minutes Carlos called back and told Elliot the ex-cop was at the Salzedo Street station. The desk sergeant, an acquaintance of his, had agreed to let Steil talk to the detainee for five minutes.

At nine minutes past two o'clock, Elliot faced a sober Tony Soto.

"Tony, what happened?"

Cold fury glistened in the eyes of the ex-cop. "I caught the sonofabitch molesting Tonito," he said.

"What?"

"You heard me."

Tonito was Tony and Lidia's twelve-year-old son; they also had two girls, the eldest from Lidia's first marriage. Tony averted his eyes, his lips quivered, a tear slid down his left cheek. The speechless Elliot felt compassion and embarrassment growing inside him. A full minute was lost.

"How can I help?"

"There's nothing you can do."

"We gotta do something. Get ready for the trial. You . . . beat the guy pretty bad?"

"I think I broke his jaw, an arm, and I kicked his miserable, tiny dick and balls so hard he'll never get it up again."

Elliot lowered his eyes to Tony's hands; knuckles scraped and swollen. Understandable paternal reaction, Elliot considered. Illegal, brutal, irrational, but understandable. No father he knew would ask a molester to please stop it, walk his kid home, then call the police.

"Okay," Elliot said. "You know Fidelia specializes in family law. She may know how to deal with your boy's side of this. He may need counselling, maybe a doctor should, you know, examine him, issue a certificate we can show in court."

"What I want, Teacher, is to put a lid on this. You want to help me out? Help me hush it up. I don't want Tonito's buddies to know. I don't want the neighbours to know. I didn't tell Lidia, but now I've cooled off, I see she has to know."

Elliot rested an elbow on the tabletop, and massaged his forehead. "I'll do my best, Tony. But you'll be tried and you know reporters trawl the courts for this kind of news."

"I know. But the child's name is confidential."

Elliot nodded in apparent agreement while thinking that the name of an adult under trial is not confidential, nor the crime. Finding out why Tony had been charged with assault wouldn't be difficult, and if the why was published, everybody would know the child's name because Tony had only one son.

"Next step is to get a lawyer," he said instead. "I suppose Fidelia can advise me on that too. Bail you out as soon as you are charged."

"You know what, Elliot? I would gladly serve time for this."

"Yeah. When Tonito needs you most, you are locked up and glad about it."

This gave Tony pause. He frowned.

"Don't talk shit, Tony. Let's see what we can do to get you out of this mess. Maybe the guy won't press charges, you know, to avoid a scandal. What does he do?"

"He's a building contractor."

"Um. Wish he'd have to protect a public image. He married?"

"Yeah."

"Age?"

"I don't know. In his forties, I suppose."

"Kids?"

"Not to my knowledge."

"Who called the cops?"

"I have no idea. His wife, a neighbour maybe."

"Five minutes, fellas." The desk sergeant, from the door.

"Thanks, officer," Steil said. Then to Tony: "You'll need that second mortgage now."

"I know."

"Can I tell Lidia you are okay with applying for it?"

"Sure."

"Good. I'm going back to your place now, explain things to Lidia, ask for Fidelia's advice."

"Fidelia's there?"

"Yep."

"She hates my guts. I appreciate her supporting Lidia, though."

"Forget about it. Don't sign anything. Don't answer quest–"

"Teacher?"

"What?"

"I was a cop for seventeen years."

"Okay. Sorry."

"Teacher?"

"What?"

"Thanks."

Elliot told Lidia and Fidelia what had made Tony go wild, then he and Fidelia spent a quarter of an hour convincing Lidia it was not a good idea to march to the boy's room and request his version. When she finally agreed, Elliot asked whether Tonito's bedroom had a window.

"Sure. Why?" Lidia paused an instant before jumping to her feet, darting to a closed door and knocking on it. Elliot and Fedelia hot-footed it after her.

"Tonito! Tonito!"

"What?" in a subdued tone.

The adults heaved sighs of relief. Elliot opened his mouth, simulated putting something in it. Lidia nodded.

"You want a sandwich?"

"No."

"You okay?"

"Yeah."

"Let me know when you are feeling hungry."

"Okay."

They returned to the living room and Fidelia worked the phone for twenty minutes. First she called a psychologist who agreed to see Tonito the next morning and to arrange for a doctor to examine the boy and search for signs of molestation. Next she talked to a lawyer who represented children and their parents at abuse cases. The man assured her that as soon as he finished with a client he would drive to the police station, hear Tony's account, and advise him.

"Is there anything else we can do?" Elliot said to Lidia.

"No, guys, you've been great. I'll manage."

"I'll call you tonight. You coming, Fidelia?"

"I'll stay a while longer. Maybe spend the night here."

"No, Fidelia," Lidia said. "That's not necessary."

It took all of ten seconds for Fidelia to persuade her she would feel better if a friend kept her company.

"Okay. I'm going back to the warehouse," Elliot said. "You need anything, call me."

"I would castrate every single one," was Sam's sole comment when Elliot told him what had happened.

October 16

Fat raindrops were pelting the taxi's roof as it cruised south down University Avenue. Even with wipers swinging at full speed, the driver (a middle-aged Pakistani? Afghan? Iranian?) was bent over the wheel peering ahead as if in the thickest fog. *Had he lost his glasses?* Jenny wondered. She turned her gaze to the rear window crisscrossed by snaking rivulets. *It's raining buckets*, she admitted to herself.

She had got in the taxi at the Four Seasons, on Avenue Road, and asked to be taken to Muzik, the nightclub at Exhibition Place where the Toronto Fashion Show's opening night was taking place. Jenny had been to the show several times, first as a model, last year as an aspiring entrepreneur. She considered Toronto an affluent, sophisticated, modern city, a mere two hours from JFK. Most important of all, it wasn't a one-gas-station town; 2.5 million people in the city, 5.1 million in the Greater Toronto Area. She wanted to keep researching this very promising market for fashion stores.

Jenny was hoping to make new business contacts, gauge the crowd's reaction to fresh concepts, and cozy up to the fashion journalists. Not tonight, though. Tonight she would just let people know she was there, make an impression, and press the flesh of acquaintances among the designers, hairdressers, makeup artists, photographers, and models working the show.

The production team had sent the program and the designers' current concepts for the spring collection to her hotel suite. Jenny sighed; as if she had the time and the curiosity to think about that. This brought to mind Oscar Wilde's observation: "Fashion is a form of ugliness so intolerable that we have to alter it every six months." Ten or eleven years earlier, when a friend quoted the Irishman, she had concluded that Wilde had been an insufferable prick. Now Jenny conceded to herself the playwright had been on to something. Not that fashion, as a concept or an industry, was a form of ugliness, of course not. Although she readily admitted that sometimes certain designers came up with pretty weird stuff. Concerning change, though, Wilde had fallen short. Now fashion renewed itself every ninety days, which meant changing colours and designs for everything: dresses, blouses, pants, hats, sleeves, collars, skirts, underwear, rings, earrings, necklaces, shoes, hairstyles, and cosmetics. Past styles almost always were imitated. She figured any moment now the A- and H-lines popular in the mid-twentieth century would make a return. Well, it was inescapable; concerning clothing, the limit to creativity was the human body. People can't wear circular shoes, garments made of gas, or cover their heads with fishbowls. She chuckled, then sighed looking at the rainstorm.

She opened her purse, took out a tiny phone book, flipped the pages, found a number, and tapped it on her cell.

"Hello?"

"Tracy?"

"Speaking."

"Jenny Scheindlin."

"Oh, darling, how nice of you to call. I'd heard you were in town."

"Yes, I am. On my way to the show, right now. But honey, it's a downpour and I was wondering if someone with an umbrella could meet my taxi."

"But of course, dear. Where are you?"

Jenny cast a glance at an electricity pole. "Street sign says Front."

"Not far. I'll send someone. Lower the window and wave when you get here. See you."

Tracy, a member of the show's advisory council, outdid herself. Like nearly everyone in the industry, she knew that Jenny had inherited many millions, and like most people in all walks of life, she wanted to be on the best possible terms with the rich. When Jenny arrived, two volunteers rolled out a red carpet to the taxi and a third guy held a huge umbrella over the former model's head; only the soles of her Manolos got wet.

People indoors started wondering who was coming when they saw attendants rushing the carpet on a cart. The chill had made Jenny wrap a light-pink pure pashmina shawl around her shoulders. Knowing she deserved and would get attention the instant she entered the foyer, she slipped the stole down her back and held it over flexed forearms. This revealed a black jersey dress by Costello Tagliapietra that emphasized her superbly proportioned body. Big soft curls of hair reached below her shoulders. She wore gold ear-rings by Dior and a multi-pearl gold bracelet on her left wrist. Her eyes were shadowed in violet and her lips painted coral. Onlookers caught a whiff of the L'Air du Temps she had sprayed behind her ears and at the back of her neck.

She made a regal entry.

Pleased by the scrutiny and the poorly concealed admiration, she bussed cheeks, shook hands, flashed smiles. Over the years she had learned to identify enemies and adversaries among her acquaintances. True allies showed restrained affection. An industry mogul in his sixties handed her a glass of champagne.

"Cristal," the man said. Jenny smiled, took a sip, and wondered if he did it to prove he knew her taste, to quell her scruples, or because he still entertained the idea of taking her to bed.

Escorted by Tracy she paced the buyer's lounge, peered at bijoux, nodded politely at explanations, went past mannequins, registered the pulsing music, eyed approvingly the lamps standing on two long bars. Her gaze swept over the huge posters portraying a beautiful actress who made a couple of million every year for attributing to one brand of anti-wrinkle cream her fine hereditary complexion. Next she did the press lounge, where she wanted to be seen. Later she went backstage to nod at and say hello to the hairdressers and makeup artists gluing false eyelashes, affixing hair extensions, blushing cheeks. She took a second sip of champagne and left the glass on a table full of cosmetics.

Her guide sat her in the first of seven rows to the right and by the start of the runway, near all the other VIPs in attendance. She exchanged introductions and nods with the women to her right and left, took in the soft illumination, the platform for TV cameramen and photojournalists at the other end of the room, the huge video screen. She also waved back to several acquaintances sitting across the runway and posed for three photographers; for the most famous of them she assumed her naughty girl expression – left eyebrow slightly cocked, a knowing, faintly mischievous side glance, the all but imperceptible promise of a smile. The camera flashed three or four dozen times. Following several requests from the loudspeakers for the audience to take their seats, attendants withdrew the plain wrapping paper that covered the runway and the show started a mere thirty-five minutes late.

As expected, white and pastels predominated. True to form, the girl with the most beautiful breasts wore a see-through dress and the boy with the nicest abs left his safari jacket unbuttoned. Short, shoulder-length, and long hairstyles were appropriately balanced; cornrows tried to make a comeback.

After the intermission, a designer came up with blouses, capes, and a couple of dresses in black that caught her eye. The same doubt she had been considering for over a year rose again to nag her. Should her stores carry designer clothing or knock-offs? Margins were huge in originals, but sales hardly ever exceeded two or three items per store in any season; in knock-offs the margin was minimal but sales were through the roof. Few customers can splurge $300 on a pair of jeans, but thousands will gladly pay $80 for jeans that look exactly the same. Jenny knew people who followed catwalk shows through photos posted instantly on the Web and emailed them to factories in

China or India, getting knock-offs delivered months before the designer version arrived in high-fashion stores. Designers were trying to outlaw knock-offs, but it was an uphill battle. Most shoppers saw nothing wrong in forking over $300 for a dress that looked exactly like an original priced at $3,000. Lawsuits had been filed; she'd have to wait for the outcome.

The second show ended at eleven. Jenny believed in the value of being missed, so she decided to skip the party. It had stopped raining. She hailed a cab and asked to be taken to the Four Seasons. As she reclined in the back seat, she wondered if people would be speculating about what better or more romantic thing she would be doing by midnight. Perhaps a rendezvous with a rich middle-aged man who would take her out onto Lake Ontario in his yacht. In a luxurious stateroom, by candlelight, he'd lick the drops of warm champagne he'd let fall on her pussy. She repressed a yawn. Yeah, keep them wondering. Should an acquaintance ask tomorrow why she hadn't gone to the party, she'd smile and say, "My lips are sealed."

Jenny slept like a log and woke at ten. Following her usual light breakfast, she received a manicure and a pedicure from a young Chinese woman. She left her room a few minutes after twelve and went to the health club for an aromatherapy massage. Around three she ordered teriyaki salmon with spinach, shiitake mushrooms, sesame ginger vinaigrette, and a half-litre bottle of Perrier. She watched a little TV before taking a long nap. At half past six she changed into a Lululemon jacket and pants and left her room for what she almost always did when abroad: a quick jog around the four blocks surrounding the hotel. She turned right on Avenue Road, took a second right at Yorkville, and trotted past its many upscale shops. Jenny was considering what to wear tonight by the time she took a third right at Bellair Street.

She had just passed the Yamato steak house when the rear door of a van stationed a few metres ahead was flung open and a masked man jumped out. Jenny hadn't the foggiest notion of what was going on when the man took hold of her arm.

"Silence or death," he said. She stared into coal-black, furious eyes.

Half-carried and half-dragged to the open door, she was forced inside the vehicle.

Am I having a nightmare? Jenny Scheindlin thought as the man made her lie down on the floor. The van started moving and she assumed an accomplice had to be behind the wheel. It felt too real to be a nightmare.

October 18

A round noon, a courier delivered a small package addressed to Elliot Steil from Trop LLC. The box was marked personal, and Frank, the accountant, placed it on Elliot's desk.

At 3:15 Elliot returned to the office and the box caught his eye. Trop LLC didn't ring a bell, but he was used to receiving small boxes with gifts from suppliers, anything from key chains to a couple of ballpoints on a marble pedestal, so he put it aside and started reading messages and returning calls. It was not until 5:45 p.m. when, alone at the glassed-in cubicle, he opened the box. He found a DVD, a cell phone, and a note.

Elliot: Please watch this DVD the moment you get it. It has vital information. Jenny.

Elliot frowned. He had never seen Jenny's handwriting. There were no DVD players at the warehouse, and he forgot that his laptop had one because he had never watched videos on it. Intrigued, he left everything on his desk and went in search of Sam. He found him at the far end of the warehouse, taking inventory of a shipment of air conditioners.

"Sam, you gotta minute?"

"Let me finish here."

"Okay, I'm in the office."

Thinking about taking the disk home, and anticipating the need for privacy, he phoned Fidelia as he ambled back to the glassed-in cubicle.

"Hello."

"Hi, Counsellor, how are things?"

"Everything is fine. Why?"

"I was wondering if there's news on Tony's case."

"No. You know I tell you everything as soon as I learn it."

"True, sorry. You going home early?"

"No. I'm not. I'll stay at Mom's. She's got a nasty cold and I don't want her to catch pneumonia."

"Okay. Call if you need me."

"Sure. Take care, tiger."

"Roar."

"What?"

"Bye-bye in tigerspeak." He punched the end button and holstered the cell.

A quarter of an hour later, Elliot was reading faxes when Sam came in and plopped down in his executive chair. His desk and Elliot's were side by side, a foot apart. Sam was aging fast, Elliot noticed. Despite snow-white hair, at seventy he had looked sixty, for all the work in the warehouse kept him in shape. At seventy-five, however, he was showing the earmarks of seventy-five. His gait had lost its briskness, his shoulders had dropped, the vital gleam that burned in his eyes was less intense.

Two or three years earlier, in a moment of unheard-of candour, Sam had complained to Elliot that the Miami Jewish community was on the verge of extinction. Population decline was inevitable when the elderly die or get priced out and many of the young and middle-aged pull up stakes, the old man had fumed. Synagogues, delicatessens, theatres, hotels, and kosher markets closed; buildings were being razed to make way for condominiums, restaurants, lounges, and clubs. Rabbis were trying new tactics to make the end of Sabbath attractive to the young, even serving cocktails at Temple House and adding drums and guitar to services. Elliot sensed that the tirade was a token of high esteem, not a request for reassurance, and had refrained from making any consoling comment.

"Take a look," Elliot said, moving the box to Sam's desktop. The old man put his reading glasses on, lifted the box, read the note, then stared at the disk and the phone.

"What the fuck is this?"

"I don't know. Is that Jenny's handwriting?"

Plotzher returned his eyes to the note and curved his lips downward. "I don't know. Maybe."

"Do you think this may be a joke?"

"Nah. Jenny wouldn't pull your leg."

"I have a DVD player at home, and Fidelia is staying with her mom tonight. I'll call you at home after I'm through."

Sam thought for a moment. "Well, if you don't mind, I'd rather go to your place; see what our boss wants you to do. 'Vital' sounds serious."

"Glad to have you over."

They drove separately to Steil's apartment. Sam looked the place over and passed on tea and coffee. Knowing that Elliot had been on the wagon for a number of years, he kept to himself that he felt like a slug of Scotch. The Cuban waved him to a loveseat facing the thirty-inch screen, slid the disk in the player, eased himself down beside Sam, and pushed a button on the remote.

One, two, three, black, blue. Sitting on something low, perhaps a stool, Jenny Scheindlin appeared to be extremely frightened. A white robe covered her whole body, except for her feet. Her forearms rested on her thighs; she held a piece of paper. Two figures stood, one each side of her, apparently men. They wore long-sleeved dark tunics, dark trousers, and *kaffiyehs* wrapped around their heads and faces, leaving only their eyes showing. Both held AK-47s and the butts of handguns showed above their belts. The light-green wall behind them was bare. The shorter man bent toward Jenny and touched her shoulder with the stock of his rifle. Jenny shuddered, turned her head, raised pleading eyes to her captor, who nodded. Jenny lowered her eyes to the sheet of paper.

Sam and Elliot, befuddled, leaned forward.

"I, Jennifer Scheindlin, an infidel, have been captured by a unit of the Islamic Army of Canada. The Nation of Islam and the Arab Nation have been victimized by the Zionists time after time, women and children have been murdered, so these heroic mujahideen by my side strongly believe it is time that a young Zionist like me, a well-known fashion model, be made to pay for those crimes."

Jenny choked, paused, swallowed, wiped away tears from her cheeks and mucus from her nose with her sleeve. Both guardians shifted their eyes from the camera to her. She went on.

"I have pleaded for mercy. I have made the mujahideen see that by taking my life they will achieve little except revenge and publicity. I have told them that I am a woman of means. I have also told them that I am willing to compensate the relatives of the Arab men, women, and children murdered by Zionists with ten million dollars.

"The Supreme Commander of the heroic mujahideen of the Islamic Army of Canada has accepted my offer. Should they receive before November 1 ten million dollars in unregistered Eurobonds of the highest possible denomination, issued by a well-known German or French private company, in Swiss francs at the current rate of exchange between the U.S. dollar and the Swiss franc, they will set me free unharmed.

"I have explained to them that the only person who can obtain these funds in Eurobonds at such short notice is the manager of my company, Mr. Elliot Steil. This video will be sent to Mr. Steil, so he can do what needs to be done to obtain my release. They will call Mr. Steil on my cell phone to give further instructions on how the bonds are to be delivered.

"The mujahideen have made very clear that if you report this to the police or to any other North American law enforcement organization controlled by the Zionist pigs, like the FBI, I will be executed. The mujahideen have proved many times that they are willing to give their lives for the Nation of Islam, the Arab Nation, and the Prophet Muhammad. Do not doubt for a second that if you try to rescue me, you will rescue my corpse."

Jenny returned the page to her knees and stared at the camera.

"Elliot, please, do all you can. My life is in your hands."

There was a three-second pause before the taller kidnapper let go his AK's trigger guard, took out a remote from his clothes, and aimed it at the camera. The video ended in blue.

Struck dumb, Elliot and Sam kept their eyes on the screen. Eventually Elliot punched a button on the remote and turned to Plotzher; the old man was sickly pale.

"Are you okay, Sam?"

"I'm okay."

Elliot slid the tip of his tongue over dry lips. "Is it possible that this is a joke?"

Plotzher swallowed before responding. "Nothing is impossible. But I'm afraid it's no joke. Jenny wouldn't play a joke like that on us. She knows you would show it to me."

Elliot nodded. "She seemed terrified to the bones."

Nothing was said for nearly a minute.

"What should I do, Sam?"

"Let me think."

Elliot got to his feet and filled two glasses with cold water from the fridge. He emptied one before taking the other to Sam.

"Thanks."

The old man drank half the glass and put it on the coffee table with trembling hands.

"We stay together from now on, Elliot. Siamese twins, you and me. Put Jenny's cell in your pocket. Where's your regular phone?"

"On the desk," pointing.

Sam got up, but before lifting the phone, he turned his back to Elliot and took his belt off. To the Cuban it seemed that the old man had peeled something from it, a thin strip of metal maybe, then put on his reading glasses and studied the narrow piece. Next, holding the cordless in his left and consulting the thing, Sam punched in a long sequence of numbers, overseas obviously.

When somebody answered, he spoke uninterruptedly in Hebrew for several minutes, then alternately listened and spoke briefly. Intonation made some responses sound like questions, others like answers. Now and then he glanced at Elliot, pressed his lips together, and nodded in a reassuring fashion; he also dropped something in his pant's side pocket; the slip the number he dialled had been written on, Elliot guessed.

Plotzher spent five or six more minutes talking into the mouthpiece, as if retelling the story to another person on the other end; there were questions and answers. Then Sam listened in total concentration for four or five minutes.

"Tell me your address," he suddenly ordered Steil.

Elliot complied.

Sam repeated it into the mouthpiece. He said a few more words and then hung up. He shuffled back to the loveseat and sank down.

"Who were you talking to?"

"Friends, Elliot. Friends with experience in this kind of problem. Okay, here's what we do. We keep together, you and me, all the time. For the moment, we don't go to the police or the FBI. I'll call my wife now and tell her we have urgent business to attend, not to wait for me. Can I sleep here?"

"You know you can, Sam."

"Thanks. Now, in a little while someone will come and take the disk away –"

"No, Sam. I'm sorry, but Jenny said –"

"Shut up!" snapped Sam.

Steil couldn't believe his ears. At a loss for words, he turned his head, frowned, and stared at the floor. One of the reasons he respected Sam so much was that the old man had never, ever been rude to him, or ordered him around.

"Let's get something straight right now," Plotzher went on. "Jenny didn't write what she read. She's scared; she has to do what they ask her to do. She appealled to you because they ordered her to do so, because they would be sending the disk to you, okay? Somehow the cocksuckers figure you'll give them what they want. So, with Jenny kidnapped, from this moment on I take full control of the company, as senior stockholder. I'm the boss now; you follow all my orders. This woman doesn't mean to you one-tenth of what she means to me. She's like a daughter to me. You don't know, you hear me? You don't know."

"But, Sam –"

"I assume full responsibility, Elliot. This is not a business deal. This is Arabs against Jews. You don't know shit about Arabs and Jews. You can't deal with this situation. I'm putting this in Jewish hands. Are you going to cooperate? Yes or no."

"Sam, listen. You are out of –"

"Elliot, please, a straight answer: Yes or no."

Elliot took a deep breath. Shaking his head in amazement he raised his eyes to the ceiling. He couldn't leave the old man alone in this. Jenny had appealled to him. "I'll cooperate, Sam."

Sam gave three steps forward and embraced Elliot. He stepped back and half-turned to conceal the wetness in his eyes. As soon as he regained his composure, he faced the mystified Elliot.

"Okay. You got a tape recorder here?"

"Audio?"

"Yeah."

"An old one."

"Let's play the disk again and record her voice. Quick, somebody will be here soon."

They recorded it once. Then Sam wanted to record it again on a second cassette. Elliot was returning the DVD to its plastic case when the buzzer sounded. With a few long paces he reached the kitchen's intercom.

"Yes?"

"Mr. Steil, a Mr. Brown says you are expecting him," the security guard in the foyer said.

Elliot glanced at Sam, who nodded.

"Send him up."

Elliot failed to get a glimpse of Mr. Brown when Sam opened the front door just a crack and surrendered the DVD. He closed the door and returned to the loveseat. *He looks a hundred years old now,* Elliot thought.

"Listen," Sam began, "we've got to get ready for the call. When these people phone you say yes to everything. You are willing to get the – what the fuck are they asking for?"

"Eurobonds."

"What's that?"

"I have no idea."

"We'll find out. Okay. You say yes to all their demands. You are willing to buy the Eurobonds and take them to wherever they want. But you say you don't know what a Eurobond is, or how to buy them. You say you have to apply for a bank loan to pay for the bonds, because the company doesn't have ten million in cash sitting in a vault, which is totally true, and if the bastards have an ounce of brain under their thick skulls, they know it's true; no company does. You insist over and over that it's impossible to get the money and buy the

Euroshits in ten days, you need a month, you beg for a month. Understand what I'm saying?"

"I do, Sam. What if they stick to ten days?"

"You say you'll try but don't guarantee anything. Ask them to keep calling so you can report your progress. Oh, fuck!" hitting his forehead with the heel of his hand. "How could I forget? Every time they call, the first thing you do is ask them to put Jenny on the phone."

"And if they don't?"

"You hang up."

"Are you out of your mind?"

"No, no. Listen, Elliot." Sam rubbed his hands and slid his buttocks to the edge of the seat. "I don't know if these people will keep their word and free Jenny if we give them the money, I mean, the damned bonds. But I'm sure they kidnapped Jenny for ransom. They won't touch a hair on her head before they have the bonds. Maybe later they'll kill her, maybe they'll free her; we have no way of knowing that. But they won't kill her before they get the bonds because they need her to talk over the phone to prove she's alive. So, you hang up, they'll go wild."

Elliot thought it over. "You have a point."

"So, the instant you answer, first thing you do is say: 'Put Jenny on the phone.'"

"Whoa, hold it, Sam. They'll first ask who's talking, want to know if I got and watched the disk, that kind of thing. I have to answer that first."

"Right. You are right. But no negotiation before you talk to Jenny, okay? Any other questions, like 'Will you give us our dough?' 'Have you called the police?' you say, 'I'll answer all your questions after you put Jenny on the phone.' Courteous but firm. They refuse, you hang up. Are we clear on that, Elliot?"

"You sure, Sam?"

"I'm sure."

"Okay. I'll do that."

"Good. Now, let me call the missus. I'm too old for this. I'm too fucking old for this. I swear to God, we manage to save Jenny, I'll retire. You better get ready for that, Elliot Steil."

Sam's cell rang at 9:15, as they were eating pizza. The conversation progressed in Hebrew until Sam turned to Steil and asked in English, "What brand is Jenny's cell?"

Elliot pulled it out of his shirt pocket. "Nokia."

"Model?"

Elliot flipped it open and pressed a button. "6555."

"Has a hands-free speaker?"

"Sure."

"So, if you are talking, can I hear the caller, record his voice?"

"Of course."

There was more Hebrew. Again Sam turned to Elliot.

"How's the battery?"

"Almost fully charged."

Plotzher said something in Hebrew, listened for a moment, then hung up.

"Brown will be here before long. He'll bring a charger, a tape recorder, and cassettes."

"Good idea."

"I'm getting pretty good advice, Elliot, from people who know how to deal with this kind of situation. Trust me on this, okay?"

"Okay."

"We know shit about this. We are very lucky to have them advising us. So we do like they say, okay?"

"I said it's okay, Sam. Who are your friends?"

"I can't tell you that, Elliot."

Exasperated, Elliot exhaled hard, shook his head. He pursed his lips in disapproval, glared at the old man.

"Sam, I don't have to prove to you that I'm not stupid. You know that. When you used my land line, you tapped a lot more numbers than are needed to call someone here in the U.S. You spoke in Hebrew. So my guess is you called someone in a foreign country, most probably Israel. In any case, I'll find out when I get the bill. So, why don't you come clean with me? Is it the Israeli police?"

"If you know why are you asking?"

Elliot beamed. The Cuban's gullibility made Sam smile.

As soon as the cassette recorder was delivered, Plotzher started reading the instruction manual. Elliot turned on the TV, wondering if, as was his wont, he would fall asleep within ten minutes. He had stopped trying to analyze why, in very stressful situations, he slept like a baby. His all-time record dated from 1994. He had slept soundly on a raft in the middle of the Florida Straits after being rescued by Fidelia's family, who were fleeing Cuba on the raft. He had been helplessly floating alone and scared shitless for nearly six hours, peeing like the Manneken Pis in Brussels, dreading that any moment sharks would chomp his legs. To top it all, before getting hauled up onto the raft, he had fractured his arm. His emotional maelstrom had included indescribable happiness for having been rescued. And in the midst of all those conflicting feelings, he had fallen asleep. Avoidance of reality? Fear? Courage? He didn't know.

Around eleven Sam shook him awake and they agreed that proper sleep was in order. Elliot offered his bed, but Sam declined and made himself comfortable on the couch. Elliot turned off the living room's light, shuffled to the bedroom, took his orthopedic shoes off, placed Jenny's phone on his bedside table, and turned in fully clothed.

The model's cell rang at 3:15 a.m. Elliot stirred, wondering who the hell was calling. He stared uncomprehendingly at the blinking and blaring phone. Full consciousness kicked in the moment Sam Plotzher, cassette recorder ready, hit the bedroom's light switch and hurried in. Elliot's overloaded pupils ordered his eyelids to close.

"Elliot," whispered Sam.

"I know."

"Remember, put on the speaker," said the old man as he pressed the record button.

Elliot sat on the edge of the bed, fully alert now, and answered the call.

"Hello?"

Nothing.

"Hello?"

Silence.

Elliot peered at Sam, who gave three fast nods.

"Hello?"

"Who is this?" A duck's voice.

"Elliot Steil."

Silence. Then: "You have the phone, you got the DVD. Did you watch it?"

"I did."

"And?"

"Put Jenny on the phone, please?"

"She's sleeping. You want me to wake her up?"

"Yes, please."

"I'll call again in five minutes."

"Okay," and he heard the call end.

To be sure, Elliot pressed the end button before addressing Sam. "Why does he need to do that?"

"Beats me. Maybe he has to wake her up in another room, disconnect the voice changer, I don't know."

"Daffy Duck has an accent. Arab, you think?"

"Could be. But a few years ago the Canadians nabbed twenty-odd Arabs stocking materials to make bombs. Almost all were born in Canada and spoke fluent English. So, you know what? Maybe he's faking an accent."

"What for?"

"Make it sound more Al-Qaeda-like."

"Probably. Sam, stop the recorder."

"Fuck."

They waited in silence until Jenny's phone flashed and tinkled again. Sam restarted the recorder, then nodded to Elliot.

"Hello?"

"Hello? Elliot?"

"Yes, Jenny. Are you all right?"

"I'm . . . as well as . . . under the circumstances. Oh, Elliot." She tried to stifle a sob, failed, and started sobbing so hard she couldn't say anything else.

The call ended.

"Hello? Hello? What the fuck?"

Sam took the phone from Elliot and pressed the end button, turned the recorder off, sighed deeply. "She's alive. She's conscious. Thank God."

"But why did they hang up?"

"Got to go back to where they called from the first time, plug in the voice changer. Bet you five he'll call in less than ten minutes."

"You're probably right. He'll call."

As anticipated, the third call came nine minutes after the second.

"Hello?"

"She's well." Again the voice was distorted. "We haven't harmed her. She's just scared. So, do you agree to our conditions or should we behead her?"

"I will meet your demands" – staring at Sam – "and go where you want me to go. I won't notify the police."

"Good. You have nine days to deliver."

"I have a problem with that, sir. Listen, listen to me. First, I don't have ten million dollars in a bank vault, no company has. I have to apply for a bank loan. I can't tell them what for, because if I do, they'll bring the police in. I have to come up with something. I'm open to suggestions, though. Any ideas?"

Sam nodded approvingly, but whoever was at the other end kept silent.

"I'll have to make up a story," Elliot continued. "I don't know what, though. I don't know how many days that may take. Then I have to find out what's that thing you want, this – Euro something, I have no idea what that is or how to buy it. Do I have to fly to Europe to buy that?"

Sam was giving an admiring look to his general manager.

"No, you don't. You can have them couriered to you."

"Good. That's great. But then I would have to fly to Canada to bring them to you, right?"

"Right."

"I can't do all that in nine days. You must understand. I need a month."

"If you go to the police, we'll behead the Zionist pig. If we don't have the Eurobonds before midnight, November 1, we'll behead the Zionist pig."

The caller hung up.

Jenny

The friendship between Jenny Scheindlin and Chris Dawson had developed and bloomed in record time because their upbringings had much in common, and because both nursed a grievance against the world of fashion.

In their teens, they had led similar lives of luxury. Like Chris, Jenny was the daughter of a rich man and grew up in a mansion. As a teenager, she acquired a taste for pricey clothes, nice cars, and jewels.

When her interest in fashion bloomed, Jenny decided to be a super-model. She was five-ten, 116 pounds, with a beautiful face and the kind of long, lustrous hair that shampoo manufacturers want in their TV ads. She also had a very becoming year-round deep tan, the result of imitating her mother, a Polish woman with an interesting past who couldn't get enough Florida sunshine. In her youth, Maria Scheindlin had learned to hate the harsh winters of her native country, so, after moving to Bay Harbor, she spent two hours daily – early in the morning and late in the afternoon – floating naked on an air mattress in the residence's backyard pool.

Unlike Chris's, Jenny's formal schooling ended at high school. She went to a top fashion agency for a casting; they were interested. She could afford the South Beach in places where the fashion crowd hung out and made friends there. She learned that the start is tough, but there's great demand for newer faces in an industry that considers people over the hill at thirty. Success stories persuaded her it was a business like any other: make an initial investment, work hard, and eventually you reap the profits. Jenny lost her virginity to a Swiss photographer who flew to Paris six hours later and she never saw again.

After Jenny graduated, Ruben Scheindlin, worried about his daughter's fascination with what to him was the pinnacle of banality, had four serious tête-à-têtes with his wife, who wasn't in the least enthusiastic about their offspring's vocation, but thought that opposing her wishes would only strengthen her resolve.

Ruben Scheindlin was born at a kibbutz in Palestine under British occupation, volunteered for the Palmach as a teenager, enlisted in Shin Bet in 1949 and then made his way to Mossad. Sent to Florida as an illegal in the late 1950s, he made a fortune working fourteen-hour days, seven days a week, fifty-two weeks a year. For forty years he witnessed the ravages of extreme poverty by frequently travelling to South America for business. Well aware that Jenny's knowledge about the real world was minuscule, he pondered how to make her peek behind the glittering sequins of triviality, and decided that the best place for her to get a notion of the social, political, and economic problems humankind confronts was Israel.

Mr. Scheindlin offered a deal to his daughter. Should she agree to spend six months in Israel, covering her expenses with the money she made working on a kibbutz in the Arava, near Eilat, he would loan her – interest free – the funds required to cover all travel and hotel expenses to launch her fashion career. She would pay him back over time, as she earned money from modelling.

On the one hand, Jenny loved and respected her father a great deal; he had indulged her every whim and she felt duty bound to please him. On the other hand, she had done a little research of her own. A round-trip ticket to Tokyo or Johannesburg cost $2,000 but, according to her model friends, novices in the business get paid only $500, tops, for a photo shoot there. The rent on a small apartment in a dilapidated Paris suburb was $1,000 a month. If you didn't have that money, the agency gave you $100 a week for cab fare (to be spent when you come out of a cast very late, or finish a job after midnight) and you'd share a bed with another girl at a bedroom in which four other girls shared two other beds; all would have to wait for their turn to use a tiny bathroom. The agency would pay for bed and board, but you owed them for everything. It would be like being an indentured servant. She wouldn't be able to afford the lifestyle she was accustomed to. Jenny would have been willing to forgo all her creature comforts to achieve her goal, but if somehow she could cir-cumvent the hardship of getting started . . . She could take a suitcase full of skin creams, shampoos, and lotions to Israel, wear long-sleeved shirts and jeans in the fields, drink lots of water, eat only organic. Jenny agreed to spend half a year in Israel.

Her father chose Kibbutz Lotan, in southern Israel, a quiet coop-erative surrounded by the desert with approximately ninety perma-nent residents, including children. There Jenny worked in the date plantation, the organic garden, and the dairy. She learned to make compost and build houses with mud, straw, and old tires. The program included touring neighbouring kibbutzim and lessons in Judaism, basic Hebrew, and the saga of post-1948 Israel. The experience transformed her. The seeds of sympathy for the land of their ancestors that her father had sown in her grew rapidly and blossomed into patriotic fervour. Predictably, she developed an uncompromising David/Israel versus Goliath/Arab world mentality.

Mossad's scout at Lotan typed a preliminary evaluation that the Israeli intelligence agency added to Jenny's file. Daughter of one of their most experienced agents, young, beautiful, immature, passionate about their country, and obsessed with becoming a high fashion model. This last characteristic made her especially worthy of note, for rich Arabs collect models as fervently as philatelists collect stamps. In the fourth month of Jenny's stay at Lotan, an experienced female recruiter – Hadara (no last name) – joined the kibbutz. Her assignment: befriend and sound out the potential informer.

Apparently in her thirties, the recruiter was short on looks but long on brains. Unremarkable at five-foot-five, 120 pounds, her smile was her sole beautiful feature. Hadara claimed to have a master's degree in labour studies from Tel Aviv university (false), that she was divorced and childless (true), had relocated to Israel from Brooklyn at thirteen (true), and was passionate about scuba diving (true).

The teenager couldn't believe her ears when she was asked if she would contribute to the defence of Israel. For an instant she paused and frowned, then asked if that would mean giving up modelling. Of course not, Hadara said in her deep contralto, on the contrary, we encourage you to excel at modelling – so young and beautiful, you are destined to be a supermodel. So Jenny put pen to paper, wrote what Hadara dictated and signed it. The single page stated that, of her own free will, she had volunteered to be a secret warrior in the defence of the Jewish homeland, and that she would keep that fact from everybody, including her father and her mother.

Basic training commenced. Now she was a soldier in Israel's secret army, Hadara explained. Soldiers followed orders. Her superior officer in the U.S., however, wouldn't be constantly hovering over her. She would see him (or her) maybe once a month and he (or she) would issue guidelines, make suggestions, recommend actions; not orders in the strict sense of the word. Yet, if Jenny did as she was told, the probability of good results would increase dramatically.

Jenny should try to meet, befriend, and obtain information from anti-Semites of any race, creed, or nationality. She would not seek out Arabs, but should some approach her, she would pretend to be pleased with their attentions.

What the man probably wanted was to fuck her, Hadara explained. She was free to decide whether to let him or not, and her superior officer would approve whatever decision she made. But for several millennia, women had learned invaluable secrets just by letting guys get horizontal. All men are sex-crazed, the recruiter maintained. In Arab countries, in the U.S., in Israel, everywhere, most men are fuck-brained; female superiority was indisputable in that respect. But it was up to Jenny to decide whether obtaining information that could save countless Jewish lives was worth the hard time, or not.

"It's easy," Hadara said with a chuckle. "In many cases you insist they wear the condom you give them – always have a few (the extra-lubricated kind) in your purse. Then you lie down, let them in, sigh with pleasure, murmur, 'Oh, my God, you are so big,' then moan, say 'ahh' a few times, and they splooge. It's all over in five minutes, sometimes less."

Moving on, the recruiter said Jenny should not needlessly tell associates that she had spent half a year in Israel. To those of her friends and acquaintances who knew she was going, or to people she met in the future that asked her if she had ever been here, she should say yes, she had spent months at a frigging kibbutz; such a huge disappointment. All work, no play, interminable lectures, insufferable heat, boredom. She had endured it to please her father, and also because she wanted him to bankroll the start of her career. Should she say she wouldn't return to that God-forsaken country? Jenny asked.

"Never overdo it," Hadara said, forefinger raised.

Having watched a few James Bond films, Jenny asked her when she would be trained in miniature cameras and recorders, cryptography, weapons, and karate. Straight-facedly Hadara said: "Not for the moment." She should sharpen her mind, though. Her two real weapons were her beauty and her brains. Jenny should take good care of her body, eat healthy food, exercise, avoid alcohol and drugs, and to broaden her horizons she should read as much as she liked. Scanning the news on a daily basis was essential, but she should also read novels, and, if possible, unscholarly books on history and politics, like the memoirs of American presidents.

The Jenny Scheindlin who returned to Miami Beach was a woman with a mission. She behaved indulgently toward her parents, friends, and other aspiring models (if they only knew!), took a liking to spy thrillers (she found le Carré dull), watched in fascination the *Mission Impossible* kind of movie, and joined a martial arts school, but fearing that an injury may affect her career, switched to aerobics after two weeks.

Mossad decided that her best possible handler, a man she loved and trusted, one of the most experienced and capable of their U.S.-based officers, had his hands full of delicate missions and should not be exposed to the emotional fluctuations of an untested novice, so for three years Jenny was guided by the middle-aged owner of a beauty salon in Fort Lauderdale. No anti-Semites crossed her path, though. Jenny felt she was doing nothing for Israel and grew frustrated. The hairdresser said not to despair; her time would come, maybe in a year, maybe in five.

It took the aspiring model two and a half years to build a book that the agency liked enough to send to the top houses. She did catalogue work for the first eight months, then did editorial for major magazines in Tokyo, Taipei, Hong Kong, Johannesburg, London, Zurich, Milan, Paris, Amsterdam, Frankfurt, New York, Toronto, and other, smaller cities. At first the work was exciting and exhausting: the long flights, the shoots, the parties, the fuck buddies, going out with whomever, whenever, hormones burning, no curfew, no hostilities; like water flowing continually. Jenny was low-maintenance, but caring for her body meant she had to watch what she ate, spend hours waxing her legs and pubes, doing her nails and hair. Some models slept in the raw to let their skins breathe, their hands covered with Vaseline and gloved, but she passed on that.

The would-be spy eventually found out that modelling was not the glamorous life everybody thinks it is. At times middle-aged, rich, powerful women went to the shows and made comments like, "Oh, you guys must love it, feel so good, you have nothing to worry about, everything looks great on you, if only I could have your figure." The models would roll their eyes, thinking, "Oh, lady, how wrong you are," but abstained from doing what the monkey in the zoo does: laugh at the humans outside the cage. After the hens leave, the chicks sit or walk around in their underwear, steal fruits from the racks, talk about the craziest things, and laugh at each other. Jenny soon learned that models quickly become unselfconscious about their bodies and develop a unique sense of confidence and a great sense of humour about themselves.

Jenny was not prettier or uglier, taller or smaller, younger or older, brighter or dumber than the great majority of aspiring models. She also tried to please others and blend in. Yet, she never made it to the inner circle. Money was the major reason she was tolerated, but not accepted. She flew business class, leased studios at wealthy neighbourhoods or booked rooms at four-star hotels, ate at fine restaurants, rented chauffer-driven cars, went to health spas, splurged on souvenirs. Her less fortunate colleagues, like the rest of humankind, were not immune to envy.

The strict limit on pleasing others that was deeply ingrained in her, as it is in most rich people, was the other reason. Jenny rejected the advances of influential photographers she wasn't attracted to, then bedded a bellboy she thought hot. She refused to pose nude. Once she hooted with laughter in the face of an agent who suggested she should have a breast implant. She left parties when she was tired or felt it was getting out of hand. Her friendly demeanour and sweet smile failed to conceal that this woman would not, under any circumstance, kiss ass. Many models, photographers, and agency scouts believed that modelling was a leisure pursuit for the Jewish American Princess, not a business, and any day she would find another pastime. She wouldn't do whatever it took to succeed, was unwilling to pay the price.

This reputation cost her dearly. When her agency forwarded a book with fantastic pictures of Jenny wearing everything from evening dresses to beachwear and lingerie to the nine biggest names in the world of fashion, none of them was interested. Her huge disappointment was followed by a crushing blow: the death of her father from cardiac arrest.

Devastated to the point she couldn't be present at his interment or sit shiva for him, it took her weeks to recover. Eventually she agreed to do a cheap catalogue, and she met and befriended Chris Dawson at the shoot. He invited her to his place for dinner and to meet his boyfriend. Jenny felt very relaxed among gay men and enjoyed their company. Chris, like many educated gays, had excellent taste, from music to clothes, and was artistically sensible, knowledgeable about the fine arts. When she mentioned La Scala, the George V hotel, Waikiki, or Auckland's Gloria Cafe Espresso Bar, Chris knew what she was talking about; he had been there, done that.

One other thing they had in common, what made them close friends, was a grievance against the world of fashion, Chris's even greater than hers. They gossiped about the supermodel who had reached the top by climbing the sex ladder step by step, progressing from nobodies to the top guns in the business from both sexes (*and she's so ugly, those horrible lips and large, hanging ta-tas. And you know what? She has to have a bikini wax in the morning and another at 5:00 p.m.*). They chatted about people they knew who shot heroin under their toenails, under their tongue, and between their toes to hide the tracks; about the alcoholics; about when Dieter found that Jean Pierre was cheating on him, confronted him, and they broke up; about the closeted gays and lesbians; about that beautiful, sixteen-year-old Russian girl, Svetlana, who hung herself in a New York bathroom; about the anorexics and the bulimics; about Peggy's tantrums. When both were in a benevolent mood, they agreed there *seemed* to be good people in the business who donated money to the needy and to defend animal rights, but they could be posturing, you know?

Hearing them talk, Valerio felt the flame of jealousy burning inside him. Chris and Jenny were bonding like brother and sister, and their relationship, inadvertently, excluded him. He could talk about Lima and the travails an undocumented Peruvian experiences before reaching New York, he could tell them about his stay in Nueva Guinea, Nicaragua. But these two were as far removed from poverty and hungry people as he was from Waiki . . . what? Óclan? They had lived inside the world of fashion, had seen it and breathed it and savoured it and touched it. He had flipped the pages of fashion magazines.

Valerio's attitude mellowed after Jenny's mother was murdered. Chris was the first person she told, over the phone, and they hurried to her place, stayed for three weeks providing moral support, cooking for her, keeping her company. In their presence, Elliot Steil, manager of the trading company her father had founded, had advised Jenny to consult with her lawyers and learn basic facts about the company, for now she was main shareholder.

"Do you have any idea how rich you are?" Chris asked Jenny several months later, as the three of them were dining at Afterglo.

"Oh, I don't know, maybe a hundred million," she said dismissively.

Despite fairly recent examples – such as the Japanese kamikazes during the final stage of the Second World War, the suicide by burning of Buddhist monks in South Vietnam in the 1960s, and the human bombs in Palestine in the late twentieth century – at the start of the new millennium, scores of influential people in the Western hemisphere were unaware that in the East many seriously considered martyrdom for country, honour, and religion. Those powerful Occidentals knew that the needy, the wronged, and the persecuted are not averse to departing for paradise as soon as possible to be near God and to get all they desire and ask for, including as many as seventy beautiful virgins. But in the West, the fact that rich, educated, intelligent Orientals are willing to sacrifice their lives for a belief had been forgotten.

The wakeup call came on September 11, 2001. The heads of the NSA, the CIA, and the FBI grasped that all their supercomputers, spy satellites, and zillions of other sophisticated gadgets developed for the Cold War could not find out in advance what small bands of terrorists were conniving. Bedazzled by their scientific and technological prowess, they had downplayed the role of humans to the point they didn't have enough interpreters to translate the telephone conversations their fantastic machines were recording.

Most heads admitted their mistakes, even if for political reasons they didn't go public with them. The NSA, the CIA, and the FBI asked their Western counterparts to extend their cooperation from lending a hand to lending both, and their feet, if you would be so kind, please. For the two friendly intelligence and counterintelligence agencies operating in the midst of Arab territory, with informers in unimaginable places – Israel's Mossad and Shabak – they had a few special requests. One had to do with the role that certain wealthy Arab men could be playing in funding terrorism.

According to German mythology, the nine giant maids who turn the mill of the gods ground things slowly but exceedingly fine, so it may well have been their doing that Jenny Scheindlin was one of the pawns that Mossad realigned to accommodate the Americans.

After her father died, Mossad entrusted Samuel Plotzher, Ruben's handler and business associate for over forty years, with guiding Jenny. Sam had been a close family friend ever since she could remember, an uncle by all measures except blood. A spot risky, Mossad knew, but Sam was an authority in his field, and they were inclined to believe that Jenny would never put in jeopardy the man who was now a father figure to her. Plotzher's approach consisted in telling Jenny that, because of his closeness to her, and considering that she hadn't achieved results, an Israeli friend with Mossad had asked him to act as go-between by forwarding instructions and reports until an experienced handler arrived. Initially, the model was pleasantly surprised by the change, but later on, when her mother was murdered, Jenny felt so utterly alone in the world that she deemed Sam her own flesh and blood and placed him above everyone else.

In November 2002, Jenny was instructed to leave the Miami modelling agency that had represented her from the start and give her business to a Manhattan agency whose executive vice-president collaborated with Mossad. Of course, she complied. The model had put on fourteen pounds and was near her peak of erotic attractiveness. In spite of this, the vice-president had to tap all his contacts to get Jenny into the January 2003 Dubai fashion show. Her reputation as a pampered millionaire acted against her, but her voluptuousness was an issue as well. Couturiers are disinclined to let mere mortals upstage the ensemble they are wearing (curvaceous celebrities are all right, for the fabulous publicity the designer garners), which explains the unsexy, unhealthy appearance of many young models. As the only one on the catwalk who was not a celebrity, Jenny imagined she would pass unnoticed, but a number of rich, heterosexual Arab males gaped in open-mouthed admiration at the stunning American.

For five years she was asked to do fashion shows in Beirut, Cairo, Amman, Dubai, Abu Dhabi, Sharjah, Ajman, Umm Al Quwain, Ras Al Khaimah, and Fujairah. She travelled every year to Riyadh (to the motor show, to stand and smile alongside a Ferrari 612 Scaglietti). She met scores of sheiks with similar names: Nizars, Mohammeds, Sultans, Husseins, Humaids, Rashids, Saqrs, Hamads, Zayeds, some with an "ibn" as a kind of middle name; she eventually found it means "son of."

Over time, out of the forty-six Arab men who put the moves on her, the CIA expressed interest in thirteen; Jenny befriended and had sex with all of them. A forty-two-year-old guy with a BSc in Petroleum Engineering from Texas Tech University had humped enough Lone Star State girls to get a sense of what American women prefer and made Jenny come. With the other twelve, Jenny adhered to her recruiter's advice. Letting them in won her a total of $550,000 in cash that she donated to Kibbutz Lotan via Mossad, and jewellery worth maybe $300,000 that she kept. But she never learned a single piece of information that provided a clue about whether the suspects were funnelling funds to Al-Qaeda through charity organizations fronting for it.

Frustrated by the lack of correlation between her sexual stresses and the intelligence she gleaned, on a hot and cloudless July 2005 afternoon she complained to her handler. They were in the ample living room of her large penthouse condominium on North Bay Road, Sunny Isles, reclining on an ultra-modern, domed leather chaise longue. The place had a spectacular view, three bedrooms, three bathrooms, and three balconies. She had bought it in 2003, weeks before selling the Bay Harbor mansion in which she had been raised.

"You can't despair, Jenny," Plotzher said, to lift her spirits. "My friend says certain agents have spent twenty years drawing blanks. Then, when they least expect it, they hit pay dirt."

"Those agents have to fuck men they feel nothing for, Sam?"

Plotzher felt that vulgarities demeaned women and shook his head in disapproval. Seventy-three and childless, he was experiencing conflicting emotions about this girl he had held in his arms when she was a few weeks old and now manipulated shamelessly.

"I don't know. Maybe," he said.

"It's not easy, Sam," she sipped from her *mojito* and gazed at the ocean. "I had such a childish notion of this trade when I joined. I thought I would be sort of a Lara Croft, shooting bad guys, jumping from one building to the other, flying planes. What I've done is give blow jobs and screw circumcized bastards who shave their pubes. I do this for twenty frigging years, I'll bust a gut."

"You are free to do as you please, Jenny. You want to throw in the towel, say the word. I'd like to see you quit this before I fall off the perch."

"Shut up."

Plotzher sipped from his tumbler. His doctor had said a daily shot of whisky was the healthiest thing in the world. Only one. Good doctor. This was his second. He knew her "shut up" meant "don't even think you are going to die on me," and that pleased him. Unschooled in reverse semantics, he didn't know that the expression had come to mean "unbelievable" among the young.

Jenny shook her head, but in despair. "When bombs and rockets blow people up, I feel I'm not doing enough, then a few days go by and . . . Oh, I don't know."

"Let me tell you something, child. You shouldn't stew over it. Want to know why?"

"Why?"

"Because it could make you jump the gun. You ask one of these Arabs if they know who is contributing to Al-Qaeda and . . . end of story. The guy will figure you are working for Israel and spread the word. A beauty like you, they'll keep asking you out, that's for sure, but they'll plant mikes in the rooms and never, ever, volunteer anything valuable. They may use you to disinform. Know what I'm saying?"

"Oh, for Chrissake, Sam, I know that."

"Just a reminder."

As her popularity among Arab jetsetters grew, and because she was with a New York–based agency, Jenny sometimes had to spend weeks at a time in Manhattan. So, she rented and decorated an apartment on the Upper West Side and made it her home away from home. A number of her sheiks frequently flew to New York and found that the place had beautiful furniture and interior decor; it was ample, cozy, and much more discreet than a hotel suite. Of course, Mossad had planted bugs and miniaturized digital cameras from floor to ceiling, thus extending the vast collection of persuasive arguments it draws on when someone proves difficult to win over.

Jenny's business acumen, perhaps inherited from her father, gradually surfaced in the Big Apple. Despite recent concerns about unhealthily thin models that might lead to fuller women on the catwalks, she realized she had grown too sexy and mature to compete with the never-ending wave of painfully thin sixteen-year-olds most fashion designers prefer. What would she do when modelling was over for her? She wouldn't even consider learning her father's business. The sole industry she had been involved in was fashion; not its business side, though. She readily admitted to herself that she lacked what it took to be a designer and had no interest in hairdressing or makeup. However, the very prestigious Fashion Institute of Technology offered a bachelor of science (BS) in fashion merchandising management. Maybe if she hit the books and got that degree she could get a sense of whether it would be prudent for her to invest a little money, a million or so, in a store, then retain Steil-like people, learn the trade, and, after a year or two, decide whether to call it quits and live a life of leisure and relaxation, or start building a chain named Jenny's Latest, or something like that.

On her first trip to Europe, Jenny had discovered the majestic, well-preserved, incredibly beautiful architecture that was almost non-existent in the U.S. After becoming an informer, to forget her scruples and frustration, she devoted most of her free time to pacing the streets and taking photos in Paris, Milan, Barcelona, Copenhagen, Amsterdam, and Athens. She would don scruffy clothing and trainers, leave her credit cards, expensive watch, and other valuables at the hotel, put a few dollars in her pocket, and spend hours lost in contemplation.

In 2005 she met Tico Monerris, a struggling, forty-six-year-old Puerto Rican painter whose watercolours no person in their right mind would buy. Total loser, kind soul, poor as a church mouse, intellectually mediocre, undersized penis. She found it embarrassing to be seen with such an unattractive, much older man, and from the start she had warned Tico, whom she eventually hired as her assistant for $48,000 a year, that her social life was off limits to him. Tico was not in the least offended by this, as the beautiful model was the miracle he had been praying for from the time he was a child in San Juan. He had no problem with remaining in the background.

She lived in Manhattan; he roomed in Brooklyn and slept at her place when she invited him to spend the night. She flew first class, he economy. She rented hotel suites for her, a cheap room for him. She sat on the limo's back seat, he alongside the chauffer. When she had dinner at the Ritz-Carlton, he waited outside. They had never been to a party together. Yet, Tico had two qualities she considered priceless. First, every orgasm with him was like diving headfirst into a warm lagoon of complete sexual gratification. Second, he made her laugh.

Before Tico, intrigued about her mild sexual response, Jenny had read four books on sex. She discovered that some women had orgasms even without genital touch. But she had never come as a sexual partner kissed her ears, neck, or any other non-genital zone. Nearly all her orgasms were clitoral, and various sexologists claimed that women unable to achieve vaginal orgasms during intercourse had an anatomical problem; others argued it was merely psychological in nature.

Jenny's gynecologist had assured her she was anatomically normal, so she believed her predicament to be psychosomatic, but she'd been incapable of determining its nature. Fear of getting pregnant or of contracting AIDS? She wasn't missing much; sex was not the ultimate sensation people claimed, so why worry about vaginal orgasms? That had been her frame of mind the evening she decided that a guy who made her laugh so much deserved something and let Tico make love to her. Instead, she got something unexpected.

Inured to brief foreplay, she kept asking guys to take it easy, offering them more wine. The delaying tactic proved ineffectual; most men grew desperate and demanding after a few minutes and some even ejaculated before going to bed. However, the first time they made out, Tico extended the foreplay for so long that Jenny, terrifically aroused, stood from the couch, took his hand, and guided him to her bedroom. Minutes later the naked Puerto Rican lay down facing her pussy and proceeded to kiss it so gently, lick it so tenderly and patiently for such a long time, that she experienced her first head-to-toes orgasm. Not one person among the several dozen men and two women she had had sex with had made her experience the marvellous commotion her body registered that evening.

Even more surprising, Tico kept postponing his climax. He lay alongside her murmuring sweet nothings for a quarter of an hour or so, then started caressing her breasts and abdomen as he kissed her forehead, cheeks, and lips. Feeling him rock-hard against her thigh, she grabbed his depressingly short organ. *What a shame*, she thought.

Out of compassion, to reward him for having taken her where no other person had, she had asked him to put on a condom and fill her. Tico was a slow poke and she experienced a second orgasm. From that day on, against conventional wisdom, any girl who wanted to know Jenny's opinion on size learned that if the handyman did the job to her full satisfaction, she couldn't care less about the dimensions of his tool.

The Puerto Rican listened patiently to her tales of her achievements, disappointments, and failures. He wasn't judgmental, and refrained from giving advice. He even murmured corny endearments no man had ever said to her. Lines like: "You are to me what sunrise is to a dewy blade of grass." "The votive offering I humbly place in your altar is my soul." Should she call from abroad he would say something in the vein of "I miss you to the point that all nights seem starless, all mornings cloudy, all trees leafless." Or "My days are as empty as my heart." Or "I shiver with cold when I wake up and you are not by my side." Always a new, beautiful, flattering seducement; just one. Jenny had no way of knowing all were verses from the lyrics of famous Latin American *boleros* that he translated, modified a little, and used shamelessly.

She kept her contentment from Tico because her mother had impressed upon her why you never, ever, tell the dreamboat of your life that he is the one and only. It's okay and highly convenient to tell all others they are formidable lovers, the greatest; but don't tell that to Mr. Amazing. The reasons, according to the late Maria Scheindlin, are five.

First, all men like to lead their women by the nose, so you tell him he reigns supreme, he figures you must indulge his every whim. Second, all lose interest once you cease to be a challenge and start looking for a new one. Third, he may be a failure in all other respects; unworthy of you. Fourth, the guy is a natural; he knows you have a great time in his bed. Fifth, the possibility of falling madly in love with such a guy is huge and you mustn't. Not even if, besides being

an amazing lover, he's young, handsome, rich, brilliant, and funny.
You don't fall madly in love, period.

As Jenny developed mentally and emotionally, she realized that
her mother had given her sound advice and she followed it to a tee
with Tico. What she had seen happen to a few famous women who
married jerks corroborated it. Her mom's fifth rule had seemed the
most difficult to her, but luckily the Puerto Rican perfectly fitted
reason number three, outstanding only as a lover, so she had kept
him under her thumb. Her agent, her friends, other models and photographers, Sam Plotzher and Elliot Steil, knew what Tico's role was.
Doormen and security guards at the Manhattan apartment building
and her Sunny Isles condominium probably suspected it as well. But
everybody pretended Tico was Jenny's personal assistant, which was
exactly how she wanted things to stand.

Because she attended classes at the Fashion Institute of Technology,
modelled at seasonal shows, entertained sheiks there, and loved the
city's sophisticated verve, Jenny was now spending between seven
and eight months a year in Manhattan. Inevitably, she lost her connection to Miami Beach and the people she hung out with there.
Most visits to her hometown were short, a few days that she spent
with Sam – making reports, receiving fresh indications, and discussing ways to carry them out – and with Elliot Steil – adamant in
updating her on how the firm was doing as often as possible. There
was little time for old friends. At the dawn of her Arab phase she
found messages from Chris on her machine and called back, but time
and distance worked their black magic and she forgot to give her new
number to the photographer when she changed it.

Chris's reaction moved from perplexity to incomprehension to
extreme anger. Valerio saw the opportunity to break up a friendship
he had never been comfortable with, and every time the subject came
up he fuelled his lover's resentment at Jenny. The fucking bitch had
turned her back on them. Following her mother's murder they had

devoted three weeks to holding her hand, drying her tears, consoling her, preparing her meals, brewing and forcing her to sip soothing teas when she woke up screaming in the small hours. They had given her massages, pedicures and manicures, cleaned her home, done her groceries, and provided advice on numerous things, from how to spot photographers that, for whatever reason, wanted to make her look bad by asking she adopt inappropriate poses or by using the wrong lighting, to recommending the colours more suitable to her complexion, which had not been easy because she had had such a deep tan.

Now that she was riding high, she had ditched them. People in the know said she had taken an "assistant" twenty years older than her, a most repulsive spic who was milking her dry and screwing her brains out. Well, nobody knows what life has in store for you, Chris mused, she could be heartbroken again and then . . . Oh, God, *then* she would clamour for Chris and Valerio, but it would be too late.

"There's nothing we can do," Valerio said, "except what Bedouins do."

Chris frowned. "What do you mean?"

"Bedouins sit patiently at the doors of their tents and wait for their enemy's dead body to pass before them."

A few weeks later, a letter addressed to Valerio de Alba was slipped under their apartment's front door.

> *Dear Valerio:*
>
> *Would you like to spend several months (or years) in a cell in Krome, then get deported to Peru, forbidden from ever again setting foot in the U.S.? Do you think Chris would adapt to spending the rest of his life in Lima or any other foreign city to remain living with you?*
>
> *I guess not.*
>
> *Would you rather split five million dollars with Chris, become a resident, maybe even a citizen of this country in a few years? Would you like to live with your loved one without a worry for as long as you wish?*

I guess you would.

I am under the impression that Chris loves his parents very much and would feel great sadness and regret should anything bad happen to either one. For instance, God forbid his beloved father is stabbed by another prison inmate, or that his mom is knocked down by a hit-and-run driver.

So, should both of you wish to live happy lives and make a lot of money, the way to let me know is to spend an hour strolling along Indian Beach Park next Friday between 7:00 and 8:00 p.m.

If you are not there, I will assume you reject my offer, report you to the INS, then call a guy I know at the prison where Mr. Dawson is serving time.

A friend

P.S. Believe me, I am your friend. Today you will be consumed with fear. But at some point you will remember this day as the best in your life.

They debated what to do for hours. Finally, dreading Valerio's deportation and fearing for the lives of Chris's parents, conceding that living together abroad would be extremely stressful, that they would not make even a small fraction of the money they made in Miami, and a bit curious about the prospect of netting five million, the following Friday they spent from seven to eight pacing the park. Nobody approached them; neither did they see anyone eyeing them from a distance.

"This may have been a prank," Chris opined.

"I doubt it," Valerio said. "Have you ever told anyone I'm an illegal?"

"I swear to God I haven't."

"Okay. Then how can this guy know?"

"Beats me."

On the Monday a courier delivered an envelope containing two typed pages that spelled out a most daring and unlawful undertaking in which no one would be injured. During the following nineteen months, Valerio and Chris got twenty-three similar envelopes with detailed instructions on what they had to learn and do to make five million dollars and get away with it. Each was delivered by a different courier service.

They were given instruction in surveillance, telephone monitoring, GPS, night vision, stakeouts, disguises, fingerprinting, bug detectors, and voice changers. Part of the course dealt with how to choose secure places for the job and for collecting the payoff. The curriculum included American and Canadian federal rules of criminal procedure, financial instruments, and banking dealings. Because they never met their pen pal, the couple dubbed him the Professor.

Each batch included a date and a place for them to leave a note indicating what they had failed to comprehend. The next delivery would include answers to their queries. They posed questions just twice.

The twenty-fourth envelope came inside a small refrigerator within a sealed box delivered by a Miami Beach courier service. Inside the freezer compartment they found twenty-five thousand U.S. dollars in fifty- and one-hundred-dollar non-sequential bills (half the operation's estimated cost). A three-page letter revealed the victim's name, habits, routines, and when the operation would take place. For several seconds Chris and Valerio stared into each other's eyes, at long last learning why they had been chosen. And for the first time ever they felt absolutely sure they could make a lot of money.

The final document pledged that, once they returned to Miami, in exchange for the payoff, their associate would personally hand them two suitcases each containing 2.5 million U.S. dollars in fifty- and one-hundred-dollar used bills. From then on, they would be on their own, the letter ended.

"Amen," Valerio said.

NINE DAYS

Toronto

Two days into her ordeal. Lying on a mattress on the floor, hand-cuffed, shackled, and blindfolded, her mind kept replaying the last forty-eight hours as if remembering every single second would show her a way out of her predicament.

On the van's linoleum-covered floor, bound and gagged, she had been sure the kidnappers wanted to rape her, and thought she could deal with that. Sliding back and forth as the vehicle rode up and downhill, she had remembered the stories of models who had been raped. Those with enough presence of mind to yield had fared better. Submission could even make the rapist frustrated and harmless, as he couldn't get an erection if the woman didn't fight back. She considered what to say to the motherfuckers. *Hey, hunks, I bet you have big cocks and I want to screw bad. So c'mon, let's see some action.* She would give them a class-A fuckathon, tell them it had been the greatest night of her life, and ask them for a date next evening. *Now drop me at my hotel, you crazy sex machines.* But she never got the chance.

Jenny shuddered at the memory of being undressed by them. They had taken her up a staircase to what she thought was a house. "Okay, okay, no need to force me. I'll lie down. I'm sure I'll have a great time. Just put on condoms," she had said. But her captors had only grunted derisively. Without uttering a word and with certain consideration, they had stripped her and slipped something velvety over her head. Her arms were thrust into sleeves and the garment dropped to her ankles.

Now she saw clearly that they wouldn't rape her. Mujahideen wouldn't descend to raping an infidel. It would be a sin. Wouldn't it? Why the grunts had been derisive.

During the first hour in the house she hadn't imagined they were Arabs. She should have suspected they were, though, because the tunic's cloth reminded her of her *abaya*, a present from a certain Zayed, a man who Mossad had been interested in. Dark blue, made of Malaki crepe, quite ample and collarless, its long sleeves covered her hands, like this one. The dress had a front closure, with snaps, and she had wondered if, like Zayed's present, it was embroidered at the sleeves' ends and along the bottom. Immediately thinking, *I'm so stupid.* Even abducted and blindfolded she wanted to know what she was wearing. *Oh, fuck!*

Later they had come for her, steered her to another room, made her sit on a stool. They took off the handcuffs and the shackles before slipping off the blindfold. She gaped at the two guys. The instant she saw their full mujahideen garb and their guns, she thought she was doomed. An Arab terrorist organization had found out that she was a Mossad agent and ordered her beheaded. She hadn't peed since leaving the hotel room and the wave of fear that suddenly engulfed her acted on her bladder. She felt urine flowing and peeked downward. The *abaya* was white. Without a word they gave her a paper to read and pointed at a video camera on a tripod. Then the taller kidnapper turned on a portable halogen lamp that bathed them in light. Following their gestures, she had read.

Afterward, the shorter mujahideen fetched a black *abaya*, signalling her to take off the wet one. She had demurred out of modesty, but eventually turned her back on them and pulled the white robe over her head; the bastards had actually giggled at her nudity! Once she put on the fresh garment she was guided back to her bedroom, where once again she was handcuffed, shackled, and blindfolded, then helped to sit on the mattress.

All that had taken place the day before yesterday. Now she decided she should, once again, consider her options. Should she confess to being an Israeli agent? Out of the question. If they asked her, she would shoot back, "Are you out of your minds?" *No, don't be offensive; just say it's not true.* The note she had read didn't charge her with spying for Israel. She was a fashion model, she was rich, why would she spy for any country? Okay, that was set in stone. Never admit it.

They had couriered the DVD to Elliot Steil, for she had recognized his voice on the phone a few hours earlier. Ten million dollars. Did these people really think Elliot could raise ten million dollars in a few days? She had never paid much attention to the Cuban's boring yackety-yack, but seemed to remember that the company's working capital was a couple of million. Would they behead her if she wasn't ransomed? She doubted it. It was gradually dawning on her that these men seemed more interested in money than in waging jihad or following the teachings of the Prophet Muhammad. Maybe they would extend the deadline. They hadn't asked for cash, though, but for stocks, or was it bonds? She should explain the difficulty of raising ten million to them. No, that would be wrong; only if they asked her. What if she offered to give them the money from her own investments? They would have to free her so she could sign papers. No, they wouldn't agree to that.

She was sure that Elliot would have shown the video to Sam, who certainly would have notified Mossad. But what could Mossad do? Nothing. And her kidnappers wouldn't wait forever. They would perhaps extend the deadline (*no, not deadline, time limit is better*) a few days. But you can't keep a hostage indefinitely. At a certain point you have to cut and run (*no, not cut, just run*).

What can I do? How can I get out of this mess? Oh, my God. Tico wanted to come to Toronto with me and I didn't let him. If he had, I wouldn't be here now. He would've jogged with me. No, wait. They would've shot Tico and kidnapped me anyway. Oh, good. Sweet, loving Tico is safe. Wait a moment. I feel for Tico? What do I feel for Tico? Am I in love with him? Oh, my God, Tico, I love you. I should've told you. Now I will die and you won't know. I've never been in love before. I've had sex with a lot of guys and I fall in love with you, you old, ugly sonofabitch. And despite all the humiliations I've made you suffer, you act as if your mission in life is to make me feel loved, to make me laugh, and to help me forget the frustrations and sad moments. I see it in your eyes: you adore me. Only love can make a man say all the sweet things you've said to me. And you've made me feel what no other man has made me feel. I know Mom would disapprove. But it's not like I'm telling you. Maybe I won't live to tell you. Oh, my God!

Miami

Neither of them could go back to sleep after the kidnapper's phone call, so Elliot gave Sam a towel, a new toothbrush, and a disposable razor, and the old man showered and shaved. Sam brewed coffee as Elliot used the bathroom, and then they surfed the Internet for Eurobonds.

While perusing various websites, Elliot thought about Ruben Scheindlin. The one good thing about his death was how he and Sam Plotzher had bonded. Compelled to get along, each of them had peered into corners of the other's personality they hadn't scrutinized before. He liked what he saw, and it seemed Sam felt something similar. They had a friendship in which mutual respect covered a lot of ground, including poking fun at each other. Yet Elliot always kept in mind Sam's triple seniority: in age, in experience, and as a shareholder.

By the time the sun came up they had more than forty pages printed; Elliot also had estimated that ten million U.S. dollars in one-hundred-dollar bills would weigh 212 pounds, give or take.

"That explains the bonds," Sam said. "Even if a hundred-franc Swiss bill weighs half what a C-note weighs, running away with a hundred-pound package is a ball-breaker. Eurobonds in the high denominations the bastards demand would weigh much less. There may even be a ten-thousand-franc denomination. I don't know how much the damn things weigh either, but a lot less than ten thousand dollars in one-hundred-franc bills, for sure. Maybe a few ounces."

"And there may be a few with a hundred thousand face value," Elliot added. "Then, ten million dollars – or however many Swiss francs that is – will fit in a briefcase."

"Right. The bastards are not stupid."

"No, they aren't."

They had learned that Eurobonds were available in various currencies and issued in bearer form. According to several websites, many European corporations had turned to the Eurobond market to diversify away from bank loans and to escape transaction fees. To their amazement, they found that even U.S.-based companies raise money by issuing Eurobonds in foreign currencies. The Eurobond market seemed to be both an international market and to a certain extent an unregulated domestic bond market for Europe. Most Eurobonds were unregistered, meaning that possession alone was evidence of ownership, like cash.

"Aha!" Sam said.

"I don't think so," Elliot said, emphatically.

"Possession not evidence of ownership? Bearer bonds?"

"It is, it is. They can't lie about that. What I don't believe is that it's like cash."

"Why not?"

"Because of the age we are living in, Sam. We've just learned that bearer bonds were made illegal in the U.S. in 1982. Money laundering must've been the reason. They survive in Europe, granted; it's why they asked for Eurobonds, because they are like cash, weigh little, and can be easily transported. But when you cash the bond, you must provide some ID, have a bank account, show something, for Christ's sake! You can't walk into a bank and say: 'Hey, I want to cash these bonds. Give me eleven million Swiss francs. And hurry up, I have an armoured truck waiting outside.'"

"True."

"That may have been possible before 9/11. But now, with the whole banking community on the lookout for terrorist financing? I don't think so. Bearer bonds are as good as cash if you are on the level. For instance, you walk into a bank and say, 'I'm Sam Plotzher. Cash this and transfer the money to account number so and so in such and such bank.' Then and only then, after they check you out, are Eurobonds as good as cash."

Sam considered this for a few moments. "But you just mentioned money laundering. What about that?"

"What about it?"

"Suppose these guys take these bonds to one of those shady little banks on an island somewhere and say, 'I have these Eurobonds, so many millions in Swiss francs, perfectly legal. At today's exchange rate it's ten million U.S. or whatever. You give me five million U.S. cash, you make a five-million profit.'"

It was Elliot's turn to mull things over.

"Suppose they contact a drug lord," Sam continued. "Drug lords lose money to launder their cash. Get seventy or eighty in clean greenbacks for a hundred dirty. This would be the opposite. They pay these bastards with dirty money and don't lose a penny. Even better, they give them eight for ten and make a two-million profit."

"Well . . . I don't know about that," Elliot said, with a doubtful expression. "There has to be a record of who the original buyer was and where he bought them."

"Not according to what I read here."

Sam started flipping through the printed pages, frequently licking thumb and forefinger. Used to seeing him do that, Elliot kept considering the supposition.

"See?" he said, after a minute. "'Most Eurobonds are unregistered, neither the issuing firm nor the underwriter keeps records of ownership. Possession is evidence of ownership.'"

"But the bonds must have a serial number," Elliot objected. "Then, after Jenny is freed, we go to the police, tell them what company issued the bonds, give them the serial numbers, and every bank in the world will be on the lookout for bonds issued in Swiss francs by . . . I don't know . . . Berlin GmbH or Follies SPRL."

Sam shook his head at Elliot's wishful thinking.

"So what, Elliot? This island's little bank cashes the bonds. Interpol goes to the island and asks, 'Who sold you those bonds?' And the bank's president, who is a suave sonofabitch in an Ormani suit, says, 'I don't remember. Those were bearer bonds. I only made sure they were not counterfeit. I paid the customer in cash, minus my commission, and they left. I don't know who they are. I'm not required to demand IDs. The bonds are payable to the bearer.' Understand what I'm saying?"

Elliot cocked his head. "Sam, you with the Sioux or with the Seventh Cavalry?"

Plotzher grunted. "I'm with the Sioux. But we are at war. And at war, you have to anticipate what the enemy will do. We have to try to think like them. Which is why next thing we should find out is why Toronto. Okay?"

"Okay. But it's Armani."

"What?"

"The banker's suit. Armani."

"Whatever. You wear that?"

"I won't dignify that with an answer."

And they shared their first laugh since watching the DVD.

Toronto

They had gone to bed after the phone calls, around four, drained and very tired. An erection had awoken Chris a few minutes after seven. He had roused the Peruvian and they had made love passionately, if hastily. Now, both felt like sleeping one more hour, maybe two. But they knew they had to get up, make breakfast, and don Arab clothes.

Chris had had a splendid orgasm, perhaps the result of several days of abstinence, but perhaps also because of the high stakes venture they were embarked on. Sex with Valerio was always superb, but pulling it off and once again living the high life may have helped his formidable sexual climax. Before long he would be living the life he had grown accustomed to, in which money is no limitation, provided you don't squander it on a personal 747 or a 400-foot-long superyacht. And he would share that wonderful future with the person who, without trying, had made him realize that the height of sexual pleasure is reached when feelings are as long-lasting and solid as your lover's cock.

Chris sighed contentedly and shifted focus to practicalities. They should remove the woman's restraints, take her to the bathroom, give her privacy there, then serve her breakfast, restrain her again. After that there were chores, including washing and drying the *abaya* Jenny had peed on the day before. They had only two; suppose she had her period? He made a mental note to get some tampons.

"I'll shower now," he said, getting up.

"Okay."

The brief exchange failed to sidetrack Valerio, who was reflecting on what they had accomplished so far and what remained ahead. Over the last two years the Peruvian had come to realize that the Professor had been right to knock into his head the importance of planning every single detail, however minute, when you were risking the two most precious things of all: life and freedom. He also had discovered the immense value of meticulous research, of expecting the unexpected and anticipating how to deal with it, of stockpiling and duplicating vital components and systems, and of trying to foresee the possible excuses and delays that "the competition" (what the boss called those ransoming Jenny) might come up with.

The Professor, in addition to conceiving the scheme, had sandpapered its rough edges and polished it to perfection. Valerio had learned from someone who, as well as being knowledgeable in a vast number of fields, was trained to think ahead. The man had anticipated every conceivable scenario, debated every alternative, planned each step.

He had argued that Jenny should be seized at a place and time when there would be few casual observers, probably in the vicinity of her hotel at dusk, the time of day when she usually jogged. It would be for the best if nobody witnessed the abduction, he had insisted in three different letters. The guy thought of everything. So, they had wandered around near the hotel a week in advance, checking for surveillance cameras. Two-block-long Bellair Street seemed to be the best spot; to the naked eye there were no cameras on it. Luck had played a part too, for the sidewalk had been nearly deserted when they grabbed the model; merely a couple of well-dressed dodderers walking arm-in-arm exchanging whispers, and a young man across the street hurrying in the opposite direction; he couldn't have seen anything.

Now the less dangerous, but more difficult part had started. Seventy-two hours earlier only he, Chris, and the Professor knew what would take place; now two more knew: Jenny and Elliot Steil. Maybe three, if Elliot had told Sam Plotzher. Perhaps hundreds of officers as well, if the Cuban had gone to the police. In which case, red and amber lights would be blinking everywhere; the phone lines of myriad police forces could be clogged with calls and faxes reporting the abduction. The probability that the FBI had already contacted the RCMP was anybody's guess. No matter. They had taken it as a given that the top abduction experts in North America would be searching for Jenny and her kidnappers, that he and Chris might well see in real life the scene depicted in so many Hollywood thrillers – SWAT teams sliding down ropes from choppers hovering above. They had not overlooked that possibility.

There was no backtracking now; the shuttle was airborne and to land safely it first had to reach orbit. Failure was unlikely, Valerio was sure. Not a soul could imagine their complete scheme. Knowing that Jenny was in Toronto, the "competition" would track their phone calls. A waste of time. Chris Dawson and Valerio de Alba – and, he felt sure, their counsellor too – were satisfied with what they had accomplished. They were more than ready.

Wrapped in an oversized bath towel, Chris returned to the bedroom.

"You want me to clean you up?" he asked, staring at Valerio's still lubricated flaccid penis and waving a wet hand towel.

"No, I'll take a quick shower."

By the time Valerio returned, Chris had dressed in pants, a tunic, and black sneakers. He had put on contact lenses to change the colour of his eyes to brown and pulled on disposable latex gloves. Once the Peruvian dressed, they helped each other with the *kaffiyeh*.

"This may be great for the desert, but in a city?" Valerio said.

Ominous-looking plastic handguns tucked in their belts completed the elaborate masquerade.

Having breakfast with the headgear on proved difficult, so they took it off and put it on again before carrying the tray to their captive's bedroom.

"Oh, thank God," cried Jenny, "I need to use the toilet, please."

The abductors' eyes locked for an instant, and compassion and a little sadness shone in them. Valerio removed Jenny's restraints but not the blindfold. Clutching her elbow, Chris walked her to the bathroom and positioned her facing the toilet, then turned her around. Valerio lifted the *abaya* to her waist and made Jenny hold it by the seams. Feeling the cool porcelain against her calves, Jenny quickly sat down. She thought it was the longest pee of her life.

"For God's sake, I need a little privacy here," in a pleading tone.

The men glanced at one another. Chris nodded. Valerio removed her blindfold. Jenny implored with her eyes. They gave her a hard stare. Then Chris made a V with his fingers, took them to his eyes, then pointed them at her. They would be watching her. The men retraced a few steps and closed the bathroom door. Jenny felt momentarily grateful to her captors.

"You know what?" Valerio whispered in Chris's ear, standing by the bathroom door. "I feel sorry for her."

Chris shook his head and shrugged.

Jenny studied the bathroom: a sink, two faucets, soap, a bathtub, shower curtain, towel, toilet paper on a holder. The small window had been boarded up from the interior. Would they let her shower? Why didn't they ever speak? Maybe not to hear her argue for her freedom. Perhaps their boss had prohibited them to speak to her, or they believed that talking to an infidel was sinful.

She had read articles on how detained mujahideen considered it sinful to see a naked woman who was not their spouse. Taking advantage of this, American interrogators had forced them to watch females in the raw. But these two had snickered at her nakedness. Exception proving the rule? Maybe. Pretty devout Arabs had humped her and other infidel females too, with no qualms whatsoever. But they hadn't been mujahideen.

As soon as the sound of flushing reached his ears, Valerio opened the door. Jenny, washing her hands at the sink, half turned.

Valerio indicated the shower.

"Oh, thanks. Thank you so much." Overjoyed.

The Peruvian closed the door.

"Onset of the Stockholm syndrome," Chris whispered to his boyfriend.

The first thing that got Jenny wondering how much her captors knew about her was breakfast: although tepid, her mug of tea tasted exactly like her favourite brand, and the slice of wholegrain toast had the crispness she preferred.

Miami

Elliot pressed the key and said, "Steil."

"Morning, Elio."

"Morning, girl."

"I got to the office two minutes ago, checked my machine, found it had a message from Stuart. The guy Tony mauled decided not to press charges."

"That's great news!" Elliot said and shot a glance at Plotzher, who was eyeing him inquiringly. The old man knew the five or six words of Spanish every Florida non-Hispanic resident knows: *hola, adiós, latino, dinero*, plus *margarita, mojito, cerveza*, and *daiquirí. Well*, thought Steil, *serves you right. That's how I feel when you talk your gobbledygook.*

"The trade-off is Tony won't charge him with molestation."

"And?"

"Tony is fine with that, provided the guy moves."

"And?"

"Stuart hasn't told the bastard yet. He'll let me know."

"Okay. Call me when you hear something new."

"Miss me?"

"Very much so. How's your mom?"

"Better. Got to go. Love you."

"Love you too."

Steil returned the cell to its holster.

"The guy Tony beat won't press charges."

"Glad to hear that. How's Tony?"

"Well, it seems this whole thing has made him . . . oh, I don't know, reconsider, or make a fresh start. He quit drinking beer and has lost twenty or thirty pounds, got a job with – wait a minute!" wide-eyed, half-smiling at Plotzher.

"What?" feigning ignorance.

"You had something to do with it?"

"Something to do with what?"

"You were behind it."

"What are you talking about?"

"Thanks, Sam."

The old man stopped pretending, smiled, and shook his head. "Least I could do. But don't tell him."

Three days earlier Tony had called Steil to say that a guy from the human resources department of Greater Miami Security Services had phoned him. The man had said Tony was a good cop going through a hard time. The firm wanted to offer him a minimum-wage desk job at its main office. Should Tony be cleared of charges or declared innocent and could again carry a sidearm, he'd be promoted to a better-paying position in an armoured truck, transporting cash and valuables.

Steil had congratulated his friend but failed to make the connection. But now it had flashed through his mind. On the few occasions that Imlatinex had needed a security firm, Ruben Scheindlin had used Greater Miami Security Services, founded and owned by a friend of his. After Scheindlin died, dealing with the security company had been one of Sam's responsibilities. The odds that somebody at GMSS, from nowhere, had learned of Tony's troubles and offered to lend him a hand were 999 to 1. Sam Plotzher had to have asked them to hire Tony.

"I won't. Appreciate the gesture, Sam."

"Guy protects his family deserves a break," Sam said. "Let's keep trying to figure things through. Jenny had done this fashion thing in Toronto in the past, so it wouldn't have been difficult to find out if she would be there this year too. These shows have organizers; people who know shit about fashion but are experts at publicity, press, invitations, that sort of thing. They make lists, reserve seats, right?"

"Right. But the mujahideen also had to confirm she hadn't cancelled. If she were still modelling they could've called her agency. Maybe they called her, or her assistant. Hey, shouldn't we call this guy Tico?"

"We'd be letting on that there's a problem."

Elliot argued that secrecy created a huge obstacle. In a tolerant tone, with raised eyebrows and tilting his head somewhat, Plotzher killed the idea of calling Jenny's "assistant."

Then he perked up. "Hold it, hold it, wait a fucking moment. That guy is a suspect, ain't he?"

Elliot shrugged. "I don't know. I suppose."

"You've met him?"

"I've seen him, if that's what you mean, when I report to Jenny. First time he showed up during one of our meetings Jenny introduced us. We shook hands, she told me he was Puerto Rican and told him I was Cuban, we exchanged a few words in Spanish, and that was it. All other occasions he came in with a tray, nodded at me, said hello, I nodded back, said hello. What Jenny sees in this guy is a mystery to me."

Sam considered Elliot's last comment for a few moments. "Probably he's not intimidated by her," he said eventually.

"Pardon?"

"Most men are intimidated by beautiful women, think they are not in their league, stare pop-eyed at them but don't have the guts to ask them out. And Jenny is a very beautiful woman. She had most likely gotten tired of the schmucks she usually meets by the time this dude who doesn't give a shizzle about women came along. If he treated her like an ordinary woman, not like a goddess, he would've swept her off her feet. Especially if he made fun of her and her job."

"Well, I don't know about Jenny" – Elliot was perplexed that Sam, married to the same woman for over forty years, held such views about the female psyche – "but concerning beautiful women, generally speaking, you may be right."

"You think I'm right, you don't give a shizzle about women either, buddy," with a mocking smile.

"Now, wait a minute –"

Sam's cell rang and he answered. While he talked, Elliot brooded on the old man's accusation. So unfair; he did care about women. They had affected his life a great deal more than men. In all those memories he would cherish until one second before dying, women had centre stage. Smiling lovingly, or crying tenderly, or running towards him, or running away from him, or caring for him when he was sick, or allowing him to knit a veil of caresses over their naked bodies. Cubans all, without exception. Beautiful? Most, yes. Correction. Every single one had been beautiful, either physically or spiritually. A few had been perfect in body and soul.

"My old lady," snapping the cell shut. "You are not gonna believe the coincidence."

"Try me."

"This Tico just called home."

"Really?"

"Esther gave him my cell number. He'll call now."

"Turn your speaker on; let's record what he has to say."

Less than a minute went by before Sam's phone rang again. Elliot held the tape recorder close to it.

"Hello?"

"Mr. Plotzher?"

"Speaking."

"I'm Ms. Scheindlin's assistant, sir, Tico Monerris. Your wife gave me this number a few minutes ago."

"Ah, oh, yes, we've met. Can I help you?"

"Well, Mr. Plotzher . . . the thing is . . . I'm a little worried. I haven't heard from Je – Ms. Scheindlin, in three days. I've called her cell and her hotel room many times and she doesn't answer. Do you by any chance know where she is?"

"No, I don't. Where was she?"

"In Toronto."

"At which hotel?"

"The Four Seasons."

"Room?"

"1519."

"Okay, Tico. What was she doing in Toronto?"

"Attending a fashion show. She has done this same show as a model for four or five years. But last year, and this too, she went to do research about starting a business, or so she said."

"Where are you, Tico?"

"Manhattan; her apartment."

"Go on."

"I called the hotel desk. They say she was there the first two nights but hasn't returned or called since. And I'm a little worried, Mr. Plotzher, because, you know, this is not like Jenny *at all*."

"Hmm. Had you noticed any recent changes in Jenny? Like she was depressed, or worried or something?"

"No, sir."

"Did you have a fight?"

"Excuse me?"

"Did you quarrel?"

"Sir, I never quarrel with my employer."

"Cut the crap, Tico. I'm not stupid. Everyone and his uncle knows you two are lovers. So, c'mon, you had a fight?"

"Ah, um, no, sir."

"Is it possible she met another guy and dumped you? Flew to Tahiti or some other place?"

A short silence ensued. Sam shifted his look to Elliot and winked.

"Well, that's possible, of course. But she would've checked out, and the desk said her baggage is still in her room. And besides, she wouldn't disappear without warning you. She sees you as next of kin; wouldn't want you to worry."

Now it was Sam who paused, considering something.

"Okay, Tico. Tell you what. I'll see what I can find out. Meanwhile, keep your mouth shut and don't call her any more; not on her cell, not in her hotel room. Last thing we need is some rag printing 'Missing Model' or some other stupid headline in big red letters. Could be bad for her future. You understand what I'm saying?"

"Yes, Mr. Plotzher."

"You have any news, call me immediately. At midnight, the wee hours, any time. If I learn anything I'll call you at the apartment."

"You have the number?"

"Of course I have the number. And thanks for the heads-up."

"You're welcome, Mr. Plotzher. Bye now."

Sam closed the phone, stared at Elliot stopping the recorder. "He could be part of it, you know?"

"Could be. But the guy sounded really worried."

"Elliot, ten million dollars is a lot of gelt; some people would do anything for 10 per cent of that: kidnap, murder, anything. And he knows everything concerning Jenny. To me he's guilty until proven innocent. Let's get to the warehouse. If we are not together and Jenny's phone rings, don't answer it. Get me, then we lock ourselves in your car or mine, and wait. Daffy Duck will call again, for sure," Sam sighed. "Wish we had someone to take care of the company till this is over. C'mon, let's go."

Toronto

Chris pulled over on a quiet street near St. Lawrence Market, got out, and locked the Cadillac. He started strolling and looking around, acting the part of a recently arrived tourist. As he came close to a storm sewer, he took out the prepaid cell phone he had used the previous night to call Steil, feigned dropping it by accident, then kicked it into the sewer. In case someone had seen him, he ran his hands through his hair and flapped his arms against his body to indicate frustration.

Next he strolled into a drugstore and bought tampons. "She always forgets," he said to the brunette at the checkout counter, putting on his Julia Roberts smile.

At the Four Seasons, the head of security, Robert McLaughlin, formerly an inspector with the Toronto Police Service, tapped Constable Mark Bowen's number, his contact at the 53 Police Division.

"Hey, Mark, Bob. How are things?"

"Same old, same old. Heard you had a fire scare the other night."

"Yeah, a drunk had a lie-down smoking. Ruined a mattress."

"So, you calling on account some other room attendant kept what she found?"

"Nah. We got a fine crew now. But in case there's a black sheep we haven't ferreted out, I spread the word we've hidden cameras in every room."

"You ferret out sheep, Inspector? That's news."

"Very funny, wise guy. Listen, this woman checked in three days ago, Jennifer Scheindlin – s-c-h-e-i-n-d-l-i-n – fashion model, seems to have left without checking out. Her things are in the room, though, including jewellery in the safe."

"Then she didn't check out."

"Well, no, I mean, she hasn't checked out but she hasn't been to her room since the seventeenth. She has stayed with us before; never caused any trouble. This guy who claims to be her assistant is breaking my balls; he's called from New York four frigging times. Said he hasn't heard from her for three days. Wanted to know if she's sick."

Bowen finished writing the name of the hotel, the date and the time, then tore the page from the block.

"What do you want me to do?" he said.

"You tell me. File a missing person report maybe?"

The policeman thought this over as he folded the paper and put it in his shirt pocket.

"Let me ask the sergeant. These models, well, Bob, you know. Maybe she hooked up with someone and has shacked up somewhere else. You file an MP, we have to start working our asses off trying to find her even as she could be snorting joy flakes, screwing, and having a great time."

"Okay, you let me know. Take care, buddy," McLaughlin said.

"You too."

As Constable Bowen made his way to the sergeant's cubicle, news that a shooting had occurred at Ramsden Park arrived. He hurried to a police cruiser, the possibility that a fashion model was really missing vanishing from his thoughts.

After washing and drying the *abaya*, Valerio prepared traditional
Arab fare: basmati rice, chicken majboos, pita bread, and tea. They
served her a meagre ration, everything thrown together, the tea in a
plastic cup, to give the impression the infidel was getting leftovers
from the kidnappers' table. A famished Jenny wiped the plate clean,
including the final few grains of rice she picked up with her fingernails. The *kaffiyeh* concealed Chris's disgust. He had seen this woman
order a $150 lobster thermidor and a $600 bottle of Belle Epoque
champagne at a pricey restaurant and leave an hour later, having
barely picked at the food and having sipped less than half a glass of
the prestige cuvée. Conflicting feelings stirred inside him. What she
was going through was uncalled-for.

They had discussed this. Perfectly possible, Valerio had said. It's
only human to root for the weak and sympathize with the victim. But
her torment would last only a few days, and they wouldn't harm a
hair on her head. Yes, she must experience anguish; believe they
would kill her unless she was ransomed and they weren't hunted
down. They could be rich and start new lives, and they'd barely dent
her wealth. Not to mention that Jenny needed the lesson. She would
learn to appreciate her money, freedom, and beauty. She would learn
to value friends and friendship.

Chris sighed. Valerio was right. If all went well, he would visit her
two or three years from now and learn about her ordeal from her own
lips. On second thought, maybe she wouldn't tell anyone. Or maybe
her silverback lover, the greasy spic, wouldn't tell her that her old
friend Chris Dawson was trying to contact her. But in any case, Jenny
would have learned to count her blessings. Without a word, he hand-
cuffed her, picked up the tray, then left the bedroom.

Miami

At 4:15 p.m. Sam crossed the glassed-in cubicle's threshold, gave Elliot a wink of complicity, and said they had to go see a client. A black SUV was stationed in front of the warehouse.

"We'll ride that," Sam announced, waving toward the vehicle, then holding out the key to Elliot.

"A rental?"

"Yep. We gotta go to the airport, pick up the experts. Wouldn't want to torture them in your bucket of bolts, would you?"

"Oh, yeah, like yours is a batmobile."

Waiting at Concourse G's arrivals gate at the airport, Elliot marvelled at how things had changed since the 1940s. Jews flying Lufthansa; perhaps the first flight out of Tel Aviv after Sam's call.

"You bring a sign with their names?" he asked Sam.

"Nope."

"You know them?"

"No."

"Then how . . . ?"

"They'll find me."

The woman came out first, spotted them in her first scrutinizing sweep of the waiting crowd. She had the elastic stride of an Arabian mare, razor-thin lips that looked as if they hadn't smiled in a long time, clever eyes that had seen too much, a firm handshake.

"Hadara," first to Sam, then to Elliot, who tried to discern whether the woman's blue, three-piece pants set concealed something worth checking out. Touches here and there, not much, just curvy insinuations in the right places. She was sporting a not-too-stylish brown bob, short at the back with a choppy fringe. A stainless-steel diver's watch on her left wrist and little gold studs in her ears were her sole adornments. She carried a leather purse, the strap over her shoulder.

"Javan," a bald man in his late forties said. Five-eight or so, 170 pounds, ears bent forward, prominent nose. Standard Israeli male attire: sports jacket over a white, open-necked shirt, brown pants. Elliot judged the man unimposing. Then a callused paw that had martial arts and iron pumping all over it seized his right hand. Yet again Elliot cursed his tendency to make snap judgments. The seemingly unimposing guy was a toughy. The overused cliché about the two partners, one all brains, the other a muscular moron, popped into Elliot's head.

During the walk to the parking garage, Sam briefed the newcomers about Elliot, in English. From van driver to general manager and shareholder in fourteen years, former English teacher in Cuba, capable, serious, responsible. The kidnappers had couriered Jenny's phone to him.

"You have the courier's box?" Javan asked. His English had a heavy Israeli accent.

The realization that he had failed to hold on to the box made Elliot curse. He stole a glimpse at Sam, who raised his eyebrows, shrugged, and shook his head in resignation.

"No, I don't. I'm sorry," the Cuban said. "I opened the box four or five hours before I watched the disk. I had no idea it would be important. I threw it in the wastepaper basket. The cleaning man empties all baskets every night. Garbage truck comes at sunrise. I'm sorry."

Silence.

From the back seat, Hadara phoned someone and said a few words in Hebrew. Elliot found her voice unusually low for a woman, almost masculine, but the intonation was feminine. When the call ended, she addressed Sam also in Hebrew. The old man nodded and turned to Steil.

"You know where the New World Tower is?"

"No, I don't."

"Okay. What about Bayfront Park?"

"Near the Port? Close to Flagler and Biscayne Boulevard?"

"That's right. Let's go there."

Their final destination was the Israeli consulate, on the eighteenth floor of a thirty-storey glass-and-steel high-rise with an entrance in terracotta-coloured marble. Elevator, hallway, nods; introductions were omitted. The door said the consulate's hours were Monday to Thursday 9:30 a.m. to 1:00 p.m. It was 5:44 p.m.

An extremely good-looking receptionist in her late thirties or early forties made Elliot lift his left eyebrow. A gorgeous woman. She and Hadara bussed cheeks and exchanged pleasantries in Hebrew before the lovely lady handed her a tightly wrapped and sealed envelope. Then she guided them to a small conference room, nodded, exited discreetly, and closed the door behind her. They settled themselves around a circular table. Hadara dropped her handbag on it, inspected the seal on the envelope, passed it to Javan for additional scrutiny. Her colleague searched for signs of tampering before nodding and ripping open the wrapping. He extracted a square plastic case, got up, seized a remote, inserted the DVD in a player, pressed buttons. All four watched in silence. At the end, he returned the disk to its case and eased himself back into his seat. Hadara asked a question in Hebrew. Sam started to answer.

"One moment, please," Elliot said.

Heads and eyes turned to him.

"I think, Sam, you should inform the lady that I do not speak Hebrew. Therefore, I would appreciate it if, in my presence, conversations are held in English, or translated into English. Would that be possible?"

Sam exchanged glances with the newly arrived; both nodded.

"Okay, sorry for that, Steil," the woman said in impeccable English with a New York or New Jersey accent. "What I asked Sam was how he learned about Jenny's abduction. Please, Sam."

The complete recapitulation, including questions, answers, and listening to four taped calls, took just about an hour. At the end, Hadara turned to Elliot.

"You have any experience concerning police methods and procedures, Mr. Steil?"

"Well, if American TV serials bear a resemblance to real police work, then I have an idea."

"Fair enough. You said at the start of this meeting that you'd appreciate it if we talk in English when you are present. Well, I would appreciate it if you are not offended by any questions I ask. Consider it standard police procedure. Okay?"

"Okay."

"For my colleague and me, you are the prime suspect. Are we mistaken?"

Toronto

"Hello?" Jenny said, loud enough to be heard outside. Nothing happened. She waited several seconds. In the living room, Chris was hurriedly helping Valerio with his *kaffiyeh*.

"Hello?" much louder. She couldn't hold it one more minute.

"Hello!" shouting now.

The door opened.

"What?" from the door frame, angrily, the man she identified as the shorter mujahideen.

"I have to pee. I can't hold it for hours on end."

Valerio unshackled her but kept the handcuffs in place. He took her to the toilet, went out and left the door ajar. Jenny lifted the *abaya* and emptied her bladder with a deep sigh of relief. After she flushed the toilet, her captor pushed the bathroom door open, marched her to her mattress, shackled her, and left.

"Wanted to pee?" Chris, standing in the living space.

"We gotta remember," Valerio said, after a nod. "I've already peed twice since lunch. Every three hours or so we gotta take her to the bathroom."

"Agreed. But you said 'What' to her."

"One fucking word."

"The Professor made clear we should speak to her only at the swap, because we must, and as little as possible."

"Okay, sorry."

"We all make mistakes. Give her the Qu'ran now."

"Okay."

Valerio went to their bedroom and returned with a copy of the Qu'ran translated into English.

"Remember to turn the light on," Chris said.

Valerio unlocked the door to Jenny's room, flicked the light switch, and respectfully placed the book on the mattress, facing Jenny, who seemed caught unawares.

"Thank you," she mumbled at last.

Valerio left.

Jenny stared at the book without touching it, wondering if they would try to convert her to Islam, which was exactly what they wanted her to think, to reinforce the imposture. She brought it to her nose. A barely discernible smell of printed paper. She wondered why she had done that. She enjoyed smelling perfumes, foods, coffee, fabrics, leather, but she had no recollection of having ever smelled a book. It's what animals do first, she reasoned. How much of an animal was she turning into? Are they supposed to convert the infidel before beheading her? She felt fear welling up.

Jenny had never imagined such suffering as being imprisoned in a dark room. Flying between continents she had known that if the plane crashed, she'd die instantly. In her first years as an informer, she had pictured herself firing guns, maybe getting shot and dying heroically. The possibility of a slow death, from cancer or other consuming disease, had rarely crossed her mind. And this, a death sentence lacking execution date and time, had been inconceivable. She was sure these people would collect the money and kill her. Maybe tape her beheading. She shuddered.

It suddenly dawned on her she was meeting tragedy head-on for the first time ever. She had never suffered. Her childhood as the apple of her parents' eyes had been glorious. She could recall stern looks from her mother when she misbehaved, none from her father. For him she had been *printsesin* Jenny. She learned the meaning of the Hebrew word when she asked him on her sixth (or her seventh?) birthday. Yes, she had been his princess and she enjoyed the title. Perhaps royal children weren't half as happy as she had been, what with the protocol, ceremonies, security. (Well, security wasn't bad.) Daddy had given her all she had asked for all through adolescence: first subscriptions to *Vogue* and *Harper's Bazaar*, first savings account, first credit card, first car, first Woody Speedster, first diamond, first everything.

And she had taken it all for granted. She had believed everybody lived like her. Well, no, she hadn't been *that* stupid, Jenny reconsidered. Every now and then, zapping between channels, she had stumbled upon newscasts or documentaries showing famished Africans with amputated arms, or half-naked Amazonian tribesmen shooting monkeys with blow guns. But she had kept on flipping, unconcerned. She also had become conscious that the Miami Beach residents making a living as servers, chauffeurs, housemaids, and in similar menial positions didn't live like her, but what the heck, they could always win the lottery!

Her immaturity had been why Dad had proposed to cover all her expenses during the making of her book, so that she would consent to spend six months in a kibbutz. She had learned a lot there: what it was to toil all day long, even with period pains, what little money people got paid, how long a person would have to work and save to afford a TV set, a fridge, or a plane ticket. She had understood why racial discrimination is intolerable, why terrorism is cowardly and despicable, why every human being is entitled to a few essential rights. Israel had burst her fairyland bubble. In Israel she had learned about real life for the first time ever.

The lesson had gradually receded in her mind once she returned to her world and as the years went by. But now, under the most demanding circumstances of her life, it was coming back to her with a rush, overwhelming her brain, shutting out banalities, leaving space only for thinking about life and death, about eating, breathing, peeing, and defecating. About those who had loved her: her parents and Tico, maybe Sam, no one else. Would she live or die? Was there an afterlife?

She picked up the Qu'ran.

All praise is due to Allah, the Lord of the Worlds. The Beneficent, the Merciful. Master of the Day of Judgment. Thee do we serve and Thee do we beseech for help. Keep us on the right path. The path of those upon whom Thou hast bestowed favours. Not of those upon whom Thy wrath is brought down, nor of those who go astray.

Miami

Most Jews Elliot knew were brutally honest. Pretence was uncharacteristic. If they liked you, they showed it; if they disliked you, you would soon find out. But this was too much. He shot an angry look at Sam, who was eyeing Hadara and shaking his head in a silent *you so screwed up, sister*. But the woman wasn't catching on; she was looking intently at Elliot, his flared nostrils, narrowed eyes, pressed lips.

"I will gladly respond to your question," Elliot began, forcing a smile, "as soon as you tell me what you are doing here. Why I shouldn't walk out that door, right now, go to the FBI and let them handle this?"

"Good point," Hadara said. "Let me tell you first why you shouldn't go to the FBI. Jenny was abducted in Toronto, which, last time I consulted a map, was in Canada. The FBI operates within the United States. Unless the Canadian government asks the FBI to assist them, they can't move a finger. And as far as we know, the Royal Canadian Mounted Police, which is the Canadian FBI, sort of, has no clue an American citizen has been abducted. If it had, we would know. Does that answer your question about reporting this to the FBI?"

"Go on."

"About why we are here, I'll offer you a deal: I tell *you* why we are here; you tell *me* why we shouldn't consider you a suspect. But," the woman paused for effect, "our reason to be here is a state secret. If I reveal this secret, you swear you won't tell it to anyone?"

"I swear nothing, lady," fuming. "I owe no allegiance to you or any state. I hate politics, I hate all the secrecy bullshit all states engage in." Elliot paused, admitting to himself he had blown his lid. He took a deep breath. "But I don't go around mouthing off about everything I know. I could give you my word I won't reveal to anyone this so-called secret, though. You want to take my word for it, okay. You don't, I get up and leave."

Hadara turned to Sam. "You vouch for him?"

"I do," with a firm nod.

She returned her eyes to Steil.

"We are here because Jennifer Scheindlin has been working for the Israeli police for a little over five years."

"Jenny?" Elliot's anger abated quickly; this was too much for him to swallow. "You gotta be kidding me."

"I'm not kidding, Steil."

Elliot turned to Sam. "Is it true?"

Jenny's handler had rearranged his expression. "How can I know?"

Then, to the woman: "Are you serious? Jenny?" Leaning forward, pretending to be dumbstruck. Javan and Hadara knew they were attending a magisterial class.

"It's true, Sam," Hadara said.

Elliot frowned. The previous evening Sam had unstuck something from the inside of his belt, read what was on it, and tapped out a number on his cordless. What was going on here? Was Sam a police informant, too? He'd ask him, but later, in private.

Hadara proceeded to tell the story she and Javan had contrived. Jenny had befriended a Brazilian model who, six years earlier, had asked her to smuggle diamonds into the U.S.; stones stolen in Tel Aviv. Did Steil know that Israel has an important diamond industry? The Cuban shook his head. Israel lacks diamond mines, but traders buy the stones rough and cut and polish them in Israel, Hadara told him. To make a long story short, Hadara went on, the Brazilian girl was in hock to drug dealers and they had forced her to approach Jenny. Not knowing that she was rich, they were hoping to recruit her to smuggle diamonds into the U.S. As a good Jew, Jenny came to where they were now and told the Israeli Consul what was going on. Eventually the IP asked her to become an informer.

"What's IP?"

"Israeli Police."

"What's your rank?"

"We are detectives, both of us."

"I want to see your IDs."

The plastic cards had their photos, but he couldn't make sense of the Hebrew words. Israeli Police, he assumed.

"Go ahead."

"Thanks to Jenny's work we've collared nine thieves and eleven smugglers, mostly Palestinians. It's possible that the criminals somehow found out that Jenny was informing on them and abducted her to get even. You get the picture now?"

"Things start to make sense, yes."

"Okay. I fulfilled my part of the deal. Now, explain to me why you can't be in cahoots with the bastards."

"You know what, lady? You are certifiable," Elliot began, in a derisive tone, tapping his right temple. "You would suspect your own mother, wouldn't you?"

"In that DVD, Jenny read what they ordered her to read," said Hadara in a soft tone, keeping cool. "They, not Jenny, put your name there. They, not Jenny, chose you as the intermediary. They couriered Jenny's cell phone and the DVD to you. You threw away the courier's package. Don't you see the chain of suspicious coincidences there, Steil?"

Elliot exhaled hard. "Listen, Har . . . whatever –"

"Hadara."

"Got it. You think I'm part of a Palestinian diamond-smuggling ring, you are crazy. That, or you don't know the first thing about me. I'm Cuban. I've never met an Arab, male or female. I've never been to an Arab country. I've never bought a frigging diamond. How the hell could I have something to do with this?"

"I'll tell you. These people are asking for money, a lot of money. They have explained in detail how they want it. They may be mujahideen, have nothing to do with the smuggling operation; that's possible. But they may be kidnappers posing as mujahideen. Kidnappers need someone inside, an accomplice. You or someone else. But at this moment you are the most probable suspect because they chose you. If you are innocent, why did they choose you?"

"I don't fucking know!"

"Elliot, the swearing," Sam, in reprimand.

"Shit, Sam, I don't believe you. They accuse me of kidnapping Jenny, and you worry about my swearing? God Almighty!"

"Are you religious?" Javan butted in.

"It's an expression."

There was silence for several moments. Elliot was staring at the tabletop, thinking, breathing heavily.

"They may have asked Jenny who could get the money quickest," he said, off the top of his head. "Or, she may have thought that Sam, well, you know, that Sam would be too upset by the news. Sam is like a father to her. Hey, Sam, give me a hand here, will you?"

Plotzher shifted in his seat. "Listen, friends, Elliot's a mensch –".

"What's a mensch?" Elliot said, irritably.

"A good man."

"Oh, am I? Really? So kind of you, Sam." Dripping irony.

"I'm sure he has nothing to do with this," Sam said to the others, disregarding the comment. "He may be right when he says they may have asked Jenny who could get the money quickest and she gave them his name. He deals with the financial side of the firm. And, yes, she may have wanted to spare me the suffering."

Hadara lifted her eyes to the ceiling, considering something, or pretending to.

"Okay, Steil. We'll give you the benefit of the doubt," she said. "You are, however, the sole link to the kidnappers and we need your cooperation to save Jenny. Can we count on you?"

"Of course you can. Her father saved my life. I'd do anything for Ruben Scheindlin, but he's dead. So, I'll do it for his daughter."

"Her father saved your life?" As if Mossad's file on Elliot Steil hadn't been consulted.

"Yes, he did."

"Glad to hear that. Good, good. Now, we have to keep together, sleep in the same room –"

"What?"

"Wait, Elliot," Plotzher said.

"Not as guards, as part of the team," she went on. "We need to be near you to tape the calls these people make, to advise you on what to say, to help out with the Eurobonds, to escort you to Toronto."

"I don't need escorts."

"He's not part of it," Javan said to his partner, following their script.

"Thank you very much," Elliot said to Javan.

"Or he's the greatest actor on Earth," Javan again, to Hadara.

"Oh, shit!" Elliot said.

"Take it easy, Elliot," said Plotzher. "You can't go there alone. You need these friends to cover your back. Otherwise, they may kidnap *you* and then ask for twenty million."

"Very funny, Sam. Very funny."

"It'll be just a few days, Elliot. Well, maybe a couple of weeks," Plotzher said. "I can take care of things here."

Elliot considered it for a moment. Jenny belonged to a world a million light years from his. But she was Ruben Scheindlin's daughter and her life was in danger. And the damn diamond smugglers had chosen him as intermediary. Why the fuck had they chosen him? *El recoño de sus madres.*

"Okay. How do I get the Eurobonds?"

"We'll take care of that, Steil," Javan said. "But I propose we start discussing what you'll say to these guys next time they call."

In Flight From Miami to New York

Nineteen hours later, reclining in seat 19-C with his eyes closed, Elliot was reviewing the most recent events. Big pieces of the puzzle mismatched the empty spaces, and a few were missing. Jenny a police informant? Hard to believe. Nothing is impossible, but can you conceive a nuclear physicist who is a Mafia don as well? That Paris Hilton moves to the slums of Calcutta to follow in the footsteps of Mother Theresa? As improbable as Jenny Scheindlin, fashion model and multi-millionaire, snitching on smugglers for five years. According to Tico, she was researching a business concern. More likely, but . . . a business? Jenny? Also hard to believe.

There were two Jennies. The beautiful model who exuded sexual magnetism, and the spoiled rich woman for whom he felt no admiration, affection, or esteem. After her mother's murder, he had felt compassion for the young orphan, but the feeling faded away as time went by and she got ahead as a model. Because Jenny inherited 79 per cent of the company's stock, Sam had asked him to teach her the fundamentals of the business, but for two reasons this was impossible. First, she spent a mere five or six weeks each year in Miami Beach and, while in the city, the farthest thing from her mind was Imlatinex. Typically, her winter breaks consisted of sunning in South Beach during the day, and partying at night. Second, when she devoted an hour to the firm – only to please Sam, he felt sure – and he reported on how the business was doing or started explaining what a quote, a manifest, or a letter of credit was, her expression was so glazed that he felt both of them were wasting their time. They went through the motions because neither wanted to make Sam unhappy.

To nab thieves and smugglers, the police need to know names, addresses, dates, routes, and means of transportation. To learn all that, the informer has to gain the trust of the criminals. Jenny would have had to do things, like smuggling stones across international borders, that Elliot doubted she was capable of doing; he couldn't picture her running those risks. She had been raised in a cocoon of wealth and security, and he doubted she had the street smartness required to dupe criminals. The more he mulled it over, the more improbable it seemed. *Okay, calm down,* he said to himself. If Hadara and Javan had bullshitted him, what the hell was going on? That she had been kidnapped by mujahideen was beyond question, also that they had asked for ten million, and that two Israeli detectives had flown over to help him ransom her. So, what could conceivably be the point of concocting the implausible story that she was an informer? To prevent him from going to the FBI? To give credence to their presence? But if Jenny was not a police informer, why had the Israeli police come to the rescue? Because Sam had called them. And why had Sam called them?

He had posed this question to the senior partner the instant he had a few minutes alone with him, after the Israeli Consulate brainstorm. Sam's explanation had been as bizarre as the smuggling story. In 2005, Jenny had presented him with a fine belt and asked him to always wear it. On the inside, glued to it, was a thin metal band engraved with an Israeli phone number. She had told Sam that, should she fall gravely ill, have an accident, or experience any other serious problem, he had to call that number and explain the situation. Sam had asked her whose number it was; she had begged him not to ask questions, just to call should anything happen to her. Like Elliot, he had learned she was an IP informer at the consulate. The old man's tale rang hollow.

The financial angle was intriguing too. From reading novels and watching films and teleplays, he was under the impression the police were against ransoming people as a matter of principle. Was it different in real life? Another thing: he had wanted to know whether the Israelis would give authentic Eurobonds to Jenny's abductors. They could have the expertise to detect forged bonds, demand to see a sample before releasing the woman, and kill her if they realized they were being duped. Hadara had assured him that, as they talked, other officers were buying real Eurobonds with real money. In Miami he had been relieved by her assurances, but now he wondered whether the Israeli police – or any other police force for that matter – had pockets deep enough to fork over ten million U.S. dollars to rescue an informer at a moment's notice. On the other hand, Jews the world over donated generously to Israel. Maybe they could afford it.

The thing that overrode all his suspicions and qualms was that Jenny risked being killed if the demands were not met. The woman could be as shallow and irrelevant as her work, but she was a human being in grave danger, just as he had been earlier in his life. In his hour of need, her father had unflinchingly stood by his side and provided armed protection, contacts, and funding. It was payback time. He had to do all he could to save her. He owed it to her father and to his conscience as well. Should he turn his back on Jenny, he wouldn't be able to live with himself.

A flight attendant walking backwards and pulling a cart brushed his shoulder; Elliot opened his eyes and clicked his tongue in disgust, the Cuban way. He preferred aisle seats because he could get up without bothering other passengers. But in the ever-narrower walkways of commercial airplanes, flight attendants frequently grazed those sitting by the aisle, in particular broad-shouldered males.

"You were dozing?" Javan asked.

Javan was sitting next to him; Hadara was in the window seat, her eyes closed but listening intently.

"Yeah, a little."

"I tried to, but can't. Keep thinking about this Tico Monerris. You know him?"

"No. I've met him, though; exchanged a few words with him."

"What kind of guy chooses to be assistant to a fashion model?"

Elliot studied the overhead fixtures. "Off the top of my head I would say a poor, jobless guy. I mean, when I got to the U.S., I would've said yes to any job offer, cleaning dumpsters included. A guy in love with the model may also accept the position. And someone that hopes to use her to gain a foothold in the fashion industry."

"In which category would you place Tico?"

"I said I didn't know him."

Javan nodded, then said, "Yeah, but cleaning dumpsters is a man's job. Assistant to a fashion model is not."

"So, he's either in love with Jenny, or an opportunist."

"Last night I tried to find the origin of the surname Monerris on the Internet."

"And?"

"Came up empty-handed. It pops up in Spanish websites and I don't know a word of Spanish."

"May I ask how is that search useful?"

"Learn the origin. Is it Latin, German, Arab?"

Elliot nodded. "You're searching for an Arab origin. It's possible. Arabs occupied most of Spain for seven hundred years or so. Many Spanish words have an Arab origin and surnames can, too. But you've heard the taped phone calls. Tico sounds really concerned. And had the kidnappers sent the video to someone else, like, I don't know, a friend of Jenny's maybe, or her banker, we would've learned of her disappearance only thanks to Tico's call. Why would he call Sam if he's an accomplice?"

"To cover his tracks," Hadara said, without opening her eyes. Both men turned to her. "To feign concern and worry," she went on, "so you trust him and tell him every single step you've taken, or plan to take, and he tells the kidnappers."

Elliot unfastened his seat belt, stood, and headed to the toilets, brushing the shoulders of several passengers.

"He doesn't like you," Javan said to Hadara.

"Tell me something I don't know."

In the washroom, Elliot mused, *She's above all other mortals. She never stole a bill from her father's wallet, never lied, never gave anyone a blow job. She's an expert in all forensic disciplines, best shooter at the firing range, solves the most complex crimes, dreams of becoming prime minister in ten years or so.*

Washing his hands, he inspected his face in the mirror. The space between his nose and upper lip caught his eye. Had it always been that wide? Not to his recollection. Not when he was young, he felt

sure. When had it widened so much? He had made peace with the
lines on his forehead and by the corners of his mouth and eyes, but
he hadn't discovered this . . . this . . . widening. Like London Bridge,
his skin and muscles were falling down. Well, as long as the soldier
managed to stand at attention when called to combat . . .

A knock on the door made Elliot dry his hands and return to his
seat.

He buckled the seat belt, lay back, closed his eyes.

"That's why, Steil, we don't mention the video to Tico," Hadara
said. "We don't know what has happened to Jenny. We know nothing.
We want him to tell us what he knows, make suggestions."

Elliot didn't turn his head, open his eyes, or give any other indication of having heard her.

"Are we in agreement on this, Steil?"

"Excuse me, ma'am," only now opening his eyes and turning to
her. "Maybe I'm experiencing an episode of déjà vu. Didn't you say
exactly that same thing to me in Miami?"

"I did, yes. But there's no harm in –"

"Didn't I agree to your plan?"

"Yes, you did."

"Detective, just so you know, I don't have Alzheimer's."

"I know. I apologize."

"Apology accepted. Now I'm going to take a short nap."

New York City

In Manhattan, on the way to Jenny's apartment, Elliot took notice
of the life bustling around him: people going in and coming out of
all sorts of businesses; merchants peddling twenty-dollar Rolexes;
homeless men asking for spare change; smokers taking a hurried puff;

signs offering palm readings; pedestrians waving down taxis; pushers
in hooded sweatshirts or wearing ill-aligned baseball caps reclining
on frontages. An endless stream of humanity from every corner of
the world wearing all kinds of hairstyles and clothes. This steel-and-
concrete jungle always brought to mind a fragment of a poem about
New York by the late Spanish satirist Enrique Jardiel Poncela:

> *Y dolor, un infinito dolor*
> *corriendo por el asfalto*
> *entre un Chevrolet y un Ford.*

Poetry is what gets lost in translation. Now, who said that? He'd have
to look it up.

Seventy minutes after getting a cab at JFK, Hadara stopped tapping
the floor with her right foot for an instant and glanced at her watch.
Guessing they still were twenty minutes or more from their destination, Elliot asked: "See now why I recommended riding the
subway?" Happy to rub it in.

Jenny's living room impressed Elliot. Splendid and exquisite, two
concepts difficult to reconcile, he thought while gazing around. To
his untrained eye it seemed that the varying styles of furniture, decorations, and colours related harmoniously; the work of a professional interior decorator, he guessed. The other rooms had to be
magnificent too, especially Jenny's bedroom, he assumed. She must
have spent three or four hundred thousand dollars furnishing and
decorating the place.

Despite having called Tico from the airport to let him know they
were on their way, when he answered the door, he had the air of
someone caught napping. A spark of astonishment briefly lit the cold
stares of the Israelis. A *This is Jenny's lover?* look of incredulity. Elliot
could identify with them; he had been disappointed, too, when he
first met the guy. At least two inches shorter and fifteen years older

than Jenny; bushy eyebrows, a life-saver around his middle, homely as hell. The salt-and-pepper three-day growth on his cheekbones was not stylish. He had to be very good at something, Elliot supposed all over again. Fantastic lover? Great poet? Wonderful composer? A singer perhaps? He had a deep baritone. There had to be a reason why Jenny had fallen for this guy.

According to plan, he introduced Hadara and Javan as private investigators from Greater Miami Security Services. Before the threesome left Miami, Sam had called the head of the security firm and requested cooperation. The man promised that should he get a call from anywhere wanting to know if two of his operatives were currently working for Imlatinex, he would ask for the person's name and phone number, then call him or her back to confirm Sam's fib. Immediately afterward, he would tell Mr. Plotzher who had called.

When Tico invited them to take a seat, the visitors stared at the sofas, unsure they were deserving of such luxury. Then Elliot spoke as they had arranged: how worried everyone was, the firm was sparing no expense to find out where Jenny was, blah, blah, blah.

"So, Tico," Elliot, putting the lid on his crock of shit, "we want you to tell us all you know, from the start, every single detail. Please."

"Have you talked to Mr. Plotzher?"

"Yes, we have."

"I told him all I know."

"We'd appreciate it if you say it again for us," Hadara said with a pleasant smile. Elliot was taken by surprise. The woman could smile? "You know, Mr. Plotzher is old and sometimes seniors forget things," with a quick look at Elliot, yanking the Cuban's chain.

"Okay, then," Tico said and leaned forward in his seat. "Ms. Scheindlin flew to Toronto on the fourteenth. She had a room at the Four Seasons –"

"Who made the reservation?" Hadara asked, taking the reins.

"I did. She stays there whenever she goes to Toronto."

"I see. Go ahead."

"She called me that evening and asked me to rank in order the bigger Canadian cities, population wise. It took me less than a minute, you know, Internet. Toronto, Montreal, and Vancouver."

"Did she say why she wanted the list?"

"No, she didn't. But I guess it had to do with her ideas for a business."

"Is she planning to open a business?"

"I think so, yes. When she got her degree in fashion merchandising management she started considering –"

"She has a degree in what?" asked Elliot, left eyebrow arched in disbelief. The interruption won him an annoyed stare from Hadara.

"Fashion merchandising management."

"I didn't know that," Elliot said.

"She got it three years ago, from the Fashion Institute of Technology."

"So," Hadara said, to get the interrogation back on track. "You were saying that Jenny is considering opening a business."

"Yeah. She's toying with the idea of a high fashion store. Several, if the first is successful. A chain, perhaps."

"In Canada?"

"My understanding is she would open the first store here in Manhattan, but Ms. Scheindlin believes Canada is like the U.S. in some respects, like, you know, language, traditions, culture, that sort of thing. She says what's fashionable here eventually turns fashionable there, so if she goes international she'd set up shop in Canada first."

"I see. What else did you talk about that evening?" Hadara crossed her legs.

"Nothing else."

"Was that the last you heard from Jenny? The evening of the fourteenth?"

"That's right."

"And you called Mr. Plotzher on the eighteenth, early morning. Why?"

"I was getting worried, very worried."

"Why?"

Tico Monerris bowed his head and seemed embarrassed. "When abroad, Ms. Scheindlin calls once a day to get her messages, or to ask me to do something for her – run an errand, call someone. Sometimes she calls every other day. I don't recall any trip abroad when she failed to call three days in a row. I wait for those calls because that's how I know she's okay. I can't call her; she's my boss. I have to wait until she calls me. But I need to be sure she's okay. This trip I hadn't heard from her in three days. That's not like her at all. I called her cell, she didn't answer. I called the hotel, I called the Toronto fashion people in her phone book; nobody had seen her since the sixteenth."

"You said you need to be sure she's okay," Hadara said, in a sympathetic tone, a supportive expression on her face, sharing Tico's suffering. *The bitch*, Elliot thought. "Mr. Plotzher believes you and Jenny are romantically involved. Is that true, Mr. Monerris?"

Tico's shoulders shook, he gave a sob, then he jumped to his feet and sped away, to the bathroom, the visitors guessed, as they exchanged astonished glances.

Elliot opened his mouth. "I think –"

Hadara shushed him. Elliot gave her a very hard look. So she pressed the palms of her hands together as if in prayer, smiled pleasantly. Elliot fought to suppress a grin and failed. Hadara sensed that, from now on, dealing with the Cuban would be a lot easier. Confrontation wasn't cutting it, and neither was proving that she was vastly superior to him. Like Gloucester in Shakespeare's *King Richard the Third*, he was "penetrable to kind entreats." Smiles also worked. The foolish macho. An awkward minute went by at a snail's pace. Legs and ankles were crossed and uncrossed, fingers interlaced, thumbs twiddled. Eventually, a disconcerted Tico returned to the living room.

"I must apologize," he said.

Voices overlapped as the visitors expressed their sympathy.

"It's just . . . it was all bottled up in here," tapping his chest. "This is the first time I discuss this with anyone. You understand?"

They all nodded.

"I'm deeply in love with Jenny. That she cares for me makes me the luckiest man on the face of the Earth. I can't figure it. I mean, I don't kid myself. I'm no prize package. Seventeen years older than she is and coyote-ugly. I know people think I'm a cuddle bunny making a living here. But Jenny is the love of my life and the thought that . . . oh, fuck. Sorry, lady. I'm desperate, okay? Haven't slept properly in three days. Because, you know, sex maniacs stalk any woman. Jenny's a rapist's dream. Every single minute I'm fighting the idea she's been kidnapped, raped, and killed. I pray God that's just my imagination. I want her to be safe. If she's dumped me, I don't care. I just want her to be safe. Oh, my God," fresh tears streaming down his stubble.

Sam's shot in the dark concerning Tico surfaced in Elliot's mind. Jenny was all over this man because he was not at all impressed by her beauty and riches, made gentle fun of her line of work. Wrong, Sam, Elliot thought, *he just loves her*. Or was Tico playing a well-rehearsed part?

"But Mr. Monerris," Hadara said, unimpressed, back in her tough woman mode, as Tico wiped away a tear with the heel of his hand. "If you want to help the woman you love, the first thing you must do is control your emotions. We need you calm and composed, because we have to ask you very important questions and we are hoping you'll give us thoughtful responses. Will you calm down and cooperate with us? For Jenny's sake?"

"But of course. I'll do anything for her. Ask away," Tico managed, before blowing his nose in a handkerchief.

"Okay. Fine. First of all. Do you know if Jenny has enemies?"

Tico considered his answer. "To my knowledge she has no enemies. But I suppose many people envy her, her wealth, looks, independence. And from envying a woman to hating her, well, I don't know, maybe it's not a big jump."

"How many is many?" Javan asked.

Tico raised his eyebrows. "I can't say. A lot. Maybe a hundred, maybe a thousand. You gotta understand," he said eagerly, hunching forward. "Jenny was a model for ten years, she's travelled all over the world. There's no way I can tell you how many people envy her or hate her."

"Okay, let me rephrase that. Give me the names of people you feel sure hate Jenny."

"No, no, no." Tico shook his head vigorously. "I can't give you names. Listen. First of all, Jenny established rules from the very beginning of our relationship. I've travelled abroad with her five times, but I have never escorted her to fashion shows, photo shoots, parties, agencies, restaurants, or nightclubs. I've never seen her with other models, or agents, or designers, or photographers. Second of all, in Jenny's words," and Tico made quote marks with his fingers, "'in the world of fashion, hypocrisy is as abundant as the grains of sand on Miami Beach. But most of the people who hate your guts pretend to love you.'"

"Did she ever mention enemies to you?"

"Not to my recollection."

Elliot wondered what that line of questioning was for. They knew Jenny had been kidnapped by Arab terrorists or by diamond smugglers posing as Arab terrorists. Why ask about fashionistas? Javan and Hadara kept pressing Tico for clues, but the Puerto Rican couldn't or wouldn't add any useful information to what he had already said. A quarter of an hour later the Israelis gave up.

"Okay, Tico, thanks," Hadara said, opening her purse and extracting a notebook. "I'll jot down two numbers for you, my colleague's and my own. You learn anything, call either one, any time, okay?" She wrote the numbers and tore out the page. Tico took the note, mumbling okay.

"Listen, I don't know how to find a missing person," the Puerto Rican said. "I don't know anything about police work, but I'd give anything, anything at all, to be part of your team and help you find Jenny. C'mon, guys, give me a break. I'll follow your orders. C'mon. Please?"

Hadara smiled. "That's not possible, Mr. Monerris. We need you here to keep watch. We need you to tell us all the phone calls you get; from friends, from strangers, the wrong numbers, all calls to the land line and to your cell. Write down who calls, at what time, what day, what the person asks or says. That's the most important contribution you can make," and she stood.

Elliot, Javan, and Tico got to their feet as well. Tico looked pained.

"You can be sure, Tico," Elliot said, "that we'll do all we can and then some to find Jenny."

"I know, Mr. Steil, I know. Jenny speaks highly of you."

"That's nice of her. Take care, Tico."

They took two adjoining rooms at a medium-priced hotel. Javan surveyed the room he'd be sharing with Elliot and, cursing under his breath, slammed down the handle of his roll-on. Elliot doubted the lever had survived the blow. Was this the man's first trip to the Big Apple? he wondered. The Cuban was used to Manhattan hotel rooms being smaller than and double the rate of hotel rooms in nearly all other American cities. Two-fifty to three hundred for a couple of beds, a TV set, a phone, and a modest bathroom, plus thirty or forty dollars in taxes. He hoped his bed was bug-free.

"It sucks, doesn't it?" Elliot said to the Israeli as he slipped out of his jacket.

Javan nodded.

Elliot was soon up to here with the living arrangement. His only private moments were when he was using the bathroom. He had been asked to shave with the door open. Every night Jenny's fully charged cell lay on his night table.

Hadara believed the kidnappers would call again forty-eight to twenty-four hours before the deadline to find out if they would get the ransom on time, and to give instructions on where, when, and how the swap would take place. But she could be wrong; they could call earlier, she had warned. It was inconvenient, she knew, but they had to be together should Jenny's phone ring in the middle of the night.

Elliot called Fidelia as Javan showered. Again she displayed her uncanny ability to smell a rat. Had Imlatinex's business in New York ballooned to the point he had to spend a full week there? Really? He had never stayed there more than a couple of days before. What was going on? In the past she hadn't known shit from shinola concerning mysterious and dangerous episodes in Elliot's life until an awful thing happened to her. And she wouldn't take it any more, especially if she found herself in the middle of something without warning. "You remember what happened to me in '94? And in 2000? You do? Great. So, if I'm in any kind of danger, you better let me know right now."

"Fidelia, you are not at risk. I'm here on business."

Fidelia promptly moved to the next topic. Did Elliot remember what she had told him at the start of their relationship? That she wouldn't stand in his way should he fall in love with someone else? All right. She was a woman of her word, so if he was seeing a woman in New York, he should let her know so she could pick up her things and move out.

"Fidelia, I'm not seeing another woman, in New York or anywhere else."

"Glad to know that," she said. Another thing that nagged at the back of her mind was that, because she was caring for her mother, Elliot had been sleeping alone a lot. Maybe he was getting horny and wanted to play the field. Should that be the case and he decided to screw a hooker, she begged him to tell her. Everybody knew Manhattan was full of hookers with AIDS and genital herpes, and as much as she loved him, she wouldn't expose herself to the risk of contagion.

"I'm not playing the field either, Fidelia."

That mellowed her tone. She said she missed him.

"I miss you too."

She wanted to be sure nothing would happen to him.

"I'm not running any risk."

Did he love her?

"Very much. You are my life companion and I'm not interested in any other woman."

Despite the fact that she wasn't as attractive as fourteen years earlier?

"Who says you're less attractive now?"

Fidelia concluded, but refrained from saying, that Elliot was resigned to her ripening.

After a few platitudes, they hung up.

Javan came out of the shower and Elliot went in. Afterward, Hadara proposed ordering dinner from a restaurant next to the hotel. Forty minutes later they were eating Chinese from containers in Hadara's room. As Elliot savoured the slightly overcooked, mild-flavoured Cantonese specialties, he wondered about Jews eating shrimps, pork, lobster, and other non-kosher fare. These two weren't Orthodox, he deduced. Not too chic either, for like him, they used plastic forks instead of chopsticks. After Javan bagged the remainder and dropped it into the trash can, Elliot tried his luck at finding out something.

"Listen fellows, I can understand your doing all you can to free a fellow Jew, especially as Jenny is a police informer. But there are two things I can't figure out. The police usually discourage paying a ransom to any kidnappers, but you are planning to ransom Jenny with real bearer bonds purchased with real money. How come?"

Javan crossed his legs and looked off thoughtfully at the opposing wall, as if answering the question was not his job. Hadara laced her fingers.

"Sometimes the only way to save the victim is to pay the ransom. In this case, the priority is to save Jenny. Once we've done that, we'll get to work on nailing the kidnappers. And when we do get them, we'll probably recover all or some of the bonds. Ultimately, the bastards will sorely regret having messed with IP, if they are smugglers, or with the State of Israel, if they are mujahideen."

"I'm sure they'll regret it if you catch them," Elliot said, remembering how the Israeli Army dealt with terrorists. "The second thing that bugs me is the money. I mean, ten million bucks is not chicken feed. Can the IP come up with ten million dollars to rescue an informer?"

Javan shifted his eyes from one talker to the other.

Hadara smiled tightly. "Mr. Steil, you are a very curious man. What is it to you?"

"To me? Nothing; it's not my money. It's just that   suppose you don't recover the money. Not only have you lost ten million, you've set a precedent. Here, the FBI would probably have to get authorization from the Justice department, the Treasury, and maybe other agencies too, before getting their hands on that kind of money to ransom an informer. It seems you do things more expeditiously in Israel."

"Yeah, we do things differently," Hadara said. "If we were American police officers, the news of Jenny's kidnapping would be all over CNN, Fox, the newspapers, and ten thousand blogs. There are no secrets here. Government officials with axes to grind call newspapers and spill the beans. The president orders the NSA to intercept the phone calls terrorists make? As soon as the press finds out, there's a scandal. Do you think it's right for a nation at war to torpedo the work of its secret services?"

Elliot tilted his head, considering whether to say what he was thinking. He opted to speak his mind.

"Well, Hadara, you know I'm Cuban. In Cuba, for half a century, the president has not had to consult with anyone to order its secret service to intercept phone calls, arrest dissenters, tell judges which defendants were to be found guilty, and if they should be sentenced to death by firing squad or sent to prison. And the rationale for this abuse of power was that Cuba is at war with imperialism. So I find it comforting that here there are strict limits to the president's authority, that he can't do what he wants whenever he wants, even if the nation is at war. That he can't order the courts to do as he pleases. That he can't have journalists jailed because they criticize his decisions. That he can't order broadcasters to suspend their programming any evening he wants because he loves to hear himself speak and will jabber on about whatever he fancies for four consecutive hours."

The editorializing won him a frigid smile. "Mr. Steil, all things taken to the extreme are wrong. Granted, Fidel Castro was a dictator with absolute power. But excessive openness results in powerlessness. You read the opinion columns and editorials in American newspapers, those guys are experts in everything and have the solutions to all the problems of the United States in science, foreign policy, jurisprudence, elections, the economy, you name it. They always know best. Even worse, they have the solutions to all the problems of humankind. From how to stop global warming to how rich and poor nations should conduct trade. It's the dictatorship of the intellectual elite; the media is their vehicle."

"Except that that dictatorship is toothless," Elliot interposed. "It lacks prisons, bombs, secret services, spy satellites. It doesn't control the courts, Congress, or the army. It's a pretty lame dictatorship, if you ask me. Although I agree that intellectuals have a tendency to think they are always right. They also disregard, or have no inkling of, a zillion conflicting interests, which leads them to believe that governments should always implement what seems fairer, or commonsensical, or decent, regardless of political or economic considerations. Intellectuals – the fools – believe the pen is mightier than the sword."

Hadara chuckled. Javan didn't seem amused.

"Okay, Steil, let's call it a draw. But to answer your question, the decision to give us ten million dollars was taken by someone, I don't know who. But I told my superiors that Jenny would probably reimburse us should we rescue her."

Elliot almost slapped his forehead. Of course. It was a loan. To a woman who had money to spare.

"I see," he said.

"Makes sense?"

"It does. It does."

The conversation turned to the weather, the price of hotel rooms in Manhattan, and other banalities. Fifteen minutes later, Elliot faked suppressing a yawn.

"Well, I'm tired. I think I'll turn in."

"Fine, sleep well," Hadara said.

"You know what, Mr. Steil?" Javan said. "I think I'll join you as soon as I send an email."

"Okay. Good night to both of you."

"Good night."

Elliot closed the door between the rooms behind him.

In Hadara's room, at the desk where her laptop lay open, Javan logged on to Walla! and typed an email in Hebrew, saying that the family was okay but rather disappointed with the Christmas Special show at Radio City because, for all intents and purposes, it was the same show they had seen two years earlier. Next afternoon they would be flying to Vancouver, to visit Uncle Asher and Aunt Faiga. He signed Joel and clicked on send. Then he turned in his seat and eyed Hadara.

"No police woman is as well-informed as you were when debating Steil, *seren*," he said reprovingly, in Hebrew.

This startled Hadara. After an instant: "I'm sorry, *aluf mishne*."

"Don't let it happen again."

"I won't."

As a civilian service, Mossad does not rank people militarily, but because most personnel come from the Israel Defense Forces, they frequently call each other by the highest title he or she had in the chain of command when transferred to the Institute. *Aluf mishne* translates as colonel; *seren* as captain.

After a short pause. "Sir, I think it's important to disinform the Four Seasons."

"What do you mean?"

It took her less than three minutes to persuade Javan that calming down the hotel's security staff was imperative, and that Tico was the perfect person to make the call from Jenny's apartment and report she was back in Manhattan. Javan approved the idea. Should Tico refuse to do it, they agreed, he was probably in the clear.

They sat in silence for a while.

Eventually Javan got to his feet. "Sleep well, *seren*," he said.

"You too, sir."

Toronto

I *was kidnapped on the evening of the seventeenth. The video was made in the small hours of the eighteenth. I talked to Elliot in the small hours of the twentieth, I think. I took a shower on the twentieth, definitely. Now, did*

*they give me the Qu'ran on the twentieth? I'm not sure. I can't remember!
That's why they took away my watch; no date, no time. Well, birds chirp at
sunrise; it's been a long night. How many hours have I slept? No more than
two or three. Worrying and insomnia go hand in hand. We must be miles
from Toronto, given the time it took to get here, the silence all around, the
birds. Haven't heard a car honk or a human voice outside. Definitely sunrise,
crack in the window letting it in. The bastards think my bladder can hold
ten gallons. And I'm not drinking a lot. Why the hell don't they let me loose
so I can go to the washroom whenever I need to? Not even a strong man
could pry open the boards on the bathroom window with his bare hands.
Fear must be the reason I'm peeing so much. Oh, my God. I wonder what
Elliot has been doing these last three days? Or is it four? How the hell is he
going to raise ten million bucks in ten days? He can't, is the answer, he can't.
Wait a minute! I know I asked him not to tell the police, but Elliot would
realize I had been forced to say that. Maybe he . . . No, Elliot wouldn't dare
without Sam's approval. But maybe Sam has gone to the police. Maybe the
Miami police have contacted the Toronto police and they are looking for me
right now. But supposing they find this godforsaken place, the mujahideen
will have plenty of time to kill me before the cops break in. I'm a dead
woman. You're dead, Jenny Scheindlin, you are dead.*

The door to her room swung open. The taller mujahideen came
into the bedroom, set a tray with her breakfast on the floor by the
mattress, and removed her shackles and handcuffs.

"Thank you," Jenny said as she hurried to the bathroom. Chris
pulled the door closed and listened to her pee. The things one does
for money, he thought. The affection, perhaps even tenderness, he
had once felt while caring for her evaporated when success had gone
to her head and she'd cut them off, but, even so, she didn't deserve
this. Well, it'd soon be over, and he and Valerio would be rich. Five
million. Sweet Jesus! They could travel the world, live anywhere:
Monte Carlo, Milan, Paris, you name it. They'd keep doing photo
shoots, to make the money last, and have fun. Ten days of Jenny's

anguish would buy them all that. She pulled the door open, a plead-ing expression in her face.

"Listen, mister, I know you don't want to speak to me. But, please listen to me. You gotta understand Elliot Steil can't get ten million in ten days. It's impossible. I could get it in ten days –"

The mujahideen grunted.

"No, no, listen. I'm not asking you to free me so I can go get the money. I know you won't. What I'm trying to say is that I have much more than that deposited with various banks. I can say 'give me ten million' and they have to. They can't make excuses. It's my money. All they can do is not pay accrued interest. But Elliot is not rich. Elliot has to ask for a loan or . . . something. He doesn't even own a house, rents an apartment, can you believe it? He goes to a bank asking for ten million, they'll want to know what for and ask him a thousand questions. They'll want collateral, that kind of thing. With Sam's help, he may be able to, oh, I don't know, sell the company. But he can't do that in ten days. You must understand any delay is not because he refuses to give you the money. It's because Elliot can't get ten million dollars in ten days. And I don't want to die."

Chris grabbed her elbow and pushed her back onto the mattress.

"I want to live. Please, don't kill me. Oh, please, mister, don't."

She kept pleading and crying while Chris put the handcuffs and shackles back on, and was sobbing uncontrollably when he left the bedroom.

"I could hear her bawling. What's the problem?" Valerio added, with a frown.

"She's totally freaked out." Chris filled him in before saying, in a dubious tone, "And she has a point. I told you, the moment I read 'ten days' it seemed impossible to me."

"And to me too. Don't forget we wrote to him about this," Valerio said, jogging his lover's memory. "And he replied that it's perfectly feasible. But he authorized a five-day extension, if necessary."

Chris bowed his head, slid both hands over his hair to the back of his neck, interlaced his fingers. "For God's sake, Val. I know that." He lifted his head and stared at the Peruvian's coal-black eyes. "I also know how banks work. If her father were alive, no problem. He'd go to his broker and order them to buy the bonds for him. Wouldn't have to explain a thing, it's his money. A week would be more than enough. But a company manager can't do that."

"Are you mad at me?"

"No, I'm not. I'm worried, that's all. Just for argument's sake, what are we supposed to do if after fifteen days we call Steil and he says he still hasn't raised the money? What do we do? Free her?"

"Stop fretting, Chris. The Prof greased the skids perfectly. We're talking payoff here. If he thoroughly researched everything else, do you really think he overlooked that? Do you think you know better than him what Steil has to do to buy the bonds?"

"Maybe you're right."

"Of course I'm right."

"But it wouldn't be a waste of time to plan what we should do if after fifteen days of this ordeal there're no bonds."

In her bedroom, feeling a little calmer, Jenny sniffled and drank the tepid tea.

New York

After breakfast, Hadara approached the desk and paid their bill with cash while Javan talked to someone on his cell phone in Hebrew. The fact that Hadara paid for everything proved she was in charge and Javan was the muscle, Elliot figured. The doorman flagged down a taxi for them. Hadara told the cabbie "800 2nd Avenue" and sat back in the seat.

"We'll make a brief stop at the Israeli consulate before heading for the airport," she said to Elliot. "Javan has to see someone there."

"Okay." *What else could he say?* the Cuban asked himself. Two people had been kidnapped: Jenny and he.

As Hadara paid the fare, the men got out and Elliot looked around. Like much of Manhattan, the block consisted of grey concrete-and-glass towers facing each other across the street; only a building painted in hot-pink on the corner of 43rd broke the chromatic tedium. The consulate was on the thirteenth floor of a long building.

Once Javan was waved inside, his companions chose adjoining seats in the reception room where other people were also waiting. Several were filling out forms, others reading papers, watching a TV set, or staring into nothingness. A few were talking in the respectful whispers reserved for government offices. Security cameras watched everyone. Elliot grabbed a copy of the *New York Times* from a low mahogany table and after skimming the front-page headlines, read the editorials. Then he turned to Hadara.

"Want to learn today's cures to some of the ills of the world?"

Hadara chuckled. "No, thanks."

Elliot replaced the paper on the table. The receptionist called a couple to her desk and directed them to a door. It struck Elliot as odd that Hadara had to wait for her guard. Whatever Javan was doing behind those walls – a telephone update by a secure line to IP brass, or informing superiors what they would do next, or receiving new orders, or meeting with a consular officer – shouldn't Hadara be doing it? Strange. How could he sound out the woman? After a few minutes, an idea came to him.

"Where's the men's restroom?" he asked.

Hadara stared at him. "I don't know. You have to go?"

"I do."

"Can't you wait until Javan comes out? In case Jenny's phone rings when you are . . . . ?"

"Will he be long?"

"I don't know."

So, the brain was in the dark concerning how long they would have to wait for the muscle. Strange.

"Well, as they say in the land of the free, when you gotta go you gotta go."

"Just to pee?"

"For God's sake!"

"Okay, okay. Should her phone ring, don't answer."

The receptionist pointed Elliot down a corridor. After seven minutes he reckoned he'd wasted enough time sitting on the toilet's plastic lid, so he washed his hands and rejoined Hadara with a relieved expression.

"He still in?" Tilting his head toward the door through which Javan had disappeared.

"Yeah. No call?"

"No call. *That* would've been a freaking coincidence," glancing at his watch. "Damn, we've been here for half an hour already. What's he doing in there?"

Hadara turned her head with deliberate slowness and stared at the Cuban. "What is it to you?"

Elliot shrugged. "Never mind. I was trying to make polite conversation. But what you said back in Miami, the 'part of a team' line, is plain bullshit. You still think I may be part of this."

"No, Steil, it's not that. It's –"

"Yeah, yeah, yeah. Save your breath, Hadara. I'm still suspect number-one."

"Listen, Sam Plotzher vouches for you, we trust you. Problem is, Steil, we're police and we've been taught to be close-mouthed, catch

my meaning? Our job demands it. In Israel we have this siege mentality: everybody is a suspect until proven innocent. I asked Javan to
go there and make arrangements for us in Toronto. I don't know how
long that'll take, okay?"

"Okay. I get the picture. Thanks for telling me."

But the explanation failed to abate Elliot's suspicions. If she was
in charge, why wouldn't she arrange whatever had to be arranged?
On the other hand, what did he care which of the two was in charge?
They were both Israeli cops helping to get Jenny out of harm's way.
Rescuing her safe and sound was what really mattered. But there was
no news. Why hadn't the kidnappers called again?

"Why haven't they called again?" Elliot turned to the woman.

"They probably fear the call may be traced."

"Down to phone and street number?"

"Phone, yes. Street number, no. But it's possible to get the coordinates down to hundredths of a second, which to all intents and purposes is better than street numbers."

Elliot mulled this over.

"You can really do that?"

"What do you mean? Javan and I? Here in the U.S.?"

"Yeah."

"Of course not. For that you need pretty sophisticated hardware
and the phone company's cooperation, granted only to local law
enforcement. We are fish out of water here."

"So, their fear is unfounded."

"Totally. But they can't be sure you didn't call the police, so they
are taking all precautions. Their next call will probably be from
another town, Kitchener, London, Newmarket, who knows. Or from
some place in Toronto pretty far from where they're keeping Jenny."

He mulled that over. "What other reason would keep them from
calling?"

Hadara thought for a second or two. "Well . . . they may have killed Jenny, or she may be wounded, or very ill, and they don't want you to know so you still ransom her and they get the bonds."

"Any other less macabre reason?"

Hadara shook her head. "Let me see. By some miracle Jenny may have been able to talk her way out of this. Maybe they freed her on condition she won't go to the police, doesn't call you or Sam until she gets back home."

"That's not likely, right?"

"I would say not."

Both fell silent until, a few minutes later, Javan returned to the reception area. They got to their feet.

"All set?" Hadara asked.

"All except Tico. He says he wants to talk to Steil."

"What?" Elliot said, at a loss.

"Let's go to the hallway," the Israeli suggested.

Once there, Javan talked in a low voice.

"Okay. Tico called the Four Seasons several times before telling Sam about Jenny's disappearance. Maybe other people called her room too. Her voicemail could be full. She hasn't been seen there since the seventeenth, and her baggage is in the room. Maids are supposed to report when a guest who has all her baggage there fails to use the bed and the bathroom two or three days in a row. If this goes on for several days, hotel security inform the police that a guest is missing. That way, if the guest turns up safe and sound, they call the cops and say all is fine, sorry to have bothered you. If she disappears, their ass is covered."

"I hadn't thought about that, but yes, you are probably right. But what has this to do with Tico?"

"I called Tico, explained all this to him. I said if the Toronto police learn that Jenny hasn't been seen for several days, the media could find out – all newspapers have ears in police stations – and it'd be much more difficult for us to rescue her. Then I said it would help us if he calls the Four Seasons and says Ms. Scheindlin is back in New York and that she'll send for her luggage in a few days and pay the bill. Would they pack her things and take them to a storeroom, please?"

"And what did he say?" Elliot asked.

"He said he wasn't sure he wanted to do that. It would be lying. And should anything happen to Jenny, he'd be the prime suspect. Then he said he wanted to talk to you about this."

Elliot nodded a few times, thinking things over. "Well, the first thing comes to mind is that Tico is not one of the bad guys, right?"

"Why do you think that?" Hadara wanted to know.

"Well, if he were, he would jump at the opportunity to keep the police in the dark. Am I wrong?"

"No, you are right. I hadn't seen it that way," Hadara lied.

"Hey, would you consider joining IP?" Javan smiled widely.

"Thanks, but no thanks. I guess you are right. If the world learns Jenny has disappeared, the mujahideen might panic, kill her, get rid of the body. You want me to call Tico?"

"Yes."

Flanked by his escorts, Elliot called Tico from a bank of pay phones on the sidewalk and said he understood the Puerto Rican wanted to have a word with him. Tico confirmed that he did. Specifically he wanted to ask Steil if he knew what the cop-for-rent had asked him to do. Steil said yes, he knew, and added that he believed it would serve Jenny's best interests if neither the Toronto police nor the press learned she had disappeared. That's why someone should tell the hotel she was back in New York, so they wouldn't report her as missing. It would facilitate the discreet inquiries they had to make. The right person to do that was Tico, for he was on record as Jenny's assistant. Would he please make the call?

"Will you serve as a witness to this should the need arise, Mr. Steil?" Tico asked.

"What do you mean, Tico?"

"Testify that I made this call because those detectives asked me to?"

"Yes, I will."

"Can they hear me now?"

"No."

"Just so you know, I taped our meeting here yesterday, and the first call about this, and this one too. I'm taping every fucking phone call I get, including those pitching credit cards. I will keep the tapes in a secure place, because you know what, Mr. Steil? Jenny trusts you, says you're really A-1. But I don't like those two guys you brought here. Especially the smartass lady. I'll call the Four Seasons as soon as we hang up. Take care."

"You too, Tico," Elliot said and hung up.

"Well?" Hadara asked.

"He'll make the call. Says he wanted to talk to me to make sure I was in agreement. Hopes you guys understand."

"Sure. No problem," Smartass said.

Toronto

"We're definitely getting short," Chris said, as he finished counting $380 in Canadian twenty dollar bills.

Valerio nodded and proceeded to unfold a Toronto street map over the kitchen table. Most of the city's downtown, and a wide swath of its eastern part, was now dotted with one-hundred-odd coloured points. Green pinpointed the supermarkets, clothing stores, gas stations, and other places where they had made purchases. Orange showed the various places they had parked the van. Violet stood for hotels and motels, restaurants, and pharmacies. Blue represented storefront businesses that changed moolah for Canadian currency. Red was for "stay away" areas, those near police stations.

They called it the "been there" map and its purpose was to prevent them from visiting the same place twice. The Professor had put in writing that Valerio's ethnicity and Chris's good looks attracted attention. Both were too easy to describe, so they should avoid going to places they had already been. Neighbours posed an unavoidable risk, the operation's brains had told the grunts, but Toronto had thousands upon thousands of all sorts of businesses.

Valerio opened the notebook and flipped pages until he found a list of currency exchanges, eleven of which had blue check marks. He checked out several unmarked addresses on the map.

"There's a Money Mart on Yonge Street, between Queen and Dundas," he said.

"All right. Want me to go?"

Valerio considered it. "No, I'll take the bus and the subway. You cook dinner, okay?"

"Okay. How much should we change?"

"Well, we should be hauling ass out of here in a few days, ten at most, so I think a thou will be enough."

"And our U.S. balance is?"

"Thirty-four hundred."

"More than enough, I guess," Chris said.

"Okay. I'll get dressed," Valerio said, pushing back his chair and getting up.

The flight from New York to Toronto was uneventful, but Elliot's Cuban passport made the turbaned immigration officer at Pearson's Terminal Three apprehensive.

"What is the purpose of your visit to Canada, Mr. Steil?" the man asked.

Having been asked similar questions every time he entered a country, Elliot was used to, but not resigned to, the suspicion. Most citizens of countries famous for something negative are suspects the instant they show their passports at an immigration booth. You might be a respected professional, a decent businessman, a famous scientist, but if you were Cuban, immigration officials presumed you wanted to immigrate illegally.

Steil pulled his wallet out, removed his U.S. Permanent Resident card, and handed it to the officer.

"I'm here on business," he said.

The man examined the card and did something beneath the counter that Elliot supposed consisted of scanning both IDs.

"You just need to show this to be admitted to Canada," the inspector said as he returned the card to Elliot.

"I didn't know that."

The Sikh handed back the passport and the customs declaration card.

"Welcome to Canada, Mr. Steil."

"Thank you."

This may well have been the instant when the nine giant German maids decided to grind Jenny's fate for the second time, for American Eagle lost the bag that Elliot had checked in.

"I can't believe this," the fuming Elliot said to Hadara and Javan. The baggage carousel was now empty, except for two suitcases that had passed before their eyes several times.

The Israelis had carried on their luggage and stowed them in the cabin's overhead compartments.

"Why did you bring such a big bag?" Hadara asked.

"Did you know how many days this would take?"

"This is why I travel light," Javan said. "Need more underwear, a pair of shoes, pants? I go to a store."

"Well, I guess I'll have to do that today," Elliot said.

Once again the possibility of a call from the kidnapper made them act like conjoined triplets. They went to the airline's lost baggage counter, reported the missing piece, and told the attendant to send the bag to the Eaton Centre Marriot, where Mr. Steil would be staying. Little was said as their airport limo took Highway 427 south, then the Gardiner Expressway. For a while Elliot could see a tall tower to his left. Mr. Eiffel was to blame; he had started it in Paris, he thought. As had happened in many other metropolises, at some point the powers that be had decided Toronto needed a big phallic symbol to feel important.

Once the cab left the Gardiner, Elliot spoke to the driver.

"Hey, mister, could you take us to a department store near the hotel?"

"Sure, sir. Any one in particular?"

"No. Any place I can get some clothes."

"Okay."

The nine giant maids may have giggled at this, but having to accompany Elliot to the store made Hadara grunt. Believing that whoever establishes a rule shouldn't break it, Javan resigned himself to it. The cabbie took them to the Bay, at Queen and Yonge, telling them that to reach their hotel they just had to cross Queen and walk up James Street. For almost half an hour the two Israelis watched as the Cuban chose underwear, socks, a pair of pants, two shirts, and personal hygiene items.

While waiting at a pedestrian light to cross Queen Street, Elliot spotted someone in the crowd of people approaching a subway entrance. In the nanoseconds that it took his retina to send the face to the visual-recognition circuit at the back of his brain, Steil was under the impression he had seen those features before. Then the precise axons and dendrites used their synapses to carry the image to whatever part of his brain stored memories. He recognized the man.

"Fuck," Elliot muttered, under his breath.

"What?" Hadara asked.

Valerio disappeared behind a glass-and-aluminum door. Elliot took a deep breath. Was he wrong? According to some people, every human being has a look-alike somewhere.

"What?" Hadara insisted.

"That light. How long does it take?"

The Mossad officers noticed that for the rest of the afternoon Elliot seemed extremely distracted and inattentive. However, by the time Javan got under the shower in their hotel room, the Cuban had made up his mind. He flipped his cell open and speed-dialled Tony Soto's number.

"Hello."

"Hi, Tony."

"Teacher! I called the warehouse and Sam said you're in the Big Apple. You back?"

"Nope, I'm still in New York. How you doing?"

"I'm fine, buddy. Coming back soon?"

"Still have to dot a few *i*'s here. How're the wife and the kids?"

"Fine. We're all fine. And I'm, like, bonding really tight with Tonito, you know? Wish I had done that years earlier."

"How's the job?"

"Okay. No big deal, though. Can't believe I'm a nine-to-fiver now."

"Good. Listen, Tony, I need a favour."

"Shoot."

"A few years ago there were a couple of gay men in Miami Beach making a living in the fashion business, as photographers, I think, but I'm not sure. One is American, white guy, handsome; don't remember his name. The other is Indian; don't remember his name either. Four or five years ago they were a couple; may have broken up, I don't know. This Indian – not from India, but from somewhere in South America – has copper-coloured skin, a head of black hair, big beaked nose. I need to know if he's currently in Miami. You think you could check that out for me?"

"Well, I can't say for sure, but with those kinda smacker, gay and fashionista, it shouldn't be too difficult. Is it urgent?"

"I would say it's pressing, yes. The sooner the better."

"Okay. I'll get on it right now, call in sick tomorrow if necessary."

"Tony, I really appreciate that."

"Dude, I owe you big time. Just ask."

"Thanks a lot, Tony."

"Call you as soon as I find out, okay?"

"Okay. Take care, brother."

By the time Javan emerged from the bathroom, Elliot was relaxed and looking satisfied with himself.

"Are you out from under the cloud?" the ex-colonel asked.

"What do you mean?"

"This afternoon you seemed worried."

"Did I? Well, probably. You know: the company, my woman, all this mess, losing my luggage. But in Cuba we say, 'Face stormy weather with a smile.' I'm hungry. What do you say we go grab a bite?"

Before Javan could answer, the room's phone rang. The desk clerk had good news: the airline had found and delivered to the hotel Mr. Steil's lost baggage. It was in the storeroom and Mr. Steil could pick it up at his convenience. At which point the nine giant maids may well have called it a day and gone to bed.

"Tomorrow's the call," Chris said.

"I know."

They were sitting at the kitchen table, drinking tea after eating Subway sandwiches, both tense and a little nervous.

"Where will you go?" Valerio asked.

"Any Niagara Falls motel; as close to the American border as possible, in case they track the call. Make them wonder if I'm on the American or the Canadian side."

"You think they can't determine exactly where you're calling from?"

"A call from a land line, absolutely. From a cell, I don't know. In any case, once I hang up I'll leave the room and drop the phone in the river."

Valerio chuckled. "But why bother with a motel?"

"Privacy. The voice changer is small, but its cables make the phone look different. Outdoors you never know who may be staring, don't you think?"

"Beautiful and attractive as you are, hundreds may be leering."

"Be serious."

"I *am* serious. But you're right about getting a room. Leave as soon as you hang up, though."

"Bet your life I will."

They were silent for half a minute, Valerio fidgeting with his mug, Chris resting his chin on the palm of his hand and gazing at the wall across the room.

"She's totally losing it, Val."

"How so?" Valerio looked up, left the mug alone.

"Yeah. I figure she's been keeping count, knows the deadline is approaching. Each time I went to her room today she cried and begged me not to kill her."

Valerio frowned. "But that's perfectly normal."

"Don't you think she's going nuts?"

"No, I don't think so. She's a strong woman; she's just upset. But if tomorrow the Cuban says he has the bonds, we'll write a note saying not to worry, Steil has what we've asked for and soon we'll free you. That should calm her down."

"The Prof warned against any sort of communication with her," Chris objected.

"But he's not dealing with this. He didn't foresee her going bonkers, okay? And he made us swear nothing bad would happen to her, right? So, we write a note to calm her down. Are we on the same page here?"

"I don't want her to go nuts, so yes, I'm for it."

"Fine. I'll take her to the bathroom now, then we go to bed. Help me with the *kaffiyeh*, will you?"

Next morning, Hadara, wanting to make sure Tico Monerris had reported to the Four Seasons that Jenny had returned to New York, asked Elliot to call him. Tico confirmed he had made the call.

After breakfast the triplets went to a car rental place where Javan chose a Chrysler 300. Before leaving the garage, behind the wheel and assisted by Hadara, he spent a few minutes studying a Toronto street map. Javan drove along Queen West, as smug as those accustomed to driving Fiat Seicentos always seem when they get behind the wheel of a big bad-boy.

In the back seat, Elliot was taking in the city's differences from and similarities to his own town. Rumbling streetcars, the many races and the ethnic attire of the pedestrians, the profusion of traffic signs, two-hundred-year-old churches, billboards advertising unknown products; all were unfamiliar sights. But just like in the U.S. there were glass-and-steel high-rises, young tattooed people with pierced bodies and multi-hued spiked hairstyles, office staff hurrying to work and drinking coffee from paper cups, steel-mesh screens in the back seat of patrol cars.

"Right on Bathurst." Hadara was acting as navigator.

The downtown lustre diminished after they crossed College Street and disappeared past Bloor Street. The tallest building now was three storeys; eighty- or ninety-year-old red brick homes predominated, a few with eight- or nine-foot-tall pines next to their doorsteps.

"Turn right at this coming side street, Wells."

"I can't; look at the sign. One-way."

"Oh."

Javan weaved a tentative path along streets lined with trees bearing the myriad tones of red, ochre, and yellow typical of the fall in temperate zones. Elliot had seen the autumn colours many times along U.S. highways and he always enjoyed it.

At the corner of Wells Street and Albany Avenue, also a one-way street, they took a left. Hadara leaned slightly forward to scan the house numbers. At a certain point Javan pulled the car up alongside the curb. All three got out. The house the Israelis had been searching for had a porch and faux brick panelling. Javan pressed the buzzer.

A blonde woman in her early forties opened the door. Hair to her shoulders, no makeup, courteous cool smile, elegant in a simple white blouse and blue slacks.

"Welcome, Hadara, Javan. How nice to see you again. It's been over a year, right?"

"Thank you, *habibati*," said Hadara. "Yes, around a year. Meet Elliot, a friend."

"Pleased to meet you, Elliot," the woman said, extending her hand. "I'm Faiga."

"The pleasure is all mine, ma'am," Elliot said, taking it.

"Come in, come in, please."

A man emerged from what Elliot assumed was the kitchen, for he wore an apron over jeans and a polo shirt and was wiping his hand on a dishcloth. Short, stocky, dark complexion, bushy eyes, fortyish.

"*Shalom Aleichem*," grinning.

"*Aleichem Shalom*," Javan replied. "Asher, meet Elliot."

Hands were shaken, standard platitudes exchanged. Faiga invited them to sit down and Hadara and Elliot chose the sofa and Javan an armchair. But no sooner had they sat down than Asher said he was preparing *matzah* ball soup for lunch. Everybody knew Javan was an exceptionally good cook. Would they mind if he stole his good friend for a moment to make sure he would be adding the right amount of oil and water to the *matzah* balls?

"Not at all," Hadara said.

For several minutes, Faiga and Hadara jumped from one inconsequential topic to the next: weather, flights, hotels, meals, the Toronto housing market. Elliot stopped paying attention, wondering why, if the Israeli cops had been here previously – a year earlier according to Faiga and Hadara – they had needed to study the street map before leaving the rental company's garage, had had trouble finding their way, and had checked house numbers on this block. During the ride into the city yesterday and at the Bay, and on Queen Street, they had looked around like first-timers. Were these guys pretending to be old friends for his benefit? Asher's stealing Javan with a banal excuse seemed strange. Who were these two? Jews, of course, but Israeli cops in Toronto? No, not likely. Collaborators then? Informers?

Preparing the *matzah* balls took around ten minutes, during which time no voices, clanking of pans, or any cooking sounds came from the kitchen. When the two men returned to the living room, Javan was carrying a bulging, olive-green garment bag. *The bonds*, Elliot supposed, smiling slightly. Javan only needed to give him a fleeting glance to realize the Cuban was in on it.

The hostess said she would make tea for all and left for the kitchen; Asher turned gracious host. After a while, Faiga returned with a whole tea service and cookies. Civility imposed fifteen more minutes of polite conversation and, after courteous goodbyes, the visitors got back into their rental.

"What a lovely couple," Elliot commented from the back seat, enjoying the moment.

Javan and Hadara glanced at one another.

"Okay," she said, turning to Elliot. "Yes, they are here," patting the bag.

"Here? What? What's in the bag?"

Javan took a left at Barton Street, stopped the car by the curb, and stared at the Cuban through the rearview mirror.

"Okay, Elliot. We know you know what's going on most of the time. We are not trying to fool you. But we must follow certain rules of discretion and, seeing that we are forced to be constantly together, we must keep appearances, too. Yeah, the bonds are here. Just bear with us, okay?"

"Appreciate the frankness," Elliot said with a nod. "Can I see them?"

"In the hotel," Javan said, then drove along.

Back in Hadara's room, the first object removed from the bag startled Elliot: a .40 Glock Model 27.

"That's not a bond," he said, apprehension in his tone.

"No. These are the bonds," Javan said and handed him a stack of documents held together by two rubber bands. He gave a similar bundle to Hadara.

Staring at the first bearer bond of his life, Elliot felt at a loss. The company's name and logo were unknown to him; the long words seemed to be German, a language as familiar to him as Mandarin. The watermarked paper was thicker than the bond paper used in offices, and he guessed it had a security graph or message ghosted into it. The amount was 10,000 and he assumed *Franken* meant Swiss francs.

"This is it?" lifting his eyes to the man.

"That stack's one million. A hundred bonds; $10,000 Swiss francs each. There are ten of those here," pointing to the bag. "And one with twenty-two bonds, for a total of ten point two million Swiss francs. Ten million U.S. at the current rate."

"And these are the real thing; not counterfeit?"

"The real thing, Steil."

Elliot returned his pack to Javan. "Okay, now, what's with the gun?"

Javan pursed his lips. "Just a precaution."

"You shoot anyone, I tell the whole story to the police."

"Understood."

Elliot's cell rang. He pulled it out and opened it.

"Hello."

"Hey, Teacher," Tony said.

"Hold on, honey."

Trying to change his expression from surprised to uncomfortable, Elliot turned to the Israelis. "My old lady. Would you excuse me for a minute?"

"Go ahead," Javan said, with a nod.

"You mind if I use your bathroom, Hadara?"

"No. But leave Jenny's cell here. In case, you know . . ."

Elliot fished out the other phone from his jacket and gave it to her, closed the bathroom door behind him.

"Go ahead."

"What's the matter with you?"

"Birds on the wire. Go ahead."

"Well, the Peruvian is Valerio de Alba; his boyfriend, Chris Dawson. No criminal records, not known as druggies or drunks, although they share a reefer and a margarita now and then. Florida driving permits, no tickets. Valerio makes a living as a social photographer: weddings, baptisms, that kinda thing. He helps Chris at fashion photo shoots. They shared an apartment on Lenox Avenue, Miami Beach. Need the address?"

"You got it?"

"Sure."

"I can't write it down now. Keep going."

"They flew the nest six months ago; told the landlord they'd spend the summer in New York but would be back in winter. Left a deposit to rent an apartment from November 1 in the same building. Haven't used their credit cards since. Their furniture is in a self-storage place. That's it."

Trying hard to stay cool, Elliot was silent for several seconds.

"Hey, Teach, you there?"

"I'm here. Thanks a bundle, Tony. You've done me a big, big favour. I'll drop by as soon as I get back. Gotta go now."

Elliot clicked the phone shut.

Okay, calm down. That Valerio is here doesn't mean he's the kidnapper. Is Chris here too? Maybe they broke up. But if Chris is in Toronto too, they may be here for perfectly normal reasons. On business, as photographers. Visiting friends or relatives. On vacation. This may be a fucking coincidence. But not using their credit cards in six months? People who don't want to leave a trail do that. Okay, take it easy, Elliot. Second possibility: Valerio is the kidnapper, maybe Chris too. Should I tell the Israelis? How would that help us find Jenny? We don't know where they have her. Knowing who the kidnappers are doesn't tell us where they have her. And suppose they are not the kidnappers? Besides, Jenny must've considered them great friends; they were the first people she called the night Maria was murdered. When I got to the Scheindlins' they were already there. It seemed they adored her. Most importantly, they are not Muslims. Well, they could have converted. No, it's impossible; Islam condemns homosexuality. Then, they could be faking it. No, gays don't kidnap people. They don't. Okay. That's it. Not a word to these two. Okay. I'm going out now. Look normal. Okay. Here I go.

"Any problem, Steil?" Hadara asked.

"No, why?"

"Your face is flushed."

"Really? It's that you women – why do you always think we are cheating on you?"

"Because you frequently are."

Believing that the kidnappers *had* to find out whether Steil had the bonds, the three of them holed up in the hotel, waiting for their call. To make a bad situation worse, they were not in adjoining rooms. Crowded in Hadara's, they passed the time absorbed in their own thoughts, sighing resignedly, reading, watching TV, making small talk, staring out the window, eating lunch, standing and sitting, crossing and uncrossing their legs, using the bathroom every two or three hours, all the time stealing looks at the unrivalled centre of attention – Jenny's cell in hands-free mode – on the coffee table.

After supper, once Javan wheeled out the room-service cart, Elliot got to his feet.

"Well, I'll take a shower and get some shut-eye. You coming, Javan?"

"Hey, guys, could I spend the night in your room?" Hadara asked.

Elliot passed the ball to Javan with a glance.

"I'd have no problem with that if there were a couch I could sleep on," Javan said. "But we only have two singles."

"Under no circumstance would I take your bed. I'll sleep on the floor. No big deal."

"Okay," Javan said with a shrug.

This obliged the men to get into bed with their pants on, as neither of them had brought pyjamas. Even though Javan gave a pillow and his bedspread to Hadara, he seemed unfazed by her having to sleep on the floor. Elliot found this strange. Well, maybe Israeli men were used to seeing women roughing it, what with female conscription and all that, he thought. But if she was his superior, a little grovelling wouldn't hurt. Another weak hint that in fact he was in charge? But what could be the purpose of pretending that Hadara was the boss if she wasn't? Did Javan think he, Elliot, would be more amenable to a woman's instructions? Well, if she looked like J. Lo, he would follow her instructions to the letter. But not even her earlobes were like the Puerto Rican's.

The woman shook her shoes off, chose a corner, turned off the lights, lay down on the carpet fully dressed, slapped the pillow twice, and, after covering herself with the bedspread, turned on her side and closed her eyes.

Elliot fell asleep feeling a little respect for her dedication and wondering how many sacrifices she had made to reach whatever step on the ladder she was standing on now. Family, husband, children, friends, vacations, parties . . . *Some people have a very strange sense of self-fulfillment* was his final thought.

His full bladder awoke him at 2:42, and coming out of the bathroom he peeked at the unmoving Israelis, both apparently sound asleep. *She doesn't snore*, he thought. Five minutes later he was dead to the world again.

A strong hand brusquely shook his shoulder.

"Uh?"

"The phone, Steil, get the phone," Javan whispered.

Elliot swung his legs out of the bed and Hadara handed over the blinking, ringing cell. Javan clicked the tape recorder on.

"Hello?"

"You have the bonds?" Daffy Duck asked.

"I do. Put Jenny on."

"That's not possible."

"Why?"

"It's not possible. But she is fine. I won't ask you if you reported this operation of the Islamic Army of Canada to the police, because if you have, you won't admit it. I will assume that you haven't. If the FBI or the RCMP are in on this, if they are hearing this now and tracking this call, the prisoner only has a few more hours to live."

"No, no, listen; I've followed your instructions to the letter. You have no idea, no idea at all, the things I've had to do to buy the bonds and be here tonight. The only other person who knows about this is Sam Plotzher. Sam is –"

"We know who he is. The prisoner told us."

"Oh, she did? Okay. Well, no other person, police or civilian, knows about this. Please, believe me."

"I never believe an infidel, but you may be telling the truth. Do as we say and tomorrow night, God willing, we will free Jennifer Scheindlin. But there are fresh instructions you must follow concerning how we will swap the prisoner for the bonds. If you have lied

to us, or if tomorrow night you don't do exactly as I tell you, the prisoner will be beheaded and we will send you a DVD of the execution.
Are we clear?"

"We are."

"Good. What's the bonds' denomination?"

"Ten thousand Swiss francs."

"All from the same company?"

"Yes."

"How much is the total?"

"Ten point two million."

"All right. Now, listen carefully. Rent a car today and buy a solid
leather handbag or suitcase that all the bonds will fit in. Has to be
leather, with sturdy clasps and handstraps. Are we clear on this?"

"I'm clear."

"Don't even think of embedding a tracking device in it."

"Embedding what?"

Daffy Duck considered the question and smiled. No, Elliot Steil
had not gone to the police. They would have discussed putting a
tracker in whatever container they decided on.

"Never mind."

"No, tell me. I don't want to endanger Jenny."

"It's a gizmo that sends a signal, shows where a thing is."

"Oh, I see, no, no. I won't do anything that jeopardizes Jenny."

"You put only the bonds in the handbag. Nothing else. I'll call you
later with further instructions on when and how we'll make the swap."

The connection went dead.

The triplets exchanged hopeful glances before Javan stopped the
recorder. Elliot pressed the end key and glanced at his watch. 3:43.
Why the sonofabitch had said *later*.

"Where do we stand now?" he asked.

Hadara turned her gaze from the Cuban to her frowning colleague, who was scratching the top of his head.

"Why didn't he ask where Steil was staying?" he said, looking at her, stopping the scratching.

"I don't know."

"Why is that so important?" Elliot asked.

"To check you out."

Elliot lowered his eyes to the carpet, reflected. "Maybe he's not interested in checking me out." Then, glancing first at Javan, then Hadara, "Didn't even think of it."

"It's the most important thing he should've asked," Javan said, and for the first time Elliot detected emotion in his voice. "They should make sure that you are alone, that no one follows you. That's the only way to confirm you haven't gone to the police, which opens the possibility of stealing the bonds; or even better, killing you and stealing the bonds. They kill you, the swap doesn't have to take place. They kill you and Jenny, they are home free with the bonds; no witnesses."

"You think so?" Elliot, suddenly worried.

"Absolutely."

"Then, why didn't he ask?" Elliot again.

"I can't figure it out."

They fell silent. Hadara was examining the carpet, as if it had the answer to Javan's question.

"Possible causes," she began. "One, he forgot."

"Impossible." The ex-colonel waved his hand dismissively.

"Two," she went on, unperturbed, "the Islamic Army of Canada has only two soldiers; the two in the DVD. The Army exists only in their minds. They can't check out Steil because there's no one else to do it. Remember how at the end of Jenny's DVD one of them fishes a remote out of his pocket and aims it at the camera? There was no cameraman. There's no one else. When one goes out – for example, to make this call – the other has to stay with Jenny. Both have to be there for the swap, one holding Jenny until the other gets the bonds and signals his partner to release her."

"Could be," Elliot said.

Javan shook his head in doubt. "No mujahideen cell I have heard about has less than three members and I doubt –"

"But our principal suspects are diamond smugglers," Hadara said, interrupting rather brusquely.

Elliot was a little intrigued by Javan's reaction to her objection. For a tenth of a second, the Israeli looked as if he'd mistakenly thrown a monkey wrench into wondrously delicate machinery.

"Yeah, that's possible. Okay, let's plan ahead," he said.

After using the bathroom and dressing, they listened to the tape and started debating likely courses of action. By dawn they had discussed three different scenarios for the swap: a crowded public place, perhaps a subway station at rush hour; a deserted open space, like a park; or two motorboats on Lake Ontario after midnight, in which case the kidnappers would make sure theirs was the fastest. This last possibility made Elliot uneasy.

"I have a problem with sailing."

The Israelis knew from his Mossad file what the problem was, but Hadara realized she had to ask.

"Oh, really? What's your problem?"

"Someone threw me overboard in the Florida Straits and sailed away."

The officers couldn't leave it at that and resigned themselves to losing a few minutes.

"Tell us why and how that happened," Javan said.

Elliot recounted the gist of it in less than three minutes. The Israelis expressed controlled amazement and said they understood why he had a phobia about sailing. They added a number of assurances concerning the possibility of a swap on open water and asked him not to worry. Then they returned to guessing what might happen.

"In any scenario," Javan said, "he'll give you instructions through

Jenny's phone. He will call at least two times tonight, maybe more. The first we will be here, all three of us, so Hadara and I will hear his initial instructions. But later you will be alone in the rental."

"But it's very important," Hadara said, seizing the initiative, "that during the first call you tell him in no uncertain terms that you won't give him the bonds or leave them somewhere so he can pick them up before making sure Jenny is okay. Tell him it has to be close enough that you can recognize her. He says, 'You'll find binoculars beneath a bench; use them to see Jenny at a window.' You say no, no, and no. Tell him she has to be near you, twenty or thirty metres tops, standing, so you can ask her how she is and she can hear you and respond."

Elliot closed his eyes, bowed his head, and massaged his forehead before staring at Hadara. "I understand your concern, I really do. But what happens if the bastard says, 'It's our way or no way'?"

With a look, Hadara deferred to her colleague.

"At that point," Javan said, looking Elliot straight in the eyes, "you've done all he has asked you to do, given in to all his demands. It's the right moment to pretend you're furious. You ask the guy if he thinks you are stupid. You insult him: 'Fuck you, motherfucker.'"

"Listen, Javan, I don't think –" shaking his head.

"Trust me, Steil. Trust me. He asks you to leave the bonds somewhere without you making sure – and I mean 100 per cent sure – that Jenny is alive, safe and sound, you call him asshole, sonofabitch, any and all name-calling that comes to mind. Say you're driving back to your hotel and calling the police."

"You sure about this, Javan?"

"I'm sure. He will yield. What this guy and his accomplice want is the dough. They know that to get it they have to free Jenny. They haven't killed her, I'm sure of that too. They may have raped her, beaten her, I don't know. But they won't do any permanent damage because she's worth ten million dollars. If they have an ounce of grey matter under their thick skulls, Jenny hasn't shaved her legs or underarms since her abduction. I'm sure she eats with plastic cutlery on disposable plates, drinks from paper cups, sleeps on a bare mattress. You know why?"

"No."

"Because they would lose it all if Jenny gets so desperate she commits suicide. So, they don't give her anything she could slash her wrists with or hang herself with. Steil, listen to me. They want the money because, if they are the diamond smugglers she snitched on, that's a hundred times more than what we've impounded thanks to Jenny's work. And if they are mujahideen, ten million buys a lot of weapons and explosives. But Jenny's corpse isn't worth a dime."

Javan paused, searching his mind for more persuasive reasons. He slid the tip of his tongue over his lips, took a deep breath, went on.

"You have to be flexible, though. You can't say you won't give them the bonds until Jenny is standing next to you. This is a negotiation and you are a businessman, so negotiate the best deal you can. But keep in mind that if they get their hands on the bonds before releasing Jenny, the possibility that she gets killed rises exponentially. Presumably she's the only person capable of identifying them, of accusing them in a court of law. You give them the bonds before making sure that Jenny is safe and sound, before asking them to let her walk towards you, they'll probably kill you too. Do you understand what I'm saying, Steil?"

Steil nodded, thinking things over. Then he said: "I want that gun of yours in my belt."

The Mossadist smiled. "I asked for it taking for granted you'd want one."

Once Elliot had left the hotel to rent a car and shop for a suitcase, the Israelis returned to Hadara's room. Javan ordered breakfast as Hadara took a shower and changed. Both were about to sip their first cup of tea when Javan raised his eyes to the woman.

"I got carried away," he said.

"We all make mistakes," Hadara, with a shrug of dismissal. "Mine was in New York."

"I know," sounding resigned. "For a whole week we've been bull-shitting him about diamond smugglers, then I start babbling about mujahideen cells as if we deal with them on a daily basis."

"I don't think he'll infer anything from that," she said.

"Don't underestimate him. He has what it takes."

Hadara placed her cup back on the saucer. "Sam said Steil has no reason to suspect that Jenny has been working for us, or who we are. Besides, we left open the possibility the kidnappers are honest-to-goodness mujahideen."

"Right, but it was a blunder. We said we are IP, and millions every-where know that the police don't deal with international Islamic ter-rorist organizations. Shabak, MI5, FBI, DST, CSIS, those are the players. Then I go and say I don't know a mujahideen cell with less than three members."

"You didn't say '*know* a mujahideen cell.' You said you hadn't '*heard about*.'"

"Exactly. It's what I've heard during coordination sessions with Shabak's Arab Affairs. He may think we are Shabakis."

Hadara chuckled and shook her head. "No, no. This guy doesn't even know that we or Shabak exist."

"I hope you are right."

Nothing was said for a few moments. Javan drank the rest of his tea. Then Hadara asked, "Do you think he'll panic and shoot someone?"

"I don't think so, but it's possible. He's helping us; he's willing to take a big risk for Jenny; that earns him the right to defend himself if he's shot at. It's better to be alive and kicking in a Canadian jail than six feet under."

"You cleared it with Tel Aviv?"

"I did, *seren*. He kills someone, we grab Jenny and him and get out of there. He gets killed, we grab Jenny and get out of there. Our people will get us through the border. Steil's nabbed, we'll see what we can do for him. Poor schlimazel. What a rotten job this is. The important thing is to rescue Jenny. Pass the toast. I'm hungry."

Javan's concern with what Elliot might deduce from his blunder was not so off the mark. Even though the Cuban hadn't the foggiest notion he was dealing with Israeli spymasters, nor that Jenny Scheindlin had been screwing and informing on rich Arabs, he dedicated only a thimbleful of his mind to filling out the form and renting an SUV, eating breakfast in a coffee shop, cruising along Bloor Street searching for a luggage store, and purchasing a big black duffel bag made of untreated leather ($230, plus tax). All that time, the part of his brain entrusted with analytical thought kept pondering a possibility and searching for a missing piece that he sensed was very important. He wanted better insight into the likelihood that Valerio de Alba and Chris Dawson had something to do with the abduction, but he couldn't think of any argument to add to those he had come up with after talking to Tony. By the time he was back in the hotel, he knew he was absolutely ignorant about an important fact, but damned if he knew what it was. He knocked on Hadara's door and put the missing piece out of his mind.

As the day wore on they tried to distract themselves. Javan carefully took apart and reassembled the spotless Glock and lectured Elliot about its important features: why it lacks an external, thumb-activated safety switch and the number of rounds in the magazine. To kill time he delved into irrelevancies, too: the unusual calibre, the gun's high resistance to corrosion and wear, the untrue urban legend that airport X-ray machines can't detect it, and other, minor details that were neither here nor there to a man who might have to fire the semi-automatic in a few hours. But, having nothing better to do, Elliot and Hadara listened intently. Both noticed that Javan used his handkerchief to wipe away his fingerprints from each major part as he reassembled the gun, then from its outer surface. Lastly, he slid the Glock across the table for Elliot to take and went to the bathroom to flush the tissue down the toilet.

Later, Hadara punched the numbers of her and Javan's cell phones into the memory of Elliot's for him to speed-dial, but that took her less than two minutes. Over lunch their chitchat was depressingly boring. They turned on the television and watched the news, then switched to the Weather Channel, then a soap opera.

"Give me a break." Javan, flipping channels past rappers, ads, more ads, FOXNews, more rappers, aliens from a faraway planet, cartoons, CNN.

"Anyone?" Javan, offering the remote.

Elliot and Hadara shook their heads and Javan turned the set off.

A few minutes after four the men went to their room, showered, and changed. Elliot took a twenty-minute nap. Javan read the complimentary copy of the *Globe and Mail*. After he woke up, the Cuban considered twiddling his thumbs but opted instead to call Fidelia. He hung up five minutes later because she had sensed something about him was different and that put her in a foul mood: "Toronto? What the hell are you doing in Toronto? You do business with Latin America." Later: "For the love of God, stop being so frigging evasive!" And just before the conversation ended: "What's the matter with you, Elio?"

"Pass me the business section, Javan," Elliot said after the call ended.

Twilight was noticeable through the window by the time they went to Hadara's room. She opened the door in her pyjamas.

"Were you in bed?" Javan, incredulous.

"No, I was doing yoga."

"Oh. You want us to come later?"

"No, I'm done. Come in."

Again the news, followed by *Everybody Loves Raymond*. A little after eight, a game show in which people jumped and hooted as they opened briefcases made them switch to the Discovery Channel. Elliot couldn't focus on the documentary being shown, and turned philosophical on sitcoms. For twenty-odd minutes Ray, Brad, Patricia, Doris, and Peter, and the writers who had come up with their lines, had made him forget the seriousness of his situation. Today, no other TV program, newspaper, or topic of conversation had done that. He had even chuckled, for God's sake!

Until this evening he, like most people, thought the money successful entertainers make excessive. Now he understood the contribution sit-coms make to mental health. What was the price of helping millions forget their trials and tribulations for a while? The show's creators, writers, and actors deserved all they earned for the therapy they provided.

And not just that show, others like –

Jenny's cell rang.

They jumped to their feet.

Javan activated his recorder and gave a nod to Elliot.

"Hello?"

"What time you have?" Daffy asked.

"Pardon?"

"Your watch. What time is it?"

Elliot stole a glance. "8:52."

"Correct. You bought the suitcase?"

"I did, and I rented a car."

"Make, colour, and plates, please."

"Hold it."

Elliot fished the car key from his pocket and read from a plastic tag attached to it. "Ford Expedition, black, AYSM089."

Silence.

"You there?"

"Jotting. Repeat the plates."

Elliot did.

"Are you carrying a gun?"

"What? No. I don't have a gun. How could I? I flew in the day before yesterday. I don't know anybody here."

"There are ways."

"Well, I don't have a gun. Should I? Do I need a gun?"

"You don't need it. But maybe you have some funny idea; knight on a white horse coming to rescue the JAP, shoots dead her kidnappers."

"Listen, I'm no hero. I'm a business manager. I don't . . . What Jap are you talking about?"

"Jewish American Princess."

"Oh, I see. No, listen. I just want to get it over with, peacefully. Release Jenny, I give you the bonds. No shooting, no argument. We swap my boss for your bonds, end of story, okay?"

"Okay. You have a city map with you?"

Javan nodded energetically. Elliot raised his eyebrows to ask where the map was. Javan mimicked steering a car.

"Yeah, sure, I have one, but not here; it's . . . in the glove compartment."

"All right. Write this down. You have pen and paper?"

Javan pointed toward the tape recorder.

"I have hotel stationery here at the desk. And, wait, let me open this drawer. Yes, a ballpoint too. Shoot."

This won him a nod from Javan. Hadara's eyes crinkled a little, re-evaluating the guy.

"Be at Woodbine, between Cosburn and O'Connor, at ten tonight."

"Woodbyne between Coxbuuurn and O'Connnooor" as if simultaneously writing and speaking. "At ten?"

"At ten. But it's Cosburn, with an *s*. Park the car on the right, kill the lights and the engine, and wait for my call."

"Okay. I park the car on the right side of the street . . . Wait, wait, the right side facing what? East? West? North?"

"The right facing north."

"Okay. Then I wait for your call. How long do I have to wait?"

"Just wait."

"Okay, whatever you say. But I gotta see Jenny, make sure she's well, standing, or better, walking towards me, before I give you the –"

Daffy hung up.

"The checkered flag is down," Javan said. "Let's get rolling."

For a little over thirteen hours Jenny Scheindlin had felt as if half her brain was filled with irrepressible joy and the other half was soaked in fear. Every few minutes, she swung from desperation to cheerfulness and back. She had wept several times, imagining that any moment an executioner brandishing a big sword would appear, force her to kneel, then cut off her head. Then her mind would turn to what to do first once Elliot took her to a hotel, police station, hospital, or wherever the brilliant, handsome, adorable, magnificent, kind, sweet, and wonderful manager of Imlatinex would take her as soon as she was free. Who should she call first, Tico or Sam? Should her first decent meal be filet mignon or lobster au gratin? Perhaps she would take a sleeping pill and stay out cold for fifteen hours. But first she would pour a whole bottle of Eclat de Velours bath salts into a half-full oversized tub and soak for a full hour. She would then get out and, still wet, drench herself from neck to toes in Huile de Magnolia body oil.

The pleasure of these thoughts inevitably led to self-flagellation. Why was she so stupid? How could she believe that Elliot was in Toronto to ransom her and that she would be released at any moment in the next twenty-four hours. There was no way Elliot could get hold of ten million dollars in ten days. It was impossible. *Don't even think about it. Don't deceive yourself!* The fanatics wanted to take the lamb to the altar feeling relaxed, exhilarated, so she wouldn't fight for her life until the instant the assassin pulled his sword out of its scabbard.

The day had started as always. The taller mujahideen took her to the bathroom, and when she was done, he walked her back to the mattress and brought her breakfast. Later, the kidnapper came to pick up the tray and gave her a piece of paper. She read, in capital letters: *Elliot Steil is in Toronto. He says he has your contribution to the fund for the parents and wives and children of our martyrs. If that is true, the Islamic Army of Canada will release you within twenty-four hours.* Open-mouthed, she had moved her gaze from the paper to the man. He snatched the note from her hands, picked the tray up, and left the room.

Nothing out of the ordinary happened during the remaining daylight, apart from her emotional hurricane. Lunch and, immediately afterward, a second trip to the bathroom. Again to the toilet when the fading glow coming through the crack in the window indicated that dusk was giving way to night. An hour or so later, the smaller mujahideen had come in carrying a hanger with the jacket and pants she had been wearing the night she was abducted. In his other hand he had the sneakers. He flicked the light switch, dropped the clothes on the mattress and the shoes on the floor, removed her handcuffs, and said, "Get dressed."

Am I dreaming? she had asked herself the instant the man closed the door behind him. She had touched the clothes, the shoes. No, she wasn't dreaming. Was it true? Had Elliot been able to raise the money to buy the shares, bonds, or whatever frigging thing these bastards had demanded? Were the mujahideen planning to take the ransom and then kill her? Elliot, too? *Oh, God, poor Elliot.* He had gone the whole nine yards for her and would pay for it with his life. She hadn't ever shown him the appreciation he deserved. She had stifled a yawn whenever he lectured her on the principles of trading and the company's inner workings. The poor guy. Maybe if she refused to get dressed these guys couldn't take her to wherever they were planning to take her and Elliot would be spared. But in the next breath she admitted to herself she lacked the guts for that. Before this horrible incident, she had not known the extent of her cowardice. She had thought herself courageous because, to save Jewish lives, she had agreed to screw men she wasn't in the least attracted to. She had even imagined herself shooting guns and rescuing hostages. In fact, she had a head-to-toes yellow streak; she was congenitally faint-hearted, weak, soft. In less than two weeks she had cried rivers and now, with trembling hands, was dressing to be killed.

Once dressed, she stood like a cornered fox beside the mattress, trembling, until eight or ten minutes later, when the man entered the room.

"Let's go," he said.

Javan retrieved the street map from the Chrysler, and in Hadara's room they pored over it, examining the area around where Woodbine ended at O'Connor.

"Hmm, this park, Taylor Creek, looks promising," Javan said.

Elliot lifted his eyes from the map. "Listen, in real life things may be entirely different, but in movies I've seen the guy with the money going from one phone booth to the next, and at each one they send him to a new place. Couldn't that happen here?"

"It's possible," Hadara said. "Maybe once you're there they'll call you and say, 'Now go to such and such street.' And from there send you to where the swap will happen."

"I don't think so," Javan said, "Elliot doesn't know the city and could get lost, especially at night. They would have ordered him to bring the map with him if that was their plan, but they didn't. But it's possible, Hadara. If they are morons. All right, Elliot, let's see. How would you get there?"

Elliot lowered his eyes to the map. "We are here," he said, a finger on Queen and Yonge. "It's not far. I suppose I can get there in fifteen minutes. It's 9:08."

"Let's say thirty minutes," Hadara, after glancing at her watch, "in case traffic's snarled up or something. Better early than late."

"Right. What will you guys do?"

Hadara's gaze kept being drawn to her superior. By now Elliot felt sure Javan was in charge. He couldn't figure why they had ever pretended the opposite.

"You leave here alone," the man said. "Drive east along Queen to Woodbine, north on Woodbine to Cosburn," tracing the route with his forefinger. "Hadara and I will take a different route, let me see . . . University to Gerrard, Gerrard to Coxwell, right on Cosburn, park somewhere along Cosburn, wait for your call. What do you think, Hadara?"

"Sounds fine to me. Elliot, let's check the phone batteries."

"Both are fully charged, don't you remember? Mine was when you put your numbers into it."

"I know. One last time, please."

Elliot took out both cell phones, showed her the displays.

"Okay. The minute you get there check signal strength," she said.

"Bastards wouldn't send him where the signal's weak, would they?" Javan said. "Listen, Elliot, the instant Jenny's phone rings, before you answer it, speed-dial Hadara's number and turn on the speakerphone, so we can hear what they say."

"Why? I can call you after they hang up."

"Suppose one of them is hiding, watching you. They see you talking on your cell phone *after* they gave you instructions, it's clear you are telling someone what you were asked to do next."

"Right. Jesus! What a profession! Distrust is your *raison d'être*."

"Is that a profanity?" Javan said. Hadara chuckled, then contained herself. Elliot shook his head, turned, marched to the bathroom and heard her saying, in Hebrew, words he assumed may have translated as: *You know language teachers. Showoffs. It means "reason for being."*

The Israelis also used the bathroom; all three drank a glass of water. Then Elliot took the gun, loaded a round into the chamber, pushed it into his belt at the small of his back.

"Very uncomfortable to drive with it there," the ex-colonel observed. "Move it to your left side once you get in the car. But keep your jacket buttoned, so no one can see it."

"Javan, I'm partially stupid, not totally."

"Sorry, sorry."

"It's okay. 9:26. I better get going."

"Good luck, Elliot," Hadara said.

"Take care," Javan said. "Don't lose your temper. Keep cool. Shoot only if you are shot at."

"Famous last words," the Cuban said, his back to them, heading to the door.

By her side, gripping Jenny's arm with his right hand, a fifty-foot roll of polyester rope in his left, Valerio guided the blindfolded and hand-cuffed woman from her prison to the garage, where he opened the van's back doors and helped her in. A white *abaya* was spread over the floor.

"Lie face down," he ordered.

She did so and got a whiff of detergent from the garment.

The Peruvian, in black from head to toes and wearing a *kaffiyeh*, dropped the roll of rope on the floor, climbed in beside her, closed both doors.

Then Chris, who, knapsack in hand, had been watching the trans-fer from the top of the steps, descended to the garage and opened its manually operated door. He also wore black clothes, but instead of a *kaffiyeh*, a black balaclava rolled up as a skull cap. He slid into the driver's seat, turned the key in the ignition, exited the garage, stopped in the driveway. He got out, locked the garage door, and returned to the van. On Halsey, he turned left and Jenny endured the first of the many slides and rolls she would experience for almost an hour as the van cruised uphill, downhill, and took multiple turns, with the sole purpose of dispelling any notion she might have formed of where she had been held captive. *It's like watching a movie backwards*, she thought.

At 9:48 the van turned onto Glenwood Crescent off O'Connor Drive. Chris came to a full stop at the intersection with Glenwood Terrace, took a good look left and front. Not a single person on either sidewalk, on the porches, or at any windows facing the streets. The photographer looked at the side and rearview mirrors next; not a soul. He switched off the headlights, drove right down the trail that wound down into Taylor Creek Park. He killed the engine and eased the van down the hill using the emergency brake. The vehicle moved at a snail's pace, for Chris wanted his pupils to adjust to the pitch-dark ravine. Raccoons, frogs, rats, owls, and lesser nighttime fauna either scurried or flew away from the big squeaking intruder. After three hundred winding metres, he made out a flight of concrete steps less than three metres away. He turned the key in the ignition and turned the van around, ready to drive it back to the street. He shut off the engine and pulled on the emergency brake before knocking on the dashboard twice.

Valerio opened the back doors. Carried by a gentle breeze, the smell of wet earth and vegetal life invaded the vehicle. The eerie silence was disturbed only by the squeaking of the old clunker's coil springs as Valerio and Chris got out.

"Sit down," the Peruvian said to Jenny, as he grabbed the rope and put his left arm through the roll, and slid it up so it hung from his shoulder.

"Don't kill me, please, please," she begged, tears welling.

"Shut up, Zionist bitch. You will be free soon. Sit down."

Free soon. Was he telling the truth? She felt a glimmer of hope. But . . . that voice, had she heard it before? Or was it the accent? Or the fusion of the voice and the accent? Jenny was thinking as she struggled to turn face up, then sit. Valerio helped her out. Her sneakers landed on soft earth. Crickets were starting to chirp timidly; a faraway hoot reached their ears.

Knapsack in hand, Chris descended the flight of concrete steps. He paused where a second concrete staircase led up to the O'Connor bridge, and pulled the balaclava over his face.

Valerio removed Jenny's handcuffs first, the blindfold next. She looked around in total bafflement, rubbing her wrists. Where were they? In the countryside? The shorter mujahideen was in full regalia; and yes, a *kaffiyeh* muffled his voice; she couldn't even make out his eyes, those hard black eyes that had glared at her for so many days. Was he going to hang her from one of those tall trees with that rope? In retaliation for Saddam Hussein's execution?

"Please, don't kill me. I have many Arab friends. I respect Arabs and, you know, these last days, reading the Qu'ran –"

"Grab the handrail and go down."

A humid chill made Jenny shiver; her nipples hardened. The metal handrail was wet and cold, but she clutched it firmly. Dreading that the whole scheme might collapse if she fell and broke a leg or, worse, gashed her head or face, Valerio took her by the arm.

A minute later, Jenny saw a masked man waiting at the end of the stairs. The taller mujahideen? *Who else, you stupid woman? And . . . another staircase?*

"Stop," Valerio ordered her. "Grab the handrail. Climb."

She did as she was told. At her side, Valerio started counting the steps. Chris turned and kept going down.

"Stop," Valerio ordered at step thirty.

The Peruvian unrolled the rope and tied one end around Jenny's waist. *What's this man doing?*

"We wait now; in silence," the Peruvian said.

She had, at a certain point in her life, definitely talked to someone with a voice like this man's, Jenny felt sure.

Chris, meanwhile, had crossed to the creek's left bank over a wooden bridge and was now crouching among shrubbery, practically invisible, next to the park's paved walkway. He took out the night-vision goggles he had purchased at a Bathurst Street store from the knapsack, adjusted them, and carefully scanned his surroundings. They were sure that no lonely jogger, or even a couple, would venture into the park after dark, but Valerio had worried that a group of high-school kids might gather here to smoke pot or drink booze. This was why he had reconnoitred this same spot five nights in a row and found it deserted each time. Tonight too. Chris heaved a sigh of relief and checked his watch. 10:07 p.m. He reached into the knapsack again and pulled out two cell phones, one pink, one black. He felt in the bag for the voice changer; it wasn't there. Must have left it at the house. Impossible to go back. He speed-dialled a number on the black phone.

Elliot speed-dialled Hadara's number and heard her say *yeah* before he took the call.

"Hello."

"Listen, Steil –"

"No, you listen to me," Elliot said, and realized he was hearing a normal male voice, not Daffy Duck's. "You hung up on me last time. That's not polite. Now, you listen to me. You must understand I have to make sure Jenny is safe before I give you the bonds. All bets are off unless I see her, as close to me –"

"Shut the fuck up," Chris said.

"No, you shut the fuck up, motherfucker," warming to the role. "I've let you break my balls for ten fucking days to save that woman's life. But I'm telling you, unless I see Jennifer Scheindlin safe and sound in front of me, you'll have to kill me to get the bonds. Are you ready to kill me, you piece of shit? Are you ready to kill me?"

"Calm down. Nobody is going to get hurt. Jennifer is safe. You'll see her soon and, once you do what I'll ask you to do, she'll walk towards you, okay?"

"Don't bullshit me."

"I'm not bullshitting you. Jennifer is in good health. We are Muslims. We haven't raped her or beaten her. We are not like you beasts. She'll confirm this in less than fifteen minutes, provided you do as I say."

"Okay. What do you want me to do?"

"Get out of the car with the suitcase –"

"It's a leather duffel bag."

"Sturdy? Firmly closed? All the bonds in it?"

"Yeah."

"Good. Walk along the sidewalk towards O'Connor. When you get there, turn right and walk toward the bridge. Start counting lamp-posts. When you reach the sixth, stop, and put the bag on the side-walk. The parapet there is over a metre high. Put your arms out and wave for ten or fifteen seconds. Then I'll call you. You'll see Jennifer; she'll wave to you. Then I'll tell you what to do next. Once you do it, she will start walking towards you. If you don't do as I say, she dis-appears again. Bye, Steil."

Chris ended the call.

"Hey! Hey you!" Elliot yelled. He stared at the phone for a moment before closing it, then clicked his tongue and shook his head in dismay.

"You heard the man?" lowering his eyes to his phone.

"We heard him," Hadara said. "You did great, Elliot. Do as he says."

"Okay. But I can't call you from the bridge so you won't be able to hear what he asks me to do."

Two or three seconds went by. Elliot suspected Hadara was con-sulting Javan.

"Don't hang up this phone," Javan said. "Put it in your shirt pocket. Maybe we can hear what goes on at the bridge."

"Okay."

Elliot grabbed the bag and got out of the rental.

"No voice changer this time," Javan commented to Hadara.

"Isn't that weird?" she said.

"It is."

After a few moments of silence, he said, "If things turn out well, how soon should we tell Jenny that we are posing as police officers? She may be so emotional and grateful she spills the beans to Steil."

"Yeah, let's think about that."

Chris put the knapsack on his back, crossed the walkway, and crouched down beside a maintenance shed. Approximately forty metres to his left were the arches of the O'Connor bridge. He pulled out the pink phone and pocketed the black.

Valerio felt the vibration and removed his phone from his pants pocket.

"Yes."

"What?" Jenny, her back to him, thought he was talking to her.

"He's coming. Get ready. Five minutes," Chris told Valerio.

"Okay."

"What?" Jenny said again.

"Shut up."

"What's happening?" she asked as Valerio closed the phone.

"You'll be free soon, you Zionist bitch."

"Really?"

"Shut up." His eyes went to his watch. 10:09.

Elliot did as he was told and walked toward the bridge. His Miami jacket was too light for the chill, but he unbuttoned it so he could grab the gun faster, should he have to. A couple of cars passed him in both directions. He started counting lampposts. Javan turned the Chrysler's ignition, drove slowly to Woodbine, took a left, parked ahead of Elliot's SUV, killed the lights.

Valerio's watch read 10:11.

"Okay, Zionist bitch," he said. "You climb the steps to the next landing. Stay there, arms next to your body. I'll be watching you. If I see you trying to untie the rope I'll pull you back so hard you'll fall down these steps and break your neck. Understand?"

"I do, sir. I swear I do. I will do exactly as you say."

"Okay. I'll tug the rope once to signal when to climb the next set of steps to the sidewalk. Then you turn left. You'll see Steil standing in the middle of the big bridge. Wave to him. Your wave is the signal. Then he will pay the ransom to one of us. When he does, I'll tug the rope twice to say you can run to Steil. If he does not hand over the ransom, a mujahideen sharpshooter across the street will put a bullet through your head."

"No! Why? I've done all you've asked me to do. Don't kill me, please."

"Your life is in Steil's hands, not ours. Now shut up."

Elliot reached the sixth post, placed the bag on the sidewalk, looked over the parapet, and waved his hands reluctantly, for doing stupid things made him angry. Who waves both hands while peering over the side of a bridge at night? The streetlamps provided enough illumination for him to see it was a park all right, with a paved path too narrow for vehicles, and . . . was that a creek?

Chris saw the Cuban wave. He called Valerio.

"Yes."

"Send her to the sidewalk now."

"Okay."

Without ending the call to Valerio, Chris put the pink phone on the grass, pulled out the black, counted to ten, called Elliot. The Cuban drew back from the wall.

"Yeah."

"Turn left."

The trembling Jenny had spotted Elliot the instant before. He was facing the park and – talking on a phone? She started crying.

Elliot watched Ruben's daughter waving at him with her right hand, her left covering her lips, and relief spread all through his body. He heaved a deep sigh.

She's dressed like she's going to go jogging! But a hand over her face? Must be crying. Yeah, she's sobbing. And what the hell's that around her waist?

"I see her. Tell her to walk toward me."

"Drop the bag over the parapet."

"What?"

"You heard me. Drop the bag over the parapet."

Without taking the phone from his ear, the Cuban hoisted the bag atop the wall. Jenny guessed that it contained her ransom. Would Elliot throw it down? She covered her mouth with both hands. Who was he talking to?

"Here it is. Tell Jenny to come to me."

"Not before you drop it, and I make sure the bag is not full of newspapers or other crap."

Elliot did as he was told. A young passenger in a cruising Toyota thought Elliot was polluting the park's environment by dumping old clothes.

"Give it to charity, you moron," he yelled at the Cuban. He couldn't imagine there was a second strange shock in store for him. He gawked at Jenny.

"That babe back there had a rope around her waist," said the astonished passenger, his thumb pointing backwards, an instant after they passed Jenny.

"New trend, probably," the driver opined.

Chris watched the duffel bag fall. It landed with a thud near the walkway. He ran to it, put both phones on the grass, pulled a small flashlight from his pocket, opened the bag, shone the beam into it.

There was a stack of bonds at the top. He made sure there were other stacks below.

He could hear Elliot over the black phone yelling, "Let her go you sonofabitch! Let her go!" Javan heard him too. The Cuban was striding toward Jenny. Chris picked up the pink phone. Javan started the Chrysler and stepped on the gas.

"Set her free, Val. I have it. Run back to the van."

Valerio tugged the rope twice. Jenny started running towards Elliot, but she fell headlong on the sidewalk. Elliot raced toward her. The Chrysler braked alongside her, its hazards blinking. Hadara jumped to the sidewalk and helped Jenny get up.

"You okay?"

"Hadara?"

"Yes, honey. It's me."

Elliot reached them.

"Oh, Elliot," Jenny cried and collapsed in his arms. He hugged her tight. Behind the Chrysler, a car horn tooted. Javan reached over and opened the right rear door.

"Get in," Hadara said. "Hurry."

For a second Elliot stared at the slithering rope hanging from Jenny's waist, not knowing what to do, then he grabbed it and started pulling it in, shoving it into the rental. Jenny squirmed from it, as if it were a snake. Then the Cuban jumped into the back seat.

Javan made a U-turn on the spot and a few infuriated drivers called him nasty names, but he had to wait for the green light to make a left at Woodbine. Jenny couldn't stop crying and kept shifting from Elliot's arms to Hadara's.

"I love you so much, both of you. I love you. I love you," between sobs.

Elliot untied the rope from her waist.

Javan drove half a block then pulled over to the curb, across the street from Elliot's SUV.

"Hey, Steil. Get in your car and follow me back to the hotel."

"No, Elliot, stay with me, please, please."

"I'll be with you in a few minutes. I'll be right behind you. Just a few minutes until we get to the hotel, okay?"

"Okay," with a resigned expression.

Elliot got out and crossed the street. Javan waited until he saw the rental's headlights come to life before driving away. *So simple*, he thought.

"Jenny, listen to me. Are you listening?" Hadara said.

"Yes. Oh, thank you so much, Hadara."

"Okay. Okay. But you are Deborah, the brave secret agent. Listen carefully. The driver of this car is Colonel Javan, from Mossad. We told Steil we are police officers and that you, Jenny, are a police informer. Do you understand what I'm saying?"

"What? I'm a what? I don't get it."

"Listen to me. It's very important that no one, not Steil, not Tico Monerris, absolutely nobody, finds out that you are an agent for Mossad. It's why we've been posing as police officers and why we told Steil that you were informing on Palestinian diamond smugglers. We flew to Miami as soon as Sam told us what had happened to you and then . . ."

Elliot reached the hotel first because Javan stopped at a pharmacy for his colleague to get iodine, band-aids, and painkillers. Once in Hadara's room, Jenny neither ordered a filet mignon nor a lobster au gratin; she didn't take a bath either. She asked Elliot for her cell phone and a little privacy, and called Tico. The first words she said to the thunderstruck Puerto Rican were a question. Could she spend the rest of her life with him? For half an hour her rescuers paced the ninth-floor hallway as Jenny and her lover cried and hiccupped and confessed neither could live without the other. Then Jenny let them back in and took a long, hot shower. By the time she came out wrapped in a bathrobe, Elliot and Javan had gone to their room. Hadara swabbed iodine over the scrapes on Jenny's elbows and knees, then gave her a sleeping pill.

Jenny woke the following morning at 8:35, after sleeping for nine hours. It was Hadara's second night sleeping on the floor. Javan, Glock in his lap, stayed awake all night in an armchair, keeping watch.

After brushing her teeth, Jenny called Sam and learned that Elliot had given him the good news the night before. Crying, she assured the old man that she would fly to Miami soon to spend time with him and Esther, take them to their favourite restaurants, make them enjoy life a little. He was, after all, a father to her and had been since Ruben died.

As all four had breakfast together, it struck Elliot that this Jenny was far removed from last night's terrified woman. She was composed but a little abstracted. When the room-service table was wheeled out, Javan asked Jenny whether she felt like telling them about her horrible experience.

The model shook her head. She hadn't been raped or beaten but couldn't provide descriptions beyond saying that one mujahideen was maybe six feet tall and the other two or three inches shorter; she'd never seen them without *kaffiyehs* and gloves. She had lived the most trying days of her life and needed time to readjust. She wanted to pick up her things at the Four Seasons, fly back to New York first, to Miami later, forget the whole thing, and count her blessings. She wondered, however, if the greatest Cuban who had ever lived would give her a few minutes alone with Javan and Hadara, as she assumed they wanted to ask her questions concerning people she knew in Tel Aviv, and it would be best if Elliot remained ignorant of an Israeli police operation that had nothing to do with him personally.

Elliot got to his feet, said that all he had wanted was to free Jenny and that he would now return the rental, take a taxi to the airport, buy a ticket for the first Toronto-Miami flight, and resume his daily routine. Jenny stood, kissed him on the cheek, escorted him to the door clinging to his arm, opened it and closed it behind him.

Hadara's cell rang and for almost a minute she talked in Hebrew with someone. Yes, she was in Toronto; marvellous city. Incredible sales! Women's nonsense, Javan thought, half-listening. He was paying attention to the sombre Jenny. Hadara said to the caller she was in the middle of something and would call her later. After, "Okay, bye," she clicked her phone shut.

Jenny crossed her legs, pulled her skirt over her knee, and calmly told the Mossad officers that she was extremely grateful for all they had done and would never forget they had stood up for her. Pause; deep breath. She was hoping they would understand that she had just gone through a life-changing experience, and as a result had decided her life would take a new course. She had devoted eleven years to the defence of Israel. Fruitless years, she regretted to say. Now it was over. She wouldn't undertake any new missions as a Mossad agent. She was over and done with pretence. She wouldn't fly to Arab countries ever again. Never again have sex with a man she felt nothing for. She asked them to get rid of the cameras and mikes they had installed at her place in Manhattan. She didn't care whether the men who had abducted her were honest-to-goodness mujahideen or common criminals. At the end of this speech, she asked whether they understood her position.

Hadara glanced at Javan, who nodded. Then she nodded.

"Can I ask you a few questions, Jenny?" Javan asked.

"Of course."

"Do you have any idea who these men are?"

"No."

"Do you have any notion where they kept you?"

"No, colonel."

"Okay. I asked you this a little while ago, but Steil was here then, so I'll ask you again. Would you be willing to tell us what happened, from the day you were abducted to yesterday?"

Jenny looked the man straight in the eye, considering the question, then said, "I will do this for you once. Tape it because this is the last time I talk about it."

Javan pulled out his tape recorder, pressed the record button, and placed it on the coffee table.

Jenny uncrossed her legs, sat back in the seat, laced her fingers, and provided a ten-minute, dispassionate story of her ordeal. Either remarkable self-control or a case of split personality. She finished. Javan nodded.

"So you couldn't recognize them."

"Exactly."

"Would you mind letting us keep your phone? We would like to see if we can find who the bastards are or where they kept you by tracing the phone calls they made."

Jenny nodded, walked over to the bedside table where her cell was, grabbed it, handed it to Javan, and returned to her seat.

"Well, I have no further questions. You, Hadara?"

"No, sir. I just want to tell Jenny that I can't put into words how happy I am that it all ended this way, and that I'm sure Mossad and the State of Israel set in great store what she has done."

"Thank you, dear Hadara. Now I have a question . . . May I?"

"Of course," Javan, with a nod.

"Were the bonds forged?"

"No. We considered it, but decided against it for two reasons. First, we didn't want to run the risk they would be able to detect a forgery. They could've said, 'Give us ten bonds. We want to check them out. In an hour go to the corner of so and so.' If they found the bonds were forged they would've killed you. Second, there was not enough time to do a good forgery."

"Then, to whom should I write a cheque for ten million?"

THE PROFESSOR

The people who best knew Steil and Plotzher – Fidelia, Sam's wife, Tony Soto, and Imlatinex's staff – had discerned that, for a couple of weeks, both men had been acting strangely. Now they were under the impression that they had returned to normal. Appearances, however, were deceiving.

The only people for whom life was now glorious were Jenny and Tico. All the others had bees in their bonnets.

The evening Jenny returned to New York, her building's doorman and two residents going out had their suspicions confirmed when she entered the foyer holding hands with Tico. The news spread like wildfire through the building. That night the couple reached previously unexplored heights when they had sex. The next few days she took her lover to the restaurants, boutiques, and other places that in the past had been off limits to him. When they flew to Miami, the Puerto Rican sat alongside her in first class.

Valerio de Alba and Chris Dawson returned to the rented house on Halsey Avenue. Earlier, they had spent ten full hours over the course of two days wiping their fingerprints off every surface, so now, without taking their gloves off, they changed clothes, picked up already packed suitcases, turned off the lights, and drove the Cadillac

to Cornwall. The next morning the Peruvian contacted Tommy
Jones, paid him five Cs, and cuddling the bulky duffel bag made it
back to Hogansburg, New York, in the trunk of Tommy's Buick.
Chris crossed the border in his car, picked up his boyfriend, and drove
to Brooklyn. There he sold the Cadillac and purchased a cobalt-blue
2001 Lincoln Continental. They drove it down U.S. 1 stopping every
time they felt like it – to rest, eat, or visit a resort – until they reached
Miami Beach. They felt no pangs of conscience; Jenny *had* to be well.
They had done a not-too-bad bad thing. Both knew, however, that
the curtain wouldn't descend until the Professor gave them five
million greenbacks in exchange for the bonds. The mysterious character had promised to meet them in Miami Beach once "the operation" had been successfully completed. Chris and Valerio spent many
hours speculating how soon that would take place. They agreed on
three things about the Professor: he was gay, had a brilliant mind,
and had access to the most private details of Jenny Scheindlin's life.

Freed of managerial duties, Sam Plotzher returned to pacing the
warehouse up and down at full steam supervising everything, from
the daily recharging of forklift batteries to taking inventory. He
smiled so often that staff wondered whether the old man had discovered Cialis and was screwing a stripper. Sam had a new concern,
though. In addition to Jenny, Arab terrorists might have others in
his immediate circle in their crosshairs. Having succeeded on their
first try, they could take a shot at kidnapping him next, or his wife,
or Jenny a second time, or burn the warehouse to the ground. That
line of thought prompted him to keep a fully loaded Colt .45 auto-
matic pistol in the glove compartment of his car. Over the phone,
Javan had told Sam they would fly from New York to Miami before
returning to Tel Aviv. Sam anxiously waited for his colleagues to have
a brainstorming session on security measures.

The Mossad agents sent Jenny's cell phone to Tel Aviv in the
Toronto Consulate's diplomatic bag and, while waiting for the report,

spent much of the next three days pacing Taylor Creek's trails along both banks of the stream, searching the public washrooms, examining trash cans. They also drove around the neighbouring streets to see if any had predominantly Arab residents, a mosque, or businesses advertising in Arabic. All in vain. On the fourth day, Mossad's report confirmed their suspicions: after the abduction, each call had been made from a different prepaid cell phone purchased in Toronto, probably under false names, and most likely discarded minutes after each call.

The following morning both officers flew to New York to interview Jenny's former modelling agent. They compiled lists of the fashion shows she had attended in Arab cities in the last five years, the hotels where she had stayed, and the limousine companies from which she had rented. At the end, they faxed seven pages to headquarters asking to cross-reference their findings with the lists of known terrorists, their places of work and residence, to see if there was any link. The next day they boarded a plane to Miami.

Work kept the kidnapping on Elliot's backburner on weekdays, but in the evenings and on weekends he kept asking himself whether he knew who the kidnappers were. Was sitting on his hands the right thing to do now? Of course not. Should he go to the police, reveal all, and let them investigate the two fashionistas? Would it be fair to cast suspicion on two individuals who might well be guiltless? Certainly not. But if they were the kidnappers, should he let them get away with it? Wasn't that cowardice? His anxiety kept him awake at night.

At last he made up his mind, called Tony Soto, and asked the ex-cop whether they could meet that evening after work at the corner of 2nd Street and Flagler. Tony said he could, around six.

Elliot left his car at a parking lot and strolled to the agreed meeting place, contemplating the blue sky, enjoying the warm weather, and wondering what the temperature in Toronto would be. Now he'd decided to act, he felt calmer. He spotted Tony and was happy to see that he had lost some more pounds.

After the handshakes, Elliot, unsure where to go, snuck a quick look around.

"Where can we talk in private?"

Tony had been on the wagon for five weeks, but he was unsure about his willpower; wasn't ready to test it in a bar. The smell of the frosty one, seeing others cracking suds. Not yet, no.

"There's a Catholic church two blocks from here."

"Let's go."

They chose a pew, as far away as possible from all six parishioners scattered around the nave. With the smell of burnt candlewick and wax in his nostrils, and under the gaze of life-sized images of saints, Elliot addressed the ex-cop.

"Tony, I have a problem."

"Who doesn't?"

"No, listen. This problem is . . . how can I put it? I think 'strange' cuts it. There are two guys I know a little who may have committed a very serious crime with a big payoff. Then again, they may be totally in the clear, have nothing to do with it. I think people in law enforcement call the evidence I have circumstantial. Oh, boy, you can't imagine how circumstantial it is!"

"Are these the two queers you wanted me to scope out for you?"

"Yes."

"What's the crime?"

"I can't tell you that."

This made Tony tilt his head, raise his eyebrows, and pull down the corners of his mouth.

"Okay," he said. "How can I help?"

Elliot took a deep breath. "Could you find out for me whether they are here in Miami Beach? If they are, I want to know if they still live at the same address where they've lived for years or somewhere else, and anything else you can find out without pumping their friends or neighbours. It's important they don't know someone is asking questions about them."

"I can do that; piece of cake. But why are you doing this?"

Elliot took a second deep breath but remained silent, considering his response.

"I mean," Tony went on, "you are not a cop, so the crime must have something to do with you, or Fidelia, or some other person you know and like, right?"

"The victim . . . is someone I know."

"And you can't say who?"

"Tony, I'm sorry. If you need to know to check out these two guys –"

"No, no, not at all, Teach. I'm just curious, and trying to keep my nose clean, because, you know, if the crime is murder, that's –"

"Not a murder. The victim's fine, now. Wasn't fine for a couple of weeks, but she's fine now."

The personal pronoun made Tony's mental wheels turn. "So, if she's fine now, wasn't fine for a couple of weeks, and it's a very serious crime with a big payoff, must've been a kidnapping, right?"

The speed with which Tony made the connection took Elliot by surprise. He realized that for years he had underestimated his former pupil's intelligence and the experience he'd gained from seventeen years in the force.

His friend's amazed look told Tony he was right.

"My wife talks to Fidelia on the phone almost daily, so I know it's not her. Is this kidnapped woman a babe you have on the side?"

Elliot doubled over, cackled, and clapped his hands several times. His overreaction was typically Cuban but it embarrassed Tony. Physically, Cuban hysterics equal a three-minute round in a boxing fight.

"Get a grip. This is a church, for Christ's sake."

Elliot controlled himself. "No, Tony, I don't have a babe on the side," still smiling. "Oh, my God, I needed that."

Grinning, Tony said, "Okay. Don't confirm, don't deny. I just wanted to be sure the fags hadn't killed anyone."

"I don't even know if they are the kidnappers, and please don't call them fags, Tony," now serious again.

"Oh, yeah, political correctness. Had forgotten about it. Nigger, fag, and butch are out; African-American, gay, and lesbian are in. But in street talk, homos are queers, faggots, fairies, fruits; take your pick."

"Tony, they are people. In Cuba I was reluctant to befriend or talk to *maricones*. My mom, though, had a bad case of hypertension, died from it in fact; stroke, boom, gone."

"Tough break. But what that's got to do –"

"Getting there. The family doctor who took her blood pressure, wrote prescriptions, and shot the breeze with her two or three times a week was a full-fledged *maricón;* the limp-wrist, plucked eyebrows, hip-swinging-walk kind. And this dude took care of my mother like she was his mother. He made me realize I was wrong. He was a fine man, caring, supportive –"

"Man?"

"Uh, I don't know; okay, person. Nowadays I discriminate against certain people. Everybody discriminates against others: blacks, whites, the rich, the poor, young people, old people, every-fucking-body. What makes a difference is the basis on which you do it. It shouldn't be on the basis of sex, race, or religion. These days I discriminate on the basis of intelligence, how the person makes a living, whether we share tastes or not, that kind of thing. I'd rather befriend a decent gay man than a heterosexual drug pusher; I prefer dealing with an intelligent lesbian than a stupid broad. I don't like ballet or opera, so I don't run with that crowd. Catch my drift?"

"Yeah, you have your mentality, I have mine," holding up his hands to ward him off. "That's enough. Class is over, Teach." He placed his hands on his knees, getting ready to get up.

"I'm not lecturing you."

"Once a teacher, always a teacher."

"You mad at me?"

"No. And you know why? 'Cause you are a fucking liberal. That's why. That's what you are. You want a perfect world. Eternal bliss, no wars, no crime, everybody in white robes singing to the rising sun in the mornings. You are hopeless."

"No, not in robes. Stark naked everybody, to ogle the babes. But think about what I said. And try not to prejudge these two. They may be clean."

"Anything else?" getting to his feet.

"No," standing, too.

"Okay. I'll get back to you as soon as I find out."

"Good, give me a call, we'll meet somewhere. Now, let's get the hell out of here."

"Bad choice of words, Teach," heading for the exit.

Chris and Valerio were anxious to get it over with, to get back to enjoying the vibrant Miami Beach life they so loved. They hadn't the remotest idea of the day or time the Professor would send a letter, make a call, or, preferably, knock unannounced on their front door with five million bucks in tow. If the courier found the apartment empty, the phone went unanswered, or both were out when the person they had come to think of as their saviour paid a visit, the swap would be delayed. Most important of all, they were following instructions to keep the bonds in the apartment, and no way would they leave ten million dollars unguarded. When Valerio went to the barber, the supermarket, or the dry cleaners, Chris stayed at home. Whenever Chris went out, Valerio stayed behind. But after three stressful months in Toronto, and the huge anxiety of the final two weeks, they were aching to go out together to the new local bars and clubs, to hear the gossip, take saunas, visit the gym, browse new titles at a bookstore; in other words, to live their lives.

One of their favourite places was a hotel lounge in the Art Deco district. They would have a ball sipping *mojitos* and taking apart the funny people strolling along the sidewalk: paper-white, blue-veined geezers in funny hats. Middle-aged, thick-waisted men in beach clothes. Moustachioed Latin Americans, gold watches and bracelets on their hairy wrists, shirts unbuttoned for the world to envy their chains and medals, their women upstaging them with the earrings and ankle bracelets the machos refused to wear. Honeymooners hurrying to their hotel rooms. Spring chickens trying to attract attention by dying their hair five colours or showcasing their sculpted bodies in gauzy clothing.

Professional buggers were easy to identify: the swollen pecs and biceps, the see-through thong designed to show the pecker was for real, the deep tan, the designer sunglasses. Mostly, Valerio and Chris contemplated those guys much like they would a nice statue they weren't interested in buying, but, every now and then one of them couldn't take his eyes off a magnificent *hombre* cruising by. Valerio pretended not to notice if Chris seemed awestruck; Chris the same when Valerio appeared spellbound. Once in a while both lusted after the same man. When that happened, they forgivingly smiled at each other.

The couple was a little frustrated because, having shared everything for several years, the kidnapping had made them even closer, which was a cause for a celebration they couldn't yet have. Instead, planning and daydreaming about it was now their favourite evening pastime. Valerio needed a Peruvian passport, and to apply at the consulate in Miami he had to show a valid Peruvian National Identification. So first they would have to fly to Peru, get Valerio's birth certificate, apply for the PNI, and once it was issued, apply for a passport. How long would that take? A month or two, maybe just two weeks if palms were greased.

Then, where first? Milan or Paris? Monaco or Barcelona? They would go online and surf the stunning visual images and read the history and descriptions of cathedrals, museums, castles, restaurants, hotels, nightclubs, and spas. They visited the websites of Dior, Gautier, Lacroix, Givenchy, Ungaro, and Chanel, and on other evenings, they visited Italy online to see what Armani, Valentino, and Versace had been doing of late, or Spain to view the latest creations by Balenciaga, Pertegaz, and de la Prada. Each evening they came closer to the world they knew, loved, and hoped to spend the rest of their lives in.

"We have to be patient," Valerio, his Inca blood talking, following one of their wish-fulfillment fantasies.

"But it's been almost three weeks."

"No matter. We have what he needs; he'll come. We wait a month, two, three. He may be late for a reason. How many safe deposit boxes have you rented?"

"Val, I showed you the paperwork."

"I know, dear. I forgot."

"Nine."

"All at banks, right?"

"Yeah."

"You said not all are big."

"We have six big ones, two medium-sized, and a small one."

"How big is big?"

"Ten by ten by 21.5 inches," Chris said, gesturing the dimensions with his hands. "That's standard."

"How much cash does each one hold?"

"Depends on denomination. If all are C-notes, I guess a million fits in a big one. If it's in fifties, maybe two."

Valerio's eyes narrowed. "In the movies, bank clerks leave you alone when you go to that part where they have the safes."

"The vault."

"Right, the vault. But these days, with all the mini-cameras and stuff, I wonder if they are watching and taping what you stash there."

"I don't know. Maybe."

"That's why we'll put the money in attaché cases, so they can't see what we are putting there, right?"

"Right. But we measure them before buying. Some are too big, wouldn't fit."

Valerio nodded, his mind racing ahead. "With all the money laundering taking place here, the FBI may have forced the banks to install cameras and give them the videos every few days."

"It's possible."

"I don't like putting our money in bank safes."

"Me neither. I've been thinking about it. But where if not there?"

For half an hour they rethought alternatives they'd previously discarded: storage company; burying all of it, except five hundred thousand or so. Purchasing valuable paintings or jewels or investing in stocks was out of the question; no respectable art dealer or broker would accept hundreds of thousands of dollars in cash; one of them might even call the police. They reached the same conclusion they'd reached before: every other option seemed riskier than storing their money in the banks' safety-deposit boxes.

No fresh ideas emerged and they were silent for a few moments, listening to an unintelligible muddle of commercials, dialogues, and music from the neighbours' radios and TV sets. The smell of the sea they had missed so much in Toronto wafted into the apartment.

"I'm turning in," Chris said after a while. "You coming?"

"Nah, not sleepy. I'll watch a little TV."

"Good night, Val." Chris kissed Valerio good night.

"Good night, beautiful."

Hadara and Javan spent their first two days in Miami at the Israeli Consulate. On the first, they arranged by date all the receipts from hotels, planes, taxis, rentals, and other purchases, then prepared their expense report. Later, they had a long session with Sam Plotzher, during which Jenny's handler learned the few things Elliot didn't know had happened in New York and Toronto. Then Javan asked him whether he had come up with any clue as to what person or terrorist organization could have planned the abduction. Sam admitted he had nothing to go on. Then Hadara asked if he had any suggestions. The old man shook his head and expressed his fear that he or his wife might be the next targets of the radicals, or that they would bomb or torch the warehouse. He asked whether his Mossad colleagues believed the kidnappers were real mujahideen or a couple of hoodlums who'd figured out a way to make a lot of money.

"According to Jenny," Javan said, "the two men seemed intent on not inflicting more physical and psychological harm than was necessary; you know, bruises on her wrists and ankles, stress, and fear. That is what true mujahideen would do; the Qu'ran condemns sex outside marriage, and I suppose it condemns torturing women, although I'm not sure, as stoning adulteresses is allowed. But kidnappers may act in the same way for two different motives: lighter charges if they are caught, which is a pretty compelling reason, and so that Jenny could truthfully say over the phone, 'I'm okay. They haven't harmed me,' to reassure whoever was ransoming her that she was being treated well."

"But Tel Aviv says," Hadara interposed, "that no terrorist organization they are aware of has asked for ransom in unregistered Eurobonds. That indicates a financial savvy not typical of mujahideen."

"All of which means that at this point you don't know," Sam said. "I was hoping you knew, because that would help me decide how to plan ahead."

"May I advise something, Sam?" Javan asked.

"Sure."

"Step up whatever security you have at the warehouse; hire a couple of guards for the night shift –"

"Already done," the old man said, cutting him short and waving aside the advice. "Elliot had extra state-of-the-art cameras installed, plus bells and whistles. He also hired six guards for three eight-hour shifts. Plus the night watchman."

"That guy hits the ground running, doesn't he?" Hadara said, but it didn't sound like a compliment.

"He's good. We owe him," Javan muttered. Raising his voice a notch, "And you've probably taken care of your home, haven't you, Sam? Guards are not your style, but I bet you have burglar alarms on all the doors and windows and have warned Esther not to open the front door to strangers and to call you if anything outside looks suspicious, right?"

"Right."

"Are you carrying?" Hadara asked.

"I am," Sam said. "Legally. I have a permit."

"Then I can't think of anything else to recommend," said Javan.

On their second day in Miami, the Israeli officers drafted and typed a detailed report, saved it, and made copies on two CDs: Javan would take one to headquarters along with the original on the laptop. The second CD would be kept in the consulate's safe until he arrived safely. Then Hadara would receive a one-word email – *shmuz* – that meant she had to destroy the CD stored in the safe and fly back to Tel Aviv. It was a standard procedure followed since the beginning, back when even the carbon paper was kept in the safe for destruction: the senior officer returned first, the second-in-command remained abroad.

On the third day, they paid a visit to Jenny and Tico. As previously agreed over the phone, Jenny first thanked the private investigators for all their efforts and asked them to please convey her sincere appreciation for what the company had done for her to the manager of Greater Miami Security Services, and to please accept this (holding out an envelope) as a small token of her appreciation. Then she told the visitors that her life companion mixed wonderful pina coladas, would they like to try his version of the famous Puerto Rican cocktail? Of course they would, Javan said; Hadara smiled and nodded. Tico got to his feet in one swift motion and made for the kitchen.

Jenny kept her eyes on him until he disappeared behind the swing door, then produced a second envelope from under her loveseat's cushion and gave it to Javan.

"This is the ten-million bank draft made out to Kibbutz Lotan, as you asked."

"Thanks," Javan said, putting it in his pocket.

"The other has a twenty-thousand cheque payable to the bearer."

Javan's lips parted to say something.

"Hold it!" the model said. "It's not a payment. What you two and Elliot did for me is beyond any price. If I gave you guys all I have, I'd still be indebted. What would please me most is that you cash it, split it, and spend it as you deem best. A couple of weeks at Eilat, pay bills, whatever, but I don't know if Mossad's rules or ethics permit it. If not, give it to the widow of an agent, rip it up, burn it, whatever."

"How much did you give Elliot?" Hadara asked.

Jenny shook her head. "Nothing yet. Sam says if I give him money I should say it's a year-end bonus, and if it's a significant amount, spread it over two or three years. He says I don't know this guy, that if I send him a cheque he'll get mad at me. He's – oh, I can't figure Elliot. He's from another time."

"Or hasn't shed all the Communist indoctrination he got as a child," Javan said, with a smirk. "Or his ego is too big. He knows he's smart and efficient, he knows people know he's smart and efficient, but that's not enough for him. Maybe he needs people to think he's highly principled, a money-is-not-all-that-matters kind of guy. I wonder. As for your gift to us, we'll take it back and let the chief decide what to do with it. But let me make something clear." He paused and shot a glance at the kitchen door to make sure Tico was out of earshot. "We did our duty. You served Israel by doing undercover work for Mossad, so Mossad has to be there for you in your hour of need. We would've deserved the strongest criticism had we abandoned you, but we don't deserve praise for rescuing you."

Jenny took a deep breath. "Okay. Let's not argue. But when the mujahideen kidnapped me, I thought you couldn't move a finger for me. So glad I was wrong."

"We also are glad all turned out for the best," Javan said. "By the way, all the cameras and mikes at your New York place have been removed."

"Good. Thanks. I'll change the locks so your people can't barge in any time they feel like it."

All three smiled.

Hadara asked how she felt and Jenny said she was considering what to do in the short term and also completely re-examining what she wanted to do with the rest of her life. No decisions, just mulling things over. A few months in Europe visiting the places she loved or perhaps discovering China and India; opening a boutique in New York or cancelling that project and returning to Miami; getting married or keeping her relationship with Tico as it was; having a child or not. A few important decisions and many of no great concern.

Tico returned with the cocktails and for a quarter of an hour the two couples chatted and sipped their drinks. Then Javan and Hadara stood and bid them farewell.

The Israelis were leaving Jenny's condo when, at Imlatinex's warehouse, Elliot pressed his cell phone's end button and slipped it into its holster. Tony had called a minute earlier to report that Valerio de Alba and Chris Dawson returned to Miami on November 9 and were staying at the small apartment building on Lenox Avenue where they had lived for five years, same second-floor unit with a living room window facing the street. Lot of jerks there; drum sets, wannabe DJs, and common hogs. Not difficult to stakeout, should the need arise, Tony had said.

Elliot planted his elbows on his desk, his forehead resting on his fingertips, thumbs at his temples, and closed his eyes. The man in charge of accounts receivable and payable and the inventory specialist squinted at one another.

That Chris and Valerio had been in Toronto the night Jenny was kidnapped could be a coincidence, Elliot thought. She had gone there to attend a fashion show; Chris was a fashion photographer. It was possible. But he had spotted Valerio on Queen Street several days *after* the fashion show ended – a real fluke. Well, maybe the couple had decided to spend a few more days in Toronto. A second coincidence was also likely. However, their return to Miami Beach a mere ten days after Jenny was freed was a third. Scores of coincidences happen every day, granted. Some were stranger than others, though. And those three were intriguing.

The nine giant maids agreed to turn the mill of his mind a little faster.

Jenny had not been raped and these two men were gay. She had not been maltreated and he had witnessed how adoringly Valerio and Chris had cared for the model the night her mother was murdered. There had been two kidnappers in the video. Jenny had seen only two kidnappers. Aside from height and build, she couldn't provide descriptions because both had kept their faces covered and their hands gloved. He could understand why the kidnappers wore masks, but the sole reason for their wearing gloves all the time must have been to conceal their skin colour, because fingerprints could be wiped. If he remembered correctly, Chris was fair-skinned and blond, a type of Islamic male in short supply. The voice of the man he had negotiated with over the phone the night of the swap had an educated, American accent. Why hadn't he used a voice changer? Perhaps because he thought that Elliot, sitting behind the rental's wheel or walking along the bridge, couldn't record his voice; or because the damn thing was too bulky or had broken down. Whatever the cause, he had heard the man's real voice.

Pause.

Elliot pulled out his phone, speed-dialled Tony's number, and left the cubicle to not be overheard. The office staff watched him hurry out.

"What the fuck's going on?" Accounts said.

"Beats me," Inventory responded.

Tony answered the phone.

"How soon can you get me their phone numbers, no expense spared?"

"You mean the fags'?"

"Yep."

"No expense spared?"

"Yep."

"Cells or land line?"

"Preferably Chris's cell; land line if he doesn't have a cell."

"Four hours. A grand."

"Go for it."

"You making a date, Teach?"

"Fuck you."

Elliot heard Tony's raucous laughter before snapping the cell shut.

Chris's cell rang at 10:09.

"Hello?"

"Listen, I know you are McKenzie's brother," Tony said with a menacing tone. "You tell the sonofabitch he either pays me back tomorrow or I'll kick his –"

"Sorry, mister, I don't have any brothers," Chris interrupted. "You got the wrong number."

"Don't cut me off. I know you are his fucking brother! You tell him –"

"Told you, dude. Wrong number."

Chris clicked his cell shut.

Tony pressed the end button and looked at Elliot.

"Teach, you've paled."

Elliot took a deep breath. "Tony, I've opened a can of worms so big it would keep a hundred cops busy for a full month."

This seemed to impress the ex-cop. "Can I help you?"

"I don't know. I'll give you a call tomorrow, after I talk to Sam. Wait a moment. Can we get photos of these two?"

"Are you kidding me?"

"Well, can we?"

"It was the first thing I did when you called from New York."

"Really? Where did you get them?"

"Department of Highway Safety and Motor Vehicles."

"What?"

"Driver licence, dude."

"Wow. I had no idea."

"Cops have friends in all county and state government departments. You throw them a lifeline when they are swimming against the tide, they help you out when you need it."

"Excellent. Make copies but don't do anything else. Wait for my call. Is that clear?"

"You talk like a homicide lieutenant in a bad TV series."

"I may need your help, but I don't want to get you in trouble with the police. So, you sit tight until I call you."

Sam Plotzher arrived at Imlatinex a few minutes after eight a.m., one hour later than usual. The previous evening he had driven Javan and

Hadara to the airport, left the woman at a rental-car agency, and waited until the man checked in. He had gone to bed after midnight. The senior shareholder poked his head into the cubicle and said good morning. The staff responded but Elliot jumped to his feet and came out.

"Hey, Sam, I need a word," the Cuban said.

"Good morning, Elliot."

"Ah, sorry. Good morning, Sam. Let's go outside for a moment."

It was a brilliant morning and Elliot put on his shades.

"How you doing, Sam?"

"I'm doing fine, Elliot. What's the matter?"

The Cuban cleared his throat. "You know where Javan is staying?" trying to sound only mildly curious.

Sam glanced at his watch. "His plane will be landing in Tel Aviv in three or four hours."

"Oh, he left?"

"I drove him to the airport last night. Why? You wanted to have a word with him?"

Elliot shook his head. "No, no, I just thought maybe . . . I mean, he's a nice guy and I was thinking . . . of taking him to Versailles. You know, introduce him to Cuban cuisine."

"Oh," not fooled at all, sensing Elliot had to have a compelling reason to talk to the officer. "Well, you can take Hadara to Versailles; she's here."

"Oh? She's here? Well, I . . . don't think so. Not that I wouldn't take her, she's a fine lady, but she may think I'm coming on to her."

"Well, take Fidelia too . . . No, wait. Of course not. How would you introduce Hadara to Fidelia?"

"That's it; exactly."

"But if what you really want is to share something with Javan rather than introduce him to fried pork and black beans –"

"No! All I wanted was to take him out to dinner."

"Hadara could forward your message."

"C'mon, Sam," forced chuckle, "there's no message. I just wanted –"

"Yeah, I know, to take Javan to Versailles. You mind if I start working now?"

"Just a second. I also wanted to talk to you because I need help with a personal matter and I was thinking Tony could lend me a hand, but it would have to be during his regular working hours. And since you got him his job, I was wondering if you . . . could call your friend at GMSS and ask him to give Tony a few days of unpaid leave."

Sam frowned and stared at Steil.

"What?" the Cuban said, pretending to be puzzled.

"What's going on, Elliot?"

"Nothing. It's a personal thing I have to deal with."

Sam lowered his eyes to consider how best to word his answer. "Listen, Elliot, when you told me what happened during your trip to Cuba in 2002, I said that your private life is not my concern, except if what's going on has to do with the company, remember?"

"Yeah."

"Okay. Now, this thing you want Tony to help you with, has it to do with the company?"

"No, Sam."

"Okay. Then, no, I'm not calling GMSS to ask them to give Tony a leave of absence. You get a job, you stick with it unless you're sick, or if there's an emergency, like a relative dies and you take a day or two off."

"Fine. I'll hire someone else."

Both men spent the rest of the day feeling uncomfortable. Elliot had expected that what he had recently done for Jenny would make Sam amenable to any request he made, however bizarre. For his part,

Sam suspected the Cuban was keeping something about Jenny's abduction from him. Elliot's lie that he wanted to take Javan to dinner was in the same league with maintaining that the Earth was flat and lay on the back of a giant turtle that swam on a sea of milk. The thought that Elliot might think him too old to be involved didn't cross his mind.

At seven that evening, Tony parked his Chevy on Lenox Avenue, across the street from the two-storey concrete building, painted in bands of flamingo and passion-pink, where Valerio and Chris lived. Tony turned to his passenger and told him that the building had twelve apartments and that "the homos'" (an improvement, Elliot thought) was on the second floor, third window from the left.

Elliot nodded, taking in the dwarf palms and the shrubs in clay pots at the front. On this street fringing the Art Deco district, one- and two-storey homes built in the 1930s and 1940s predominated – half a million the cheapest, a few in the three-million range. Several were protected from curious eyes by tall well-trimmed hedges, others had landscaped front lawns and back patios. Apartment buildings were few, and it seemed none had more than twenty units. Nearby, at Flamingo Park and Alton Road, was a cluster of stores.

"You want to keep an eye on the homos, right?"

"Yeah."

"Okay. I have buddies that do a little snooping on the side. I checked with one of them about tonight. He charges fifty bucks an hour. He can be here at nine; has to leave at six. That's four-fifty."

"What about tomorrow?" Elliot asked.

"I'll call in sick."

"No, Tony. You go to work as usual, pick me up around five-thirty, and we take over from six to nine. But I need one or two guys here all day, from six a.m. to six p.m."

"Okay. Let me see."

It took Tony nine phone calls to find two cops willing to do two shifts, six a.m. to noon, noon to six p.m.

"That's settled," Tony said, shutting his cell. "Now, you tell me what my bulls should be on the alert for."

Elliot licked his lips. "I want them to take note of all their comings and goings, if they move packages, bags, or suitcases in and out, any visitors they have –"

"That's impossible. They can keep their eyes on the entrance, but there are twelve apartments there; you can't figure who is going to which apartment."

Elliot mulled that over. "True."

Tony shifted to better face Elliot. "Suppose the honeycakes do nothing suspicious for a week or two. How long can you keep this stakeout running on all cylinders, forking over twelve hundred dollars a day? I mean, Teach, you gotta consider your options, catch my meaning?"

Elliot nodded and scratched his right temple.

"At some point you gotta make a decision," the ex-cop went on. "You either walk into a police station and charge them with kidnapping, or you leave them alone. Simple as that."

"You're right, Tony. But let's give it a shot for a couple of days. Then I'll decide what to do. Now, do all these cops doing the stakeout have your cell number?"

"Of course."

"Ask them to call you the minute something strange happens."

"Define strange."

"I don't know. If it looks like they are moving out, or if they come out carrying suitcases. I want to know if they have a fight, give a party, buy a brand-new Lamborghini, dance naked in the middle of the street. You follow?"

"I do."

"Okay. Stay here until your friend comes at nine and call me a taxi. I'll be waiting on the corner of Alton Road and Eleventh."

"Will do."

When Elliot got home, Fidelia was taking a shower. He thrust his head into the bathroom, said hello, stripped to his underwear, put on a bathrobe, and sat down at his desk in the living room. From the numbers stored in the phone's memory, he chose that of Jenny's Miami condo and punched the call key.

"Hello."

"Tico?"

"Yes."

"Elliot, here."

"Hey, *cubano*, how are you?"

"I'm good, thanks. How are you?"

"Never better, *chico*. You want to talk to Jenny?"

"If she's available."

"Let me see."

The phone made a soft clatter as Tico put it down.

"Psst," Fidelia, from the bedroom's door, one hand on her waist, the other grasping the door frame.

Their hair dryer had conked out two days earlier, so the towel around her head meant she hadn't yet replaced it. The partially opened bathrobe suggested she had nothing else on, the pose and the look confirmed beyond a shadow of a doubt she felt like making love. His testicles contracted.

"Hi, Elliot, glad to hear from you." Jenny, in a pleased tone.

"Hi, boss. You sound in high spirits."

"I *am* in high spirits. And you are responsible for that."

"Well, glad to be of help. Listen, I . . . think it's time to give you a quick overview on how we are doing, and I was wondering if you could give me fifteen minutes of your time tomorrow morning."

"Sure. Would 10:00 a.m. be okay?"

"Ten's fine. See you then. Bye."

"Bye, Elliot."

He placed the cordless on its base.

"You take a shower, I'll soap your back," Fidelia, still in pose.

"My back? My back?"

"And maybe something else."

That same evening Jimmie Haskins – the first cop on the job – glanced at his watch the moment the thin man in the pinstriped suit got inside the apartment building. It read 10:14. The guy had got out of a Fort Lauderdale Yellow Cab, pulled out two roll-on cases from the back seat, and dragged them to the building's entrance.

Once in the foyer, the man pressed down the retractable handle of both pieces of luggage, grabbed the ordinary handles, and climbed the stairs to the second floor. In the hallway, he got his bearings from the metal numbers nailed to the nearest front doors, extracted the retractable handles, rolled the bags to apartment 8's front door, and pressed the buzzer.

Moments later, Chris peered through the door viewer. He saw a well-dressed guy in his mid-thirties with dark hair combed back, high-shine low-colour lipstick, traces of makeup on an otherwise unremarkable effeminate face. Wrong apartment, Chris reckoned before opening the door.

"Yes?"

"Good evening." The voice had a feminine cadence.

"Good evening. Can I help you?"

"I believe I have something for you," as he lowered his eyes to the carry-ons.

Chris's jaw dropped. He closed his mouth, moistened his lips with the tip of his tongue.

"Oh, my God. Val!"

"Yes, dear?"

"Come here, hurry! Please, come in, sir, come in."

The caller smiled and stepped into a sparsely furnished living room, pulling the roll-ons behind him. Chris closed the door. Valerio appeared and stared at the visitor. Who was this? Why the luggage?

"Val, meet the Professor," Chris, overcome with emotion.

"Is that what you call me?" noticeably pleased.

"Oh yes, you taught us everything we had to know to . . . successfully complete our . . . operation. You are the greatest professor I've ever had."

"Thank you."

The startled Valerio managed a shit-eating grin. He shook hands with the visitor and felt a surgical glove.

"Pleased to meet you, Professor," he said, glancing at the gloved hand.

"Yes, gloves," the Professor, with a fresh smile. "Fingerprints on the handles, Valerio," again pointing at the pieces of luggage. "As I told you many times, no single detail should be overlooked."

"Of course, of course. But please, sit down. It's such an honour to meet you at last," Valerio, waving the visitor to the couch. "Would you care for a glass of juice, tea, a drink maybe?"

The Professor raised his hand. "Thank you, dear friends, but no, I won't stay long. I'm in a hurry. Could you please bring the bonds?"

"Of course," Valerio said and hurried to the bedroom.

The visitor returned his eyes to Chris. "I know you two are deeply in love. But I guess this" – tapping the carry-ons – "will allow you to enjoy your affair even more, don't you think?" with a wink.

"Oh yes, we are very much in love . . . Sir?"

"I'm Eve to friends."

"We always suspected, Eve, that such a brilliant plan could only come from an extremely bright and bold gay mind. Like Alexander the Great, Julius Caesar –"

"Oh, please, stop it," patently pleased but dismissing the compliment with a wave. "The idea was mine and I trained you for it, but *you two* executed the plan without a glitch. You chose perfect places to keep the woman and make the swap. So, let's split the merit fifty-fifty."

"That'll do. We are so grateful that you chose us for this venture, and that no one was harmed and we made so much money."

"Thank you, Chris. Remember my first letter? It said that at some point you would consider that day the best in your lives, remember?"

"Oh, yes. How could we forget?"

Valerio returned with the black leather duffel bag and placed it at the feet of the visitor. "There you are, Professor."

"Thank you, Valerio. There's two and a half million dollars in each of these two cases," patting the roll-ons' handles. "You may want to count it, but it would take hours and I can't wait. I assure you it's all there. Will you take my word for it?"

"Of course we will," Chris said. Valerio nodded.

"Now, I want you to take either one, Valerio. You take the other, Chris. Give me space to open this and see what company issued the bonds. Meanwhile, you take a peek at your cash, okay?"

"Okay," Valerio said.

The couple reached for their roll-ons and stood back a few paces. The visitor placed the duffel bag on the coffee table. Valerio, surfing a gigantic wave of happiness, bent over and started unzipping his piece. Just as delirious, Chris knelt on the floor and did the same.

The Professor pulled out a Walther P22 semi-automatic with a silencer from a shoulder holster and shot Valerio first. The bullet went in through the right ear and wreaked havoc in the brain before getting stuck in the left temporal bone. The shooter swung to Chris, who was stunned to the point he couldn't think. The slug the American caught in his lower jaw perforated his neck in its downward trajectory. The visitor gave a step forward, took careful aim, and put a third bullet in Chris's temple, and a fourth in Valerio's. Both men collapsed to the floor. The Professor then drew close and shot each in the heart.

Hadara took a step back and watched the spreading pools of blood until all movement ceased. From the roll-on Valerio had chosen, she pulled a cheap cotton tote bag and a flashlight from an external pocket, placed the gun in the tote, and put it in the duffel bag with the bonds. Then she turned on the flashlight and, in less than a minute, recovered and pocketed five of the six casings; locating the last one took her almost eight minutes. Before opening the front door she took a deep breath, inspected the cheap lock and unlatched it with one quick twist of the wrist. She went out and closed the door behind her.

Jimmie Haskins found it strange that the same taxi that had dropped off the man in the pinstriped suit returned to the building and waited six minutes until he came out with only one piece of luggage. But as he wasn't one of the fags under observation, Jimmy was unconcerned. His watch read 10:35.

The décor of Jenny's Miami condo was the polar opposite of her Manhattan apartment's. Here, ultra-ultra reigned. The two Italian benches in cherry with curved backrests and padded seats appeared uncomfortable, so Elliot sat down on the leather chaise longue. Jenny and Tico chose armchairs. The oak coffee tables were extra-low; the hanging lamps had multi-coloured blown-glass stems. A cabinet crafted in black ash with mother-of-pearl details caught the Cuban's eye.

Elliot reckoned that the antiques in the New York condo had to be considerably more valuable, but what Jenny had chosen for her second home wasn't cheap. Judging by what he had seen online a year or so earlier, the day Fidelia had tried to convince him to buy modern furniture for his apartment, the cabinet's price tag was probably five thousand dollars, the Italian benches ten thousand each.

"Forget it," he had told Fidelia. On the subject of interior design, as on many others, Elliot was neither a traditionalist nor a modernist, but he preferred Jenny's New York antiques to this avant-gardism.

Elliot had planned to tell Tico he needed to talk to Jenny alone about confidential business deals, but following a cup of espresso and a five-minute chat, the Puerto Rican, not wanting to abuse his new status, asked to be excused for he had things to take care of. Jenny gave him a loving smile. Then Elliot spread charts and reports on the coffee table, and for around twenty minutes updated Jenny on sales, margins, profit-and-loss statements, taxes, and other company matters that would serve as a peg on which to hang the questions he hoped he could ask.

"And that's it, Jenny. Any questions?"

"No, Elliot. You say the company is doing fine, I believe you. I trusted you in the past; now I trust you even more."

"Your father liked to say, 'Trust is good, control is better.'"

"Yeah, I know. Some exceptions apply, though."

Elliot thought Jenny looked stunning in the simple white cotton blouse, navy-blue shorts, and flip-flops she was wearing. The kind of woman that looks fantastic even in rags. She was approaching the years at which, in his opinion, female magnetism peaks – the mid-thirties.

"Before I learned you had a degree in management, I thought all this was mumbo-jumbo to you."

"It is, it is," she said with a dazzling smile. "My degree is in fashion merchandising management, not trading. I learned a little about accounting, but most of these things you talk about are Greek to me."

"Fashion," said Elliot, seizing the genie's bottle, getting ready to uncork it. "I haven't told you that, because you were a fashion model, I kinda took an interest in fashion and fashionistas, read a little about your line of work, surfed the net –"

"Really?"

"Really."

"That's sweet of you, Elliot," crossing her legs.

"No. I was trying to learn a little about a world I was perfectly ignorant of. It made me sort of reconsider what I thought about models and gay people. I thought all models were superficial and hedonistic and sluttish. Gay men seemed all that to me, and incapable of being supportive and caring. I know there may be sluttish models, but you and other models are fine people. And there may be callous and unhelpful gay men, but there are very nice people among them, like those two friends of yours that were there for you that . . . horrible night when your mom . . ."

"Oh." Her eyes clouded.

"True friends, those two," getting out of there fast. "They came the minute you said you needed them. I don't remember their names."

"Chris Dawson and Valerio . . . his last name was . . . doesn't come to mind. I think he was Ecuadorian or Peruvian. Not sure."

"Yeah, he looked Indian. I saw him in Toronto, you know? Or a man who looked like him."

"You saw him?" with a frown.

"I did."

She uncrossed her legs, leaned forward. "You talked to him?"

"No, no. He was across the street, going into a subway station."

Jenny raised her eyebrows, wondering. "Well, maybe he relocated and –"

She paused mid-sentence. A voice saying, *Would you like a cup of chamomile tea, darling?* An identical voice ordering her, *You climb the steps to the next landing. I'll be watching you.* The Spanish-accented English. The voice saying, *Zionist bitch.*

Jenny paled and drew a sharp breath. Shocked, her unseeing gaze went to the vast expanse of sea and sky that filled the floor-to-ceiling window. Valerio? Had Valerio kidnapped her?

Further confirmation was unnecessary. "Jenny, look at me," Elliot said.

She returned her dazed eyes to the Cuban.

"Let me come clean with you. I invented an excuse to come here today because I wanted to tell you that in Toronto I bumped into a man who was Valerio's spitting image. I wasn't sure if it was him or his double. Now I *know* it was Valerio. I find it very strange that he was in Toronto when you were abducted. Knowing that, do you remember anything to indicate he was one of your two kidnappers?"

She shook her head in incomprehension, not denial. "I can't believe it. Why?"

"Jenny, do you remember anything that would prove he was in on it?"

"Something in the man's voice."

"What man?"

"The man who tied the rope around my waist that last night. He gave me instructions. His voice sounded familiar. No, not just the voice; the voice *and* the accent. I spent hundreds of hours with Chris and Valerio here in Miami; they were my closest friends. I remember their voices. That night I was terrified and couldn't place it, but now – if you saw Valerio in Toronto, I think –"

"He did it."

"He did it, Elliot?"

"He and Chris."

"Chris too?" her face a study in amazement. Their snickering at her nakedness resurfaced.

"Yes, Chris too."

"This is unbelievable. How do you know?"

"Because I checked. They live together. They left Miami seven months ago, saying they would spend the summer in New York."

"Oh, my God."

"They kept their faces covered and their hands gloved all the time because they didn't want you to identify them. That explains why they never spoke to you until the last night."

Nothing was said for a few moments. Both minds raced as they stared into each other's eyes.

"The first thing I feared when I was kidnapped was being raped, but of course, they are gay . . ." harking back to the first night. "Oh, my God. The Qu'ran. The clothes, the *kaffiyeh*. There was no Islamic Army. It was a charade." Now her face flushed. "But if they posed as mujahideen . . . They knew I was an Israeli intelligence agent. How could they? The fucking fags." Burning rage was consuming her now. "The fucking fags!" shrieking.

Elliot frowned. Had he heard it right? Intelligence agent? Tico came running into the living room.

"What's the matter, Jenny?"

Elliot got to his feet. "Tico, please, it's a confidential business matter. She's angry about a deal that went wrong. I need privacy here, please."

The Puerto Rican turned to the woman. "Jenny?"

She took a deep breath, nodded, shot a downcast glance at her lover. "Yes, Tico, it's a business matter, and we need to sort things out. Please, darling, give us a minute."

Tico turned to Elliot. "Easy does it, okay?"

"Okay, Tico."

Without taking his eyes from Jenny, Tico backed out of the living room, then disappeared.

"Start at the beginning, Elliot, please."

Speaking in a quiet voice, the Cuban came clean. He had been completely clueless about who the kidnappers were before accidentally spotting Valerio. He recounted the lost luggage incident and the shopping at the Bay. That same evening, fearing he may have bumped into Valerio's spitting image, he had called a friend in Miami, an ex-cop, and asked him to find out whether Valerio was here. His suspicions grew when this friend reported that Chris and Valerio had gone to New York months earlier but said they would be returning to Miami for the winter. However, all this was circumstantial, he couldn't be completely sure that Chris and Valerio were the kidnappers, so he had kept it all from Javan and Hadara in case the gay couple had nothing to do with the abduction. Eventually his update reached the previous evening.

"There's a man keeping an eye on the place where they live," wrapping it up. "I'll get a call the minute one of them, or both, leaves the apartment. We can go to the cops now, have them charged with kidnapping and maybe recover the bonds. I know a guy with the Bureau. What do you say we give him a call?"

At which point Elliot realized she wasn't listening.

"Jenny?"

"Yes?"

"I was saying I propose calling a guy I know at the FBI, tell him all that happened –"

"I heard you. Give me a moment, okay? I'm thinking."

For over a minute she considered repercussions. Elliot watched her. Anger made her lose her attractiveness. It peaked when she spoke softly and smiled.

"I think," she said at last, "we should first tell Hadara and Javan, ask for their advice, because, you know, they came here thinking my kidnapping had to do with the Arab-Israeli standoff and now it turns out it's two sons of bitches wanting my money. But if we go to the police, or the FBI, we have to tell the whole story. I mean, we can't say you rescued me all by yourself. They'll ask where you got the ten million to buy the bonds, where you bought the bonds. Can you lie through your teeth about that?"

"No, Jenny," shaking his head for emphasis, "we have to tell the cops everything. I don't know how all this squares, but Javan and

Hadara told me they were here because you were snitching on Palestinian diamond smugglers. Now you say they came thinking that your kidnapping had to do with the Arab-Israeli conflict. A minute ago, you asked how Chris and Valerio knew that you are an Israeli intelligence agent. Well, are you a police snitch or a spy?"

Jenny took her third deep breath and exhaled hard before saying, "Elliot, please, don't ask questions I can't answer truthfully. I don't want to lie to you. I love you almost like I love Sam; like an uncle. But Sam has been part of my life since I was born. You earned that love overnight, by risking your life for me. You didn't know if the kidnappers would kill you and take the bonds, but you went ahead. And thanks to you and to the fact that I'll never forget Valerio's voice that night, now we know who did it. But because I love you as if you were my own flesh and blood, I ask you, please Elliot, please; let it be."

"I can't believe you're saying that. You want them to go unpunished? Lose ten million dollars?"

"No, no, that's not what I mean. What I mean is you've done a lot. Thanks to you we know who did it. Now, let me talk to Javan and Hadara about how to deal with them."

"Javan flew back to Israel."

"And Hadara?"

"According to Sam she was still here yesterday. Today, I don't know."

"Okay. I'll find out. If she's here, I'll tell her what you've found out. Elliot, believe me, this is a very delicate situation. If the police learn that instead of calling them when I was abducted, Sam called Israel, and Javan and Hadara flew to the rescue, relations between Israel, the U.S., and Canada would suffer. Israelis conducting a kidnapping investigation on their own, without informing the authorities? That would be a scandal. Do you understand that?"

"Yeah. I hadn't thought about that."

"Tell you what I'll do. I'll see if Hadara is still in Miami. If she's here, I'll tell her the whole story and ask her how she thinks we should deal with Chris and Valerio. She may want to talk to you personally. You would tell her everything like you just told me, right?"

"Totally."

"Okay. I have your numbers. I'll call you as soon as I get an answer from her."

"All right," picking up the charts and reports from the coffee table.

"And from the bottom of my heart, thank you, Uncle Elliot."

An hour later, at his apartment, Elliot set his laptop to hibernating mode and pushed himself out of the desk's kneehole. He had learned from Wikipedia that *ha Mosad le-Modi'in ule-Tafkidim Meyukhadim*, The Institute for Intelligence and Special Operations in English, often referred to as the Mossad, meaning the Institute, was Israel's main intelligence agency. There were also Aman (military intelligence), Shin Bet (internal security), and enigmatic-sounding "other agencies." He also learned that in the past Israeli spymasters had been in serious trouble with the governments of the U.S. and Canada. The whole world knew that in the 1980s they recruited a U.S. Navy intelligence agent who had passed secrets until he was caught and sentenced to life in prison. It was also public that, in the 1970s, the Israeli assassins who murdered Arab assassins (including a case of mistaken identity) in Europe and Jordan had carried fake Canadian passports. The sneaking suspicion they had executed a Canadian scientist working on a supergun for Iraq had surfaced too. Other embarrassing incidents may have not been made public, Elliot thought. So, Jenny was right. Should it be known that two Israeli intelligence officers and a dim-witted Cuban had conducted investigations in Miami and New York, behind the back of the rightful law-enforcement agencies, before orchestrating the rescue of Jenny Scheindlin in Toronto, diplomatic fallout would be unavoidable. He risked being tried and sentenced to prison, or, as a U.S. resident, getting deported.

Elliot felt certain that Jenny Scheindlin had been, or still was, a spy, that Sam Plotzher collaborated with her, and that he himself, to put it mildly, was a world-class shit-eater. Was he? Maybe a wicked witch had put a curse on him, because every few years he was shaken to the core by people trying to assassinate him or involve him in thefts, contraband, espionage operations, and now a kidnapping. But as he didn't believe in the supernatural, the most probable explanation was he had been a victim of circumstance. Not sure of that, either. He could have rejected the offer to be smuggled out of Cuba, turned down the chance to steal cars and deliver illicitly imported CFCs, declined to collaborate with the FBI, refused to work together with the Israelis in Jenny's rescue, so almost certainly he was stupid to the bone.

Was Imlatinex a front for Mossad? Had Ruben Scheindlin been a spy too? Who could imagine that a young, beautiful, multi-millionaire woman is a spy? It was unbelievable. Was Jenny crazy? And where did all this leave him? What should he do next? After a few minutes he concluded he should move on. Jenny was safe now, and whatever she and her colleagues wanted to do concerning Chris Dawson and Valerio de Alba wasn't his concern.

The cell vibrated on his waistline.

"Hello."

"Hi, Steil," Hadara's contralto voice.

"Oh, hi, Hadara."

"Listen, I'm with a mutual friend. She wants me to hear a very funny story you told her. I've had a lousy morning and would love to laugh my ass off. Could you join us today? Any time that's convenient to you?"

"Ah, you know, ah, I have to go to the warehouse now. But if Jenny tells you the story exactly like I told it to her, I'm sure you'll bust a gut."

"Nah. C'mon. You are the funniest guy in Miami. After work, maybe?"

Elliot remembered he had promised Jenny to tell Hadara the whole megillah. But he had things to do at Imlatinex, and later, at six, he had to meet with Tony Soto across the street from where Chris and Valerio lived.

"Okay. Where are you staying?"

"The Port of Miami Holiday Inn. On Biscayne Boulevard. Room 508."

"Does nine-thirty work for you?" jotting down *HInn, BysB, 508.*

"Sure."

"I would like Jenny to be there too, if possible."

"Hold on."

A few seconds.

"She'll be there."

Hadara clicked her cell shut and stared at Jenny.

"I'm sorry, Hadara," the model said, for the third time.

"I understand. You were overwhelmed. Maybe I would've said the same things."

They were in Hadara's hotel room, sitting on white plastic chairs, forearms resting on a matching plastic table. Jenny was wearing a multi-hued, bare-shouldered, ankle-length beach dress that contrasted sharply with Hadara's no-nonsense white jacket over a pink dress shirt and jeans. Jenny wore leather sandals; Hadara, moccasins.

"Can't I tell him I was confused?"

"No. Steil's too smart for that. Now he knows."

"So, how can we contain this?"

"Let me think; give me a moment."

Jenny's tale of the Cuban's findings had tested Hadara's self-control to the limit. Fortunately, the revelation required her to act amazed, so she had gaped at the model, interjected questions like, "But who are these guys? When did you meet them?" Now, staring at the table-top, Hadara realized that she needed much more than a moment to consider her options, but she had only a minute or less to check out the angles. She distinctly remembered the dark Mercury clunker parked on the other side of the street from Chris and Valerio's apartment building.

Three whole years of meticulous planning put in jeopardy by the concatenation of several strokes of incredible rotten luck: one, a missing carry-on had, two, made them go to a store, three, whose nearest exit to their hotel led to a street with, four, a pedestrian light they had to wait at and, five, the final, mind-boggling coincidence that, the very minute and second they stood there, Steil had spotted the Peruvian. What were the chances? And why hadn't she seen the fucking Indian? What was he doing there? She'd never know. Had Elliot told her then and there, she would have been forewarned. But the loathsome Cuban had kept it to himself! Even worse, he'd launched an investigation of his own, the sonofabitch!

To top it all, Chris, the stupid fairy, had forgotten to bring the voice changer to the swap. She couldn't believe her ears that night when, sitting with Javan in the Chrysler, she had heard his real voice. According to Jenny, Elliot only felt sure he knew who the kidnappers were when his mysterious friend, a former cop, called Chris and the Cuban heard his voice for the second time. Had the godforsaken faggot taken the voice changer to the swap, Elliot wouldn't now be raising hell.

The only two men Hadara really hated – her father, for raping her at twelve, and her husband, for trying to sodomize her at twenty – had disappeared from her life many years earlier. Her mother had had the good sense to kick the scumbag out the day she told her; three months later, mother and daughter had relocated to Israel. Completely traumatized by the rape, Hadara had abstained from sex until, upon successfully completing her masters at Tel Aviv University, Security Studies Program, she got married. On the wedding night, the seemingly courteous and harmless Israeli Army captain had tried to overcome his erectile dysfunction by forcing a thick, eight-inch-long dildo into her anus. She'd smashed a vase on his head and started divorce proceedings three days after tying the knot. Now, for completely different but equally frustrating reasons, she was considering adding Elliot Steil to her short list of loathed men.

On her return to Miami she had acted quickly and decisively. That gave her the upper hand. She had scouted Chris and Valerio's apartment building five nights earlier to be sure there were no security cameras. The casings and the gun were stuck in the cold muck at the bottom of the Port of Miami. Dressed as and acting the part of an effeminate gay man, she had driven her rental to Ft. Lauderdale's airport, taken a taxi back to Miami Beach, returned to Ft. Lauderdale in the same cab, and driven the rental back to her Miami hotel. The cheap carry-ons and the packages of bond paper in them were untraceable. She hadn't left a fingerprint anywhere. Whoever had stood watch would report that the previous night, at a quarter past ten, a queer thin man of average height hauling two carry-ons had arrived in a taxi, licence plate so-and-so, and entered the apartment building; but from the street he couldn't determine which apartment she had called in on. The lookout could add that half an hour later the same taxi picked up the guy, this time carrying a duffel bag. But how many people had gone in and out of the building that evening? A dozen? Two dozen? Hadara felt sure that getting tracked down wasn't one of her worries. Her useful idiots had nothing to say and the bonds were safe.

Raising her head she searched Jenny's eyes. "You did great when you mentioned the political consequences if this whole shebang were on everyone's tongue. What did he say?"

"He said he hadn't thought about it."

"Probably. Tonight I'll talk some more about that and ask him, as a favour, to keep his mouth shut. Concerning what happened after the rescue, tell him that we begged you – beg, it's important you say beg – we begged you to go along with the police-informer story. Give it to him straight. He's not stupid. He'll realize we couldn't let him know you were an agent. Make it clear that you are now over and done with us. He did what he did for you because he feels he owes your dad. He wouldn't deliberately harm you, so he'll probably keep quiet."

"Okay, let's hope that takes care of Elliot. Now, what about these two. You think we can recover the bonds?"

"Well, you said Steil's staking them out, so . . ."

"He didn't use that word. He said a man's keeping watch and he'll get a call the minute one of them, or both, comes out."

"Good. You know what? When I met Steil he seemed a little bit difficult to get along with. But he's proven to be quite a stand-up guy."

"Oh, Hadara, he's great. Dad liked him a lot."

"I'm sure he did. Now that we know where the perps are, we stand a very good chance of recovering the bonds. They may get away with the abduction because we can't accuse them, but most certainly we can try to recover the bonds."

"You're right," Jenny said. "Now let's talk about what we'll tell him tonight."

At 4:35 Elliot's phone vibrated. He left the cubicle before answering.

"Hello."

"Hi, buddy."

"Hi, Tony. Give me news."

"Well, they haven't gone out."

Elliot frowned. "Isn't that strange?"

"Strange? Why? They have all the food and lube they need, why should they go out?"

Elliot chuckled. "Jeez, dude, you are so 1950s."

"Yeah, yeah. See you there at six. And bring the dough for my bulls, okay?"

"Sure. I'll run to the bank and get a couple of thousand."

"Good. I'll pay them tomorrow. Tonight I'll keep watch until midnight."

"Why's that?"

"Only guy available can't be there before twelve."

"Oh, okay. See you at six, then."

Elliot closed Tony's passenger door at 6:22.

"What's up?"

"Nothing. They are holed up."

Pause.

"If they took off in the wee hours, how can we be sure your friend wasn't having a siesta?"

"Elliot, for Christ's sake. We can't be sure we'll be alive tomorrow. But these are trained cops doing a little overtime. They are used to supervision; they know that if I, or the client, catch them snoozing, they won't be making green stuff from me any more."

This failed to relieve Elliot's worries, but he grasped it would be useless to keep arguing. He stared at the building in silence.

"Cat got your tongue?" Tony said.

"I was thinking . . ." returning to the here and now, "how coincidences change lives."

"Oh, my God, another philosophy lesson?"

Elliot smiled, racked his brain for a few moments searching for a good example.

"Correct me if I'm wrong. One day, on a Sunday morning, having nothing better to do, you drove to the beach to swim a little and see if you scammed a babe, right?"

"Right, but I did that a hundred times, not one day."

"Okay, Don Juan. But on this particular day you spotted a woman, approached her, introduced yourself, asked her for a date. Today she's your wife, you have two children with her, you've been with her – how many? Thirteen years?"

"Fourteen. But what's your frigging point, Elliot?"

"My point is neither you nor she had any idea, any idea at all, that by going to Miami Beach that day at that time you'd meet, get hitched, have kids. Had you or Lidia gone anywhere else that day, chances are you would've never met. Sheer coincidence changed your lives, right or wrong?"

"Right. But that sort of thing happens a million times every day, everywhere."

"True. But not only do people meet people. Think of all those who are still alive because on a certain day they missed a plane that crashed and all passengers died. Think of nine-eleven. Guys who overslept, caught a cold, or had to take their wives to the hospital at seven because they went into labour. All those that for any unforeseeable reason didn't go to their office at the World Trade Center."

"So?"

"Nothing. You asked what I was thinking. That's what."

Tony sighed hard to show exasperation. "Okay, okay. Now I'm supposed to have learned something from that, right?"

"Maybe. I don't know."

"Oh, c'mon, what's the lesson, Teacher?"

"No lesson. Just a thought. But we are sitting here because of a coincidence."

"Oh, now I get it. You met these two at the beach; one slathering Coppertone on the other."

Elliot chuckled, then pulled out an envelope from his breast pocket.

"Here's two thousand. I'm going home to rest. Gotta be somewhere else later."

Starting at when and where he had met Chris and Valerio, Elliot finished his story at 9:55 by explaining why he had kept the Toronto finding to himself. Hadara nodded twice. Jenny kept shifting her eyes from one to the other.

"I can't make up my mind," Hadara said, shaking her head. "Half of me holds it against you for not telling me about these two in Toronto, or telling Javan, if you don't trust women. The other half says kudos to you for stumbling upon Jenny's kidnappers and having people keeping an eye on them. But all that is water under the bridge. Now I must ask two more favours of you. May I?"

"You may ask, Hadara, but I'll have to think about whether I can do what you ask."

"Fair enough. Jenny explained to you what the repercussions might be should it become known that Javan and I came here and did what we did. She is absolutely right. It's why we couldn't tell you we were intelligence officers. So, the first favour I want to ask of you is to keep the whole thing under wraps."

Elliot stared at the opposite wall while he considered the request. "Well, if American and Canadian authorities don't learn about this," now looking squarely at Hadara, "okay, I won't say anything to anyone. But if one day I'm detained, or subpoenaed and interrogated concerning this whole . . . thing, I would have to admit what I know. You can't expect me to go to jail for Mossad, or Israel, or you."

The swine. "Fair enough. But the people staking out the perps, do they know what happened?"

"No, Hadara, they don't know. They are keeping an eye on them but don't know why."

"No problem then. Now, the second favour. Because this can't be known we can't press charges, so these two can't be bagged, tried, and sentenced. But neither Jenny nor I think there's justice in this world if they go unpunished and get to live the life of the rich and famous. Jenny has told me you share that view. Is that right?"

Elliot nodded.

"Okay, now that you know why we can't call in the cavalry, what would you do?"

"Me? You asking me? I have no idea. You are the cloak-and-dagger person here."

"Right. But I want to see what you would do if I weren't here."

"I suppose I could go there and confront them. No, wait. I wouldn't go alone to see these two. I would find a friend –"

"You call a friend, he learns what happened. And we are in agreement it would be best if no one else knows."

"Right. So, Javan and I could go see them."

"Javan is in Tel Aviv, Steil. I would have to send him an encrypted message telling him all you told me tonight. He'd have to inform our chief, get an approval, board a plane. By the time he gets back here the perps may have flown away."

Elliot grinned, knowing the words she wanted to put in his mouth and admitting to himself it was the best, perhaps the only, quick-fix solution. "Okay, then we go together and tell these two they either give back the bonds or Jenny will report them to the FBI. Scare the hell out of them."

Hadara flashed him her pleasant smile. "Turns out you're cloak-and-dagger too."

"No, I'm not. It's the logical and fastest course of action."

"Exactly. There's no other way. They don't know we can't accuse them. They don't know I'm an Israeli intelligence officer. So, what do you say we go there right now, throw them a scare, and see if we recover the bonds tonight? I mean, these two will shit their pants when they see you."

Elliot lowered his eyes to the tabletop, thinking of the angles. Jenny and Hadara exchanged glances several times, shifted in their seats, crossed and uncrossed their legs, but respected his silence.

"You still have the Glock?" Elliot asked Hadara.

"No. We returned it to our friends."

"What happens if they pull a gun on us?"

"Good point. You own a gun?"

"Nope."

"Jenny?"

The model nodded twice. "I have a pistol at home. A . . . friend gave it to me on my twenty-fourth birthday."

"Well," Elliot said, "if Jenny loans you her gun, I would say let's do it. But I keep the magazine in my pocket. I need to make sure you won't shoot these two bastards on the spot."

Hadara's hearty laugh caught Jenny and Elliot by surprise. After a moment she managed to compose herself.

"Elliot," still smiling, "do you really think I'd shoot these bastards? You think I'm crazy?"

"No, but I think –"

"Take it easy, okay? I promise you I won't shoot them. But I need the gun ready to fire in case they pull a gun on us."

"You promise?"

"I promise I won't shoot them if neither pulls a gun on us. I suggest we do this. I knock on the door. Does it have a peephole?"

"I don't know."

"You've never been there?"

"Of course not. I didn't want to risk a chance encounter."

Hadara had been trying to find this out since the beginning. Perhaps the corpses had been found. Perhaps Steil's spotter had told him and, suspecting she had murdered them, he was ambushing her. But his opposition to a violent outcome, coupled with his admission that he had not been inside the apartment building, made it very possible she was overstating Steil's cunning. Yeah, probably. The Cuban was an open book. Not a single acting gene in him.

"Wish I had a reverse peephole," she said.

"A what?" Jenny said.

"Exactly that. You place it over the peephole and see what's going on inside. All police forces have them. Now, Steil, if the door has a peephole, you stay out of sight. If they ask who it is, I'll say . . . give me a second." She paused to pretend she was cobbling together the course she had chosen hours earlier. "Jenny, quick," snapping her fingers, "the name of a big Miami Beach model agency."

"William Morris."

"I'll say William Morris needs urgently, for midnight, a fashion photographer and they sent me to find out if Chris . . . What did you say his last name is?"

"Dawson."

. "Got it. The guy supposed to do the shoot had a heart attack. The agency wants to know if Chris Dawson would be willing to fill in. I could add that I have a car outside ready to drive him to the site. That'll make them open the door. Even to say no, Chris would open it, out of courtesy. Then I go in, gun in hand, and scare the bejesus out of both. You can stay outside or go in, Steil, as you wish, but I'd prefer you go in with me, because your being there will overwhelm them. The rest, you know. I pull out my cell, threaten them with calling the FBI immediately. Then, because they were Jenny's friends, helped her during difficult times, and because they didn't hurt her in Toronto, I say Jenny won't press charges if they return the bonds."

Elliot gave it a couple of seconds. "Hadara, you shoot one of these guys, the whole thing blows up and I'll have to tell all I know."

"Trust me. I won't shoot them."

"Jenny stays at her place," Elliot stipulated.

"Okay."

"Then . . . let's do it." .

Twenty minutes later they were at the model's underground parking lot, Jenny sitting in the back of Hadara's rental, a shoebox in her lap, as the Mossad agent, behind the wheel, checked the gun – a Beretta Jetfire, seven .25 ACP rounds in the magazine – before putting it into her purse. Elliot, in the passenger seat, turned to Jenny.

"Does Tico know what's in the box?"

"No, he doesn't. I keep it in my safe, in the walk-in closet."

"Good. Now go back to your place. We'll give you a call later."

Elliot asked Hadara to park the vehicle three blocks from the apartment building and they walked the rest of the way.

"Which of those is your man's car?" Hadara asked mid-block. Tony had parked beyond the building, and was using the car's mirrors to keep an eye on the entrance and the window of the couple's apartment. Five other vehicles were parked behind him.

"The deep-blue Chevy."

"You want to let him know we're going in?"

"Yep. Wait for me in the foyer, please."

Tony recognized Elliot as he was crossing the street and lowered the window.

"Hey, Teach. What you doing here?"

"I'm going in," grabbing the window frame with both hands and bending down to Tony's level, "with the woman standing at the entrance. We'll have a talk with those two and try to reach . . . an understanding. I don't foresee any trouble, but you never know. You hear screams, a fight going on, anything that may make the neighbours call the cops, start the car and get the hell out."

"You want me to go in with you?"

"No. And that's a very definite and final no, Tony."

"Okay."

"Do I have your word you'll beat it if there's any trouble?"

"Yes."

Elliot crossed the street and joined Hadara. They climbed the stairs, got their bearings, approached the apartment's front door, and knocked. A radio or CD player was blasting rap; from a TV set came the audio of a Mexican soap opera. It smelled musty. Hadara let thirty seconds slip by before knocking again. She knocked four times in all before moving away from the peephole.

"You sure they haven't flown the coop?" in a whisper.

"My people say they haven't gone out," also murmuring.

"You have a handkerchief?"

Elliot pulled one out from a pants pocket, gave it to her.

"C'mon, woman. Nobody leaves the front door unlatched."

"Let's make sure."

She returned to the door, covered her hand, and turned the handle. She opened just a crack, peeked inside and recoiled in feigned shock, confusion, astonishment.

"What?"

She swallowed hard, lowered her eyes to the carpet, gestured inside.

"What?"

"Take a look."

The scene took Elliot's breath away. He pulled back wide-eyed and pale.

"Let's get out of here," he whispered.

"Right," she agreed and pulled the door closed.

They had taken a few steps when Hadara stopped.

"Wait."

"What?" turning.

"Let's see if the bonds are there."

"Are you out of your mind?"

"No, listen. Maybe it was a lover's quarrel. Maybe the bonds are still there. Let's go in and search the place."

"I can't believe you're . . ." in a low voice laden with fury and astonishment. "Lady, for Christ's sake, there are two corpses in there. Forget the damn bonds."

"I'll take a peek."

"Hey, no, listen."

But she turned and went in.

Welcoming the opportunity to cover her tracks, Hadara carefully tiptoed around the pools of congealed blood and through the living room, the bedroom, and the bathroom. The night she killed them, an hour before driving to Fort Lauderdale she had heavily gelled her hair, so it was unlikely that crime scene investigators would find a strand inside the apartment. Should one be found, tracing it to her would be highly improbable. But if all the bad luck in the world descended on her, Steil could testify she had gone in when both men were already dead. Back in the hall she found the Cuban enraged and perplexed.

"I couldn't search every nook and cranny, but it seems the bonds are not there."

Elliot looked daggers at her.

"Let's get the hell out of here," he said and stomped to the stairway. She chased him. As he was turning in the landing she grabbed his arm and pulled.

"Wait, Steil. Let's think this over."

He shook himself free and kept going down. She caught up with him at the foyer.

"Wait, goddamn it. Wait."

Elliot turned towards her.

"What the fuck you want?"

"I want you to think. What are we going to do and say?"

Elliot took a deep breath, raised his eyes to the ceiling. "I don't know."

"Me neither. I'm supposed to keep calm in this sort of situation, but I'm dead from the neck up. They were shot, but there's no gun there. So, they were murdered. And you know what? There were two roll-ons there stacked with – you are not going to believe this – packages of bond paper."

"Bond paper?"

"Hammer something. Isn't that weird? Listen, let's get to my rental and try to figure this out."

A moment of pondering. "I guess."

"Okay. Maybe you tell your man we've talked to the perps, every-thing is all right, he can go home."

"Good idea."

Elliot crossed the street and approached the Chevy.

"So?" Tony asked.

"It's okay, Tony. Call off the guy who's coming at midnight and tell him he'll get paid anyway. Then you go home. We talked to these guys and all is clear now."

"All is clear, Elliot?"

"Yeah."

"What does that mean? All was resolved? The kidnappers got away with it or they returned the money?"

"Tony, don't yank my chain."

"Hey, what did I say?"

"Just go home. I'll call you later and explain."

"Are you sure?"

"Tony, just start the car and drive away. Please."

Elliot's serious expression and tone made it sink in. "Did some-thing happen up there, Elliot?"

"I'll call you later." Elliot turned and started walking. He heard Tony's car start and pull away before joining Hadara.

"Okay, Hadara, let's try to think this out."

Their brainstorming lasted half an hour. Elliot told Hadara that all the men on the stakeout were police officers, friends of a friend. Regardless of when the corpses were discovered – tomorrow, in a week or in a month – one of them would remember he had been shown photos of the gay couple, and had been paid to watch the apartment where they were murdered, report on their comings and goings. Chewing on this, Elliot added that he wasn't sure, but supposed that cops were not allowed to work as PIs on their spare time. And, if so, the rule breakers would face discharge, which might give pause to anyone thinking of blowing the whistle. But the magnitude of the crime might prompt one of the hired cops to make an anonymous call to Homicide from a pay phone and reveal who had hired the officers to keep the deceased under surveillance. Elliot's friend would be inter-rogated and forced to say who had paid for the stakeout.

Hadara begged to disagree. Unless he was mentally retarded, she argued, the hypothetical stoolie would be aware that Elliot's friend would be questioned, if not detained, and offered a choice: keep mum and get charged as an accessory before the fact or make a list of *all* the cops who had been hired. Was she right to assume that Elliot's friend would choose naming names over being thrown in the clink? The Cuban nodded. Then, Hadara went on, before making the call, the theoretical dime-dropper would realize that his name would be on the list and his superiors would interview him. To cut a deal and stay in the force, the whistleblower would have to admit he had made the call and exposed his buddies. He would take the blame for their discharge. The man would be known as a rat among fellow officers and those wronged would try to get even. Many criticisms could be levelled against the police in Miami Dade, but recruiting mentally retarded individuals was not one of them. No, Hadara said, she felt sure that when the bodies were discovered, none of the cops involved would reveal that he had been keeping watch on the place. The impli-cations were enormous, and what would that clear up? Nothing, probably. Had one of them heard the shots, seen the killer, and let him get away with it? That would show him as incompetent to the nth degree. And if the killer went undetected, what would be gained by revealing that the place had been under surveillance?

Elliot conceded to himself that Hadara's reasoning was faultless. But saying so was beyond him, so he merely told her she could be right. Then he added that for damage control he had to see his friend. He would call him as soon as possible. Hadara asked how he would explain her presence at the scene. The Cuban said he would tell Tony that she was a lawyer: Hadara recommended instead saying she was the American financial adviser who had purchased the bonds. No, Elliot said, lawyer sounded more believable; a lawyer with a minia-ture recorder in her purse to record the exchange. Hadara yielded.

The next topic was whether to tell Jenny that her abductors were dead. In a matter of seconds they decided against it. They would tell her they had knocked several times and nobody had answered. Maybe the couple had flown the coop unobserved. It was a mystery. Hadara would drive over, return the gun, and explain things to her.

Sam Plotzher came next. Not a word to the old man either, they agreed. Hadara would fly to Tel Aviv tomorrow and file a full report. The bonds were gone and it would be Jenny's loss, for she doubted that Mossad would not cash her certified cheque. It was possible that someone had learned about the bonds and killed Chris and Valerio to get them. Another possibility was that the gay couple had stored them somewhere, like a safety-deposit box in a Canadian or American bank. In that case maybe the CSIs would find a receipt and get a warrant to open it. Should that happen, they would learn about it sooner or later, for in this country everything eventually was made public.

Their discussion at an end, Hadara turned the key in the ignition and drove away.

Each of them was planning their next moves and neither spoke until Elliot, still unable to take in the murders, broke the silence with a string of questions. Why had Chris and Valerio done what they did? Who had killed them? Why?

"Beats me," Hadara said.

She dropped off Elliot near her hotel, at the parking lot where he had left his car, and drove straight to Jenny's to return the gun and tell the model that apparently her kidnappers had vanished into thin air.

Elliot drove to Asturia Avenue, parked in front of Tony's home, lowered the front window, killed the engine, and dialled his friend's land line. Would Lidia hold it against him if her husband put some clothes on and came out? He needed to have a word with him. A few moments later, Tony, a robe over a T-shirt and pyjama bottoms, descended the porch's two steps. Elliot reached over and opened the passenger door for him; Tony arranged himself in the seat, closed the door.

Tony thought the news a sick joke. He knew his former teacher thought too much, took life too seriously, hardly ever kidded around, but this *had* to be a prank.

"It ain't funny, Teach. I was sound asleep. The wife got up too."

"Tony, I'm not joking."

The grave expression, the tone, said Elliot was serious.

"Murdered? Murdered?"

"Murdered, Tony. I saw the bodies with my own eyes."

"Did you fall off the wagon, Teacher?"

"Tony, I'm fucking serious, man. Listen up."

After Elliot finished the whole story, Tony asked the questions any policeman would have asked. Elliot responded as truthfully as he could, under the circumstances. Then the ex-cop fell silent, staring across the windshield.

"What is it with you?" he said after a few moments.

"What do you mean?"

"It seems you are like a magnet for crime, tragedy, and disgrace. For Christ's sake, man, go find a *babalao* and ask him to give you a *despojo*."

In Cuban Spanish, *despojo* is the name of a religious ceremony based on African rituals and deities in which a man who reputedly has magical powers – the *babalao* – runs a recently uprooted shrub of basil, or a torn-off sprout from the shrub, over the body of someone (usually a person, but occasionally an animal, for instance,

a Thoroughbred or a greyhound on the eve of a big race) to assure
a favourable outcome in almost any endeavour: conquering the love
of someone, winning a sports competition, make a show a box-office
hit, bring in huge profits in business, accomplish a political landslide,
or, like in Elliot's case, end a streak of bad luck. Making illness go
away would be another reason to go get a *despojo*.

"You want me to ask some *babalao* to rub me with some plants and
blow smoke in my face? What use would that be? What I want to
know, Tony, is what the chances are your buddies won't blab when
the bodies are found."

Tony checked his memory for the traits of the four cops involved.
"Pretty good, I guess. None of these bulls is Y3."

"Is what?"

"Yada, yada, yada. A fat lip. Besides, they'll figure it out, like you
said. But you know what, Teach? You never know."

"Okay, what can we do to make sure?"

"Well, off the top of my head, I could come clean with them. Talk
to each separately. Tell them the two birds didn't show up because
they are dead and that any day the corpses will be found. I'll swear
on my mother's grave that neither I nor my client did it. Then sort
of draw them a picture of what could happen if there's an indiscretion. I won't offend them by saying I fear one of them may rat on
me. They are straight shooters, all of them. And then you and me
pray they keep quiet."

Elliot filled his lungs with fresh, dead-of-night air. "Well, dude, I
guess that's it. Sorry to have woken you up."

"No, no, you did right. I'll dress, get on my wheels, and start
waking up and chewing this over with the guys not on the graveyard
shift. Tomorrow I'll see the others. I'm sorry I thought you were
kidding, Teach."

"It's okay, Tony. I'm sorry I got you involved in this."

"No problem. Gotta go."

And with this Tony got out of the car, trotted all the way to the porch, went in, and closed his front door.

Elliot turned the key in the ignition and headed home.

Hadara came into her hotel room, dropped the magnetic card into her purse, bolted the door, and hurried to the bathroom. It took her just a minute to empty her bladder and wash her hands. The second she left the bathroom a fist hit her in the centre of her forehead. She instantly blacked out and crumpled to the floor.

The man who hit her had chalked up a 580 pound/force impact when throwing his fist forward at 40 miles per hour along a ten- to twelve-inch trajectory. But on this occasion he'd pulled his punch for he had some things to talk over with Hadara. Crouching, he pressed his fingers on the woman's neck, watched her breathe, then got up. After readjusting the shower cap on his head, he inspected the medical examination glove on his right hand. The blow had torn it. He snapped it off, stuffed it into the left pocket of his suit's jacket, fished out a new glove from the right pocket, pulled it on. Then he bent, slid both hands under Hadara's armpits, and dragged her to the centre of the room, the friction pulling her moccasins off. He sat her on an armchair by the bed and tried to hold her steady; she kept slumping forward, head lolling. Gripping her shoulder with one hand to prevent her from falling, he pulled free the top sheet from the unmade bed, passed one end lengthwise underneath her breasts, grabbed the other end, and tied a knot behind the seat. Retracing two steps, he observed the inert woman and gave a self-approving nod. At a certain point he'd need a bright light, so he turned on all the lamps. He placed the other armchair a few feet from Hadara, facing her. He glanced at his watch, then sat to patiently pass the time.

Hadara remained motionless for almost ten minutes. Then she moaned and slowly raised her head. The man leaned forward the better to see her rose-pink, swollen forehead; nothing incapacitating, he felt sure. Still groggy, she glanced around with half-opened, expressionless eyes, trying to figure what had happened.

"Oh."

The man's sole reaction was to blink once. Hadara's brain cobwebs were clearing and she tried to change position. Immobilization wiped the last traces of confusion. She tried to focus on the person in front, batted her eyelids, refocused.

"What happened?"

The man just stared at her.

"When did you return?"

"I never left," he said.

She frowned: never left? "Did you tie me up?"

"Yes."

"My head hurts. Did I take a fall?"

"No, I hit you."

"You hit me?"

"I did."

"Why?"

"Because."

Hadara frowned, looked around the room, spotted her shoes.

"I don't get it. Why did you hit me and tie me up?"

"You deserved it."

"I deserved it?" Something was very wrong, Hadara realized.

The man gave two solemn nods.

"You hit a colleague because you felt she deserved it? What's going on, *aluf mishne*?"

He scoffed and looked away, an I-can't-believe-this-woman expression on his face. "You don't know what's going on?" now looking intently at her, sneering.

"I don't."

"All right, allow me to enlighten you. You made the worst mistake a person can make: to think that he or she can fool every other man and woman on this planet. Very common among the dim-witted; not so common among the highly intelligent. The sad thing is, you're brilliant. It's the worst mistake because it causes many other mistakes. Makes me think of a string of Chinese firecrackers; once the first pops, there's no way you can stop all the others from popping. Until the final firecracker pops. Tonight, right here, your string of mistakes ends. This is your last pop, *seren*."

"May I learn what I'm being charged with?"

"Nothing, nothing at all. But to satisfy your curiosity I can reveal that you've been under observation for two years, give or take a few weeks, ever since the FBI nailed Marty Seligman. We cross-referenced Marty's file and it emerged you had been classmates at a primary school in Brooklyn."

"Marty who?"

"Seligman. He was charged with gathering and unlawfully transmitting national defence information. Found guilty; sentenced to twenty-five years in prison."

"Now, I remember! The DIA analyst passing documents on Iran's progress in missile technology. We went to the same school?"

"You did, dear. We had to make sure you were not an FBI mole, had nothing to do with his getting rolled up; you know we had to, it's textbook. So, *aluf* Dekel's people started watching you. They found one intriguing thing: you exchanged secret messages with your lover."

"My lover?"

"Tali Kline."

Hadara's eyes narrowed. A look of faked incomprehension fading to uneasiness.

"Tali is not my lover. We are friends, not lovers."

"Oh, I see. Well, your sexual preference is not what made us keep you under the microscope once we were sure you had nothing to do with Seligman's case. The Institute couldn't care less. You know the service needs all kinds of people; you know we have several openly lesbian case officers. Tali had nothing to fear either. She's a divorced, childless secretary at the Consulate; she can do what she wants. If being known as lesbian wouldn't have any adverse effect on your careers, why were you so fucking secretive about your relationship? It made Dekel's boys wonder. There had to be a reason, they concluded. Time went on and on and on; nothing came up.

"Then Jenny was kidnapped. Brilliant, work of a genius I would say. I take off my hat to you, *seren*. You managed to do an enormous amount of research without missing a beat in your work, and without us getting any wiser. Uncovering that Chris's father was in jail was nothing; a kid trawling the Internet could do it. But we still haven't got a clue how you learned that Valerio was an illegal, for only Chris knew that. It's amazing. You knew everything about these two poor bastards and they only met you the night you killed them. And you manipulated them like a master puppeteer.

"You mapped out every step of the way. Making them pose as mujahideen ensured that Mossad would try to rescue Jenny, and that you would take part. You knew I would have to call in and consult with the only person in Tel Aviv who knew Jenny personally, her recruiter. 'No, kidnapped?' you said, wide-eyed and open-mouthed, then added you felt morally obliged to rescue her. Logical, understandable, even admirable, I thought. In a matter of hours you came up with the cover story, how to recruit Steil, what to do about the bonds. What a fantastic improviser! I thought. You knew our people would monitor our cell phones to keep abreast of what was going on. And you kept the ball rolling impeccably until nineteen days ago when Tali called you. Remember? The morning after? We were in your room in Toronto, beginning to debrief Jenny."

Hadara didn't say a word; she just looked at the man's shoes.

"And you chatted about seemingly trivial things, the weather there and here, what a great time you were having, the bargains you had found. You were trying to tell her all had gone like clockwork without saying so, hoping she'd infer it from your tone and cheery chit-chat. But maybe beautiful Tali has a conscience, sort of; maybe she was worried that something bad could have happened to Jenny. For whatever reason, she asked a question that made people in Tel Aviv jump in their seats. 'Is she all right?' And you said, 'Okay, bye.'

"It's second nature for us. We're taught from day one that passing on information is the riskiest thing the agent does, and we become extremely distrustful of all sorts of communication, even in our private lives. You know what? The wife calls to find out when I'll be getting home, we've agreed I'll say a time that's one hour later or sooner, according to whether the day is odd or even, than the actual time I expect to be home. We're a bunch of paranoids. All of us. And realizing that Tali had slipped, you cut her off.

"There was no way Tali could have known about the kidnapping. You hadn't called her in three months, not since your last trip to New York to debrief Richard. She hadn't called you either. The email account where you left unsent messages in the draft folder didn't have a word concerning Jenny, the fashion industry, or the kidnapping. At the consulate, only Ephraim had watched the DVD and he put it in an envelope that he wrapped and sealed. You and I inspected the seal before opening it, remember? It hadn't been tampered with.

"Dekel was baffled. He asked me, 'How could Tali know?' I said the only possible way was that you had told her. We assumed you had another means of communication we knew nothing about. We still haven't found it, and that's another credit to you. But if we still don't know how Tali learned about Jenny's kidnapping, how do we know you masterminded the whole thing? Let me show you how we know what we know."

Javan stood, took two steps, and retrieved the woman's stainless-steel diver's watch from her left wrist.

"What's inscribed in the back of your watch, *seren*?"

Hadara didn't say anything.

"*With love, Mom.* Now, take a look. You see it?"

The man turned the watch over and showed it to Hadara. She peered closely, paled, turned her gaze away.

"Any inscription there?"

Hadara hung her head.

Javan returned to his seat with the watch.

"Nobody knew whether your Eterna Kontiki had an inscription or not," he went on, "which made an exact replica impossible, not with us here and the experts in Tel Aviv. But nobody reads the inscriptions on their rings and watches every time they put them on or take them off, so you didn't find out that Dekel's boys had this one," lifting and balancing the watch in front of her eyes, "ready for me. After Jenny was rescued and we returned to New York, when we got back to our hotel the next evening, I said I needed to use your laptop. Remember?"

Hadara had turned into stone.

"I'm sure you do. We went to your room. I had been pestering you for over an hour when you grew impatient, took off your shoes, left your watch and earrings on a bedside table, and went to take a shower. I swapped watches on you then. This one, *seren*, is state-of-the-art molecular nanotechnology. Cutting edge of Jewish science. For eleven days, it has transmitted every single word you've said to a receiver that can be as far as ten kilometres away."

Javan ran the tip of his tongue over his lips. Hadara was unblinkingly staring at the carpet.

"No need to tail you. We heard the address you told the Fort Lauderdale taxi driver to take you to, what you said to the *faigeleh* before killing them. We heard you asking for a big safety-deposit box at the Palmetto branch of Coconut Grove Bank, we heard Steil telling you when he spotted the Peruvian *faigeleh* and how he found out they were back here. We also heard your amazing performance when you took him to the *faigeleh*'s apartment and 'discovered'" – Javan gestured quotation marks around the word – "the bodies. Enough is enough, Dekel said, and one of his boys gave me the magnetic card to this room. But I'm impressed by how you handled this whole operation, and I'm going to propose making it a case study. You know which image my mind keeps replaying over and over? After the swap, you at Taylor Creek, searching the trash cans and trails for evidence, without stopping, swigging from a bottle of water, missing lunch. What a superb performance!"

Javan kept talking. He mentioned that he had found it strange, for instance, that Chris had been uninterested in knowing the Toronto hotel where Steil was staying; Hadara had excluded that from her instructions to him and Valerio because she would be there too. He listed other things that he had failed to spot, like her insistence on telling the Four Seasons that Jenny had returned to New York, so that they wouldn't alert Toronto police.

Hadara had stopped listening. She was sadly remembering the four years during which she and Tali, separated by thousands of miles, concealing their feelings, and sacrificing living together, had tried to come up with a foolproof plan for a financially secure future, once both resigned their positions and got married. She had promised her soulmate that she'd find a way. Because she lived in Miami, Tali's collaboration had been invaluable, but Hadara had tried to insulate her as much as possible from the real risks and the necessary unpleasantries. Hurting Jenny physically had been excluded from the start. The model would merely be made, albeit unwillingly, to contribute to their future happiness. She had instructed Chris and Valerio to treat Jenny as humanely as possible, to make sure her living quarters and her food were adequate. She had also banned firearms; real-looking plastic guns had been used for the DVD and to intimidate the victim.

The one important fact she had kept from Tali was that the photographer and his Latin lover would have to die. The woman she adored was incapable of hurting anyone and would have backed out immediately, would have begged her to cancel the whole thing. But it was inevitable; she couldn't come up with their half before cashing the bonds. The kidnappers would have had to be crazy, and they weren't, to hand the payoff to a total stranger who promised to come back weeks or months later with their cut. Killing them and taking everything was the only way.

"But, dear colleague, you failed," Javan said after a long silence.

His tone, more than the remark itself, brought Hadara back to the present. She lifted her eyes and stared at Javan. "I did not, *aluf mishne*. You got lucky. If the FBI hadn't nailed Seligman, you wouldn't have put me under surveillance. If Steil hadn't seen the Peruvian, you wouldn't be here now. And even if all that happened, if Tali hadn't asked the question, you wouldn't have figured it out, you thick-headed sonofabitch."

Javan tilted his head, considering her words. "Probably," he conceded.

"So, take your string of firecrackers and shove it up your ass, you lousy kike."

Javan tilted his head left and right, as if pondering the suggestion. "I don't think I would enjoy that."

"Try it. Maybe you are a closet *faigeleh*."

"Maybe. But I'm also your superior officer, *seren*, and as such I am responsible for your actions. I have recommended you for promotion on two occasions, so what you do reflects on me. The Institute will probably send me to jail, or promote me; I'm not sure how they'll take what I'll do to you. Remember, this watch is transmitting everything we've said here tonight. And one of Dekel's boys is recording it."

"I know what you'll do. The shower cap and the gloves speak volumes. Go ahead. I'm ready."

"I will, with a heavy heart, you should know," pocketing the watch. "But I will, right now. I'm sorry. Do you want a moment to pray?"

"You're so full of shit. In this business nobody believes in God. Get it over with."

Javan stood. With three steps he placed himself behind Hadara and visually estimated the distance. She closed her eyes and pictured Tali. He also closed his eyes, took a deep breath, concentrated. Then, with a sharp exhalation, Javan shot his right fist at around forty miles per hour against the nape of Hadara's neck. If measured, the impact would have been in the six-hundred-pound force range. Two vertebrae snapped, damaging the spine, the windpipe, and causing asphyxiation. Staring at the carpet, Hadara gasped over a dozen times; within a minute she was dead.

Javan waited another minute before untying her, letting her body down to the floor, bending over to check for a pulse, and resting his ear on her chest. Then he sat on his haunches, slipped his arms under her shoulders and knees, stood, and crossed to the marble-topped bedside table. Holding the corpse as high as he could, he let it drop. The back of Hadara's head banged against the edge of the marble top, and the lamp on it fell to the floor. He arranged the body in the position he considered most probable had she died as a consequence of tripping and hitting her head. Then he pulled out Hadara's inscribed watch, slipped her hand into the band, clasped it around her left wrist. After that he searched the woman's purse and removed two keys to a safety-deposit box from a keychain. Javan surveyed the room looking for other things he should take care of. He lifted the bed sheet from the carpet. It took him close to five minutes to leave the unmade bed as he supposed it would be if a person lying on the left side of the mattress had pulled aside the top sheet and got up.

Before leaving, he reviewed all his actions from the moment he had entered the room. He decided against moving the shoes from where they were – a tired woman shaking off her moccasins – but slid his foot over the microscopic trails the back of her heels had to have left on the carpet when he dragged her across it. Satisfied, he returned both seats to their original positions, took a final look around, and unlocked the door, placing his shoe between the door and the jamb. He took off both gloves and the shower cap, put them into his jacket pocket, opened the door with his elbow and left. On his way to the elevator he heard the door click shut.

EPILOGUE

H adara's corpse was found around noon the following day. The maid, having knocked on the door on three occasions without getting a response, reckoned the guest had left early. Homicide and crime scene investigators did their thing. A desk clerk tipped a journalist and the following morning the *Miami Herald* reported:

The body of a middle-aged woman was found in a room she had rented days earlier at Port of Miami's Holiday Inn.

An Israeli passport and other identifications were found in her purse, but her name is being withheld until relatives are notified.

Homicide investigators, speaking on condition of anonymity, said the body had signs of violence; an accident is also possible.

MPD spokesman Roy Simpson said, "We have not made a determination yet as to the status of the case."

Guadalupe López, the maid who found the body, said she had passed the time of the day with the deceased two or three times.

"She seemed a nice lady . . ."

The same morning the body was discovered, the Israeli consul paid a visit to the office of the MPD's chief to get photocopies of the genuine passport, the bogus driving licence, and a ten-print card of Hadara's fingerprints. Meanwhile, at the consulate, Javan and Ephraim – Mossad's legal man in Miami, under cover as vice-consul – had a seventy-minute heart-to-heart talk with Tali Klein. The gist of it was that the two officers knew everything. They were under the impression that Hadara, taking advantage of Tali's feelings for her, had shamelessly manipulated the secretary and made her an accessory before and after the fact. Weeping and hiccupping, Tali swore she had begged Hadara not to carry out the plan. That she had predicted they would be tracked down and caught; the photographer and his friend first, she and Hadara as soon as the kidnappers confessed. But her girlfriend never once doubted that the plan was infallible.

Well, Tali had been right, Ephraim said. They suspected the secretary's role in the scheme was unimportant and motivated by love, not greed. She'd done nothing more serious than maybe making a few phone calls or couriering messages to Chris and Valerio, right? At this point Tali thought a small lie permissible and swore she hadn't met the kidnappers (true), mailed or couriered things to their place (false), or phoned them (true). What she had done over and over and over was try to persuade Hadara not to go ahead with the scheme (true at the start, not so true after a few months, untrue in the final stage).

"It's what I figured," Ephraim said, with a sympathetic nod. "I know. I told Javan your case is typical: decent, hard-working person under a bad influence."

Sending her to prison would be legally correct but morally wrong, for she was also an injured party, the vice-consul continued. Tali deserved understanding, compassion, and support; she ought to have an opportunity to rebuild her life. Concerning her present position, however, he had no alternative. The consul had to let her go; she would be barred from working for the State of Israel in any capacity. A shame, but there was nothing he could do. A secretary as good as she would find a job with any first-class Tel Aviv firm a day or two after applying. And she shouldn't exclude from her résumé that she had worked for the consulate; Personnel had agreed to provide a glowing reference. All this, naturally, was contingent upon her making amends and cooperating in redressing Jenny Scheindlin's grievance.

"How?" Tali asked, pulling out a seventh Kleenex from the box and blowing her nose.

Javan cleared his throat before explaining that Hadara, upon finding out (God only knew how) that the police were looking for Chris and Valerio, had vanished into thin air. Eventually, in a week or a month, Mossad would find her and bring her to Israeli justice, but right now nobody had any idea where she was. Her disappearance prevented him from returning the bonds, currently stored in a safety-deposit box, to Jenny Scheindlin. But Tali could help them do that because, when Hadara leased the safety-deposit box, she had named Tali as the other person with access to its contents.

"She did?" the weeping Tali asked.

"Yes, she did," Javan said, and paused to offer the secretary another sip of water, a fresh Kleenex, and to reflect a little on the vagaries of love. Tali Klein, an extremely beautiful woman, intellectually was ten steps below Hadara and emotionally she didn't have an ounce of her lover's steely control. Do opposites really attract?

When Tali regained her composure, Javan continued. A bank vice-president well-known as an ardent admirer of Israel had been instrumental in providing a key to the safety-deposit box. Should Tali wish to avoid being charged and hauled into court, should she want to get on with life and gain Mossad's pardon and gratitude, she needed to accompany them to the bank right now and recover the bonds.

At 11:54 a.m. Tali walked out of the bank branch holding the black leather duffel bag, followed by Ephraim and Javan. Inside the car, Javan took a peek at the bag's content.

"Thank you, Tali," he said, and sighed.

That same afternoon Ephraim drove the beautiful Tali Klein to the airport and got her on a plane to Tel Aviv. The consul had no clue why his secretary had been sent home, but once Ephraim told him it was a security matter, he thought best not to ask any more questions.

After lunch Javan called Jenny, said he had news, asked if they could meet in private. Of course, she said; Tico would understand. Around four, maybe? So, at 3:35 the Mossadist drove to Sunny Isles, and a few minutes before the agreed time was admitted to the penthouse. It was a luminous, clear day, and he drank in the spectacular view over the Atlantic, said hello to Jenny's paramour, and accepted a pina colada. When the Puerto Rican asked to be excused for he had to run to the supermarket for groceries, Javan stood, put a smile in place, shook the man's hand. Once the elevator door closed, the ex-colonel wiped off his smile, sat back down in his seat, and without a word produced the certified cheque and handed it to Jenny. She looked at it, frowning.

"Why are you giving me this?"

"We recovered the bonds," he explained.

"Really?" wide-eyed.

"Really."

She stared at the cheque for a few more moments. "Well, that's great! I had resigned myself to being ten million poorer. But how come? I mean, Hadara said the bonds weren't in the apartment. Where were they?" putting the document in the pocket of her beach shorts.

"At a safety-deposit box. Okay, Jenny. Listen to me carefully. I know this is going to be a shock. Hadara killed your kidnappers."

Hoping she had misheard or misunderstood, Jenny slid to the edge of the seat and leaned forward. "Did you just say Hadara killed Chris and Valerio?"

"Yes."

"You had two men killed for ten million?"

Javan shook his head vigorously. "Jenny. This will be hard to believe, but it's the truth. Hadara was the brains behind your kidnapping."

The model's lips parted as if to ask something, but disbelief and shock had left her speechless. She slumped back on the sofa. For an instant the image of Chris and Valerio helping her all those years ago flashed in her mind; tears welled up and slid down her cheeks. She sobbed, and for a minute not a word was said. Eventually, she stood and hurried to the bathroom. After almost three minutes, more composed, she returned to the living room.

"Javan, please. Let's go back a little. I met you, when? Three weeks ago?"

"Give or take."

"Okay. I met Hadara thirteen years ago, in Israel, while working at Kibbutz Lotan. Hadara recruited me, she was my first instructor. Until you said what you just said, I thought of Hadara as a great patriot, a heroine, a friend I couldn't spend time with because of the nature of the work she and I were doing for Israel. She is one of the three people who risked their lives to save mine. I appreciate all you've done for me, but compared with her, you are a total stranger. Why should I believe you?"

Javan heaved a deep sigh, then, slowly and carefully, he began to tell her what he could. He knew that neither Jenny nor Elliot would be able to make sense of what had happened without seeing the whole picture, but he also knew that the most revealing and amazing part would remain one of Mossad's many secrets. First, he told her about Hadara's relationship with Tali Klein, then explained that she had volunteered to help rescue Jenny the minute she was informed of the kidnapping.

"Why did you tell her?" intrigued.

Because all informers' files include the name of their recruiters, Javan said. Hadara was aware, he added, that she was the only person at headquarters who knew the asset personally, so she would be informed of the kidnapping and asked for her opinion of Jenny's likely reaction to being threatened and physically abused. Would Jenny confess that she worked for Israeli Intelligence? Would she reveal the names of the Arab men she had been asked to inform on? They had to know the recruiter's opinion because, if Jenny confessed, the mujahideen might videotape her and post it on the Internet.

Hadara had taken a few calculated risks, Javan added. She had gambled that Elliot Steil would show the DVD to Sam Plotzher and ask the old man's advice concerning whether to go to the police. Mossad had opened a file on Steil, Javan revealed, when he joined Imlatinex. Hadara had read it and felt 99 per cent sure the Cuban would consult Sam before doing anything.

"The minute I called Hadara to my office she knew she had the upper hand," Javan said and drank what was left of the pina colada. He placed the empty glass on the coffee table and went on.

Hadara's seemingly spur-of-the-moment suggestions had seemed reasonable, including her certainty that Jenny would gladly pay for the bonds if rescued alive. All were well-received by him and his superiors. Skipping over what the model already knew concerning the rescue, he told her of the phone call Tali made to Hadara, which had prompted Mossad to send him the watch with the hidden transmitter. Then he spoke about what had been learned once Hadara started wearing it, including the conversations between her, Steil, and Jenny in this same room and at Hadara's hotel room.

Having reached the point where he had decided to bring up Hadara's death, Javan took out the *Miami Herald* article, unfolded it, and handed it to Jenny.

"This is from today's paper," he said.

Jenny read the first three lines, lifted her head and stared at Javan. Incredulity shone in her eyes.

"You killed her, Javan?"

"I did not."

"You had her killed?"

"No. The Institute asked me to find her and arrest her, then get her on board a plane, a freighter, whatever. She was supposed to stand trial. I have nothing to do with her death."

Totally mystified, she shook her head. "Then, who did?"

"I wish I knew. First of all, read on. It may have been an accident. The police are not sure."

Jenny read the rest of the newspaper piece, then stared at Javan, wordlessly asking for clarification.

"My guess is," he said, "she was killed by someone we know nothing about. Maybe someone who has nothing to do with your kidnapping: a rapist or a thief who somehow got into her room. Maybe it was an accomplice who felt deceived or betrayed. Which brings me to the question of why I have told you the whole story. I could have kept you in the dark and couriered you the cheque. And the answer is that until we know if it was an accident or a murder, I want you to hire round-the-clock protection from a security company. If we find out that she was murdered but the killer is loose, then I very strongly recommend that, wherever you are – here, in New York, or anywhere else – every time you go out, make sure you have two bodyguards watching out for you."

It wasn't sinking in. Jenny was still overwhelmed by grief and emotion and she kept shaking her head in denial. Javan moved on to the real reason that had brought him here today: the necessity of keeping it all under wraps. He would tell Sam and Elliot that Hadara had flown to Tel Aviv. All of her documents had been under an assumed name, so even if the name was published, nobody would be able to figure out it was Hadara.

"It's why I am now asking you to tear up the cheque, right here, now."

"Why?"

She should keep everyone believing, Javan explained, that she had bought her freedom. If Tico, Sam, or Elliot learned that she had got her money back, they would demand an explanation. That would unleash a string of questions. When? How? Where? Who had recovered the bonds? One thing would lead to the other.

Jenny tore the cheque into little pieces and gave the scraps to Javan. He put them in his pocket.

"Where are the bonds now?" she asked.

"In the consulate's safe. They will be flown to Tel Aviv in the diplomatic bag, with the transmitter that made it possible for us to find out the whole scheme. Any other questions?"

She shrugged. "None right now. Later a thousand questions will pop into my mind, but you won't be here, right?"

He assembled a so-sorry expression and shook his head.

"Jenny, I speak in the name of the Institute when I say that we are deeply embarrassed, saddened, and angry that one of our officers put you through all this anguish and suffering. We are extremely grateful for all you did for Israel for so many years."

Jenny nodded and tucked a strand of hair behind her ear.

"I need to know how all this ends," she said. "I suppose the consulate will eventually learn whether Hadara had an accident or was killed. Forensic experts here are supposed to be good. Maybe the killer will be caught. I need to know because I'm a very private person. I love to take walks, to pass unnoticed. I hate the idea of having a couple of beefy guys in mirror shades following me everywhere."

"You can be sure I'll personally tell you any news," getting to his feet.

"Well, thanks for everything," standing too. "I'm . . . overwhelmed. Three lives. I mean, why?"

"Who knows? Maybe the wrong kind of ambition. I'm not a psychologist. It's been a long time since I stopped trying to understand human nature."

"I think I'm getting near that point too."

"Move on, enjoy, count your blessings, and be happy, Jenny."

"Oh, you bet your life I will, Javan. You bet your life."

Before returning to Tel Aviv, Javan had a final talk with the man who, until his retirement in 2006, had been Israel's senior spymaster in South Florida: Sam Plotzher. A Palmachnik at fifteen, a Mossadist ever since the foundation of the Institute, Sam was one of the seven living legends of Israeli intelligence.

Nobody could set a parabolic listener and tape their conversation at some place they had never been before, so Sam chose to talk with Javan at the Fairchild Tropical Botanical Garden, in Coral Gables. On their way there, Javan didn't ask where they were headed; he knew it would be a secure location. Anyone who operates undetected for fifty years has to be an expert on safe places for a rendezvous. The changes in surveillance technology since the 1950s had been mind-boggling, so Sam must have kept researching and studying the new developments – after ten-hour workdays. Not for nothing had Sam Plotzher been awarded all the service ribbons and decorations the State of Israel confers.

As they ambled along the paths, among fruit and palm trees, vines, and other tropical plants, Javan told Sam the unvarnished truth, including Hadara's execution – at which point the veteran nodded his approval. Then Javan asked two favours. First, should Jenny commit any indiscretion concerning this whole mess in the immediate future, or if she needed counselling, would Sam report it to headquarters?

"I would," Sam said. "But in all likelihood she won't tell anyone. I think I've managed to convince her that certain things you keep to yourself. She knows three people were killed. My guess is she won't tell anyone, not now at least, not this good-for-nothing Puerto Rican who's swept her off her feet, not me, not Elliot. Maybe when she's an old lady, she'll want to get it off her chest and confide in a son or daughter. But by then you, me, Elliot, this Tico, we will all be six feet under. Everyone else connected to this whole mess will be dead, too. If I were you, I wouldn't worry about her blabbing about this."

"Well, no one knows Jenny better than you, Sam. I hope you are right."

They had reached the area of tropical rainforest, home to the ferns and anthurium that grow on huge tree trunks and branches, the paved path and identifying labels spoiling the intended effect of a wilderness.

"Now, about Steil. When the bodies of the *faigeleh* are found, will the cops he hired to stake out the place keep their mouths shut? That's what Hadara thought."

"Well, her reasoning, as you explained it, seems pretty solid to me. But we can't be sure."

"I think we should be prepared for the worst. Suppose one of them talks and Internal Affairs gets to Elliot. What will he do?"

"I don't know."

"Can you scare him off?"

"Well . . . I could say that if he talks whoever killed the others may want to get him out of the way."

"Not bad."

They strolled in silence for a few moments, searching for alternatives.

"I could add," Sam, remembering the meeting with the officials from the Customs and Border Protection agency, "that if the police learn about Jenny's abduction and his participation in her rescue, he may be sent to jail and then deported to Cuba later."

"No vain threat," Javan concurred. "And a good one."

"But we should give him a credible reason for staking out the fags that he can feed to the cops."

"Yeah."

They kept walking in silence, contemplating their surroundings as they considered a justification that would hold up.

"He wouldn't admit being gay himself, would he?" Javan asked.

"No."

"Because that would give him an ironclad reason: jealousy."

"Forget it."

Sam was feeling a little tired when, a few minutes later, he came up with an idea that seemed plausible, although far from perfect.

"What do you say I go to an Internet café, type and print a letter, unsigned, asking Elliot to be at a certain place, on a certain day, at 8:00 p.m. 'Someone' will approach him and offer something for sale. If Elliot isn't interested, he'll sell it to the tabloids."

Javan thought for a moment. "Okay, it can be done, but the envelope would be postmarked today at the earliest, and the autopsy will prove Chris died days earlier. How would he explain the fag posting the letter after he was dead?"

Sam smiled. "Elliot can say he threw away or lost the envelope. He threw the DVD's box in the wastepaper basket, remember?"

"All right. What did Chris want to sell?"

"Photos of Jenny in the raw."

Javan considered it. "Not bad. Steil met Chris somewhere. He remembered him from the night Jenny's mother was killed. Chris's story was that one evening Jenny had drunk too much and he had taken shots of her naked and using sex toys and stuff. He said he was broke and needed money. He wanted fifty thousand for the prints and the negatives. Wait, wait. Why did he call Elliot? It would've been easier to blackmail Jenny."

"Jenny was in New York." The old man, patiently. "Chris didn't know her number or address here or there."

"Okay. So Elliot was furious but he kept his cool and told Chris he would have to think about it. Then he followed Chris and found where he lived."

"Right. And he had the place staked out because he was considering the best way to tackle the problem. Tell Jenny? Tell me first? Buy the photos? Go to the police? Eventually he told me and I advised him to end the stakeout and wait until the fag contacted him again. But there were no more letters, no phone calls. Then he read in the paper that Chris and his partner had been killed. I'll sandpaper the rough edges and tell him, but should one of the cops rat on Elliot, I guess the story would hold up."

"Hey," Javan said, looking relieved. "Maybe he could go to the police when the papers publish the news and give them that story. Pre-empt the snitch, know what I mean?"

"Never overdo it," Sam said with a raised finger.

For the next seventeen days, the first thing Elliot did after getting up was log on to MiamiHerald.com and scan the crime pages. On the eighteenth morning he learned that, because residents had complained about an unbearable stench, yesterday morning the superintendent of a Miami Beach apartment building on Lenox Avenue had let himself into a unit and found the decomposing bodies of two males.

On his way to work he rang Tony Soto.

"Yep."

"How are things, Tony?"

"Hi, Teach. How you doing?"

"You at work?"

"On my way."

"You finish at five?"

"Sure."

"What do you say we meet and decide once and for all if we want to join or not?"

Short pause.

"Sure. I'll meet you at the warehouse."

Around six, Elliot's Nicaraguan neighbour admitted both men to the Presidential Country Club. Hoping that during their second visit the Cubans would decide to apply for membership, he handed out application forms (a subtle make-up-your-minds hint; this ain't a fucking public park) and let them take a second stroll around the lush lawns.

"They were found today," Elliot said.

"Really? Who found them?"

"The super."

"The stink, almost certainly."

"Right. You talked to your buddies?"

"Of course I did."

"Should I get ready to be taken in?"

"You have nothing to worry about, Teach. Everyone knows we'd all be up shit creek without a paddle if someone blows the horn."

"You sure?"

"As sure as I can be. I can't guarantee it, though."

Elliot sighed. "Okay, Tony. If worse comes to worst I think I could beat the rap, provided you button up concerning the kidnapping."

"You know I won't say a word about that. But what crap would you feed the bulls?"

"It's better if you don't know. If this explodes and they ask you who paid for the stakeout, you name me."

"You sure?"

"I'm sure. You did me this favour because I'm your friend but you had no idea why I was staking out those two."

"Okay. But I feel pretty sure none of my buddies will turn me in."

"That's great. How's the family?"

"We are doing fine."

"How many pounds have you lost?"

"Forty-one. Had to buy a whole new wardrobe."

"You look five years younger, Tony. Best thing I've ever done was quit the booze."

"No preaching, please. Let's get out of here."

New Year's Eve

The party ended when the sole remaining employee turned off his outdated CD player, gathered together his discs, put everything in a gym bag, waved goodbye to the big shots, and left. It was ten past six. The best thing about New Year's Eve company bashes, Elliot thought, is that folks are looking forward to a long night of boozing and gorging on delicacies, so at work they drink moderately and leave early. The watchmen (triple hourly wage tonight), the catering crew (cleaning up), and the three shareholders were the only people left at Imlatinex.

"Hey, Sam," Jenny said, "I don't want to rush things, but Tico's plane lands at 7:30 and I promised I'd pick him up. What do you say we start now?"

"Sure; the party is over. Let's go," Sam said, and headed to the cubicle. Jenny and Elliot tagged along.

Jenny looked fantabulous, Elliot thought. White long-sleeved blouse, jeans, scuffed trainers; no bra, no lipstick, thin eyeliner. So sparingly had she dabbed perfume behind her ears he had only gotten a whiff of it when she kissed his cheek – for the first time since the rescue. The less elegantly a beautiful woman dressed, the more attractive the Cuban found her.

The old man had dressed in a white shirt, a horrible, sixty-year-old tie with multi-coloured amoeba-shaped motifs, and an off-the-rack brown suit. Everybody at the party had been wondering if Sam was delirious. "Been here sixteen years; never saw him wear a tie,"

one forklift operator had remarked, summarizing the staff's bewil-
derment at Sam's attire.

"So, where's Tico?" Elliot asked Jenny, making small talk as they
followed Sam to the office.

"Oh, he went to San Juan to see his mom. Ninety-three, the *señora*,
can you believe it?"

"Lucky lady. Mine died at fifty-nine."

"Mom was even younger when she was killed."

"I know."

In the cubicle, Sam unbuttoned his jacket and plopped down in
his executive chair; with a wave Elliot offered his to Jenny. "No,
thanks," she said and rolled out an office chair from beneath a desk,
positioning it so she faced Sam.

"Well, I'm sure you two have plans for tonight, so I'll cut to the
chase," Sam said. "I want to make an announcement: Effective
tomorrow, I'm retiring."

Both Elliot and Jenny had known the day would come some time,
but the news still took them by surprise. Unsure what to say, they
looked at each other for a second, then opted for silence.

"To you Elliot, I want to say you've worked hard, put your hide on
the line for the company and for Jenny. You've made money; not as
much as you deserve, but some. I've taught you all I know. In my
opinion, nothing here needs recalibration or fine tuning, you are ready
to go it alone. Only thing you've got to watch out for is" – Sam raised
his forefinger – "your temper and" – his middle finger went up – "your
concept of friendship. Let's suppose . . . oh, I don't know . . ."

Sam raised his eyes to the ceiling, pretending to be searching for
the right words, when he'd known just what he would say for several
days.

" . . . that some bastard at customs accuses you of smuggling, makes
you so mad you punch him in the face and get busted. Or suppose
you don't hit the s.o.b., but are so pissed off you drive away recklessly,

run over a drunk crossing a street, and get thrown in jail. Who would call the shots here? I suppose I could cover for you for a few days or weeks in an emergency, but what if I've gotten my ticket punched?"

"Shut up," Jenny, with a frown.

"C'mon, Sam. You're the healthiest senior in Florida," Elliot said.

"Yeah, yeah, yeah. Reassure the dodderer. Let's move on. Friendship and business are mortal enemies. Keep your friends away from the business. Wine them, dine them, loan them money – best way ever to lose friends – but don't give them jobs here, don't do business with them. You control your emotions, keep your friends outta here, you can make this company grow. Have I made myself clear?"

"You have, Sam," Elliot, with a nod. "Now, may I have a word?"

"You may not. You're gonna say how much you've learned from me, that you respect me and love me, that you'll be there for me anytime I need you, and that you'll be pallbearer Number One at my funeral. I know all that, so let's cut the crap."

Elliot was taken aback. Jenny repressed a giggle as Sam turned to her.

"My dear, for several years now I've been trying to imagine what your father would have advised you to do with the company the day he retired. But he didn't retire; death seized him right there," pointing to Ruben Scheindlin's desk. "Your mother is dead too. I reckon you are so out of luck the closest thing to a father you have is me."

"You are the greatest and I'm very lucky and honoured to have you, Sam."

"Yeah, yeah, yeah. Now, listen to me, Jenny. You don't know shit about this business. Not because we've kept you from learning it, but because this isn't what you like to do in life. I can understand that; I respect that. You want to sell Imlatinex, I won't hold it against you. It's the company your father built from scratch, but he's history and you are not. It's your life; do what you think is best for you, for your future. Think it over; make a decision.

"If you decide to sell, you own 79 per cent of the shares, so you can do as you please. But I'd appreciate it – and I suppose Elliot too, on account he owns 1 per cent – if you'd consult him and me on the price per share. But if you decide not to sell, from now on you gotta pay attention. Elliot is a very good manager, but you *own* the company. When I say pay attention I don't mean come here every day. I mean take an interest, force yourself to learn the basics of the business. I mean personally check monthly results, not retain a CPA to do it for you – well, I suppose you could hire one to translate Ari's mumbo-jumbo into English, but you gotta make an effort to take in what's going on. I also mean come here every time Elliot wants to discuss something with you. I'm sure he won't be calling you every week or every month. He may call you twice in a week and then months may go by before he asks you to drop around again to know what you think about some important matter. Every time he asks you to come over, he'll have a good reason to consult with you.

"Regardless of what you decide, Elliot needs a raise. I would recommend 100 K, to take him to 350, effective tomorrow. If you sell the company and the new owners make an offer to Elliot, he could make it contingent on getting a raise. In your place, I'd sell him some of your shares, too."

"As many as he wants."

"Good. You two sit down next week and negotiate price, quantity, when, and so on. The money we've been paying him, I'm sure he can't afford many shares, but you discuss that. To both of you I say: You need my opinion concerning something, give me a call; I'll drop over. I don't want teary farewells. I'm the only one talking here tonight. Let's get out of here. Now."

Sam got to his feet and with an agility that belied his years dashed for the door. Elliot glanced at Jenny, who nodded and stood.

From their long faces and the softly said happy-new-years, the watchmen deduced that something unpleasant had taken place inside the office. The threesome walked over to Sam's car. At the driver's door, Sam turned and shook Elliot's hand.

"It's been a pleasure working with you, Elliot."

"Thanks, Sam. But listen. You taught me that nothing, uh, compromising should be said in the office, and I have to say something that's, well, related to what happened to Jenny in Toronto, and here in Miami."

"Go ahead."

Intrigued, Jenny searched Elliot's eyes.

"I hate politics," he began. "I think most politicians are despicable sons of bitches. Two parts of politics I find especially repulsive: war and espionage. I don't want to know what you and Jenny did, are doing, or will do for Mossad. I just want to say that, in the future, don't count on me for anything that smacks of espionage. Even if it has nothing to do with Mossad, the CIA, or any other agency, if I *think* it's espionage, I won't move a finger to help you. If the firm is . . . duty-bound to be involved in any sort of secret activity, I want you to tell me here and now. If it is, I'll resign tomorrow morning and sell my shares to either of you at a fair price. I won't tell anyone. I'll keep on being your friend. I'll be there for you should you need my help. But I don't want to be conned ever again into anything that's remotely related to spying for any government or cause."

Sam and Jenny exchanged a look and a smile.

"That part of my life is over, Elliot," Jenny said. "You may have noticed that I shed the bodyguards; it's because Javan called me last week and told me I don't need them any more. I'm done with Mossad, but not with Israel. I haven't been there in a long time because, well, it wasn't convenient. But now I'll visit frequently, help orphans, widows, sick children. But whatever I do, I'll do it above board. No more spooky business, I promise."

"Thanks, Jenny. Sam?"

"I've just resigned. I'm a private citizen. Whatever I do with my life doesn't concern the company, so I don't have to give you assurances."

"Fair enough," Elliot said and pulled open the door for Sam. "Happy New Year and happy retirement."

"Thanks," Sam said. He took Jenny in his arms and hugged her. She broke down and sobbed.

The old man got inside his car, buckled up, turned the key in the ignition. Not wanting them to see him cry, he drove off without a backward glance.

Jenny wiped her cheeks with her fingers.

"Once you make up your mind concerning the company," Elliot said, "let me know. No hurry, though. A month, two, whatever time you need."

She stepped forward and hugged the Cuban. "I'm so grateful, Elliot," she whispered in his ear.

"I know."

She pulled back. "I don't share Sam's opinion regarding friendship. You are my manager and my friend. If you ever have to choose between being one thing or the other, quit being my manager, please."

"Thank you."

"Happy New Year."

"You too."

Jenny turned, got into her Mercedes, and drove away.

Elliot watched her taillights disappear before starting up his bucket of bolts.

Following the custom in Spanish-speaking countries, Elliot, Fidelia, her mother, her son, and the good-looking Cuban girl the young man was dating welcomed the new year at midnight by popping a grape into their mouths with each peal of the bell – twelve peals, twelve grapes, one for each new month – then clinked their glasses and sipped hard cider (7Up for Elliot). Around 12:30 Fidelia tucked her mother in, kissed her son and his date good night, and left arm in arm with Elliot.

"You seem far away," Fidelia said, while waiting for a light at Flagler.

"I do?"

"Yes."

Green. He stepped on the gas pedal. "Sam Plotzher retired today. Now I'm fully responsible and the only one accountable. I'm a little worried."

"You'll be fine."

"I hope you're right."

"The walking mannequin won't find a better man to run the company."

"She's not a walking mannequin."

"Oh, no?"

"No."

"So, what is she? An expert in eyelashes and mascara? A cult figure for the rich and stupid women of the world?"

Elliot forced a chuckle. Every time Jenny came up in conversation, the scorn in Fidelia's tone said she felt not only jealous, but threatened. If she thought Jenny was a possible rival it meant she judged him stupid.

Fidelia knew that her concerns about Elliot and Jenny Scheindlin were based on the hundred or so married couples she had seen divorce as a result of the man falling for a much younger and more attractive woman. Yes, many of the men were dickheads, literally, but some were as intelligent and mature as Elliot. One in particular, much brighter than her man, at age fifty-five had married a twenty-eight-year-old stripper who started playing the field as soon as the honeymoon was over.

But this wasn't what they wanted to talk about in the first hour of New Year's Day, and both decided to pour oil on troubled waters.

"Jenny has changed," he said. "She is not a model any more, and she has fallen very much in love with a Puerto Rican. She plans to get into the fashion business, open a high-end store or something."

"Really?"

"Really."

"Well, she's too old now to compete with much younger models. She's what? Thirty-five?"

"I don't know." He knew Jenny was thirty.

"Well, I hope she realizes she won't find a man who knows the company better than you, who's more efficient than you."

"She may think so. Gave me a 100 K raise today."

"She did?" *Is she trying to lure him with her money?*

"Yep. But she may sell the company. She's not sure what she'll do."

Oh, Holy Santa Bárbara, make her sell the fucking company. "In any case, the raise makes you much more attractive. You know what, *macho rico*? I feel like giving you a good time tonight."

"Not a bad way to begin the year."

Acknowledgements

Several people who are thoroughly acquainted with the inner workings of the fashion industry and with the life of professional models
shared with me memories and experiences that make this novel
factual in some respects. I am deeply grateful to them all.